Tak

The A**hole Club Series

Ivy Harper

Perceptive Illusions Publishing
Bayshore, New York

Ivy Harper/Perceptive Illusions Publishing, Inc.
PO BOX 5253
Bayshore, NY 11706
www.AuthorIvyHarper.com

Publisher's Note: This is a work of fiction. Names, characters, places, and incidents are a product of the author's imagination. Locales and public names are sometimes used for atmospheric purposes. Any resemblance to actual people, living or dead, or to businesses, companies, events, institutions, or locales is completely coincidental.

Cover design by Covers by Combs

Ordering Information:
Quantity sales. Special discounts are available on quantity purchases by corporations, associations, and others. For details, contact the "Special Sales Department" at the address above.

Tak: A**hole Club Series/ Blue Saffire. -- 1st ed.
ISBN 978-1-941924-08-2

Dream hard, work hard, and never doubt yourself. No one can limit you, only you can limit yourself.

—Ivy Harper

Let It Burn

Tak

Fuck my life. The night I decided to end it, of course, there'd be a fucking race. Of course, God would fuck me over.

"Line up your bets."

Pushing my earbuds in deeper, I cursed. It was that shitty Ol' Seth who had set the shit up. He stood on the back of some dick's truck, yelling out numbers. All the fuckers from the two universities my uncle kept bitching about me going to were in attendance. I bet his ass wouldn't have been so happy if he knew this was the shit they did.

I quickly sidestepped a few chicks, running toward some dude who looked like a walking, talking Ken doll. His entire demeanor said, *Fuck you, I'm rich.*

I held back the instant need to puke. Another visible reminder of what I wasn't. Not a perfect son, not a perfect white kid. When would I get a fucking break?

Wait, that's right, when I was dead.

Walking on the outside of the noisy crowd, I shoved all that shit to the back of my mind. The music in my ears blasted as another drumbeat rolled through. It was a shitty song. The lyrics weren't worth spit, but the drummer and guitarist knew what they were doing.

Bypassing a few more drunk college dicks, I spotted my target chatting up big tits and a smile. Tanner—the dealer who liked to shove drugs into his brother, Ricky's pockets to sell at school. Ricky had been blowing my phone up to come by. At first, I was going to tell him to fuck off and shove his drugs up his well-used asshole, but then it occurred to me.

It was my last night on earth. Why play by the pussy rules set by some crooked adults? The corners of my lips kicked up, when I thought about fucking Tanner's night up.

The best fucking part about being a loner was the ability to snatch shit from arrogant fucks. The crowd around Tanner was thick, filled with ass kissers and ball strokers. Walking past them, keeping my head down, I bumped into someone and staggered, falling into the person next to me.

"Shit," I said.

Someone slammed their hands against my chest. I fell back, hitting the ground with a grunt.

"Watch where the fuck you're going."

I kept my head down, my eyes focused on the duffel a few inches away. A pair of black Converse moved to block my sight. I looked up to see a flushed and angry face.

"Hey, did you hear me?" The guy looked like he was ready to fight, but I didn't have time to play with him.

Standing, I lowered my head when he closed the space, shoving me once more. I retreated two steps, even when I didn't have to.

"I said, can you hear me, fuckface?"

I looked up and met his stare head-on. "Yeah… I can."

"What—"

"Enough, Jeremy." His buddy clapped a hand on Jeremy's shoulder and squinted his eyes at me as he smiled. It wasn't friendly. "Let's go, we got a race to win," the friend added.

The Jeremy guy looked from his friend to me. I knew he wanted to jump. I curled my hand around the rock I'd picked up. *Jump bitch.* I wasn't some little shit at six feet, I'd been one of the tallest seniors at my high school and I wasn't lacking in the muscle department. Skinny, Asian kid my ass.

I was already pissed. With my earbuds hanging down, I'd missed another good guitar riff.

"Shit," Jeremy exclaimed, shoving past me. His friend followed not saying a word.

I watched them in case they decided they wanted to jump me from behind. Seeing they really weren't coming back, I glanced over at the bag, expecting to have lost my chance, but it seemed tits had pulled Tanner toward the front of the car. The druggies eager for a drop of his generosity were now between us and the bag. Walking over to it, I bent down and grabbed it, then smoothly walked away like nothing happened.

Using my free hand, I pulled my earbuds up and replaced them. Once more the sound of the world fell away. Walking along the sidelines, I kept expecting Tanner to come chasing after me, but nothing happened. At that point, he might have been getting his dick wet with another STD.

I walked the distance of the night's track, stopping only when I could see the finish line. I dropped the bag to my feet and unzipped it. I released a whistle at the hot shit inside. Weed, ecstasy, heroin, and blue pills that had to be Xanax. Ricky hadn't been shit talking when he said his brother had a good bag. Too bad it was mine now.

Grabbing a tiny bag filled with blue pills, I then opened it and pulled two out. Unfortunately, I'd have to take them with no water. I chewed them up, wincing at the bitter taste that filled my mouth.

"Fuck, that's nasty," I said aloud.

I reached in my back pocket and pulled out a pre-rolled blunt. After placing it between my lips, I dug around for a lighter. Releasing a silent sound of triumph when I found it, I flicked it on. I inhaled the familiar flavor deep. Walking along, I muttered words that came to me on the tail end of a major drum solo. Time seemed to almost slow down, but I knew that was the effect of the drugs.

I stared at the street before me. This was where Takuya Nakamura would come to an end. I took a step forward and then another until I suddenly felt the rush of adrenaline when a car flew past me. My earbuds filtered all outside noise, blocking out the roar of engines. My heart jumped, I looked after the car as I stood out in the street.

Lucky bastard and here he could have lived knowing he cut my life short. Turning away from the ass who'd failed to kill me, I faced forward only to be met with the sight of a car flipping. The music in my ears eerily matched the scene to a T. I almost felt numb as I watched the car jump into the air. Those blue pills and blunt made me smile instead of shitting my pants.

Not believing what I was seeing, I spit out my blunt and ran toward the accident. I only paused for a second when the car that had passed me earlier came flying back. Seeing that it was going in the same direction, I ran faster.

Still, it seemed like I couldn't get there fast enough. Everything slowed down. My legs felt like lead. I would have thought it was hours later when I did get there and caught up to the now empty car that passed me.

My gaze landed on a chick who stood behind the dicks pulling a guy from another car. I noticed her just as an explosion erupted. Before I even fucking thought, I ran for her and blocked her figure.

My body lurched as something hot and heavy slammed into my back. I rolled my eyes at the fiery pain that exploded. For once, being high came in handy. The pain wasn't as bad as it could've been, I'm sure.

"Oh god, he was still in there." My ears rang from her scream.

"Fuck him," an angry looking guy yelled. "He caused this shit."

Nice fucker, that one.

I was nothing more than a fucking puppet in the wind as another guy started to give out orders. They were coming way too fast for my brain to keep up. I gave my head a shake.

The self-proclaimed leader, Mister Hero said, "Let's get him in my car. We all need to get out of here."

I wanted to help, but my body wouldn't follow my orders. My vision blurred before me as they gathered around dead guy. I staggered forward.

The girl or two girls. It was getting hard to keep up with the people in front of me. "We have to take him to the hospital," she said, panic coating her voice.

Apparently, that's not what asshole barking out orders wanted to hear. He yelled at her.

"You need to get the fuck out of here, anyone connected to this shit is going to jail. Go."

I would've, but something about the ringing in my ears, the double vision, and the occasional sensation of falling forward told me I wasn't going anywhere.

I watched them move the guy to a car a few steps away. They shoved dead guy in the back seat. They were talking, but I didn't hear shit.

I was too busy trying to make sure I could breathe, that's when the sirens sounded in the distance. I was basically shit out of luck. If I would have known my night would end like this, I would have gone to prom instead.

"Dude, fucking leave." I looked away from the cars driving off to the person speaking, only to realize the speaker was asshole again.

I took a few staggering steps forward before stopping as I swayed back and forth. I pointed with my chin to the flashing lights of the cop cars getting closer.

"Too late."

Releasing a sigh, I turned and fell to my ass. I heard him release a hiss. "Your back."

"Yeah, I know."

I was pretty sure I was sporting a back covered in burns because I no longer felt my T-shirt or my leather coat, just the chilly air. My brow was coated with sweat, and my hands were shaking.

"Damn, you're fucked, kid."

"Sure am," I said as casually as possible. Otherwise, I would have screamed my fucking head off and we already had one injured fucker halfway to hell. "I suggest you let me get fucked in peace."

First, and last time I'd ever say those fucking words.

"I'll take the heat as much as I can. You were just out for a walk. You got it?"

The sirens were on us. The doors burst open as EMTs rushed out. Their voices all came together in a wave that crashed over me. My vision kept coming in and out. The last thing I saw was the burning cars.

That should have been me. I thought right before unconsciousness saved me from the pain.

CHAPTER ONE

Friends

Tak

About two months later...

I lifted the neck of my shirt and sniffed. Grimacing, I let it go. It smelled like the hospital.

I stood at the hospital counter waiting for Skittles, who'd offered to take me home. Originally, I had planned on declining her offer, but she'd been so pushy I'd given up. And it wasn't like I was holding out for my shitty father to show up.

"Mr. Nakamura, can you sign these release forms for us?"

The nurse behind the counter set a clipboard down with my paperwork on it. I picked up the pen she set next to it and signed my name. With my attention on the paperwork in front of me, I flinched when someone tapped me on my shoulder.

"What the fuck?" I turned around to meet the amused gaze of Skittles. She poked my cheek.

"Is that how you talk to your older sister?"

"Older sister," I repeated, turning my attention back to the paperwork. "I don't remember my family taking in someone so annoying."

"You know, I'm insulted. I give you nothing but love and sweets, you twerp."

I rolled my eyes, tossed the pen down and turned around to fully face her, seeing an amused Kelex standing behind her. I quirked a brow. Looks like the dead guy wasn't so dead anymore. "Yo, you've been kidnapped by her too?"

He laughed, walking over to my side. "You'll get used to it. Skittles decided to collect all of us into her friendship circle."

"Right, all my life I wanted to be a premium collector's item."

Skittles cleared her throat, giving us a warning look. "Are you both done talking shit or what?"

"No, but since you're my elder, I'll give you a break," I said as I bent slowly to pick up my duffel. The injured skin on my back pulled and I grimaced at the uncomfortable feeling. Straightening up, I caught the look of worry in Skittles and Kelex's eyes. I pretended not to see it. "So, are we leaving or what?"

"Yeah, but shouldn't you call your parents before we head out? Just so they know you're headed home," Kelex asked.

"There's no point, they haven't cared about me for a long time, and they're not going to suddenly give a shit now." I didn't feel anything weird about saying this. It didn't take a genius to notice I hadn't been visited once over the last two months by my family.

The two of them shared a look as if coming to some kind of agreement, leaving me completely out of the loop. Kelex and Skittles each took a stance on either side of me. Skittles took my right arm, while Kelex stood at my left.

"Let's go get something to eat, I'm starving," Skittles said as she started to drag me toward the exit and Kelex followed.

"Um, can you drop me off before you do this?"

"Not happening," Kelex said. "I get indigestion when I don't eat with more than one person."

"Are all old people as shameless as you two are?" I knew he was joking, but from his expression, the fucker didn't care what I thought.

Both frowned. Kelex's face turned annoyed. "You know we're not that old, right? Where'd they get you from?"

Skittles poked my neck and complained. "Exactly. Ignore him. I think he bumped his head during the accident and now shit just falls out of his mouth when he speaks."

Instead of playing into their silly banter, I pulled away from them and made my way out. "Weren't we going to get something to eat?"

"That's the plan," Skittles sang with excitement.

Together the three of us left the hospital.

***

A few hours later, I tried to get Skittles to leave my driveway. Her car was running and Kelex maintained a monk-like silence as she continued to shout questions at me from her driver's seat.

"I already told you, I'm fine. You can go," I repeated for the sixteenth time.

"Are you sure? I just don't feel right leaving you home alone. Especially when you're not done recuperating."

I rolled my eyes. "Skittles, my family employs a full staff of servants. I'm not alone."

"Shut up, you're a baby in a houseful of strangers," she said, eyeing my house like it held nothing but people with evil intent.

"I'm an eighteen-year-old with more money than Bill Gates," I said with a deadpan expression.

I ran a frustrated hand through my hair as I tried to think of how to get rid of her. While I couldn't help feeling flattered at the amount of care Skittles showed me. There was also a bit of annoyance. So what if she visited me at the hospital and tossed a few snacks my way. She didn't know shit about me or about the fucked life I lived.

"How about we come by tomorrow to visit you?" Kelex's voice cut through the dark thoughts in my mind. I looked at him, disgruntled. My first reaction was to say no, but the way he steadily looked at me told me to rethink my answer.

"Whatever," I said.

"Then we can bring some movies and hang out," Skittles added cheerfully.

"Glad you're happy, now leave." I gave them my back and walked toward the entrance of my house. The door opened up and my housekeeper stepped out.

"See you later, Tak," Skittles called as she revved her engine and drove out of my long driveway like a bat out of hell.

I paused and turned watching as the taillights of her car got further and further away. Shaking my head, I turned back around and handed my housekeeper, Linda my duffel bag.

"Young master, your father called and wanted me to tell you he was sorry for being unable to pull away from his business in the city to pick you up. He wants you to call him as soon as you get a chance," she said.

"Tell me the truth, Linda," I ordered as we entered the place I called home.

It was similar to the rest of the mansions in the neighborhood with its many floors and sprawling size. It was originally bought by my father's family to be a place where everyone with the last name Nakamura could have a reunion.

It was open and airy, following all the rules of feng shui. Something my grandfather had gotten into a few years back. Unfortunately, the only one who enjoyed it was me, the forgotten half-breed.

Linda's expression turned dark before she lowered her eyes to the floor. "The third son had a baseball game and your father didn't want to miss it. So, he told us to take care of you for him."

All the warmth I'd felt from the time I'd spent with Skittles and Kelex evaporated in an instant. "You can go," I said to Linda and headed up to my room.

I couldn't believe I'd almost forgot about the stark reality of my life. I couldn't help resenting Skittles for showing me something different. I was better off not knowing what it felt like to have someone care about me.

CHAPTER TWO

Movie Night

Tak

The next day I laid on my bed staring at the ceiling. I'd spent the entire night thinking about how my existence to the world was so fucked up. I searched my room for the stash of drugs I'd bought way before I'd gone out to the race that ruined my death.

Once I found it, I enjoyed a wonderful high after having told the entire staff to fuck off for the day. The large, cold prison called my home was empty and I was the only human within its walls as I got high as a kite.

I should feel bad for going right back to my old habits, but it wasn't my fault the universe decided to have my father fuck my mother eighteen years ago. Resulting in me, the half-Asian kid who was a bit too Asian for this perfect fucking world, but also too White, too much like my mother for my father to like me.

I lifted my right hand and stared at the tendrils of smoke that floated from the tip of the blunt I'd rolled up. A slow piano sound started to fill my head, followed by the strings of a melancholy violin. "Shit."

I pressed the heel of my left hand to my forehead as the music grew louder. "Turn it off," I shouted to no one.

Fuck it. I sat up and took another hit of my blunt and then got to my feet. I walked over to the side table and placed my blunt on the ash tray. Since the music didn't want to shut off on its own, I'd turn it off myself.

I'd turned on my stereo, releasing Kurt Cobain's angst ridden voice into my room, but it only managed to dull some of the sound in my head. I'd read somewhere once about a guy who had gotten off on suffocating. He'd often use his belt to do it.

That is until the one time he'd passed out and strangled himself to death. It was an embarrassing way to go, but since my wish for a fiery death on prom night had been canceled by a car accident and some fuckery, this was the next best thing. Luckily, I was wearing a belt since my stint in the hospital had caused me to lose weight.

Undoing it, I pulled it out of the belt loops, letting my jeans hit the floor. I was so caught up in my imaginations of choking to death, it caught me off guard when the door to my bedroom suddenly opened. Whipping my head around, I stared speechlessly at the two people who stood there.

Skittles and Kelex looked at me from the doorway. It took a minute for my high mind to understand what was going on as the silence stretched.

"W… what are you guys doing here?" I asked flustered.

I went to turn around fully, completely forgetting that my jeans were around my ankles. With a startled shout, I tripped and fell forward, hitting the floor with a hard thump. I swallowed back the cry of pain that burned at the back of my throat, causing tears to come to my eyes.

Fuck.

I was so embarrassed, I refused to look them in the face. "How did you two get in?" I asked, my voice muffled by my arm.

My question set them both off as they released choked laughter. It was Skittles who answered first, her voice sounding strained. "We spotted your gardener. He saw that no one had answered the front door, so he let us in through the garage."

I'd totally forgotten about dismissing the outdoor staff.

"We're sorry we interrupted your time alone with your right palm," Kelex said before he released another bark of laughter.

I pushed up and glared at them both. Skittles leaned on him with her arms wrapped around her middle as tears of laughter slipped down her cheeks. The both of them were like a curse.

If it hadn't been for them, I'd have gone out in a fiery ball of glory two months ago. And now the two annoyances had unknowingly stopped me from going out peacefully. The universe must have created these two fuckers for this very purpose.

"I wasn't jerking off," I denied through gritted teeth. Not caring about the two idiots in my doorway, I kicked my pants off and got up. "Why are you here?"

Recovering her composure, Skittles said, "Don't tell me you forgot we said we would be coming over to watch some movies?"

"From that look on his face and the smell of pure snunk in here, he did," Kelex said with smirk.

"You got something against weed?" I asked as I gave them my back and walked over to my dresser and pulled open the top drawer. I grabbed out a pair of sweats and dragged them on. Finished with that, I turned off my stereo.

"If you do, it's going to turn our budding relationship sour very quickly."

"I'm not here to judge. You have enough to roll another one?" Kelex asked.

I turned around to find both he and Skittles had taken up residence on my bed. "I'm starting to think you two don't understand the word personal space."

"Personal… what?" Skittles said as she kicked off her shoes and slid back on my bed, giving me a fake innocent look. "What did you say, little buddy?"

"You know what, never mind you both said you were here to watch a movie. Let me show you our entertainment room."

I left my room and didn't check to see if they were following me. The faster I got the two idiots away from my room the better. Otherwise, I had a hunch more than just my weed would be taken. Kelex and Skittles looked a little too comfortable on my bed and Skittles seemed like the type who'd take a guy's hoodie.

***

"I can't believe you haven't ever seen *Dirty Dancing*," Skittles said as she shoved another handful of hot sauce laced popcorn into her mouth. She sat on the long couch between Kelex and me. She'd forced me to sit next to her because she's said it would make us closer.

"That's the fifth time you've said that." We'd already watched four movies and ordered takeout twice. I couldn't remember the last time I'd eaten takeout. My family's cook had always been a simple request away from making anything I wanted.

"Tak, your movie experience is sorely lacking," Kelex said as he took another hit of my weed.

"Whatever, I've always been more into music then movies anyway."

"What kind of music?" Kelex asked.

"All of it," I said, pursing my lips together.

I looked at the two of them, seeing curiosity written all over their faces. I found myself talking about my interest and it wasn't long before I realized I'd forgotten all about the darker thoughts that had consumed me only hours ago.

CHAPTER THREE

Ski Trip

Tak

Six months later...

They were all asleep. I stared at the five assholes who'd passed out drunk around the cabin living room. Not only had Skittles banned me from having a drop of alcohol because I was *underage*, but she'd also taken my stash of pills from my suitcase so I couldn't have a pleasant high. Unbeknownst to her, I'd slipped a blunt into my inside coat pocket before she'd snatched the pills.

The most fun I'd had that night was watching everyone have to take their clothes off during strip poker. That was until I'd found myself sans my pants and shirt. I smile at the memory.

Deacon looked at me. "Damn, you're skinny. You can't be skinny and look like a pretty little bitch too."

One day I was going to put sand in his beer.

Listening to the sound of their snoring, I figure this was the best time to smoke and got up to walk across the living room. I grabbed my snow coat and boots and stopped in the foyer to pull them on, then tiptoed out. I took my blunt and lighter out of my pocket.

The entire resort Skittles had brought us to looked like something from one of those movies she'd forced me to watch. I took a moment to light up before I shoved my lighter back in my pocket and followed the path from our cabin to where there was another sidewalk that led into the woods a few feet ahead of me. Since it was nighttime, there weren't a lot of people outside.

I purposely walked on the less crowded path in order to get some quiet. Soon it was just me, my weed, and the snow-covered forest.

I was still reeling from the fact I'd told five strangers everything about me and my damn cousin. It felt like I'd torn open a wound and I wasn't sure if I'd ever stop bleeding out. I knew Skittles said I wasn't to blame for my parents' shit, but it wasn't something easy for me to believe.

Especially when I'd seen my father play the role of good dad to my step siblings. Why couldn't he give me even a quarter of the attention he gave them? No matter what I did, he only called or sent emails. It was getting to the point where it would be hard for me to recognize him if he showed up one day.

I stopped at a fork in the path and read the signs that hung above. The one on the left read, Reed's Cliff and the one the right, Bunny Slope. Making a random choice, I headed toward Reed's Cliff.

It didn't take me long to reach it. There was a low stone wall. It was the only thing between me and the edge of the cliff.

I took in the night view of the town in the valley we'd driven through earlier in the day. The lights looked similar to the stars overhead. I looked away from the village and down at the drop below the cliff into nothingness.

Immediately, I was reminded of the ending of *Crouching Tiger, Hidden Dragon*. I wondered if I'd feel the same peace the heroine felt when she'd decided to jump to her death, letting go of everything. I took in a deep inhale of my blunt.

Staring down into the darkness, a reckless thought hit me. I'd just told a room of people I'd only known for six months all about my shitty life. Jumping from here would be the perfect period to my short life.

At least that's what my high mind told me. With my choice made, I climbed up on top of the stone wall and took my blunt out from between my lips and dropped it. I watched it fall until I could no longer see it and released an impressed whistle.

"Shit, I'll probably pass out before I hit the ground," I muttered to myself.

Closing my eyes, I spread my arms wide and inched forward.

"This is it," I said as I leaned forward.

A weird noise came from behind me. I crinkled my brow as I paused and listened. Hearing nothing, I leaned forward a little more only for the sound to start again. This time I could make it out. It sounded like a kid crying.

Opening my eyes, I then turned around and got down, giving a look around the perimeter of the forest. Not seeing anything, I assumed it was my imagination and went to climb back atop the wall.

A child's scream was the only warning I got before something came running at me from behind and slammed into my legs. With a startled yelp, I staggered forward. I braced myself on the wall to keep from falling completely over.

Looking down, I found a little kid in nothing more than pj's and a snow coat, clinging to my legs. He cried and buried his face.

My high evaporated into smoke.

Regaining my balance, I nervously patted his head. "H… hey, kid. What are you doing out here alone?"

He released another ear-splitting cry. "Lost, I'm lost."

Yeah, I kind of figured that.

Realizing the universe had screwed me over again, I decided to comfort the kid and get him back to whoever his parents were. Sending the stone wall one more look, I turned my full attention to the crying kid attached to my legs.

An hour later, the snot-nosed kid was being comforted by one of the staff from the resort. His legs swinging in a chair as he drank some of the hot chocolate she'd made. All while I finished writing a statement for the report they'd written up. Signing it, I handed it back to the man who stood behind the desk.

"Is this all you needed from me?" I asked.

After everything that had happened, I was tired and just wanted to sleep.

"Yep, and don't worry the kid's guardian is on their way to get him. It's a good thing you'd decided to take a walk in such a secluded part of the resort. Kid's lucky he found you," the guy answered.

"Maybe."

Heading toward the door, I reached out to open it. However, it was shoved in, forcing me back, so I didn't get hit by it.

Two young women ran inside. One of them had on only silk pajamas and flip-flops. Her snow coat wasn't zipped up and her hair was a mess around her head. She looked frantically around the cabin.

"Rani?"

The little kid shouted, "Cousin, I'm here."

"Rani," the two girls ran over to his side. "How could you sneak out on Jazz and me?" she angrily asked, motioning to the young woman who stood next to her. Unlike the messy one, she'd wrapped herself up completely so I couldn't really see her face.

"Wait 'til I tell auntie about this. I swear, I'm not going to be able to sleep after all the anxiety you've stirred up," the messy looking one exclaimed.

"Calm down, Trisha. He's okay and that's what matters."

I quickly made my exit. If I stayed, I was sure the two workers would tell them I'd been the one who'd found the kid. I headed back to the cabin eager to forget this entire night happened.

CHAPTER FOUR

The Chase

Tak

Fourteen years later...

Standing outside, I flicked the end of my cigarette with my ring finger. The lights of the traffic below zoomed by. If I had been smoking the good shit in my pocket, I probably would have been humming some old tune and seeing fairies.

Instead, I was sucking down menthol flavored smoke. Better that than have Skittles up my ass. It was her day after all and I could trash these smokes later for the good stuff.

"Star gazing? Really, when we're here to celebrate? How long are you planning on staying out here?"

"As long as it takes for you fuckers to remember tying your dick to one person is a fucking curse," I said, dropping my cigarette and stomping on it. I turned, giving Luke's dumb ass a once-over. "But enough about you and Pit's shitty mistake. Is there a reason you're checking on me?"

"Worried about you. You're looking glum for someone who should be happy one of his best friends is getting married."

"Fuck that, I said I would attend the wedding and party, not fuck her friends. And if I stay in there, one of them is going to get their feelings hurt."

Luke smirked like he knew something I didn't. "Quit lying. There're at least two pussies in that room you've exchanged bodily fluids with." Luke sighed, giving me a solid pat on the back. "Don't be shy, you can tell me you're feeling lonely with Pit and me engaged."

I stiffened. I refused to admit aloud that that's what I'd been thinking. With Luke being the second one to get engaged, it was quickly becoming clear the world I'd been surviving in was crumbling. Shit, I'm not even sure how I'd managed to make it to my thirties.

When the nights get too fucking long and the demons in my head get too loud, I would either shoot up or hold the piece of metal I got from Deacon in my hand. Sitting on the edge of my tub, listing all the reasons why I shouldn't pull the trigger.

Deacon had asked me why the fuck I needed a gun. I gave him some half-ass excuse about an angry drug dealer I'd stiffed. Thankfully, that was the end of that.

"Come back inside. The champagne's not much but it'll take the edge off," Luke said.

"Nah, I'm going to cut out early. Time to find me a piece of ass to wipe away this nightmare of marital bliss." I moved to walk past him.

"You're going to miss the best part—the sappy retelling of how they met."

"I was there for it." I brush off his words with ease. "Tell them my stomach hurts," I added sarcastically, pushing the doors open.

I gave a nod to Deacon and my other brothers, who all looked the opposite of how I felt. Ignoring the obvious come-hither stares from my usual fare, I moved for the exit. Right as I reached the door, Pit called out, "I have an announcement."

I turned away from the door, curious.

"As a wedding gift, I purchased a lot to build a new house for half pint. We break ground in two weeks," he continued as he looked down at Skittles on the makeshift dance floor. "She has me moving back to Bridge Lake."

And I thought the Bugatti was an outrageous engagement gift. Once I heard what Pit had to say, I felt worse than I had before. I walked out of the party room and into the hallway, my aim the elevator across the way.

Pit was moving home. Something I thought none of us would do. I ignored the sensation of a headache building behind my eyes. My phone buzzed in my pocket.

Entering the elevator, I answered it. "Speak."

"Is that how you're answering the phone now?"

The annoyed sounding voice belonged to my manager, a hard-tit bitch who ran me and my other band members. "Chelsea, have you finally given up women and want to explore my dick?"

"If I wanted to be disappointed, I'd go watch *Avatar* again."

Leaning my head back, I released a short chuckle. I liked a woman with sass. "You'd be surprised, so... why the hell are you calling me on my very, very rare vacation?"

"Because Danny... you remember him? Kole's personal assistant."

I groaned, thinking of that wimpy waste of space.

"Yes, I know the leach," I growled.

"Well, the company you declined to do that commercial for has returned with a better offer and he called me about it."

"The one I already said no to?"

"Yes," she grudgingly admitted. "At first, I wasn't going to bring it to you, but I really think this deal is too good to pass up."

"I don't repeat myself often, but for you I'll do it this one time. I will not work with them. I will never work with them. Hell, I will do a commercial for adult diapers before I ever work with them."

"Tak, this is a lot of money you're saying no to."

A loud ding of the elevator alerted me I'd arrived at the garage floor. The doors opened and I stepped out into the hotel's garage.

"Ah. I get it now. Kole's pushing this." I took out my key fob from my back pocket with my free hand.

"Well, the label would get a percentage of the money if you take this deal," Chelsea said. "He's not the type to lose out on a chance to make some money."

"The answer is no," I said. "Now, go do what I pay you so much for... disappointing Kole."

"Wait, Tak."

I hung up and shoved my phone into my back pocket. I paid her to handle the annoying shit. Like Kole's constant desire to make money for me, stemming from his weird desire to pay me back for helping build JS records with him.

Reaching the back of the garage, where I'd parked my Ferrari, I pressed the button to unlock the doors. I stopped in disbelief.

"What the fuck do you think you're doing?"

The person who'd caused my brain to short-wire, stood on the driver's side of my car with my door wide open, a slim piece of metal at their feet. I couldn't see their face because of the black face mask they wore. Their eyes met mine, wide and filled with what seemed to be disbelief. The two of us stood in tense silence, not moving.

"I said, what the fuck do you think you're doing?" I shouted when I snapped out of it.

Raising my voice seemed to be the perfect thing to trigger the fucking car thief because with no word and a lot of speed, the fucker took off.

"Wait," I yelled after him.

If he thought he'd out leg me, he had another thing coming, but the bastard was quick. He dodged behind a car, so that I had to run around it. Then he slid across the top of a lifted Ford truck.

"Dammit." It was like I was chasing a squirrel. The overhead lamps and the enclosed parking garage walls were the only reason I didn't lose him.

At some point, it occurred to me I could stop the chase and call the cops, but I felt more excited than I had in days. I loved the feeling of adrenaline pumping through my veins. I nearly grabbed the back of his coat, but the fucker performed some wushu martial arts and legit spun out of my hold.

The sound of our shoes hitting against asphalt became its own melody in my head. Usually when that started, I would lose myself to it. Dragged down to the bottom to add words and chords, but I ignored it, the music turning into silence behind me.

I chased the fucker out onto the street. Moving through the Vegas crowd was the only thing slowing us as we drew closer and closer to the heavy traffic in the street. He paused at the end of the sidewalk.

"Might as well turn around and take this can of whoop-ass like a man," I panted, feeling the sweat coating my back. I would beat his ass. The crowd around us would probably record it, but at that point who gave a shit. "Come, I'll only break your hand."

The thief took off. The sound of car horns filled the air, followed by the sharp sound of squealing tires. I couldn't believe it. He'd seriously ran across the street through speeding traffic. The rush I felt was indescribable.

I watched his back. I was invested in whether or not he'd make it to the other side. Would he? Wasn't he afraid of dying?

Was I afraid of dying?

The questions tumbled down like puzzle pieces, before they clicked, and I took off. The rush of not knowing if the drivers would stop or whether I'd be too slow was everything. Maybe I wouldn't beat the thief too bad.

He'd given me something I'd been lacking as of late. The feeling of being alive, the challenge of overcoming my fear. Right as I reached the other side, I stopped at the sidewalk.

The thief's eyes widened as if in amazement. I couldn't help smirking. "So... what's next?" I asked to taunt him.

He didn't react right away, but when he did, it caused my smirk to drop. He took off toward an alley. I followed close behind. I couldn't lie, I was eager to see what he'd pull this time.

He turned a corner and jumped like a spider monkey. I came to an abrupt stop as he leapt up and grabbed the lowest bar. He swung himself across to a second bar above, pulled himself up, and landed with a solid thump onto the fire escape.

My mouth dropped. "Son of a bitch."

He stood and turned, looking down at me. There was no way my ass could do such gymnastic shit. Shit, I didn't know if I was pissed because this chase was over or because the adrenaline pumping through my body would fade.

"Fuck it," I said about to turn away and leave.

I was so occupied staring up at him, I didn't hear the sound of someone coming up from behind me. My only clue was the explosion of pain in my skull when something landed against my head and my vision went black.

Jazzy

I crouched down low on the fire escape, moving into the shadows, hoping I hadn't been seen. Luck was on my side as I wore all black and the alleyway was darker and more secluded than the main street.

Holding my breath, I leaned forward a bit to get a better view of the two men who'd seemingly come out of nowhere. The one who'd knocked my pursuer out was tall and grim faced with a notably bent nose. He tossed the baton he'd used to his partner.

Who caught it and gleefully said, "Shit, I didn't think he'd come running to us. I'll text Mitchell and let him know we caught him, Bradley." He pulled out his phone. The bright light coming off it gave me a clear view of his face and the red scar on his chin.

"Yeah, tell him to meet us in garage one of the Spires hotel. I've already paid off someone to keep the way clear for us, so we can use it and get up to the room," Bradley said. He squatted down and lifted up the unconscious guy by the arms, dragging him back toward a black van inconspicuously parked at the entrance of the alleyway.

Finished with texting, his partner followed him to the back door of the van.

"Shit, he's heavy," Bradley exclaimed.

"Wonder where the guy he was chasing went?"

"Beats me, help me get his ass in the back." He turned sideways so the feet of the person he was holding faced the other guy. "Here, help me get him inside, Tony."

Opening the doors, Tony tossed the baton in and turned around to help him. "Here, on one."

Once they finished shoving the body in the back of the van, they slammed the doors shut, quickly walked around to the front and got in and took off. Slowly rising, I stared after them. Jumping down from the fire escape, I landed lightly before standing and walking over to where Tak had been.

Spotting a wallet, I bent and scooped it up. Opening it, I pulled out the ID. Reading the name, I felt my stomach clench. "Takuya Nakamura." Instantly a pair of attractive brown eyes and a sarcastic smile came to mind. "You're shitting me," I muttered aloud.

It was Tak. I wasn't imagining things. The chances of me trying to steal the car of one of my old high school classmates had to be one in a million. The chances I'd try to steal my favorite singer's car tripled those odds.

Replacing the ID in the wallet, I then shoved it into my back pocket and pulled my cell phone out. I quickly dialed and I pulled my mask off. After a minute my call was sent to voicemail. Rolling my eyes, I dialed another number.

The sound of a sleepy feminine voice pulled my attention from my rapid musings. "Hello?" my cousin answered.

"Trisha, is Dutch awake?"

"He should be, let me go check," she said, the sluggish quality to her voice fading. The sound of something shifting was followed by the noisy click-clack of what I assumed to be her slippers.

"What do you need him for?" she asked, just as the sound of a door opening and a series of moans and groans filled my ear. I pulled the phone back staring at it in both shock and amusement. Soon there was a loud masculine shout, cutting the pleasured noises off abruptly.

"Trisha, what have I told you about just walking into my apartment?" Dutch asked angrily.

"The same thing you say all the time, but the only way I'll stop doing it is if you move out. Don't glare at me just because you can only get off to cartoons."

"Stop before he kicks you out," I said.

Out of the five of us cousins who lived together in a five-apartment brownstone, Trisha and Dutch were like oil and water. Especially when no one was home to get between them. I wouldn't have called Trisha if Dutch didn't have the habit of not answering his phone.

"Fine," Trisha said. "Dutch, Jazz is on the phone. She wants to talk to you."

There was some shuffling and cursing, before Dutch finally answered. "You're the reason this virus broke into my apartment?"

I laughed as I quickly walked to the end of the street, making sure no cars were coming. I crossed it. "It's for a good reason, I'm going to text you a hotel and a name, I need you to see if you can find them for me. It would be a bonus if you could tap into any cameras around them."

There was a moment of silence, swiftly followed by, "I want you to take this virus out of the brownstone for two days."

"Deal," I said as I quickly texted him the name and hotel.

After a few seconds, Dutch said, "Got it."

The steady typing of keys tempered the small bit of anxiety eating at my stomach. I bit back my need to tell Dutch to hurry up.

I reached the corner and started to think over what I would do next. Dutch cursed and a sound of scuffling filled my ear. Trisha having successfully taken the phone from him, loudly asked, "Why do you have Dutch looking up Tak?"

If I told my cousin why, I knew exactly what she'd say. I debated it for a second before I finally said, "I might have seen him get kidnapped."

"Oh God, not again. Listen Jazz, you don't have to make up a fake reason to see him. I know you love him, but you can't recklessly invade his hotel room. You need to control your fangirl tendencies."

Irritated, I snapped. "What exactly do you think of me? I'm not lying, he was kidnapped."

I must've been on speaker phone because Dutch added his two sense. "She's not, he's getting carried into a private elevator as we speak."

Hearing this, I threw caution to the wind and rushed to the hotel I'd been approaching.

"Is he a guest there?"

"I found his reservations."

"Can you tell me what floor his room is on?" I asked.

"It's 1103. They've just exited the elevator."

As I entered the hotel, I walked toward the counter. Arriving there, I was met with the disdainful gaze of the hotel staff behind the desk. She gave me and my attire a long look. "Ma'am if you're looking for one-night stays, there is a Best Value hotel down the street."

I'd met plenty of people like this, who easily judged someone based on their appearance. Unfortunately, I didn't have the time to deal with it. I reached into my hoodie pocket and pulled out my wallet and placed a black card on the counter. "I want a room, on the eleventh floor, the number should be between 1104 to 1106."

Her eyes dropped to the card and I watched as she blanched. Only the extremely wealthy carried this card around with them. The only reason I kept it on me was because it made it easier to book rooms when traveling. It took out all the fuss of identifications and reservations.

I enjoyed her expression immensely, but instead of savoring it, I brushed off her sudden switch in behavior and grabbed my key. Racing for the elevator, I got on and headed to the top floor.

"Dutch, what are they doing now?" I asked, returning my focus to my call.

"I can't see into the room," he said, aggravation clear in his voice. Another round of tapping filled my ear. "Shit, the camera across from the room is busted."

"Okay, don't worry about it. I'm almost there anyway. Bye." I shoved my phone into my front pocket.

It didn't take me long to reach the floor Tak was staying on. I exited the elevator and headed in the direction of room 1103. Just as I turned the corner, I immediately staggered back as the door to his room opened and two men stepped out, their expressions grim.

I recognized one of them as Tony. The one who'd knocked Tak out in the alleyway, but the other one was new to me. His features were plain and almost boring.

"How long do you think it will take?" Tony asked, keeping his voice low, but I was able to pick it up since I was so close.

"Shit if I know but bleeding out might take longer for such a big dude. It won't matter." The two made their way toward me. "Let's take this exit, it leads out the back."

I stiffened and turned around to run for the exit. Pulling my phone out, I proceeded to call Dutch as I pushed the exit door open and started running down the steps.

"Again?" he complained.

"Call 911 and I don't care what you have to say just get them to that room," I ordered.

"What, are you serious?"

"Just do it," I said as I exited onto the tenth floor and ran to the other side where I quickly reentered a stairwell and ran back up to Tak's floor. Reaching the eleventh floor, I walked toward 1103 and banged on the door.

"Takuya," I yelled, but no one answered.

"Hurry, Dutch," I said harshly into the phone.

"Done, they are on their way," he answered.

I took a retreating step and looked from the elevator to Tak's door. A few minutes went by. "Where are they Dutch?" I demanded angrily. My anxiety growing.

"They just arrived, they're entering the elevator now," he said, his voice calm.

"Calm down, Jazzy. He's going to be okay," Trisha said, cutting through the panic filling my mind. Dutch must have handed her the phone when he heard the trace of hysterics in my voice.

Her consoling words were enough to dull the panic inside of me. The elevator dinged and two police officers and a hotel staff member came around the corner moments later. Relief poured through me and I hung up the phone, shooting Tak's room one more look before I left.

Entering my room not too far away, I cracked the door just enough, so I could watch as they banged on Tak's. Seeing there was no response, the two cops gave each other a nod before they asked the hotel employee to open the door.

The yell of shock that followed their entrance was all I needed. My heart tightened. I exited the room and walked past them, giving the room a brief glance. Not able to see anything, I looked away. However, I was able to hear the sound of the people speaking inside.

"Mr. Jensei, Mr. Jensei, can you hear me?" One of the cops asked. "Direct the EMT here now." His voice held urgency.

I moved out of the way of the officer who ran behind me toward the elevator. Forcing myself to remain calm, I continued forward catching the next elevator in numb shock. The faces of the three men from before appeared in my mind.

Someone had tried to kill Tak, but why?

When my phone rang, the soothing sound of Rejected One filled the silence. I bit my lip. Rejected One, Tak's band. Pulling my phone out, I answered.

"How's everything?" Trisha asked me.

I quickly reigned in my chaotic emotions. "Not sure, but the officers are here now."

"Thank God," she exclaimed.

"Hey, can you ask Dutch to look into Takuya for me. See if there is anyone who'd be considered an enemy to him."

"He's a celebrity, anyone and everyone could be his enemy."

"I know, and I want to know who those people are."

"Are you thinking about getting involved? Zeno told you to keep a low profile and not give your dad a chance to stir up trouble."

"I will, but I need to do this. I don't think I can go back to my life without making sure he's safe." It was the least I could do for the singer who'd saved me from the dark.

The doors of the elevator opened as what looked like a wedding party ran past. I watched them go before exiting. "I won't drag it out, besides it's not likely I'll ever meet him. I'll just gather the evidence and send it to the proper authorities."

"Hmm, right. Something tells me I should tell you no, but as the daughter of Carter Liberiu, I enjoy chaos way too much to do that."

I chuckled at that. All my cousins lived up to their last name. Anyone with the last name Liberiu couldn't be called boring.

"Exactly. I'll be catching an early flight back to Vander in the morning. Can you pick me up?"

"Sure," she answered brightly.

"See you then, bye."

Hanging up, I headed out of the hotel. There weren't a lot of things in this world that I loved. Lucky for Tak, he happened to be one of them.

CHAPTER FIVE

Welcome Home

Jazz

Another announcement came over the sound system at the Vander City Airport as I picked up my bag off the carousel, avoiding bumping into another traveler. Pausing next to the exit, I checked my pockets to make sure I hadn't forgotten anything.

I picked up my bag and headed to the pickup area. I took my phone out of my purse and checked a few messages from my cousins. The first one that caught my eye was the one from Trisha that was in all caps and read, HERE!

Before I finished reading it, my name was shouted from the street. "Jazzy."

Looking up, I met the excited gaze of my cousin, Trisha Liberiu. Her long braids haphazardly piled on top of her head and her large golden circle earrings shaking. Her bright smile contrasted with her mocha-colored skin. Her entire body radiated a bright and friendly aura. Which was probably a factor as to why her restaurant did so well. "About time you arrived, hurry up."

"Stop rushing me," I said back, smiling.

I walked over to her black Lexus and opened her back door. Tossing my bag into the back of her car, I then shut the door and opened the one to the passenger's side and got in. Before I could buckle my seat belt, she tossed a tablet into my lap.

"Here, looks like the god of luck is helping you out. The security division for Tak's label, JS records is hiring."

I didn't bother buckling up and picked up the tablet, quickly swiping through the information.

"Seriously, do you think they're doing this because of what happened yesterday?" I wondered aloud.

"If they are, they're moving pretty fast," Trisha said as she pulled out, joining the steadily flowing traffic.

I frowned. "Did Dutch find anything?"

My other cousin Dutch owned an IT security firm and spent most of his time in front of a computer. The only reason he'd agreed to move into the brownstone we all shared was to avoid his mother's constant attempts at setting him up with someone. Unfortunately for him, Trisha had taken the place of his mother in annoying him.

"Ha, it's Dutch, of course, he did," Trisha said smugly. "It's after the application and let's just say the man is no angel."

"I don't think he ever was," I muttered as I went through the information about Tak.

Tak had never been considered an angel. Back in Bridge Lake his name had been synonymous with trouble. The man hadn't changed much from the teen who'd recklessly jumped the school fence to skip class.

I stared at his profile picture. It was a lot more normal than the poster of him that decorated my room. His shoulder-length black hair was pulled back haphazardly, his deep brown eyes shined with a bit of reckless light and his thin lips were twisted in a sarcastic smile.

From the picture alone, you wouldn't know once those lips parted, a voice that could temp angels to forsake heaven would come out. I absentmindedly brushed my fingers along those lips.

"Jazzy, you're staring," Trisha teased.

Covering Tak's face, I whipped my gaze to her and felt my cheeks heat in embarrassment. She laughed. "I'll pretend I didn't see you mooning over your favorite singer and ask you once more, are you sure you want to get involved with him?" Her amused expression turned serious.

"I do," I said.

Closing Tak's information, I started the process of filling out the application for the security company. I decided to use my fake identity as Jazz Ryland, just in case my father had his dogs on the hunt. I'd have Dutch doctor up my background check and anything else I'd need for the position.

"Then I won't stop you and now that I've done my duty as the older cousin, hurry up, and apply. I can't wait to get my hands on some Rejected One merch," Trisha exclaimed. "I saw online yesterday that a pair of his old jockey's got sold for like five thousand."

I tried to keep my expression empty of any emotion. I wasn't going to the label to steal Tak's items and resell them. Though if I ever did get my hands on something of his, I'd enshrine it on my Rejected altar. Realizing immediately where my mind had gone, I mentally shook my head and focused on applying for the job.

I'd leave it to destiny on whether I got the job with Tak's label or not.

"Is Daddy dearest going to send a limo over for tonight's banquet?"

I froze up. In all the talk about Tak, I'd almost forgotten about why I'd come back to Vander City. "Yes."

Trisha muttered something before she said, "Well, I don't have anything to do tonight. Do you want me to come and help you deal with our favorite cockroach, Clark Bennington?"

I thought it over. "Yeah, as long as you promise to behave."

She lifted her hand and made a symbol with her three fingers. "Scouts honor, I won't harass your evil father."

I only smiled at her words. We both knew how I felt about him. The faster I got the unpleasant meeting over with, the better. What a way to spend my Saturday.

***

Later that night as I watched the hairdresser behind me finish my hair with a few last touches, I kept thinking back to Tak's picture.

"Wow, they took the post down," Trisha said from where she sat cross-legged on the vanity counter. Her tablet in hand, she'd been quietly tapping away on it while I'd been getting ready for the ball. We were in one of the many dressing rooms of the event center.

"What, already?" I asked confused. "Didn't they just put it up this morning?"

"Yeah, maybe the company changed its mind," she offered up as an explanation.

I bit my lip in consternation. "Then I'm going to have to find another way in. Is JS hiring for anything else?"

"I don't know, let me look." She skimmed before she gave me an amused look. "They're looking for a janitor and a cook."

I grimaced. "Nothing else?"

Out of all the jobs, security fit me the best. At least with that I had experience. I'd been trained by my uncle and cousin Zeno in self-defense since I'd arrived on their doorstep at the age of eighteen. Both men were paranoid my father would one day make a move against me and didn't want me to be completely helpless.

She laughed. "Don't be like that. Maybe you could go to one of those ritzy star parties and pull a Cinderella. I can imagine it now. It would be called the story of Vander City's hidden heiress and the rock and roll rake falling in love. It would sell hundreds of newspapers."

Sometimes I seriously wondered what went on in my cousin's head.

"I don't think I'm cut out to be anyone's Cinderella. This dress alone is testing my patience. I feel like I'm about to burst out in hives," I complained. "And as far as the job's concerned, let's just wait it out. I'll check my email over the next few days to see if they send me a confirmation or a rejection."

"Fine, that makes sense." Trisha gave my dress a look of displeasure. "And I agree with you about the hives. With the amount of tulle under your dress, you could start a forest fire. In fact, I think in some states it's even considered a fire hazard."

She looked me over, her lips turning into a frown. She set her tablet aside and grabbed up the box off the counter that held shiny pink diamond earrings, turning it back and forth. "I don't know how you do it. I'd lose my mind if I had to be dressed up like a doll for these events only to have to spend time with that disgusting cheating trash," she said.

"What makes you think I haven't?" I asked, watching as the last curl of my long hair was pinned into place. I met Trisha's eyes in the mirror. "I just hide it very well."

A knock on the door followed by the sound of my father's voice caused Trisha to place the box down and swiftly move to hide behind the bathroom door. She hated my father and the last time they'd met she'd barely been able to say hello without cursing him out. It was better for us both if Trisha stayed out of his line of sight.

The dressing room door opened, and my father entered. As usual, those who'd helped me dress left the room quickly. My father, Clark Bennington walked over and stopped behind my chair. He looked over my reflection in the mirror.

"Make sure you're on your best behavior, I've invited the senator's son, Gerald Harrison. You should get closer to him."

"I'm always on my best behavior," I said. Keeping my face empty of any emotion. I reached forward, picking up the earrings Trisha had set down. "However, whether or not I get close to anyone cannot be dictated by you. The only reason I'm here is because of grandfather's memory. Don't waste your time scheming for anything else from me. I won't let you have your way."

Not looking at him, I removed one of the earrings and placed it in my right ear. "Also, why exactly do you need me to be nice to Harrison's son? Is there something going on that you're hiding from me?"

He glared at me. His gray eyes were probing, similar in color to the eyes I saw daily in the mirror and wanted to rip out. I hated them because they were clear proof, we were father and daughter.

"I have nothing to hide and no matter how difficult you act; it won't change that you're my daughter and I am your father."

"No." I placed the second earring in my left ear before getting up and turning to face him. "It won't change that your filthy, adulterous blood is running through my veins."

His expression darkened turning his handsome face unpleasant. He curled his fingers into a fist at his side. "You know just what to say to piss me off."

I smiled, ignoring the anger that lit in me. The rage I dared never show to the public because it would ruin my mother's name. I was trapped in this superficial world of the rich because of my last name and my mother's will had bound me to stay in a relationship with this man before me.

"Funny, I can do better. You're always going to be a poor, worthless man who couldn't even keep his marriage vows."

He lashed out his hand. I caught his wrist, gripping it tightly. I could see the anger in his eyes.

"Please control yourself, I would hate to have to redo my makeup." I tossed his hand away and walking around him, I paused next to his side. "If you try to hit me again, I'll forget any semblance of civility between us and ruin you."

Continuing forward, I opened the door and stepped out. I gave a small smile to those who had dressed me and done my makeup. Walking along the hallway, I could only count the minutes until I left this stifling place.

Reaching the end of the hallway, I turned and faced the large banner that hung above the entrance that read, *Welcome To the 40ᵗʰ Annual Roarke Celebration.* I looked at the name, feeling my throat tighten.

My grandfather's name, his foundation. A foundation my father ran well, unfortunately. The primary reason I dealt with him was because of the foundation my mother had willed to him.

My father used me and the Roarke name to keep his little black book of connections for business. The foundation my deceased grandfather used to run had the biggest names in business on its board of directors. They only respected one thing, my last name.

I was nothing more than a figurehead to my father. At the age of seventeen, I'd learned that truth the harshest way.

A hand appeared in my peripheral. I looked down without any emotion and laid my hand in his. We walked toward the opened double doors. The MC spotted us from the stage and announced our entrance.

"And here to celebrate this fortieth anniversary are chairman and CEO of the Regency Conglomerate, Clark Bennington, and his precious daughter. Also, the beloved daughter of our former chairwoman, heiress, Alicia Jasmine Roarke. Please give them a hand."

CHAPTER SIX

Hide Away

Tak

Two weeks later....

"No one has seen Tak Jensei since he reportedly signed himself out of the hospital over two weeks ago. Sources say—"

I turned the TV off, not wanting to hear any more of what the media had to say about my supposed disappearance. Tossing the remote onto the couch, I then picked up my cell sitting next to me, debating on whether or not to put my manager out of her misery.

There were a bunch of messages and missed calls from my brothers and Skittles. I had been ignoring those as well.

My mostly healed wrists grabbed my attention. I stared at them waiting for something to spark. A memory, any memory. Just one.

Someone poked my shoulder. I glanced over it to find Jeff standing a distance away with a broom in his hand. "What the fuck are you doing?"

"Seeing if your real or not," he said. "I thought I'd had a nightmare about you coming over." He retracted the broom and leaned on it. "I'm still wondering why you decided to come here and not go to one of your dickhead friends."

"Because you're not going to ask me a bunch of questions," I said as I got up and walked into his kitchen.

I'd invaded Jeff's house for one single glaring reason. Jeff hated everyone and with him hating everyone, he wouldn't snitch on me to the others. "You should be honored, you're such a big asshole the others don't want to fuck with you."

"Wait, is that supposed to hurt my feelings? I know who the hell I am." Jeff stared at me like I was some interesting toy. "I'm not the person who hangs out with a bunch of guys called *The Asshole Club*."

I glared at him. "Why are you making it sound so lame?"

"Because it is lame," Jeff answered with a serious face.

"Someone sounds like he wishes he had friends." Deciding it would be more fun to fuck with Jeff, I walked toward him with my arms open. "You need a hug."

"No, I don't," he said his expression threatening.

"Yes, you do. Let's hug it out."

"I will shoot you."

"And here, I wanted us to get closer." I changed direction, heading into his kitchen once more and opened the fridge. I smiled when I saw the little bags of marijuana decorating the bottom of it.

"What is that?"

I didn't bother turning around as I answered. "The last of my fucking stash. These little babies will carry me through this scandal and fucked-up moments of self-reflection. I've been trying to stretch them out since I can't seem to get any deliveries."

I'd wanted to go out and refill my means of facing reality, but the shit that had happened in Vegas had ruined my plans for a lot of things. Speaking of which, I needed to replace my ID.

"Get out," he said grimly.

"Yeah, after I've finished one more bag."

Jeff had told me to get out at least twice a day for the last two weeks. He'd have to pull an act of God to get me to leave his house. I wasn't leaving this bomb shelter no matter what.

"Tak, are you there?" A familiar voice filled the kitchen.

I paused and whipped around to find Jeff with a shit-eating grin on his face. He had my cell phone facing me so I could see exactly who'd he'd called.

"Tak," Chelsea, my manager called my name again with a trace of hysterics.

On any other fucking day, I'd have told her to go fuck herself and gone about my business. Sadly, I knew she'd lose her mind if I didn't answer her. It was the least I could do after signing myself out of the hospital without telling anyone and escaping to Jeff's place.

I decided to give two shits and answered her.

Snatching my phone from Jeff, I said, "What do you want?"

"Tak, if you don't get your ass back to your house. I swear to God, I will send your phone number to every ex you've fucked in the past year."

I frowned. "Are you saying you want me to have an orgy? Is this a new kink of yours?"

There was a beat of silence, before I heard something break. "Okay, stay in fucking hiding, but don't blame me when Kole hires an entire security team to watch you."

My blood turned cold at her angrily spoken words. The last thing I ever wanted was to have people watching me. One, I did way too much shit that could get me locked up. And two, my demons had demons.

I'd already dodged one attempt at getting me psychiatric help. Hence, me leaving the hospital in the middle of the night and flying back to Vander. My biggest fear was I'd find myself tied to a comfortable chair, sitting across from some wizened looking Dumbledore therapist talking about my feelings.

I shuddered. "He wouldn't?"

"He hasn't yet, but he sure as fuck had the security team put an announcement out two weeks ago. And we got so overwhelmed with applications in under twenty-four hours we had to take the announcement down. We didn't even mention your band, just that JS Records needed new security," Chelsea answered smugly.

"That motherfucker," I glared at the phone. "When are the interviews?"

"I'll tell you everything you want to know when you come back home," she said.

"I'll think about it."

"Tak." I hung up the phone and glared at Jeff.

"I'll remember this."

He smirked. "Good, now get the fuck out."

Jazz

Sitting at my computer desk in my room, I scrolled through the most recent posts from JS Records. It had been two weeks and I was starting to lose hope, not to mention Tak was in hiding so I wasn't sure how much I could learn with him off the grid. However, since they'd taken the announcement down and with Tak's disappearance, the fan forum boards had been filled with conspiracy theories.

Some fans believed Tak had given it all up and secretly retired from the pressure. Others believed the sudden hiring of security at the company involved Tak's stint in the hospital. Which led to speculation about what exactly had put Tak in the hospital to begin with.

The most popular theory was that he'd been attacked by an overzealous fan. The least popular theory was Tak had attempted suicide which unfortunately, had been the narrative that had caught the media's attention.

Since I knew the real reason he'd gone to the hospital I ignored most of it. My anxiety was solely built around the fact he was still missing and I still hadn't gotten anything other than a confirmation email about the job.

I was just about to watch another compilation video of Rejected One's best moments in concert when I heard my apartment door open.

"This is the reason living with you is a problem," I said, already knowing who it was entering my place. I turned my seat around to meet Trisha's excited face.

Her eager gaze turned into a glare. "I wasn't the one who pushed the idea for all of us to live together."

"If I could go back, I'd keep my mouth shut," I said, not meaning it. "But if Uncle Carter hadn't been worried about you, I wouldn't have suggested it."

Uncle Carter was my disowned aunt's husband. My grandfather hadn't approved of his business and had immediately ended his relationship with my aunt when she'd insisted on marrying him. Ironically, that had worked in my favor when I'd run away from home after I recovered from my shock-induced emotional coma. Clark Bennington could only gnash his teeth in frustration as my uncle ensured he couldn't reach me.

My aunt, uncle, and cousins were a blessing. The family I never thought I had before I turned up on their doorstep. They showed me what family was really supposed to be like.

It was because of that me and my cousins bought three attached brownstones and renovated them, turning them into one large home. Which is why it was extremely hard to have full privacy. Especially when it involved the intrusive Trisha.

"Is that how you feel? Fine, I won't tell you that one of the fans posted that not only has Tak reappeared, but JS Records has started sending out the times for the interviews."

"What?" I stood, knocking my chair back.

She gave me a coy look. "No, it's okay. Go back to watching your precious Tak Jensei through a screen."

"Trisha, don't make me put you in a headlock," I threatened as I took a step toward her.

Huffing, she tossed her tablet to me. I caught it and Googled Tak sighting. Right away, new images popped up. With a squeal, I quickly logged in to my email to see if I'd gotten one from JS Records. Spotting it, I couldn't help but exclaim.

"Are you kidding me?"

She laughed. "It looks like their posting the job opening wasn't a mistake at all. Your chances of running into your favorite singer has increased."

I read over the information and spotted the date of the interview. "The chances may have increased, but it's not likely."

She walked over to my side and clapped a hand on my shoulder. "You have to be positive minded about this. Imagine it. You're standing in the hallway as he passes by with those long legs, delicious body, and rock and roll swag." She placed her other hand on my other shoulder and turned me around so I faced her fully.

"Jazzy, you can find out what Tak Jensei smells like for the community. We need to know if he wears Axe or is he a Prada man."

"What about finding his would-be killers?" I asked.

She waved me off. "Semantics."

Both of us shared a look before we started screaming like the Rejected One fans we were.

"What are you two screaming about?" Zeno, Trisha's brother demanded from my doorway, his expression disgruntled.

I could tell from the heavy bags under his eyes he'd just gotten back from being out all night. Probably working with Uncle Carter on something. The less one knew about what Zeno did at night, the better. Realizing Trisha had left my apartment door open I shot her a look out of the corner of my eye.

Seeing it, she stepped forward to quickly explain. "Nothing big, Jazz just got a limited edition of Rejected One's album."

He shook his head. "You two are crazy. Isn't it about time you both focused on getting a boyfriend or something?"

Trisha rolled her eyes. "I don't even know how we're related. Way to sound like a chauvinist male, Zeno."

Zeno ignored her and turned his attention on me. "Jazz, Dad said he's thinking Clark's up to something. He's been associating with too many people of the crooked variety lately. He wanted me to give you a heads-up about it, but he also said not to worry. He's got his eyes on it."

The excitement from earlier disappeared as I listened to Zeno.

"Zeno, you're timing really fucking sucks," Trisha said, anger clear in her voice.

"I just wanted to let her know she doesn't need to worry about anything," he said. "Dad promised this will be the last few months you'll have to deal with Clark."

"Okay, tell him I appreciate it."

"Jazz," Trisha called, clearly feeling bad for me.

I waved her off as I continued to speak. "Tell Uncle I'll text him later."

He tapped the doorjamb. "Got it." And with that, he left.

Trisha ran and shut the door to my apartment before she returned to me. "Are you really okay?"

"I am. Besides, don't I have bigger fish to fry, or did you forget about the interview already?"

Trisha's expression went from anger to excitement. "You're right, I can't believe you got selected. If you don't get the job, there is no justice in this world."

My only goal was to save Tak, so if I got the job great. Otherwise, I'd simply have to think of another way to save him.

CHAPTER SEVEN

Jazz

Two days later, I sat in a cold AC-filled hallway that was in sharp contrast to the hot summery weather of Vander City outside. Sitting in a confining chair, I lightly rocked back and forth trying to warm myself up a bit from being inside for too long. I looked at the line of applicants seated along the wall who were dressed like me.

Their business attire black and white and expressions tense as if their lives depended on this single moment. Everything rested on them passing the interview. I bit my lip, feeling like an imposter. I reached up and brushed the back of my neck. My newly cut hair something I was still getting used to.

What was I thinking? I shouldn't have applied. The two double doors across from us were all that separated us from the people who'd decide our fate.

I avoided looking directly at them as if the people behind the steel doors would sense my nervous glances. Tapping the toe of my heel against the carpeted floor, I couldn't kill the desire for gum. I seriously needed something to chew on.

The entire process stirred a level of stress I'd never thought I'd have to endure. The doors clicked before they were opened as a woman came forward. Her tight figure was wrapped in a pink silk shirt and a dark tan skirt.

Her hair was in a close pixie cut, dyed platinum. Her eyes were cat-like. She looked over us.

"Numbers eleven thru fifteen, please come forward." Her smooth voice had a slight country lilt that was quaint in comparison to her appearance. "It's your turn."

Rising swiftly, I mentally cursed when the papers on my lap slipped down, hitting the floor. Quickly, I bent over and grabbed them up before rushing forward. The woman eyed me before turning her attention to the other candidates who entered.

Pressing a hand against my chest, I followed them inside and took a free chair at the end. It squeaked. For some reason, it sounded louder than any of the other squeaking chairs. Straightening, I eyed the people who were seated before me.

The woman walked around the long table and took a seat next to a lean male who wore wire glasses. His dark gray eyes were focused on the packets laid out in front of him. He tapped one, his lips pursed as he brushed a hand along the lapel of his dark blue suit jacket.

Another older gentleman who had the bearing of a soldier sat next to him. The man in the blue suit lifted his gaze to look us over. He introduced himself once we'd settled in our seats.

"Hello, I am Kole Stone, JS's CEO. As some of you have heard my label has recently suffered from a scandal due to one of our artists. I'm looking to increase the security at my label.

"In particular we're looking for someone to work one-on-one with one of our artists." The tension immediately climbed at his words. "I don't expect an exemplary education, but I don't like liars."

The hairs on the back of my neck stood up. His voice drew tight before he released a sigh. He cleared his throat.

"I'm going to ask a single question, don't waste our time by trying to impress us, just be honest. What do you think we should change in order to protect our artists from others and their selves? If you answer in a way that satisfies me, I'll let you stay, otherwise." He motioned toward the door. "You'll be asked to leave immediately."

There hadn't been mention of a quiz on the application or on the site.

"Sir, I would reduce the time they spend alone without supervision," one applicant volunteered. His chest lifted and expression serious. "As their handler, I would ensure they were never alone."

"And if they're a female? Will you enter the bathroom with them?"

The guy blanched at Kole's question. Seeing his failure, the others quickly raised their hands. Many offering similar words.

The artists should be watched, and their time strictly regulated. The more they offered, I couldn't help losing more and more confidence. A part of me felt silly for being here, but I couldn't leave now. I'd stepped out of my comfort zone to be here.

"You."

I quickly lifted my gaze from my lap to the people at the table, I widened my eyes when I was met with the serious stare of the man interviewing us. He looked down at the folders on the desk before turning back to me.

"Ms. Ryland, right? You've not offered anything, what would you do?"

Feeling out of place, I glanced at the others who looked at me with a mixture of annoyance, irritation, and impatience. My mind blank, I blurted the first thought that came to me. "B… be their friend."

"Ha." The girl next to me released a laugh. "Seriously, they don't need a friend. They have plenty of friends, famous ones. How can you be a friend with them and protect them at the same time? We're not here to play, we're security."

Stiffening, I lifted my chin. Since I had said the words, I wasn't going to back down now. "I'm saying that if you treat them less like a duty or obligation, they will warm up to you and willingly come to you when they are emotionally stressed or troubled."

Feeling more confident as the man across from us hadn't interrupted me, I continued. "I'm saying, if I'm going to be there for every waking minute of their life, the least I can do is let them know I see them as them and not a poster."

"Pfft, why not make them hold hands and sing kumbaya while you're at it," a guy at the end said rudely.

I curled my hands into fists in my lap. "I could do that and still hand you your ass on the mat," I retorted only to remember where I was a minute later. "Well, that's what I think."

"Hmm." Kole tapped the table before looking away from me to the woman who sat next to him. "He definitely needs a friend, but he isn't exactly the friendly type. What do you think, Chelsea?"

The woman with the pixie cut quirked a brow. Her lips lifting at the corners as she tilted her head to the right. "He has more fuck friends than he does friends." She stood, grabbing her cell from the table. "But I'm always down with being amused." She turned her attention to me. "Hey, can you cook?"

"Y... yeah, I mean, I do well enough for myself."

She nodded, tapping away on her phone as she walked around the table. "What do you think about having casual sex with your client?"

I frowned. "I think it's unprofessional."

"What if they swear they're in love with you?" This time she met my eyes and her steady tapping stopped. "Stars have a habit of confessing love to get what they want. No matter what they say though, it's nothing more than a casual fuck to them. At the end of the day, you're the one who suffers from their one night of fun."

I tried to control my features, but my displeasure slipped through. What exactly did she think of me for her to continuously press me on the subject? I had no intention of sleeping with anyone I guarded.

I must have been silent for too long as she returned her eyes to her phone as she spoke. "I'm not attacking you. We've had a few issues in the past despite their being a clear clause in the contract about not fraternizing with the artists, but your reaction tells me everything I need to know." She hummed as she continued typing. "Okay, so I want you to show up to this place in two days, after you're finished with HR."

My phone vibrated in my suit coat pocket. I couldn't believe how quickly everything was moving. Reaching into my pocket, I pulled out my cell. Thankfully I'd taken off the usual case it resided in—a well-crafted rhinestone work of art of Tak's face surrounded by hearts. Looking from the text to her, I couldn't help asking. "A… are you saying I'm hired?"

She smiled, but it wasn't a kind one. It felt like it was used to deal with stupid questions. "I don't know what Kole's thinking, but if he wants to hire you." She shrugged, crossing her arms. "I can't say anyone will be expecting a woman, but it will be amusing to watch what Tak does with you."

Everyone in the room sucked in a quick breath. On my part, my heart pounded so hard I could barely hear anything else. "T… T… Tak," I blurted, my mouth suddenly dry. I couldn't believe it. My hands were sweating.

The job announcement hadn't stated a specific artist. It had been broad and even when Mr. Stone had spoken, he hadn't mentioned Tak. Chelsea smirked.

"The rest are going that way, but you, my dear, are special." She turned away from me and spoke to Kole.

Facing me once more, she nodded. "JS Records' CEO wants to put you with Tak and I can't argue. See you then." Without another word, she walked out of the room, leaving my mind in chaos.

For a moment, I wasn't sure it was real. I wanted to pinch myself, but that wouldn't be professional. Mr. Kole stood and motioned to the man beside him.

"Mr. Brooker will sort through the rest of you, and Ms. Ryland?"

I jumped in my chair, before standing. "Yes."

"You may leave."

I glanced at the others, seeing the annoyance and envy in their eyes. I wanted to dance, but I held myself together and gave a small nod. "Yes, sir."

I grabbed up my purse and turned quickly to leave the room, walking out into the hallway. I leaned against the door, staring into space in disbelief. Had I seriously gotten the job to guard Tak?

Looking up and down the hallway and seeing no one, I released an excited shriek. "Yes."

CHAPTER EIGHT

No Babysitters

Tak

Of all the shit I could be doing with my Thursday morning, I was storming into JS Records ready to kill. I walked out of the elevator, I didn't greet the secretary who sat behind the desk, nor did I pause as she clumsily tried to stand. Walking past her, I went straight to the door, drew back my foot, and kicked it in.

"Where's that fucker Kole?" I yelled, stopping at the sight of Kole with a woman in his lap. Twisting my lips, I held back my amused smile. "Ah-ah, now aren't we already working on your big bag of sexual harassment cases?" I asked, crossing my arms as I peered down at them. "I wonder what our shareholders would think of this side of you?"

The woman hopped out of his lap. I appreciated the sight of her breasts jiggling as she attempted to cover them and grab her clothes up at the same time. "Don't rush on my account, continue on." I turned, moving toward the door. "I'll explain to your secretary that you're too busy fucking the staff to—"

"Tak," Kole called in warning.

I glanced over my shoulder, feigning innocence. "Hmm?"

Kole stood, the fucker had already fixed his shirt and tie. He focused his cold eyes on me from behind his glasses. I couldn't understand why women wanted to fuck him. He looked like a fucking nerd.

"Fucking you would be like fucking a monk," I said aloud. I gave a shiver.

"I'm glad you feel that way," he said. "Now that you've decided to show up, what do you want?"

I turned around to fully face him as the hastily dressed woman ran past me and shut the door behind her.

"I came about some very, very disturbing news," I said, moving over to his desk. I turned and plopped down on top. Losing my joking tone, I continued. "You hired a babysitter for me?"

"You signed yourself out of the hospital and took off for two fucking weeks."

"I don't need a babysitter."

Kole walked around the desk and stopped beside me. Leaning over, he grabbed up a newspaper from off his desk and held it out to me. "This and your behavior of late tells me differently."

Snatching the newspaper from his hands, I looked at the headline. "Rocker returns after spiraling out and a failed suicide attempt." I crumpled the newspaper in my hands. "I told you already. I. Didn't. Try. To. Kill. Myself," I snarled, throwing the crumpled paper to the floor. "It wasn't me."

"Then who was it?" he asked, staring at me with those eyes filled with both skepticism and worry. He looked at me like he was the older brother I never asked for. "Tell me, who the fuck is bored enough to stage such a scene around a drugged-up rocker?"

"Fuck you, I'm your best earner," I retorted, barely holding myself back from yelling.

He nodded. "Yeah, you are, but you're also a good friend. Which is why I won't watch you fuck up your life like this. I want you watched twenty-four seven, you're worth too much for me to just leave you on your own."

"So, which is it, are you doing this as a friend or as the CEO?"

"Can't it be both?" Kole argued.

I laughed. "If it's the CEO, I can just buy you off. I have plenty of money without being an artist. And if it's as a friend, I can tell you to kindly fuck off."

"That might be true," he admitted. "But the other artists signed with us aren't as fortunate to be trust fund babies. Many of them have lost possible sponsors and advertisement because of you.

"As the lead singer of Rejected One and the first artist I ever signed, don't you think it's only right you do what you can to rectify this issue? No more drugs, no more wild parties. It's time to grow the fuck up, Tak. And honestly, as your friend I care enough about you to force the issue and not *fuck off* as you so nicely put it."

There were many things I hated. Being told to grow up was one of those things. He didn't know shit about me or my life. He only knew about the strung-out kid who'd come to him with a demo, not thinking about the consequences because he'd thought he was going to be dead by the age of twenty-five.

People always looked at me as if I was a third-grade puzzle, easy to figure out. I don't know what happened that night. A part of me knew I could have done it, but the method wasn't my style at all.

If I was serious about dying, I would have used the gun I kept tucked away in my bedroom. Let's face it, the slices to my wrist weren't even done right. I've looked it up enough to know the proper way to take myself out.

Besides, I wouldn't have done something like that on one of the happiest nights of Skittles' life. I had done a lot of fucked-up shit in my life, but I wouldn't dare to mar Skittles and Pit's bachelor and bachelorette party with my death.

Kole pressed a finger against his temple. "Look, if you can stay out of trouble for three months, I'll tell Chelsea to move your bodyguard somewhere else. Then maybe we can talk about you seeing someone."

He looked at me and immediately I felt the urge to deck him. Pity. He was looking at me with pity.

"Don't look at me like that." The tone of my voice turned dangerous. He tensed, averting his gaze. I could see the guilt on his face. "Keep your fucking guilt, I don't need it or want it. I won't take him."

"It's a her," he said.

"I don't give a fuck if it's an oompa fucking loompa. I won't have someone, a stranger, in my house, watching me and following me around. I didn't choose this life to feel like I'm trapped." I pushed off his desk and marched toward the door.

"I'm serious, Takuya," he stressed behind me.

Hearing my full name caused me to stop. No one, literally fucking no one called me that.

I curled my hands into fists at my side. Whipping around, I moved toward Kole. He knew better than anyone how I felt about my full name. The aggressive need to plow my fist into his smug face rode me. I was abruptly stopped in my tracks when he lifted a slim piece of paper.

"You will let her into your house, or I will not only put a hold on your band's activities, but you'll be getting my resignation today. And while you won't suffer, Jay and others will. Those guys' main income is endorsements and advertisements that my connections and reputation get them. And since you've refused to reenter the studio for the last few months. They'll put the entire blame of their loss of income on you."

He used his free hand to push his glasses up. "You like to act like you don't give a shit about anybody else, but we both know you give way more fucks than you'd like others to know. What will it be, Tak?"

Without speaking, I walked toward him and grabbed him up by the collar. "You know I fucking hate you, right?"

He didn't bother to defend himself against my move. "Don't worry, I love you enough for the both of us."

I mentally ran through the pros and cons of pushing for the bodyguard to be fired. I knew one thing for sure about Kole. He wouldn't back down. Both of us were bullheaded, the two of us had a habit of focusing on the end goal.

"Shit." I shoved him away, turning my back on him. "Fine, I'll think about it."

He coughed. "No, you won't think about it. You'll do it."

"Fine," I spat as I glanced over my shoulder at him. "If one of them loses a single deal, I'll come looking for you."

With that, I slammed out of his office. Storming past his secretary, I ignored the woman and entered the elevator, staring ahead blankly. Fuck Kole and the day I handed my fucking music to him. I'd been high out of my mind and had thought to leave behind some musical confession.

Banging the back of my head against the wall, I wanted to wrap my hands around that fucking car thief's throat and squeeze. If it hadn't been for that man, I would've been living my life as usual. Instead, I was assigned a babysitter.

What the fuck? I already had my brothers and Skittles demanding answers and blowing up my phone. Not that I answered it. One thing at a time, please.

"Fuck," I shouted and scrubbed a frustrated hand through my hair.

How could I explain, yes, I'd contemplated killing myself? Yeah, I'd pushed a little harder on the gas. And fuck yes, I'd smoked and swallowed more drugs than were healthy and had lived to tell the tale, but no, this one fucking time, I didn't sit my happy ass in a bathtub and slice my wrists. Telling anyone this would be admitting to being weak enough to have those thoughts.

And what I hated more than Kole was fucking pity. Seeing that look on my brothers' faces would make my stomach turn. I'd fought so hard to be a part of their world. I cursed and drank as much as they did and sped my cars as fast as they did. I wanted so much to belong—

Shit.

I didn't want to think about it. What I wanted was to clear my head and remember that night so I could prove my innocence.

With a ding, the doors opened. I pulled my sunglasses out of my pocket before putting them on. I stepped outside.

"You're here?"

Chelsea, my manager gave a nod as she scrolled through her tablet. "You've got a photo shoot tomorrow at seven a.m. and an interview with Music Review at the end of the week. Danny has sent another email asking for your agreement to do that commercial."

"No. No and fuck no," I said.

She paused in scrolling and looked up at me. "Yes, yes, and I'll work on it."

I side-eyed her. "I should fire your traitor ass. How could you let Kole hire a fucking person to watch me?"

She pursed her lips, squinting her eyes up at me. "Because it will be funny."

"Bitch," I muttered.

"Asshole," she whispered back, smiling up at me brightly. "Also, could you give your clingy ex a call? She's annoying the fuck out of me. Apparently, she wants to make sure you're okay." She rolled her eyes. "Not that she couldn't just check online to find that out. I don't know what it is about you that makes women lose their common sense."

"If you weren't allergic to dick, I'd show you," I said as we drew closer to the exit of the building.

"You don't have to," she said, placing her own sunglasses on. "I know why. It's in your back pocket." She pushed the door open. "Now, smile for the cameras."

The sound of screams and shouts from the paparazzi filled the air as I stepped out past her. Immediately my sight was filled with the backs of guards as they held off the fans of my band and the reporters who crowded forward with their phones out to record the words I wouldn't say.

"Tak. Tak. Have you recovered? Where have you been?"

"Is it true you were in rehab?"

"How are you feeling after your failed suicide?"

"Tak, we love you. We love you."

Entering the car and shutting the door, cutting off the many voices, I released a tired breath and leaned back. "When is she coming?" I asked.

"Tomorrow," Chelsea, who sat in the front didn't bother turning to look at me when she answered. One would think she paid herself.

"Right." So, I couldn't do anything about the person coming to my house, but it wasn't like I couldn't figure out a way to get rid of them.

"Great."

CHAPTER NINE

Mr. Jensei

Jazz

Catching a taxi to the place where Tak lived was a surreal experience. I still couldn't believe I was moving in with him. He lived in a well-known gated community, with its sprawling mansions and groomed lawns. It was my first time in the neighborhood, but I spent more time looking at my cell phone than looking around.

I feared I'd get a message telling me I'd been mistaken about everything. That I wasn't really hired by Tak and they'd meant to hire the dick who'd had something to say about my words.

The taxi came to a stop right when I convinced myself I should tell the driver to turn around. I was reckless and I enjoyed stealing cars but pretending to be someone else was a whole different thing. What if they figured out I wasn't really the woman on the resume—she didn't exist?

However, I was the only one who knew someone was out for Tak's life. I was the only one who knew the faces of the two who'd taken him. If I didn't step forward, who would?

Taking a deep breath, I grabbed the car door handle and got out. I'd left the delivery of my bags to Leonard. I figured lugging it behind me wouldn't look good when meeting Tak for the first time.

I finished paying the driver and took in the front of the house and the cars that were parked in front. The loud music emanating from the house, along with the yells of a large group of people were a clear sign there was a party going on.

I walked up the steps unsure if I should enter. Stopping on the top step, I reached out to knock on the door only for it to be pulled open.

"You're here," Chelsea stated, looking me over.

I tugged at my white shirt. I'd worn a white wrap shirt, with flared black pants, and low kitten heels for an altogether professional look. She lifted a brow.

"Okay, well, here's your first test. He's been told no partying, so… stop it." With that, she turned and left me looking after her in shock.

"What? Wait, Ms. Chelsea." I chased after her.

I was stunned at the sight of the people who were clearly drunk, lounging here and there. The house was full to near bursting. Models strolled past me as they paraded through the living room, where a few people were making out.

Unsure as to what to do, I continued forward, hopping over the writhing bodies. Muttering a curse, I staggered, nearly tripping on the shag rug. Annoyed, I walked outside to where there were people hanging around the pool.

I squinted as I scoped it out. Spotting my target, I was momentarily stupefied. The fan in me losing my grip. It was really him.

I almost sighed, but I didn't. Instead, I checked my mouth for drool. Takuya Jensei was a work of art and no one could tell me differently. Since he'd released his first album as a freshman in college, I'd followed him closely.

Too closely as my cousins would say, but who else in life was as beautiful as him? He was a god walking amongst us filthy humans. At six three, he stood taller than most of the men surrounding the pool.

His skin had a warm glow. His handsome features were only outshined by his natural charm. His black hair was pulled back in a low bun and every time he smiled his canines would pop out.

He didn't look like a guy that was knocked unconscious two weeks ago. It was a shame he wasn't singing. To me, his voice was like the call of a siren.

The sudden scream of a woman as she was tossed into the pool took my attention away from him. I immediately reminded myself I was there for a job. I needed to act like a professional and not a teenage fangirl.

"Control yourself, Jazz," I whispered to myself.

Straightening, I made my way toward him. A semicircle of what I assumed to be his friends surrounded him. As I drew closer, I continued my mental pep talk.

Reaching him, I stepped forward, ignoring the dirty looks some of them sent my way. I introduced myself, praying I wouldn't choke midway.

"H… hello, Mr. Jensei, I'm supposed to be starting today as your bodyguard—"

"Who?"

For a second, I didn't hear his question. All I could hear was his voice. It was smooth deliciousness, poured over chocolate. Tak, the lead singer of Rejected One had just spoken to me. I was so occupied with that I barely heard his next words.

"Looks like we've got an intruder. You guys know what to do," he said, pointing at something behind me.

The two men beside him took a step toward me. I looked them up and down in confusion. Returning my gaze to Tak, I attempted to explain. "I… I'm sorry. I misspoke, I was recently hired by—"

"I…" He closed the space between us. Leaning down, he used a finger to tug his sunglasses down. "Don't know you," he iterated, his gaze boring into mine. Pushing his glasses back up, he gave the curt command. "Toss her."

"Wait." Before I could argue my arms were grabbed and I was lifted up. I struggled, cursing myself for being so starstruck I'd let them get a hold of me.

"Wait, stop. Mr. Jensei," I shouted his name, but he only waved at me. A wicked smile decorating his lips. "Son of a bitch I… agh." I released a scream as I was tossed into the pool.

The water swirled overhead. My purse exploded open around me. I was so shocked, I let myself sink for a second.

He'd barely let me finish my introduction. Takuya Jensei apparently didn't like the idea of having a new bodyguard around.

Ms. Chelsea had said this was my test. Kicking off my heels, I swam up, breaking the surface. The laughter of those around me only fired my anger higher.

"I don't know who sent you, but I don't want or need you, so leave," Tak shouted at me from where he stood at the edge of the pool.

He shot me a smile, before turning away, treating me to a view of his nice ass in swim shorts. Swimming to the steps, I then made my way up them. He didn't want me here, okay. However, I refused to leave, and I was going to do whatever I needed to do to stay.

Brushing my hair back, I muttered under my breath, disgruntled. I'd have to wash it again. Sans shoes, I looked for a way to pay Tak back for his punk ass act. Spotting one, I smirked. Marching over to a high table, I grabbed the ice bucket that sat on top of it.

I followed behind him. "Hey."

He stopped making his way to the DJ, turning around. He looked me over before smiling. "Now, now, I'll gladly fuck you if

I can fit it into my schedule… it would have to be a quick fuck though."

Keeping my face blank, I walked toward him lifting the bucket. He frowned. "What are you doing?"

"Nothing," I said innocently. Passing him, I stopped right in front of the DJ who hadn't noticed me yet. "Just fulfilling my assignment." I let the contents pour out over the DJ's turntable.

"What the fuck? Are you crazy?" the DJ said. Shocked, he retreated from the sputtering equipment.

A hand landed on my shoulder. Dropping the bucket, I grabbed the wrist and dove under the person's arm and twisted. "Agh, shit. Let go," they shouted in pain.

I kept an innocent face and met Tak's astonished expression. "Ah, look at that. It looks like it's time for your party to end. How sad is that?"

"Shit let me… argh," Tak's goon cried out. I lashed out with my foot, forcing the guy in my hold to his knees.

"So… Hi, I'm your live-in bodyguard, Jazz Ryland."

There was only silence after my introduction. I took a deep breath to clear my head and groaned.

I'd snapped again.

Tak

Who the fuck was this woman?

She'd had the balls to pour ice over the turntable like it was nothing—a few thousand dollars' worth of equipment. She apparently wasn't the least bit worried about what I would do to her after what she'd just done. Instead, she glared at me from between the strands of her wet hair, holding Dereck's hand like he was a toddler.

He kept cursing, but she'd completely stilled him. Looking at the hold she had on him, I couldn't help being impressed. Not many could subdue a guy over six feet.

"Impressive, what makes you think hurting him will make me stop the party?" I asked.

She lifted her chin. "I don't think anyone would have a lot of fun after one of their guest's arm is broken."

Dereck released another pained cry. "Fuck, Tak. Tell her to let me go."

I met her gaze. Her eyes were hard. I searched for the anger I usually experienced when a plan didn't go my way, but it was nowhere to be found. Who had fucking hired her? Oh right, Kole, the dick.

"Let me think about it," I said, drawing out the time.

I'd thought a dip in the pool would run her off, but instead she'd proven to be more difficult. I searched for what step I would take next. Clearly, she wasn't the type to be easily deterred. Kole had found a real stubborn one, hadn't he?

A part of me couldn't believe Kole had actually hired her to work for me. The woman wasn't the behemoth or over-muscled stallion that I'd imagined. She was curvy and somewhere around five nine. She had almond-colored skin and brown eyes. Her chin-length hair was plastered to her head.

Swiftly, I went through the pros and cons of giving in. It would be in my favor to go along with her, for now.

"Shit," I cursed aloud. "Fuck it." I looked at the DJ behind her, who'd grabbed some towels in an effort to dry his equipment. "Brody, I'll pay you for it, leave it."

Brody looked from me to his stuff before sighing. "Fine." He shot Jazz a dirty look before he tossed the towels down and left.

She didn't seem happy with my move. She gave a pointed look to those who still hung around. "I think you should dismiss your other guests," she said, releasing the man at her feet. Moving back, she turned and grabbed up a towel. "I would hate to give them the same treatment as your friend here."

"You bitch," Dereck yelled.

"Enough, take your people and go," I ordered.

"Are you seriously letting this bitch walk in here and call the shots?" Dereck questioned, looking from me to the crazy lady. He stood. "Nah, fuck that."

"Call me a bitch one more time and I'll knock out your teeth," she said as she rubbed a towel over her short hair. She let the towel drop, giving him a hard smile. "I don't know why, but I'm a little on edge."

Nope, I wasn't getting hard because she just threatened to dentist Dereck's teeth, shit. Two things occurred to me immediately. One: this bodyguard of mine wasn't easily intimidated and two: I found her very attractive.

Kole had made a fatal mistake in sending her to me. I decided I wouldn't put my energy into bullying her, but into seducing her. I grinned.

Then, she'd get fired. Win-win for everyone. She wasn't lacking in the looks department with soft brown eyes that narrowed at the ends, a cute straight nose and delicately curved lips. Ms. Bodyguard looked a lot softer than she acted.

"Tak—"

"Fucking leave, Dereck," I ordered, glaring at him before turning my glare on all the others still hanging around. "All of you, leave."

There was a beat of silence. "Leave," I shouted.

Finally, the leeches realized I was serious. Oh yes, please, they needed to go so I could get my bodyguard comfortable and tap her 'til she couldn't think about anything else. Shit, I would have her on her knees, calling me her daddy before this day was through.

Turning back to her, I bit back a hiss. She'd taken off her shirt altogether. Giving me a glimpse of the lacy bra she clearly wasn't shy about showing.

I loved a woman who was bold. Time to turn on the charm. I closed the space between us, but closed my eyes and prayed for patience when I heard my name.

Releasing a groan, I turned. "Yes, my dear and lovely cockblocking manager."

I won't admit to the level of hate I feel for Chelsea aloud, but if I did it would be as big as the fucking globe.

"Cockblocking?" Chelsea repeated, looking me over before her amused gaze found mine. "I don't know what you're talking about. I need to show her around your home."

I took a step closer to Chelsea and pointed at her. "Aka cockblocking," I whispered, glaring at her.

She rolled her eyes, walking around me. "Ms. Ryland, follow me. I'll get you a change of clothes, hopefully your luggage arrives before the end of the day."

"Hopefully, I'm sorry for the inconvenience," my new bodyguard said brightly.

"Don't worry, I was expecting some type of mess from your first meeting with Tak. Lucky for you, it's only wet clothes."

I groaned, watching as Jazz was escorted away by Chelsea. Her hips swayed in her wet slacks. "Jazz, that body is pure Jazz," I said, already hearing the smooth soulful saxophone explode in my mind. Wincing, I looked away from her. "Dammit."

I'd thought the music had calmed, but it was back. Distracted from the interesting addition to my staff, I quickly left the pool and made my way to my studio. Until the music turned off, I wouldn't be able to focus on anything else. It was my blessing and curse, but it was also the time I felt the least lonely.

However, once I dealt with it, I'd turn my attention on Ms. Jazz. *Mmm.* She would be out of here before the end of the week if the hardness of my dick was anything to go by.

CHAPTER TEN

Sassy Lady

Jazz

"I'm impressed with you," Chelsea said as she led me along the hallway, past the large windows that gave a view of the large yard that rested around the pool. "I wasn't sure if you'd be able to handle the situation." Her heels clicked along the marble floor as we turned right. She stopped, looking over her shoulder to face me. "Tak can be stubborn, and he has no problem saying what he thinks. Not too many can stand up against him."

I bet. He wasn't some small child. I wouldn't call him stubborn, more like an asshole who was used to getting his way, but that didn't stop the part of me that cheered because I'd seen him in swim shorts. In fact, if his manager wasn't staring at me, I'd probably be halfway to imagining him without them.

I brushed a hand over my cheeks feeling the heat there. "Well, I'm tougher than I look. I've dealt with my fair share of stubborn VIPs." I couldn't help giving her a dry smile. "I just can't believe

I thought it would be easy to be friends with him. I feel kind of stupid now for answering the way I did at the interview."

She shrugged, facing forward as we continued on. "Your answer wasn't bad. If you like your work, you'll get close to those you work with. Tak and I clash because I'm the one who tells him what he doesn't want to hear. So, we'll always clash, but you still have the chance of becoming his friend." We entered what looked like a den.

"There are ten bathrooms, including the one that will be your room. There's a studio located in the north wing. That's where Tak locks himself away when the music comes to him.

"You'll have to urge him to leave when he's really into it. There's a gym down the hall from your room and his rooms are located in the southern wing." She paused in front of a bar giving me a long look. "I don't think you'll be called over there more than maybe once a day. That's only if he's bored enough to keep working on getting rid of you."

I bit my bottom lip and nodded. Not only was I going to have to pay attention to finding out who was after Tak's life, but also to the man himself. It was pretty obvious he didn't want me around.

"Outside of him calling for you it's best to routinely check on him. He has a habit of sneaking away and causing mayhem," Chelsea continued. "Make sure you maintain a line of professionalism, even though you're both living together, don't become too comfortable with him."

Hearing this I felt both excitement and anxiety.

Any fan imaginings of being the love interest of Tak had already been dashed with his tossing me into the pool. I wasn't so sure I'd like to be in any kind of relationship with the ass. All my dreams and obviously unrealistic desires had washed away with the pool water.

"You don't have to worry about that, I follow all the Rejected One's edicts."

Hearing this, her stare turned probing. "I didn't take you for a fan. I usually only hear that from Tak's top fans."

I'm an idiot. How could I have exposed myself so easily? Rejected One edicts were the rules put out by the biggest fans of the band.

Rules we adhered to for both their and our safety. One of those rules was never to covet the members, they belonged to everyone. Laughing, I waved the end of my towel.

"No, no, I'm not a fan, my cousin is. She's actually one of the portal leaders for the fan board and she told me about the job opening. That's how I knew about it."

My underarms prickled as she looked me over. A part of me felt like she could see through my small lie.

"Hmm, well that's good. If you were, we'd have to move you out ASAP."

"Ha ha, well, I'm definitely not a fan. Not me." I laughed nervously.

She turned on her heel. "Good, I'll be taking you to your room. I had one of the staff bring you some of my spare clothes. I've had to stay a few times overnight, but hopefully your own clothes will arrive before you have to use them."

"Thank you," I said.

"No problem, I will tell you your duties now. You're a bodyguard, your job is to protect Tak from outside threats, but you also will protect him from himself. Which means, while I do not expect you to hang out in his wing. You will wake up with him, you will ensure he eats, you will make sure he makes his appointments, and that he keeps to his agreement with the label. Don't worry, it's not every day, you've been given Monday off for personal time.

"The job sounds more like one for a manager," I said jokingly.

The more I listened to her, the more it felt that way. She paused and glanced at me. We stood in front of what I assumed to be my room.

"Well, the way I see it, me and my wife wish to try for a baby and I can't do that chasing him down all the time. So, why not have his live-in bodyguard take care of in-house things? Don't you think so?" She smiled like the cat who'd gotten the crème.

She opened the door and entered. "Your room has all the comforts. There's an intercom system from his wing to your room, when he presses the button in his room, he will be able to call you if he needs you, but it shuts off at eleven p.m. If he really needs you after that, he'll sound an alarm.

"After all, anything that's happening after eleven p.m. isn't going to be good. On the desk is a tablet and phone. You'll use those to communicate with me, Tak, and others who work for the label.

"Otherwise, don't use it. The tablet will be updated daily with his schedule and appointments. Also, there will be a list of people who aren't allowed to meet him. Or more so, if he meets them, we'll have another scandal to deal with." She turned around and crossed her arms, smiling. "Any questions?"

I swallowed and shook my head. "No, I… I don't have any."

"Okay," she said, moving toward me. "The shower is free for use. Hopefully, it has everything you'll need. And that's it for your introduction, welcome to the Rejected One team." With that, she passed me and left the room, closing the door behind her.

I stood in the bedroom wondering what had just happened. It felt like time had been speeding forward with no brakes and suddenly it had slowed down. I took the towel from around my shoulders, tossed it on the bed beside the set of clothes that'd been dropped off and gave a heavy sigh while looking around the room.

I, Alicia Jasmine Roarke was in her favorite artist's home "I—"

I brought my hands up, covering my mouth to keep from screaming it out. I did do a little hop before taking a deep breath a few times so as not to hyperventilate. It was like I'd become the main character in a teen romance drama.

This was awesome.

Turning, I tossed myself onto the bed and stared up at the ceiling. Giving a slight wiggle, I hopped off the bed and ran into the bathroom. It was nice with black tiles and a sleek silver design. Taking my bra off and undoing my pants, I let them drop. Walking into the shower, I turned the water to hot and washed up. Once I was finished, I grabbed a gray towel and wrapped it around my body.

Stepping out, I looked at my short haircut. It was getting frizzy. They might have had a bar of soap that actually smelled good, but it looked like that's where my luck ended.

Groaning, I grabbed the extra towel from the wall and began rubbing it through my hair. Opening the door, I stopped. Parting my lips in silent wonder.

Tak Jensei sat on my bed. His ringed fingers going through my belongings that must have been delivered by the staff after they'd gathered them from the pool. He glanced up, and I swore his eyes were like fiery stones that seared me all over before they met mine.

"Hi, I wanted to see if you needed anything and to apologize for my earlier actions."

Now, there was something the top one percent of Tak's fans knew better than others, and that was when he was lying. His left eyebrow that had a slice through it—an old injury from when he was twelve and wanted to fly—would twitch, and it was twitching now.

I was caught between being amused he'd thought I'd believe his bullshit and being fascinated with how he fit so well into holey black jeans, a black T-shirt with a deep V cut—that should have been banned—with a dark gray cardigan. He had changed out of his shorts. I decided not to go the super fangirl route. Which involved screaming and throwing myself at him.

"Okay, then apologize. I'm not stopping you," I said, pretending not to be bothered by the fact he was in my room, while I was only wearing a towel. I approached the bed focused on changing into the clothes that were behind him.

His jaw worked as he narrowed his eyes. "You're a tough one, aren't you?"

I stopped beside him. "I'm supposed to be the wall between you and those who'd want to harm you. It's to be expected. What—"

He grabbed my wrist suddenly and pulled me to his side.

"What if I wanted you to be a little nicer to me?" he whispered, his gaze on my lips with a level of heat that was mesmerizing. "You don't have to keep your guard up against me, you know."

I wouldn't melt under his sultry gaze. "I'm not. In fact, I believe you're the one who needs to soften up here."

"Maybe I was shy. I'm not used to meeting new people. How about we forget about it and start over. We could do something pleasurable that only requires two players." He smiled. "Or more than two if you're feeling adventurous."

The wealth of bullshit that had come out of this man's mouth was astonishing. My mind that had been spinning in the web made by his voice became clear as glass when he mentioned a ménage. I took my hand from his weakened grip.

"I have no reason to lose my job over a casual fling. Mr. Jensei, if you don't mind, could you leave my room so I can finish dressing?"

He leaned back, covering his mouth, he took me in for a long moment. "You're not gay, are you?"

I flushed. "No, I'm not," I said, trying not to hit him.

He hummed, looking me over, then motioned to himself. "Then, what's wrong? Am I not your type?" He gasped. "Are Asian's not your thing? That's racial discrimination, you know. I feel like you're ignoring my sexual identity because of my race. I'll tell you now, I'm packing." He winked.

"Were you dropped on your head when you were a baby?" His eyes widened the same time as my own as I realized what I'd said.

"Sorry, I spoke without thinking," I quickly said to save the situation.

Tak

By her shocked expression, Jazz hadn't meant to let that question slip out. She faced me, so clearly astonished by her own words, I wanted to laugh. Lucky for her, I found her refreshing.

I'd been insulted by women before. Mostly over my lack of desire to continue seeing them.

Deciding to play with her a little more, I seriously asked, "And if I had? Is that something you should ask your employer?"

She snorted, before freezing. "Sorry, again."

"You really aren't good at hiding your thoughts, are you?"

She offered me a sheepish look. I refused to acknowledge the warm feeling that invaded my chest. I was a hard-ass fucker who ate pussy for breakfast, lunch, and dinner, despite my current diet, thanks to Kole's rules.

Shit, I wasn't feeling warm because chocolate, cocoa deliciousness here was smiling at me.

"I'm not used to controlling my emotions on my personal time."

"Personal time?" I repeated, realizing just how I would torment my new bodyguard. "There is no such thing when you're with me," I said, standing so the space between us would disappear.

She looked up at me with suspicion. I shouldn't have felt as good as I did from the knowledge that she was a few inches shorter than me. "I'll offer you two choices. Either quit and leave now or quit and leave later in tears."

She lifted her chin. "I'm staying and I'd appreciate it if you'd stop asking me to leave."

I leaned down, using my height to let my presence fill up the space between us. She tried to move back but her legs bumped into the side table. She looked down, giving me the chance to get close enough, so my lips brushed her cheek. "Baby, there are only two possible outcomes for you if you stay here. You'll either run from here screaming or you'll be in my bed screaming. I, of course, have my own preference." I smirked, flashing my teeth at her as I straightened.

Jazz huffed. "Or you'll be screaming because I've broken your wrist for sexual harassment."

"I'm not Dereck, sweetheart, don't bite off more than you can chew."

"Is that a bet?" She tossed her head in just the right way that showed off her throat.

On my grandmother's grave, I'd be putting a hickey there. "Oh, do you want it to be? I rarely pick a losing side."

"There's a first time for everything, now get out." Jazz motioned with her chin to the door.

Of course, but first. I grabbed the top of her towel and yanked. She yelped, too slow to slap my hands away.

She released a shrill screech. "Tak."

I laughed, turning before I could get a full view of her body. "Now, now, Ms. Ryland, I just wanted to make sure there wasn't any bruising from your dip in the pool," I said, walking toward the door.

"Son of a bitch," she cursed as the door shut. I leaned back against the closed barrier, lifting the towel. I took a deep breath.

"Hmm, she smells like me. Good."

Humming, I left her side of the house.

I decided to stop cursing Kole. He'd sent me something amusing to play with, while I got to the bottom of my missing memory and supposed suicide. The sooner I found that thief, I'd feel less stressed.

Dropping the towel in the hallway, I headed back to the studio. However, my phone vibrated. Taking it out, I looked at the name on the screen and grunted in annoyance.

Debating on whether or not I should answer, I swung the phone between my fingertips. Well, I guess this would be as good a time as any to deal with the person on the other end.

"Hello, my least favorite band member. How is your dick-filled life?" I crooned as I changed my destination from my studio to my bedroom.

"It would be great if the lead singer of the band would get his shit together." Came Jay's annoyed response.

I shook my head. "Sorry, that's something that just can't happen. It would ruin his image."

"Tak, you're about to have no image if you don't stop being reckless," he nearly growled on the other end.

"That's incorrect. I would have an image, just a shitty one," I continued, ignoring his warning tone. Silence met my words. "Ah fuck, don't be so sensitive. I'm following the Kole commandments to a T."

"Is that so, then why did pictures of you at a pool party pop up all over the net?"

Because I was plotting to piss off my bodyguard. Something told me that explanation would only piss Jay off more. Usually, I didn't care about what others thought, but Jay had been one of the few friends I'd made outside of the five I called my brothers and sister. He'd welcomed my offer to join Rejected One, when we were nothing but freshmen and starving musicians with a dream.

"I just wanted to celebrate a bit before I was put under complete house arrest."

"Right, and now I have to deal with Kole trying to get me to keep track of you. I already have a man in my life I want to keep track of, and that's my boyfriend."

I smiled from ear to ear, getting Jay pissed was my special talent.

"Aw, and here I thought I was the only special guy in your life. Damn, there goes my crush of ten years," I said, grabbing the remote off my bed and hopping on it. "I'm now suffering from heartache. Let's keep this short, why did you really call?"

"Urgh, why are we friends?" he complained.

"Because of destiny and fate. We're tied by a red string, but unfortunately you left me for that evil Connor, the uptight—"

"I'm calling to tell you not to forget what Ark said. He's not coming to another rehearsal—whenever that is—unless you apologize to him."

I dropped my hand, making a thumping sound on the bed. "You're fucking kidding."

"I'm not," Jay deadpanned. "He's been bitching about it at my house. Crying on and off about how you don't trust us and should have told us about your pain."

I groaned. "I swear to God, I curse the day you added that emotional ass to our band."

Jay sighed. Yep, I'd been the one to write songs and music, but Jay had been the one who'd pushed me to actually build something out of it. Ark was our Irish drummer, who'd been the best in the area.

He was all about comradeship, fucking rainbows and shit. He and I clashed like oil and water. I called shit how I saw it, and he cried about shit.

"You should call him and reconcile."

"Reconcile what exactly?" I asked, rubbing a frustrated hand down my face. "I don't understand why anyone believes the shit on the news. I didn't slice my wrists. No, scratch that. I've been low, Jay, you've been there. Have I ever been the type to sit in a bathtub and do something like that?"

Jay was silent for a long time. I wanted to yell at him, the urge was so fucking strong it felt like not doing it was giving me a headache. "Jay," I snapped.

"I don't know what to believe."

I stood up. "Shit, I—"

"Listen to me, Tak. Listen. All I know is that for the past year it's felt like you've been running from something. I don't know what it is, but I've watched you and when I heard what happened, a part of me couldn't help thinking you'd finally done it.

"You'd finally succeeded at leaving behind whatever demon that's been riding you. I won't pretend to understand everything about you, but since college you've always been the guy who everyone thinks doesn't give a fuck about anything. I'm one of the few people who knows you're not that person. So, yes, if you told me you had a moment of weakness, I wouldn't not believe you because you were there for mine."

I closed my eyes, trying to repress the urge to lash out. I wanted to cut ties and tell him to fuck off, but that would hurt one of the few fucking people who called themselves my friend. I couldn't do it.

Actually, I could do whatever the fuck I wanted to, but I wouldn't do it. Jay didn't deserve any of my anger. My anger was for the blank space between the chase in the parking lot and waking up in the hospital.

"Look, I'll have to call you later." I needed to get off the phone.

"Wait, Tak—" I cut the call, staring ahead.

My mood was shit now. I didn't want to see Ark, the kid band member whose selling point was being nothing like me. He'd always given me a huge helping of the one thing I couldn't stand, pity. I lifted my phone, pausing when I spotted Deacon's number.

Shaking my head, I tossed my phone down on the bed. Deacon had been calling me since the party and my lackluster attempt at death. The last person I needed was him breathing down my neck.

"Shit, what am I going to do?"

I still hadn't called any of my crew about what had happened. I'm sure they were chomping at the bit. I probably only had the luxury of being left alone because Skittles was holding the others back. A part of me felt bad for not at least texting her.

I'm pretty sure if I were to see Pit, he'd rip me a new one, but the one I really didn't want to face was Deacon. Nope. No thank you. It wouldn't do shit for my confidence to get my ass beat by that asshole.

A knock on the door brought me out of my churning thoughts. "What?"

"Mr. Jensei, your band member, Mr. Ark is here. He says y'all need to talk." The voice of Jazzy oddly calmed me, but I wasn't of the mind to explore that because that emotional fucker Ark was in my house.

I marched over to the door and wrenched it open, ready to rip into him. Instead, he threw himself at me. Even if I wanted to dodge, I couldn't.

"Tak," he cried, his blue eyes watering over.

I stood my ground, closing my eyes, praying for patience. "Please tell me you're not crying." He sniffled. I stiffly placed my hands on his shoulders and pushed him back. "You're crying."

"Don't be an asshole and hug me," he said, rubbing at his face.

I didn't want to hug him. I didn't even want to be near him. The real reason I felt uncomfortable around him was his constant need to express his thoughts. I kept everything in, he told the whole world how he felt.

"I was so scared you'd died," he wailed.

"Well, in this moment, I wish I had," I muttered to myself.

Feeling someone's eyes on me, I turned just in time to catch Jazz's amused stare before she looked away. I narrowed my eyes. At least someone was enjoying the fiasco.

"Do you mind leaving us?" I asked as Ark's wailing had changed to a slight screech.

She shook her head, pursing her lips together. "I... I'll leave you guys to it."

She beat a quick retreat, but not fast enough for me not to see the tail of a tattoo on her thigh peeking out from beneath her shorts. I tilted my head sideways, ignoring the fact that Ark had wrapped his arms around me again and pressed his wet face into my chest. The tattoo was a welcome distraction from the revulsion that ran through me.

I wondered if she'd let me see the whole thing one day. Then I answered my own question, of course, she would. She would show me everything. After all, I was motherfucking Tak.

Averting my attention, I lifted my arms and brought down my elbows on the back of the annoyance clinging to me.

"Agh, what was that for?" Ark demanded as he staggered back, his arms crossed as he pressed his hands to his shoulders.

I gave him a blank stare. "Sorry, I was aiming for your throat."

With a look of alarm, he placed his hands around his throat. "Are you serious?"

"Yes," I said, fed up with playing with him. "I thought you weren't going to see me anymore until I apologized."

"I wasn't."

Sensing a but in there somewhere, I gave him a probing look. "But?"

"Jay told me I should come over and at least hear why you did what you did," he admitted.

I made a face at that. "I have a better idea. Let's let bygones be bygones and I let you borrow one of my cars as an apology for being a bad band member?"

"Are you seriously trying to buy me off with a fucking car?"

"Is it working?" I would do anything to not have to apologize to the crybaby before me. Anything. Emotional conversations weren't my cup of tea.

He flushed as he glared at me. "You know you're fucked up for not reaching out to us and leaving us in the dark, right?"

I barely held back from rolling my eyes. "Yes, which is why I'm offering up one of my cars to you as an apology."

"I shouldn't take your offer."

"No, you really, really should," I pushed. The faster he took my offer, the faster I could get back to enjoying my bodyguard.

He glared at me. "Fine, I want the Lykan Hypersport."

This fucker. It took everything in me not to punch him square in the face. Out of all the cars that lined my garage, he had to pick my newest toy. I inhaled deeply through my nose and said, "And you'll come to practice?"

He nodded. "It's been like a few months since our last one, but when you finally drag us back. I'll be there."

Reluctantly I agreed. "Fine, you can borrow it. The keys are hanging near the front door."

"Okay, but don't think you can buy me with a car if you do this shit again," Ark warned before he left.

With a tired sigh, I shut the door and pressed my back against it. I glared at the phone that still remained on my bed. Next time, I wouldn't hang up so abruptly and let Jay finish. If I had done so earlier, I would have known the jolly leprechaun was coming. Grunting, I took off my cardigan and waterlogged shirt and tossed them both in the trash.

CHAPTER ELEVEN

Sweets

Jazz

I'd expected Tak to leave at some point during the day, but since his friend, the drummer had come and gone he'd spent the day by himself. Seeing the two together had caused my heart to squeeze.

Ark was the blond angel of Rejected One. The youngest and all-around favored amongst the fans for his willingness to communicate on social media and take pictures with them. If it wasn't for the dark draw of Tak, Ark would have way more fans. In fact, those who stanned Ark were almost psychotic with their level of devotion.

I paused in the hall to hug myself. My fingers ached to type this up and post it on my forum, but I couldn't. That would be violating the NDA I'd signed, but boy did I want to.

Inhaling deeply, I straightened, dropping my arms. "Clear, calm, and pure thoughts," I muttered, before I finally choked the life out of my inner fangirl. Clapping my hands together, I made my way to the kitchen. "Time to see what food rock stars eat."

"You've got to be kidding me," I murmured moments later, staring at the back wall of the fridge.

There was almost nothing in it. My stomach released a grumble. How could he only have water and microwaveable rice? How the fuck did a man who was six-three with two hundred pounds of muscle survive on nothing but water and rice?

I bit my lip, closed the fridge doors, and squeezed my eyes shut. Once again, I opened the doors. Still empty.

I closed the doors and moved to the cabinets. Opening them, I found junk food in abundance. I couldn't believe it.

From Ho Hos to Twinkies. He even had a large ass bag of gummies. Apparently, he survived off sweets. The one thing in the world that would destroy the figure I'd worked so hard for. Ugh, an addiction was an addiction and apparently his was sugar.

Letting the cabinet doors close, I turned around and stared in absolute terror at the counter. This would be the reason I quit. Not because of his harassment and not because I was discovered. No, because of the temptation of Twinkies in the cabinet.

I had to do something. Thinking hard, I spotted my cell and then a mental light went off. Grabbing it up, I then searched for the app I'd been forced to download by Dutch—who left his house only when there was a death in the family or his mom was coming over, causing him to hide in Trisha's apartment.

Spotting the green app, I released a cry of happiness. I could order groceries and have them deliver it here and from there I'd be able to feed myself. And here I'd thought musicians were so anal about their diet they'd keep a chef on call.

Then again, maybe it was only the people in my life who had their own chefs. Speaking of which, after ordering groceries, I made my way to my room and made a phone call.

"You rang," Dutch answered.

"Did you hack the cameras already?" I asked, chewing on some gum that had been in the drawer in the kitchen. "I tried to hold off calling until there weren't many people in the house."

"Am I Dutch? Do I not hold the most tags for computer invasions?" he bragged.

I laughed. "Are you also the asshole who burned my Rejected One poster?"

His arrogance diminished there. "I told you it was an accident. I was trying to see if the cloth from my cosplay costume was flammable or not. I didn't think it would turn into a firestorm."

"Excuses," I said as I threw myself on the bed. "I still owe you for the crack in Tak's first guitar."

I heard Trisha yelling in the back before Dutch released a curse.

"How was it?" Trish shouted. I moved my head back, staring at the phone, annoyed. "Did you steal his underwear yet?"

"And why would I steal that?" I asked, insulted.

I was a true Rejected Fan. We'd steal something way more valuable than some underwear. Ah shit, now the thought of stealing his underwear filled my mind.

"Because you're capable of anything when it comes to your favorite band," she said sarcastically. "I still think you're going to spend at least one day breathing in his shirts."

I flushed. "Can you put Dutch back on the phone, please?"

"Oh Jazz, you didn't."

"I didn't," I snapped. "Can I speak to Dutch?"

"I'm back. That shrew invaded my apartment again. I swear, I'll have to seal my door one day."

"Whatever, that's on you. Did you tap the cameras?" I asked, eager to get this phone call over with.

"Yeah, I have a tie into the feed, and I've been looking at the old footage from the cameras around his home. I thought I'd have better luck there."

"What do you mean?"

"At first, I thought I wasn't getting a hit because the Las Vegas police hadn't taken prints because they ruled it a suicide. They wrapped up pretty quickly, since Tak's label pushed it.

"But then I cleaned up the images we have from Vegas and expanded the search. I ran them through the criminal databases, but nothing popped up. It's almost as if someone blacked out any trace of them. It's like they disappeared. I've tried over and over for those last two weeks. Nothing. You have to have a lot of power and money to do that."

I bit my bottom lip at that news, banking the information. "What about his rivals or his bandmates?"

"From what I could find and there isn't a lot. There isn't really anything about his bandmates that gave me a red flag. Now, he does have six friends he hangs out with the most during his downtime, but again I couldn't really find much on them accept their names and professions. Oh, and one is the mayor's daughter."

I lift a brow but say nothing. Before my mind can take off, Dutch continues, taking my thoughts in an entirely different direction.

"Though after a bit more digging, I found a report of an incident that happen when he was in high school, but it literally has almost zero information on it. It's like someone started a report and didn't finish it."

"Okay, when was it filed?" I asked, curious.

Dutch hummed along to the sound of his fingers clicking against the keys. "It looks like whatever it was is buried pretty well. The only thing I can find is that it happened the night of your prom…" He stopped abruptly. "Ah, sorry."

I didn't react, instead, I said, "Look into the accident and see if it might connect to someone who's near him now. And can you do me a favor and ask Julius to call me."

His tone turned subdued. "Sure, but why?"

"I've been getting a bunch of electronic invites from father about meeting Harrison's son."

"Okay, and Jazz, I'm sorry. I didn't think."

"Don't, it's fine, Dutch. I'm going to call you back later. Okay."

"Okay, bye."

It wasn't Dutch's fault my prom fell on the night of Tak's unknown incident. I hadn't paid attention to much around that time.

I released a heavy breath, rolling over to my side. There were a lot of things I wanted to forget about Bridge Lake. That night was one of them, my life became hell after prom.

Closing my eyes, I tried to push down the memories that wanted to draw me in. Maybe tomorrow would be better, but I couldn't think of anything better than being in the same house as my favorite singer and old crush. Eventually, I fell asleep.

CHAPTER TWELVE

Not the Same

Tak

Lying on my bed, I contemplated what I would do first to my bodyguard that morning. I'd slept in since I'd spent the night in the studio. Hearing the sound of my phone buzzing on my nightstand, I reached over and picked it up.

Skittles: Come to the front door.

I read the message, then read it again. The last thing I wanted to do was see Skittles.

Since I'd been home for four days and no one had busted my door down, I'd thought they'd all silently decided to give me space. Obviously, my assumption had been wrong. This was the exact thing I'd been avoiding when I'd run to Jeff's place.

As I contemplated whether or not I would answer the door, my phone buzzed again. This time it was a call from Pit. I stared at his name before I answered.

"Hello?"

"We know you're inside, kid. Come to the fucking door. Otherwise, I'm coming inside, and you're not going to like what happens to you if I have to break in," Pit nearly growled.

"I'm coming."

"Good." He hung up.

"Shit."

I tossed my phone down and got up and dressed in a robe and pajama pants. Finished, I went out to let Pit and Skittles in.

Ever since Pit had asked Skittles to marry him, it was like they were attached at the hip. I should have fucking known if Skittles decided to come confront me, he'd be with her.

No matter how old I got or the amount of muscle I put on, Pit still intimidated me. I still couldn't pick out what exactly Skittles liked about him. Maybe it was the whole bad boy persona he pulled off.

I'd tried to work through the messed-up feelings I had when I saw the two together. It wasn't like I wasn't happy for them, but there was also this feeling of having someone precious to me stolen. I knew these thoughts were childish, which is why I hated feeling this way.

They were both good friends to me. Skittles had become like the older sister I'd never had. However, the feeling of resentment was still there and then Luke had gone and decided to follow in their footsteps. Thinking this, I opened the door to the pissed-off expressions of both Skittles and Pit.

"It's only you two?"

"The others are too busy to deal with our spoiled child today," Skittles said as she walked in followed by Pit. Her colorful hair eye-catching as usual. "Besides, we're enough."

Closing the door behind them, I then led them to my living room and took a seat. Instead of following my example, they remained standing across from me. I played it cool and asked, "So why did you come?"

"Because you've been acting like a little bitch since Skittles, and I got together. Now this bullshit. It's time we talk," Pit said, holding back nothing. "Do you know how worried Skittles was when she saw the news? And then your little bitch ass decides to hide at Jeff's like I, of all people, wouldn't know where the fuck you were."

"Pit, enough," Skittles said.

The two shared a look. During their silent conversation, I felt my mood turn sour. It was shit like this that made me feel the ever-turning wheels toward a time where I would no longer be needed by any of them. One day I would call, and everyone would be too busy for Tak.

My jaw clenched as anger swept through me. They finished their silent exchange and Skittles turned her attention to me.

"Tak, I've been meaning to talk to you for a while."

"Oh?"

"I get your family life was shit growing up, they abandon you, but that bullshit has nothing to do with who we are. I vowed to you a long time ago, you would always have me and the assholes, we'll always be your family.

"Just because Pit and I have changed our relationship, doesn't mean we're tossing you to the curb. Nothing changes with us. The day you became my little brother, you were stuck. No take backs. We're all finally growing up, but that doesn't mean I'll ever stop caring about you," Skittles said.

"I wonder about that." I felt the anger that had been simmering in my gut rise when she mentioned my family. "You see, I know for a fact once people start changing it doesn't stop. Promises are nice to hear, but when it's time to keep them, I doubt that they'll be kept."

Skittle's expression darkened. "Make me flip your ass. When have I ever failed you? When have any of us ever left your ass hanging? You really think you can't count on us?"

I didn't answer her, letting my silence speak for itself.

"You know what? I don't know what else I can do to prove to you we aren't going anywhere," Skittles finally said, sounding tired.

I looked back at her.

"This time, it's not about you or Pit or any of the other assholes. It's something I have to work through on my own. Right now, what I need the most is for everyone to back the fuck off and stop trying to *help* me."

I felt like I'd gone back to the teen who'd pushed everyone away so they couldn't hurt him by leaving, but for my sanity, it was the only thing I could think to do. I pretended not to see the hurt in Skittles' eyes. However, I wouldn't change what I said, even if Pit punched me.

"You know what, let's give the kid what he wants," Pit said, his expression cold. "Yo, since you want us to leave you alone, we're out. Call us when you're ready to grow the fuck up, find your balls, and want to face your demons because this pussy shit ain't it."

He flexed his fists before he grabbed Skittles' hand and pulled her along with him. "Wait, Pit. Hold on," Skittles yelled as she twisted, trying to get out of his hold. "We can't leave him like this."

"Yes, we can. You can't always be his mother," he said. "It's time he figures this shit out on his own."

He pulled the front door open and left. I could still hear Skittles yelling at him as they hadn't shut the door behind themselves when they left. I leaned back and blankly looked ahead.

"Mr. Jensei?" Jazz slowly walked around the corner. Her curious gaze looking from where Skittles and Pit had left to me. "Are you okay?"

Looking at her worried expression, I felt oddly less messed up. "Yeah, I'm fine."

"Who were they?" she asked as she walked deeper into the living room. My eyes were immediately drawn to every step she took in her tight leggings and the peek of stomach that flashed me from her crop top.

"Friends. What are you doing?" I asked, trying to change the subject.

She gave me a small smile. "Just looking around to get my bearings in your house."

"Why, when you're only going to be here for a few days?" I said just to see the angry flush come to her skin.

"Well, I believe I'll be here a lot longer than that," she said. I enjoyed watching her try to hold back her temper.

I came to my feet and walked over to her. "There's a difference between being positive and being delusional. We'll figure out which one you are by next weekend," I said, stopping in front of her.

She lifted her chin. "We surely will."

I dropped my eyes to her lips. As if sensing danger, she deliberately put space between us and narrowed her eyes on me. "I'll be continuing my tour of your house, please call me if you need anything."

I quirked a brow. "And what if I need you now?"

She gave me an insincere smile. "I hope it's for something that's covered in my job description."

Right as I was going to tell her just what type of job it was, the sound of her phone going off distracted her. She pulled her cell phone out.

"Hello?"

I frowned as she quickly left the living room. Shit. I couldn't catch a break.

I decided to go back to my room and get some more sleep before I fully committed to driving my bodyguard crazy. I walked over to the still-open front door and closed it, pushing what happened between me and Skittles to the back of my mind.

I'd address it once I had my head straight. I just needed time.

CHAPTER THIRTEEN

Heiress

Jazz

"Hey, Julius, what's up?"

Julius was another cousin of mine who lived in the brownstone. He was a prosecutor who spent most of his time in his office located downtown. He also did some work for my uncle Carter under the table, but that was to be expected since he was part of the Liberiu family.

"When are you coming by your office?" he asked.

I entered my room and closed the door behind me. "I should be there tomorrow, why?"

"Dutch told me you wanted to talk to me about Senator Harrison."

"Yeah, Clark has been sending me emails since I got back from Vegas about meeting the man and his son. I have little interest in doing anything involving him, but it's a red flag, nonetheless. I need to know why he thinks my getting closer to the Harrisons will help him."

"Got it, I'll come by your office. Can you let the others know I won't be home for a while? Uncle Carter is going to be making moves soon against the Ripaldi family, which is going to increase the work I'll have here at the office."

I laughed. "I'll tell them, but you already know what Trisha's going to say."

"The same shit she says all the time. That Uncle's going to ruin my chance of ever meeting anyone and I'll never get married. My chances are ruined even without him, my own work is time-consuming on its own."

"Completely agree, talk to you later."

"Yeah, see you tomorrow."

Finished talking with Julius, I tossed my phone onto my bed and looked over at the two suitcases that sat at the end of my bed that I needed to unpack. I walked over to them and grabbed one. I would put my things away and once done, I'd make something to eat.

Since it was my second day on the job, Chelsea had let me know I could spend it getting comfortable with my surroundings.

And since I was off tomorrow, I decided to take care of everything in-house today.

***

A half an hour later my stomach felt like someone was pinching it. Placing the last of my folded clothes into the drawer, I decided to go make something to eat. Walking out into the hallway, the house was silent.

Making my way toward the kitchen, I relaxed when I saw he wasn't there. At least for a few minutes I wouldn't have to deal with Tak's advances and provocations. Entering the kitchen, I opened the fridge and looked over the items in there.

Thinking it over, I decided to make pastrami sandwiches with a French onion soup dip. I took out the pastrami meat, mushrooms, provolone cheese, and an onion. Placing the ingredients on the counter, I walked over to the pantry and grabbed the hoagie bread out from where I'd squeezed it next to Tak's large supply of Twinkies.

My mouth watered as I thought of what it would taste like once I was done. I got to work and soon the smell of my French onion soup filled the kitchen, along with the pastrami sandwiches that were baking in the oven. Seeing that everything was cooking fine, I turned my attention to cleaning up after myself.

Hearing someone enter the kitchen, I glanced up and frowned to see Tak hovering over my soup pot. "Do you need something, Mr. Tak."

"Oh, baby, no. Don't call me that," he said in a fake pained voice when he looked at me. He had gotten rid of the loose pajama pants and robe. Replacing them with a loose T-shirt and ripped jeans. "I've already reached thirty. I don't need you adding years to me by calling me Mr. Anything."

"I'll remember that," I said, thinking that the man could make anything he said sound sarcastic.

"What is this you made here?"

"French onion soup," I said, cleaning off the cutting board I'd used and placing it in the dish rack next to the sink. "It's going with my pastrami sandwich."

"Mm, sounds good." Tak walked over to the fridge and pulled open the door. He reached inside and took out a bottle of water. "Can you make me a plate too?"

"There might not be enough," I said to pay him back for tossing me in the pool. "And I'm not sure you'll like it. Maybe you should order something instead." I tried to maintain a polite expression.

"Oh." He turned away from the fridge and walked over to the stove and opened it. "Look what we have here, more than enough for us to share." He looked back at me. "You weren't planning on starving your kind boss, were you?"

I didn't even have the energy to roll my eyes. The word *little* and Tak shouldn't even be in the same sentence. "No, the thought never crossed my mind."

Closing the oven, he walked over to my side and tapped my shoulder with his bottle of water. "Something tells me you're being sarcastic."

I glanced at him. "You could tell?"

A wolfish smile took over his face. "I like a woman with a talent for sarcasm, makes things interesting."

I swallowed, trying to keep my eyes above his collarbone as the smell of his cologne entered my nose. Dammit, he was too close. He stared into my eyes with those deep brown eyes of his, derailing my train of thought.

I was angry and irritated with him. I had to remember this was the man who'd decided to make it his mission in life to get rid of me. I had to do something to break whatever was stirring up between us.

"And I like a man who doesn't throw me in a pool when we first meet," I said, putting space between us. I walked around him over to the oven and turned it off. "The foods done."

I'd thought he'd go back to his room while I made his plate or at least leave the kitchen. Instead, he watched me move around the entire time. Just as I went to pick up two bowls, he asked me a question.

"How old are you?"

"Huh?"

Tak

Watching Jazz move around the kitchen filled me with a strange
sensation of warmth. I'd barely used it over the few years I'd lived
here. Aside from hosting a few parties, and having Skittles over,
the kitchen barely saw any action. Most of my meals were ordered
from a health club in the city.

She reached up and pulled an escaped lock of her short hair
behind her ear. I'd pretended not to notice the pointed looks she'd
been sending me since I'd taken up a permanent spot next to the
counter. It was amusing to watch her try to hide her thoughts.

It was obvious she wanted me to leave so she could finish
making my plate without me observing her. The longer I watched
the more curious I grew, which is why I blurted out such a
random question.

Recovering, she answered. "Twenty-nine, a few months
behind you, I think."

She wasn't that much younger than me.

"Are you originally from Vander?" I asked watching her pick
up the two bowls and place them next to the pot.

She paused for a second. "No."

I tapped my index finger against the kitchen countertop.
"Then where are you from?"

"I was born near Bridge Lake," she said as she finished pouring
the soup into the bowls and set them down on the plates that held
our sandwiches.

"Oh, then you're from the same town as me. We might have
even met before." I tried to think if I'd ever met a Ryland, but I
gave up shortly after. For me, Bridge Lake was a place that held
only dark memories.

"I doubt it, I left and moved in with my aunt and uncle when
I was a teen."

Replacing the ladle into the pot, she then pushed one of the
plates toward me.

"Here you go, I hope you like it."

She picked up her plate and headed toward her room. I stepped in front of her. "You're not planning on making me eat alone, are you?"

Jazzy's confused expression was starting to grow on me. "I... I wasn't really planning anything. I was going to watch a movie and eat."

"Then let's watch it together." I took her plate and picked up my own. "Grab me a beer out of the fridge and let's hang out."

Biting her bottom lip, she squinted her eyes in suspicion.

Donning a phony innocent look, I said, "I promise I'm not up to anything. I just want to hang out with my new bodyguard. Is that so wrong?"

"Again, the same bodyguard you're trying to have fired by the end of the week," she said, sounding skeptical.

"Look, would you join me if I said I promise to not pull anything tonight in exchange for your cooking for me?"

I could see the cogs working behind those lovely brown eyes before she finally answered. "Fine, I'll hang out with you, but only if you agree that I can punch you if you try anything."

"Agreed," I said. Those delicate little hands of hers probably hurt a lot less than taking a punch from Luke.

"Cool, let's do it then." She gave me a bright smile.

I pretended my stomach hadn't tightened the minute I saw it. I turned around and walked toward the entertainment room on my side of the house. I heard the fridge door open, followed by a clinking sound before she followed behind me.

"What movie were you planning on watching?" I asked when she reached my side.

"*Dawn Of The Dead*, I've been really into zombie movies lately."

An hour later as a rotting corpse limped across my flat screen and our dishes sat empty at our feet, Jazz cuddled into my side completely knocked out. Her nose wrinkled every time one of the characters released a high-pitched scream. Instead of waking up, she simply snuggled closer to me.

I looked over to the other end of the couch where she'd originally been seated. I wasn't quite sure how she'd gone from more than an arm's length distance to attach to my side. Every time I attempted to move, she followed me like a koala clinging to a tree.

Seeing she wasn't planning on waking up anytime soon, I picked up the remote and turned off the TV, immediately cutting off the noise. Thinking over what I would do next, I stood up and bent down to pick her up easily. She didn't even flinch, I couldn't help but release a laugh.

This was the woman Kole had hired to watch me and it took less than a half a beer and good food to knock her out. Shaking my head with amusement, I carried her to her room and laid her down atop her bed. Leaving the room, I shut the door and headed back to the studio to do some work.

CHAPTER FOURTEEN

Chilling

Jazz

Waking up in my room had confused me when the last thing I remembered was watching a movie with Tak. I rolled over and looked at the alarm clock that sat on the nightstand. I was relieved when I saw it was only five in the morning.

Getting up, I frowned as I stretched and felt a twinge in my lower back. I rubbed my eyes and cringed when my contacts moved. Luckily, they slipped right back into place. I'd traded out for these day-and-night-wear colored contacts so that I could keep my identity hidden.

I walked into the bathroom and started getting myself ready for the day. Twenty minutes later, I headed out with a small book bag on my back. I stopped at the door to make sure I had everything. Just as I placed my hand on the door, Tak came up behind me.

"Where are you going?" he asked.

I turned around to find him holding a cup of what smelled like coffee. I looked up and saw there were dark circles under his brown eyes. I bit my lip to keep from laughing at his appearance.

He wore a dark red Snuggie and he looked like he hadn't seen sleep in years. His shoulder-length black hair was all over his head.

"It's my day off, I've got some errands to run. Chelsea's sending over my replacement in about an hour," I explained.

Those sleepy looking eyes turned clear as his lips twisted with displeasure. "Who approved this? I didn't say you could abandon me today."

I pursed my lips together to keep the first thing that came to mind from coming out.

He shuffled toward me, staring down at me. "Jazzy, don't leave me. Let's have another movie night."

I took a step away. "I'll be back tonight, Mr. Jensei."

I turned, opened the door, and ran out to catch the Uber I'd ordered.

"I told you not to call me Mr. anything," he shouted after me.

I ignored him and ran down his driveway and spotted my ride at the end of it. I waved to the driver before I opened the door and got in.

I only dared to look back once we were on our way. Tak was no longer in the doorway. I hoped he'd stay out of trouble while I was away.

***

A few minutes later, I was dropped off at my favorite café.

"Ms. Roarke." I turned my head to find my assistant, in a neat and clean suit, standing next to my limo.

I smiled as I walked toward him. "On time as usual, Leonard, and here I was looking forward to getting some breakfast before you arrived."

"I already bought your favorite. Salmon on a rye bagel and a chai latte made with skim milk and two shots of espresso. It's in the car. And we'll be stopping by the boutique so you can change your clothes before we arrive at the office," Leonard said as he opened the car door for me.

Leonard was the best thing I'd inherited from my mother. He was almost forty years old, with a resume that put the mayor's right-hand man to shame. I'd offered him early retirement several times, but he'd refused each time. Aside from my cousins, he was the person I trusted the most.

I took off my backpack and held it out to him. "I heard that my father has been approaching some of the stockholders with interest in purchasing their shares."

Taking the backpack, he said, "Yes, I've been keeping my eye on it. I'll explain the situation on our way."

Getting in, I waited for him to shut the door. Seeing a stack of folders, I murmured a curse so that Leonard couldn't hear it. Another reason I'd tried to make Leonard retire early was because he loved working me to near death. Well, once he got his hands on me that is.

I picked up the contact case that set next to the folders and quickly took out my contacts. Once done, I turned my attention to the files.

Picking up the first one, I opened it and read through the information there. This kept me busy until we stopped at the boutique. Placing the paperwork aside, I got out and was escorted into the boutique by Leonard.

Inside, James greeted us enthusiastically. He was a young man who looked about thirty. He wore a double-breasted suit jacket that was open over his mickey mouse T-shirt and well-made slacks and loafers.

"Alicia, what were you thinking, not telling me you were back in town?"

I laughed at his words. "James, you know I barely have time to breathe when I come to Vander City."

"Hmph, don't complain when I give away our shop's best newest styles to Emily Rotherson. You know she's always stalking me online to dress her."

"No, you wouldn't."

James averted his gaze from mine. "I don't know, I just might."

"Come on, you know I love you. Leonard, give James our gift."

"Ms. Roarke ordered this especially for you," Leonard said as he stepped forward with a brown box that read Bvlgari and handed it over to James.

"Oh my god, what is this?" he asked, wiggling his eyebrows at me. "You didn't have to."

"It's the least I could do since you're letting me use your boutique like a changing room."

He opened the box and released a tiny gasp at the Bvlgari Serpenti Viper bracelet inside, before he closed it and gave a look around. He closed the space between us and whispered, "Are you serious?"

I patted his shoulder. "Which changing room is mine?"

Recovering from his shock, James led me to the back while Leonard remained in the front.

"Everything is prepared and don't worry." He made a zipping motion to his lips. "I won't tell anyone what I've seen today. And thanks for the gift." He waved the box before he quickly left me to change.

I entered the changing room. I found it a bit surreal when I stared at my chin-length wavy bob and cheap athletic wear. The only thing missing was the brown contacts I wore. I looked completely different from the heiress known as Alicia Roarke.

Turning around so my back faced the mirror, I started the process of turning back into the heiress of the Roarke family. A few minutes later, I stepped out. The long wig I wore brushed the center of my back. It felt like I regained a limb I lost as the familiar weight was back.

James exclaimed in approval. "You look delicious, my dear. What do you think of my choice?"

I glanced at the mirror that sat against the opposite wall of his checkout counter. I took in how my body looked in the Saint Laurent, deep V jumpsuit and six-inch red bottoms. A long necklace of black metal hung down my chest, contrasting with my skin tone.

"It's passable," I said as I looked away from my reflection and walked toward the exit. "I'll be back next Monday. I'll see you then."

"P… passable?" James sputtered as I walked past him. Leonard followed me out.

After getting in the car, I checked my watch and was relieved I wasn't late for my meeting with Julius.

***

When I entered my office, I greeted Julius who sat waiting for me. "I'm sorry, the minute I walked in a few of the managers wanted to speak with me." I walked over to the seating area that was set up in the center of my large office.

I set my wallet down on the coffee table and sat down on the leather couch across from his love seat. My other assistant, Gail, entered carrying a tray with two cups of tea.

Julius' lips quirked up in the corner. "No matter how many times I see you like this, I can't help but feel impressed by the contrast to you at the brownstone."

Gail set the two cups down and left once finished. I leaned forward and picked one up, removing the top. "I'm never against impressing people. So, tell me about Harrison and what my father wants from him."

Looking amused, Julius continued. "Well, there wasn't much I could find. Which means whatever Harrison can give your father is something he's hiding very well. I've asked Dutch to put some feelers out on Clark in regard to his financials, and since he's been looking at buying shares of your company, Uncle Carter told me to have Dutch look into buying shares in his company."

I blew gently on my tea. "Uncle Carter is a firm believer in tit for tat. I wish he'd stop trying to keep me from getting involved."

"You know why he's adamant that you stay out, Jazz. He doesn't want to see his niece get hurt, none of us do," Julius said, his expression stern. "And no matter how many times you ask to get involved, the answer will be the same."

"As I've told you before I'm old enough to take care of myself."

"Old enough, yes, but there isn't any reason for you to when you have us here to take care of him for you. Liberiu protect their own," he said.

We shared a long look before I finally looked down into my teacup. "Fine, I guess I'll leave it to you guys to deal with."

"And here I thought you'd put up more of a fight."

I rolled my eyes. "You're all too stubborn. I know when to give up. Besides, you're right. I trust you all to handle it."

Standing, he gave me a mischievous look. "As you should."

I would leave it to him, Zeno, and Uncle for now, since I was focused on dealing with Tak and his would-be killers. However, once that was solved, I'd turned my full attention to my father and what his relationship was with Harrison.

Julius walked around the coffee table over to my side and leaned down to give me a small kiss on the cheek.

"That's my favorite cousin," Julius said. "See you later, and don't forget to let the others know I won't be home for a while."

I waved him off. "Yeah, yeah, go away you traitor."

He laughed as he pulled back and swiftly left my office. I had just finished my tea when my office door opened and the sound of what seemed like a struggle going on reached me.

"Mr. Bennington, I've already told you Ms. Roarke said to make an appointment if you wish to see her."

I looked up to see my father forcing his way into my office past Leonard. "Let him in," I said, replacing the top on my teacup and setting it down on the coffee table.

My father shot Leonard a scornful look. "Alicia, it seems like your staff is under the impression they should block me from coming into your office." He moved his gaze to me, his look becoming one of arrogance. "Surely they're mistaken. You wouldn't let that Liberiu scum have entry over your own father, would you? I just past one of them in the hallway and he had the audacity to act like he didn't hear me when I asked him why he was here?"

I stood up and walked over to him, stopping him from fully entering my office. "Julius is a man of few words. He doesn't like wasting his time when he doesn't need to. What brings you here uninvited?"

I waved for Leonard to leave.

"I heard that you've been spending less and less time here at the main company and since you got back from Vegas, it's gotten harder to see you," my father said.

Keeping my expression carefully blank, I silently wondered who'd sent him this information. It looked like I would have to have Leonard comb my employee roster.

"And?"

"I thought I could offer Aaron up to assist you," he said giving my office a once-over. "As your father, I'm always concerned with your well-being. Of course, I don't wish to hinder you, but at your age, running such a large business can be tiring. Especially since there's no one for you to rely on."

He offered me a fake worried expression and took a step forward. He placed his hands on my shoulders. It took all of me not to shudder in disgust when he touched me.

Clark Bennington was a two-faced rat. To imagine this was the same man who called me spoiled and a waste of space not even a few weeks ago. I also had suspicions he had something to do with my mother's death and my comatose state after.

Unfortunately, there had never been enough evidence to prove it. I kept my voice cold as I offered him a sarcastic smile.

"I'm not so stressed here that I need the bastard child of my father's mistress turned wife to come here. And I would suggest you stop wasting your time trying to pretend to be a loving father. It makes me sick."

Stepping back so that his hands fell from my shoulders, I gave him my back and walked toward my desk. "I don't know where you got your information, but I assure you I've not wavered once in dealing with the legacy my mother left me, nor will I."

Reaching my desk, I pressed the intercom button on the phone.

"Yes, Ms. Roarke." Leonard's voice filled my office.

"Please send security to escort my father out."

"Yes, Ms. Roarke, they're on their way right now."

I turned around, dropping my smile as I took in my father's angry expression. "And please, don't forget to make an appointment next time. Unlike the Liberiu scum, you're not welcome here."

CHAPTER FIFTEEN

Tak

I sat in my living room watching the sun sink down in my back yard. My assigned bodyguard had yet to return. Her replacement had been some angry man on steroids.

He'd spent most of his time hanging out in my living room on his phone. The urge to do something to him had rode me, but I just wasn't as inspired as I was when bothering Jazz.

"Hey, what time can I get rid of you?" I asked him from where I sat across from him on the couch.

He didn't look up from his phone when he said, "Twelve midnight or when Ms. Ryland comes back."

"It's midnight, get the fuck out."

"It's not."

I smiled. If Chelsea had been here, she would have told Mr. No Neck this was a bad sign.

"Sorry, let me repeat that. I must've not been clear. Kole pays your wages, I own Kole. You have two choices, you no-neck fucker. Either leave with the hope of a check or leave with the knowledge that not only did you fuck up and lose money, but you'll never get a job protecting anyone in the music industry again."

Finally, he lifted his pin-shaped head and stared me down with his beady eyes. "You're pretty mouthy for a strung-out rock star."

"And you're pretty fucking dumb for a steroid-infested bull man." I added a wink to make him feel special.

Just as he got to his feet, the door to my house opened. "Looks like you won't have to worry about losing your job after all, Bull Man."

Jazz came walking in and I immediately felt a small— exceedingly small amount of happiness at the sight of her. Of course, this was because I enjoyed fucking with her. She looked a bit frazzled and she wrinkled her nose as she saw me and Bull Man who was putting his cell phone in his back pocket.

"Are you Ms. Ryland?" he asked.

"Yeah, thanks for covering for me. Sorry, I couldn't tell you when I'd be back when Chelsea asked," Jazz said to him, not sparing me a single glance.

Irritated, I glared at her. "And what about me? Don't you have an apology for me?"

She looked away from the big fucker to me. Neither of us bothering to offer to escort him out.

Goodbye, Mr. Mountain.

"Why would I apologize to you?" she asked as she took off her backpack and set it on the couch where the bull man had been sitting. "Today's my day off. I honestly didn't need to come back until tomorrow."

I stood up and walked over to her, stopping short when my nose caught a whiff of something familiar. Frowning, I closed the space between us, grabbed her shoulders, and buried my nose in her neck. Shit, it was what I thought it was. Men's cologne.

"What... Tak?"

I ignored her cry of surprise and her immediate attempt to pull out of my hold. I couldn't believe it, while I'd been stuck here with that blob of muscled flesh, she'd been out with some guy with shitty taste in cologne, having a great time.

She twisted out of my hold and shot me a fulminating glare. "What's wrong with you?" she demanded. Her cheeks flushed with anger.

"Nothing," I said, immediately cooling my expression. "I hope it was worth it."

"What are you talking about?"

Not bothering to explain, I turned on my heels and headed back to my room. I'd promised Chelsea and everyone who could hear I was going to make my lovely new bodyguard miserable and now I had every intention of doing so.

I ignored the small trace of jealousy that popped up at the back of my mind. She'd gone out with some unknown fucker. I plotted on how I'd make her life hard.

CHAPTER SIXTEEN

Let's Run

Jazz

Over the next two weeks, it turned out there were thousands of things I could think of that were better than being in the same house as my favorite singer and old crush. Everyday he'd done something else to drive me up the wall. From honey in my body wash to being picky about what I cooked. Tak had become more annoying than a two-year-old.

This time I had to deal with being awoken by his loud yells. He was apparently a morning person, something his profile hadn't mentioned. The man had somehow found a foghorn and had decided to use it to wake me up.

I'd been so shocked; I'd fallen out of the bed and slammed my elbow on the corner of the nightstand. While I lay on the floor, contemplating murder, he'd burst into my room in a black tracksuit.

I hated him on sight. The least the fucker could do was sleep in like a decent rock star. Instead, he looked down at me with a cocksure grin and pointed at the night sky. There was no sun. Why the fuck was he up and there wasn't any sunlight?

My brain was so filled with questions, I could only grunt when he said my name.

"Ms. Ryland, it's time to go running. You weren't thinking of sleeping in, were you?" He clicked his tongue, shaking his head as he feigned disappointment.

Finally regaining my tongue, while still lying on the floor, I asked, "And you couldn't go on a run alone?"

He gasped. "Without my protector with me? No way, I wouldn't dream of leaving without you. We have to be together, twenty-four seven." If a devil had a smile, it would look like the one on this demonic asshole's face standing in front of me. "Come, come, I would hate to have to tell Chelsea you're slacking."

"I bet you would," I muttered. I got up and walked to the closet only to realize something. Turning around, I stopped short when I found Tak had followed me. "Space would be nice."

He stared at me like he didn't understand my words. "Huh, but what if you get lost?"

"Lost?" I repeated, trying to find the patience I was not known for. "I'm sure I won't and I'm sure you're the last person I'd call for help."

He took a step closer, forcing me back. I placed my hands behind me. I couldn't punch him. I loved him—platonically—and hitting his face would be a sin. I'd also lose my job, but if there were a god, he'd stub his toe before this day was out.

"That hurts. I'm known for my charity work."

"Well, I'm not a charity case." I nodded toward the door. "I'll meet you in ten minutes."

"Five," he challenged.

"Five," I agreed.

He grinned. "What a good little girl you are."

I smiled. "Always, sir." He left and just as the door shut, my smile dropped. I'd show that misogynistic jerk. He said he wanted to run, well, let's run.

Tak

I'd thought I was getting back at that annoying woman forcing her to run with me. Instead, I questioned my own sanity for making such a suggestion. The minute she'd come outside with that look in her eyes, I should have known something was up.

My watch went off for the third time, followed by me releasing a gasp for air and staggering to a stop. Sweat dripped down my face. Squinting down at my watch, I could see we'd already reached the five-mile mark.

"Are you still good to continue?" she asked with a customer service smile as she lightly jogged in place next to me. Looking me over, she then creased her brow. "Would you like to stop?"

"I... I think I should—" I panted out only for her to cut me off.

"But don't you run five miles every morning?"

Something in her words sounded like doubt, which pissed me off. I wasn't some bitch. I would keep going. It'd be a cold day in hell before I let her have the satisfaction of seeing me quit.

Even though it'd been two years since the last time I'd gotten up early and ran five miles. My lungs felt like they were collapsing. Running on a treadmill hadn't prepared me for running up and down the hills of my larger than necessary neighborhood. I swore the minute I got her ass home and I could breathe again, I'd toss her over my knee and spank the shit out of her.

I forced myself to straighten and together we ran the last two miles home. God, I hated running. She released a cheerful whistle as she ran beside me.

I swore I'd pay her back for this. One way or another.

CHAPTER SEVENTEEN

Disturbance

Tak

As we drew closer to my house, I could see my plans from earlier would have to change. Kole's red Corvette sat in my driveway. Fuck, this day was really taking a shit on me.

"Sir, do you recognize that car?" Jazz asked as her posture turned defensive.

Impressed, but also annoyed, I nodded. She thought she could protect me. I could protect myself. I placed a hand on her shoulder.

"It belongs to someone from the label."

Hearing this her posture relaxed. "Okay, then I'll escort you inside before going to change."

"You don't need to. I can take care of myself."

She snorted. "I don't doubt that, but it's my job to make sure you don't have to."

"Oh, aren't you feisty," I teased.

"You'll come to appreciate it someday," she tossed over her shoulder as she made her way inside. I followed her to find Kole and Danny sitting in my living room.

"Hello, Ms. Ryland," Kole greeted Jazz as he stood. "I hope you're enjoying your new job. Tak's not giving you any problems, is he?"

I didn't appreciate being talked about as if I wasn't in the room, but I was also curious to hear my bodyguard's answer. And having gotten a taste of her personality, I knew she wasn't the type to mince her words. I had been a nuisance—on purpose—but a nuisance, nonetheless.

"Everything has been wonderful, Mr. Kole."

I looked at her to see an almost too bright smile on her face. She looked away from Kole just long enough for our eyes to meet. A silent conversation passed between us. Amused, I shot her a knowing look.

She used her eyes to tell me to keep my mouth shut, I decided to keep the peace and remain silent. Though I badly wanted to stir the pot, my desire to get Kole out of my house outweighed my wish to antagonize Jazzy. Walking around Jazzy, I bumped my hip against hers, forcing her to move aside. Overhearing her low murmured curse was the icing on the cake.

"I don't think you've said what made you show up here unannounced. I thought we spoke at length about these surprise visits."

I didn't bother looking at Danny. The man was like thin air. Kole placed his hands in his pockets as he lifted his chin.

It was his favorite pose. He probably thought it made him look intimidating. Instead, he looked like a *Sam I Am* punk with small dick issues.

He offered me a smile. "We did. Although from what I remember of our conversation, you agreed to respond to my emails and answer my phone calls in trade. You failed to do so. So, I decided to do a face-to-face. Danny?"

"Yes." Danny perked up immediately, bringing a packet from out of his battered leather briefcase. He gripped it in his hand, nervously glancing between us.

"Give it to him," Kole ordered.

Danny held the packet out to me. Stuttering, he said, "H... here, M... Mr. Jensei."

I didn't take it. Hell, I didn't even look at him. "I already said I won't work with them."

Kole narrowed his eyes. "I heard, but the amount of money they're offering isn't something you can easily turn down. Working with them as their model will improve your image, which is something you need right now." He took the packet from Danny and slapped it against my chest. "I expect to get this back from Chelsea, signed."

"We had an agreement when I signed my contract. I was given the right to choose the businesses I would work with."

I refused to take the packet. I would cut my arm off before I accepted this deal. The familiar revulsion intermixed with hate filled me. Memories I'd long ago locked away in my mental closet, rustled once more. I damned Kole for his role in bringing them back to life.

"Yes, we did. There was also an agreement about protecting the label's image." He stepped forward, leaning in so he could whisper in my ear. "Drug abuse and recklessness doesn't protect it."

He took a step back and let the packet fall to the floor. "Read it, sign it, and then we'll schedule the first shoot."

He glanced behind me. "I'm glad you're enjoying the job, Ms. Ryland. Come, Danny." With that, he shot me a warning look before he turned and left.

"Coming, sir." Danny ran after him.

I stared after them and then looked down at the packet at my feet. My mind raced trying to figure out a way to get out of having anything to do with the Nakamura family. My throat tightened as my hands grew sweaty.

I needed to take in more air, even though some part of me knew I was breathing fine. I still felt like I was suffocating. A black abyss yawned open before me.

The faint sound of a young child crying filled my ears. I would have much rather had the music back. The never-ending tinkling of piano keys to block out the sounds of the past.

"Mr. Jensei?"

Jazz's voice cut through the overpowering black that threatened to swallow me up. I sucked in a quick breath and looked at her. She looked at me with worry in her large brown eyes and reached out a hand toward me.

"Mr. Jensei?"

Before she could touch me, I moved out of the way. I ignored the flash of hurt in her gaze. "I need to make a phone call."

Entering the hallway, I nearly ran to my wing. Stopping once I got close to my room, I collapsed against the wall. Reaching up with a trembling hand, I covered my eyes.

Nervous laughter spilled from my lips. I needed to regain control. The shadows refused to retreat. The black ether consumed my poisoned mind, revealing images of the two who had abandoned me.

"Leave, go away, I don't need you," I whispered to no one.

The shapes withered. Their faces becoming blank slates as my memory failed to render their faces fully. Inhaling deeply, my chest tightened. I dropped my hand, forcing myself to straighten.

"I'm okay." The shadows retreated as the pain in my chest lessened. "I'm okay."

My back tingled from the cold sweat that had broken out. I glanced at the mirror that hung on the wall and flinched at the look of fear on the face of my reflection. Smiling, I forced the cocky persona of Tak forward.

"Fuck it, I'm fine. I'm Tak Jensei. I do what I want. Fuck Kole if he thinks he can dictate my actions."

I didn't owe anyone a damn thing. Not my fame, nor my presence. The Nakamuras would die before I let them see me again.

Jazz

I watched him storm off. Worry filled me at the sight of his pale expression. He had been vehement about not doing the commercial.

I bent down and picked up the envelope and glanced over my shoulder to make sure Tak hadn't come back. Opening it, I gave the document inside a brief look, the top of it read *Agreement with Nakamura Co.*

Immediately, I wondered why he didn't want to work with the Nakamura brand.

From what I knew, Nakamura was an LA based design company. It was one of the many companies owned by the Nakamuras, who had immigrated from Japan to America back during the sixties. The apparel company was the most popular. It boasted a reputation similar to Christian Siriano and Ivy Park, and it was still growing every day.

Tak's image would fit them perfectly. Dark grunge with a rebellious edge that made me both desire and feel wary of him. The most confusing piece was that Tak himself was a Nakamura.

Not many people outside of Bridge Lake knew that because he'd changed his name after he'd signed with JS Records. Quickly closing the envelope, I placed it on the coffee table and took my phone out and texted Dutch.

Seeing Tak's reaction to being forced to work with them told me they were worth looking into. Midway through my text, I received a message. I paused to read it.

"Fuck, we're late," I released a shout.

***

Three hours later, I apologized to Chelsea in the lobby of Stone Magazine headquarters. She didn't even look at me, her eyes were on her phone. "You're three hours late."

I straightened up. "I'm sorry, I tried to hurry, but Mr. Jensei needed a little more time to get ready." I bit my lip at her hard look.

She waved me off. "It's actually good. He didn't even show up for the last interview. Which is why I came by before heading to the office."

"Because they ask the same questions," Tak cut in, abrasively.

I turned around and bit the inside of my mouth. He looked so good in his suit pants, a blue T-shirt with a torn neck, and an edgy long peacoat. The scarf he had carelessly put on swung as he removed his sunglasses. He pointed them at Chelsea.

"I told you I didn't want to do it, so of course, I didn't come," he continued.

"Has anyone told you, Tak, the world doesn't revolve around you?" someone said from behind me. I turned and clasped my hands together as Ark, Omar, and Jay walked toward us.

I could die happy.

Ark was cute as usual. He'd seen his barber recently. His edges were lined up, the blond curls were wild on the top of his head. He gave a small salute in greeting. I gave him a bright smile in return.

"No, I can't say they have, but then again, it would be a lie," Tak answered, only turning his head as Jay came to a stop beside him.

Jay was pale-skinned with round eyes and stood about an inch shorter than Tak. His hair was long and brushed the collar of his thin burgundy sweater. Trying to regain my composure, I tried to put some space between myself, Tak, and Jay, who continued their argument.

"I should post a video of your real personality online," Jay threatened.

Tak laughed. "You mean, like every video of you in college I still haven't deleted."

Jay let out a gasp. "You fucker, you told me you deleted that shit."

"I lied."

"Who's this?" someone asked from behind me.

A hand landed on my shoulder, forcing me to turn fully around, meeting amber colored eyes. I retreated a step. My view expanded to the rest of Omar. His beautiful rosewood skin flattered the bright smile he gave me. He tossed his head and his sun-bleached dreads fell behind his shoulder.

"Is she the new bodyguard?"

"I… I." Shit, it felt like my brain was frying. I was surrounded by the men of my favorite band. For the past eleven years, I'd been in love with them.

I was definitely Tak's biggest fan, but I still couldn't believe I was surrounded by the four members of Rejected One.

Tak stepped between us blocking my view of the other three. "She's *my* new bodyguard."

I quietly checked my pulse. My heart was still beating, my lungs were still working. I was definitely still alive.

Once I was finished checking that I hadn't died from the overwhelming presence of my favorite band, I turned my attention to the offending back between me and the other three band members. I glared at it.

He really was being an ass for no reason. Was I not allowed to even speak with the others? I poked him, but he didn't move. I did it again. He reached behind his back and slapped my hand.

"Omar, I heard you're getting married, is that true?"

Hearing the tone of Tak's voice, I moved to the side of him in time to see Jay's expression stiffen.

"Tak, not here," Omar warned.

Tak chuckled. "Hey, you can't blame me for asking. I can't help feeling bad for the girl. Does this make it four times now that you've cheated on her?"

"Why don't you worry about that burn in your pants and not my fiancée," Omar retorted, his eyes narrowed on Tak's grinning face.

"Hmm, but your drama is so much better," Tak taunted.

My ears stung from what they were saying. They were in the middle of the lobby. Anyone could be listening.

Taking a deep breath, I stepped between them. Tak was obviously looking to start a fight. And Omar seemed more than willing to give him one.

Where the hell did Chelsea go?

"I think it's time for you guys to head upstairs," I said as a crowd started to grow a few steps away. I smiled. "After all, I would hate if everything your saying gets published."

"Well, it can't beat trying to kill yourself, right Tak?" Omar quipped, ignoring me. He gave Tak's wrist a pointed look. "How's the hand? Can you even hold a mic with that?"

Tak laughed, but he clearly wasn't amused by Omar's words. He drew his fist back. I stepped forward because it was my job to—it wasn't because I wanted to be squashed between the two band members bodies.

I turned and caught Tak's punch. The force caused my back to hit Omar's chest. Tak looked startled to see me in the middle of them. I squeezed Tak's fist.

"Let stop this here."

He looked from me to Omar. "Fuck."

He withdrew and grabbed my wrist and yanked me forward. Taken off balance, I fell into his arms, my cheek pressed against his chest.

"Fine, but if you say that shit again, I'll remove your wandering dick and make you eat it, Omar."

With that, he turned, maintaining his hold on my wrist and dragged me behind him to the elevator. I twisted my arm in his hold. "Mr. Jensei, let go, please." He ignored me. "Mr. Jensei."

Being dragged behind such an overbearing man wasn't what I would call fun. He didn't respond as we entered the elevator. Not waiting for the others, he pressed the close button right as Jay reached the door.

"Catch the next one," he said cheerfully as he flipped him the bird.

"Fuck you, Tak."

The door closed. Finally, alone, I ripped my hand out of his. Rubbing my wrist, I contemplated the good and the bad of not washing it ever again. I really needed to figure out how to engrave these fan moments into my mind.

"Why do you call me Mr. Jensei?" he asked out of nowhere.

I wasn't sure why it mattered what I called him. It wasn't like I was unprofessional. "Because you're my employer."

"Kole's your employer. I want you to call me Tak. It's weird hearing my last name all the time. I've already told you I hate being called that."

I thought over his words for a second. I called him Tak in my head, but it would be weird to call him by his name out loud. It would imply a closeness we didn't have. "I'm sorry, Mr. Jensei, but that would be rude."

"It's rude to ignore your employer's orders."

"Didn't you just say Kole is my employer?"

He glared at me. Clearly, he wasn't in the mood. I decided to annoy him a little more. After all, he deserved it for trying to cause a scene earlier.

Let's not forget he had his goons throw me in a pool with all my belongings. And made me get up at dawn to run. I'd tease him a little more before I gave in to his request.

"I don't think it would be right. I think of you as my boss or a client I work for. I would prefer to call you by your last name."

I offered him my famed Mona Lisa smile. It worked on dignitaries, CEO's, and senators. My own subtle sign of death.

"No, call me by my first name, otherwise..." He gave a sexy smile.

He grabbed my hands and lifted them above my head, my back and hands were pressed against the wall with the move. I felt the surrealness of having Tak, lead singer of Rejected One so close. My heart raced and I could feel my cheeks heating. I had been wall slammed by Tak Jensei.

I closed my eyes and puckered my lips. I would write in my diary tonight that I got kissed by Tak Jensei. In big bold letters.

Then it hit me. If I gave in, then he'd treat me like the other bimbo's who threw themselves at him all the time. I didn't hate the idea of kissing Tak, but I despised the idea I'd be another notch in his belt.

I wasn't there for romance. I was there to save his life. I opened my eyes to find him staring at me. A wave of dizziness hit me, but I refused to lose to the fangirl within.

"I'll do it," I shouted.

"Do what?"

My words tumbled over each other as they rushed out. "I'll call you Tak from now on."

He released my hands. "The one time I wish you'd been more stubborn." He flicked my nose gently, a cocky smile decorating his face. "Next time, I won't stop."

The elevator released a loud ding before the doors opened. I watched him go, feeling overwhelmed.

"I don't think I can survive this," I muttered as I sagged forward, dropping my arms. Scrubbing a hand down the side of my face, I wished desperately to go back to being only a fan of Rejected One. Instead, my eyes watered in regret as I thought about my missed opportunity to get a kiss from *the* Tak.

Sniffling, I straightened and chased after him.

CHAPTER EIGHTEEN

Ol' Bull

Tak

I replayed the moment over and over in my head. Jazz closing her eyes and puckering her lips, more than ready for my kiss. I almost chuckled in amusement.

She had recovered fast. I had expected a sharp slap, and a few choice words. Instead, she'd conceded to calling me by my first name.

She'd given in a lot faster than I'd expected. I didn't know whether to be amused or annoyed. Kissing her would be nothing, but the fact she'd rather call me my name then kiss me rankled.

Even as the interviewer droned on, I watched her beneath my lashes. Her expression had changed from excitement to sympathy when Jay spoke about his youth. She had given several sympathetic nods.

She acted like a fan, her reactions so animated and eye catching. I wondered if she really thought no one could see her in the corner she stood in. I immediately didn't like the idea of anyone else seeing the multitude of different expressions she made.

"Tak?"

Startled, I looked away from her to the guy who sat across from us. Haines, he was well known for having critiqued other bands in the past, like Linkin Park and Avenged Sevenfold. He tapped his pen against his notebook. "It looks like we've been boring you."

I smirked. "Somewhat, but I'm often bored at interviews."

"Tak," Jay warned, but he knew I wasn't one to lie about how I felt. Most of the time I didn't lie, other times lies kept me together.

Haines eyes flashed with irritation. He glanced at Jazz before those beady eyes met mine. A slow carnivorous smile coming to his lips.

"After the scandal, it looks like your label was quick to shut down any inquiries into you're failed suicide. Tell me, are you still suffering depression, or have you recovered as your CEO has said to several news outlets?"

I hated Kole for that fucking press release he held. I told him I didn't do it. He just threw flames on the fire of that fucked-up rumor.

This fucker wanted to play games. Okay, I'd bite. I shifted in the chair.

"Depression doesn't go away, so it's weird to ask that question. Feelings of loneliness and lack of emotional connection is something many people suffer from. Shouldn't you be more sensitive with your wording?"

The silence after my words was the sound of sweet victory. The producer who sat nearby, wriggled in his seat nervously. Obviously wishing Haines hadn't asked the single question that had been on the do not ask list.

"Yes, you are right of course, but one would think you'd want to share your experience with the media in order to help others suffering with it as well. It's always good for the public to feel like they aren't alone in their struggle."

Haines wanted me to put a period in his career. I uncrossed my legs and leaned forward, pausing when I felt a hand settle on both sides of my shoulders. I glanced to my right to see it was Jay and looking on the other side of me I found Omar.

Both of them weren't sure what I would do. I would have told the two wussies I wasn't going to do anything but that would have been a waste of breath.

So instead, I released a heavy sigh and smiled. Yeah, I fucking smiled because smiling when someone was trying to piss you the fuck off, pissed the person off more. Asshole Move 101.

"Haines, I'll answer this question since you seem like a prostitute looking for a dollar about it."

He narrowed his eyes. That's right bitch. I had his number.

"I don't share my problems with the media because instead of it getting to those who need help and those who'd gain strength from my story, it would be used as sensational news by publications similar to your own. The idea that my mental illness would be turned into a story about me trying to gain attention from the public sickens me. Depression, loneliness, and self-hate are not emotions to be used for other's amusement."

The hands atop my shoulders slipped away and I continued. "And people like you, who use it as a petty way to trigger me because I won't suck your dick for clout are the worse because you don't really give two shits about my mental state, you want a story. Well, here's one."

I stood, shoving my hands in my pocket. "In two months' time, Rejected One will be doing a concert at the bar that started it all and the money will go to charity for those fucked-up people who are like me. Now, go fuck yourself and have a pleasant day."

With that, I made my way out. I wasn't surprised my bandmates followed me. We were a lot of things, friends, enemies, but we weren't disloyal.

"Fuck, Tak, that was fucking wow," Ark exclaimed as we entered the elevator. "But you really want to do a concert at the Ol' Bull?"

I was too busy questioning that myself. Shit, what was I thinking? I had completely dropped my persona. Let's not forget, it'd been half a year since we'd all rehearsed together, and I had just fucking announced a concert. The only upside to this entire shit show was that Kole was going to be pissed.

"You really just do what you want," Jay said from the back of the elevator. "Are you even going to ask us if we want to do the concert?"

"Don't you all need the money? A concert would bring in major commercials," I jeered.

"Pfft, all the deals you don't take, we do," Omar said. "And before you call us vultures, we're not going to ignore a deal worth millions."

Jazz hesitantly asked, "So how do you think Chelsea will react?"

I didn't groan like the other pussies behind me. I wasn't scared of that witch and I didn't feel a sense of relief that she'd gone back to the office after she'd made sure I'd arrived at the interview. I'd handle my business and she'd get it done.

***

I looked out at Vander City with my back to everyone. Music on a low hum as the traffic below zipped by, creating visual notes, like black sheet paper and colorful ink. I'm almost lost to the growing sound in my head when Chelsea's voice yanked me back.

"Are you fucking stupid?" Chelsea nearly screamed. She had made us come to her office right after she heard from Jay what I'd said. "Do you think I'm fucking Houdini?" She finished.

I wasn't avoiding her stare because I was afraid. No, I was looking at the pleasing view of Vander City because I appreciated it.

"Tak?"

"Hm?"

"Didn't we say not to do anything reckless?" she said. "This is considered reckless. And you." She turned on Jay, who immediately lifted his hands as if to fend her off. "Aren't you supposed to control him?"

He offered her a sheepish smile. "I mean, Haines was rude. He asked Tak a question that was on the *don't ask* list. What did you think Tak would do? Honestly, it's better this way. At least he didn't hit him, right?"

"Shouldn't you be happy I'm finally getting back to work?" I asked, thinking about all the times she'd complained to me over the last few months about not committing to talking about a new tour.

Chelsea glowered at me.

"This isn't exactly the way I saw it happening. Not only did you say you wanted to make it a charity event, this event won't even make any money for us."

"Then take the money from the next job we do, and… let's do it in memory of Mira, this was the kind of stuff she'd dreamed of doing once she made it big."

"Tak." The fire that had been in Chelsea's voice diminished.

I ignored the sympathy in her words. Mira had been a young talent I'd personally discovered. I'd love watching her on stage.

She'd been completely different from me when I was young. I swore she'd be the next big thing, but just when she'd gotten her big chance. A snake I'd never given the time of day came along and ruined her life.

Three years later, people still hesitated before mentioning her name in my presence. Chelsea groaned and turned her back on us. She lowered her head, settling her hands on her hips before she suddenly turned around giving us a confused look.

"Where's that damn bodyguard? She should have stop this."

Jazz

I'd been told by the band members to stay below in the lobby as they followed an obviously pissed Chelsea upstairs. I was sitting in the café, holding a cup of hot cider. I couldn't believe the words Tak had said.

It was hard to remember he wasn't a complete idiot, despite being a grade A asshole. Hearing my phone buzz, I looked down at my smart watch, seeing a message from Chelsea. I stood and tossed my drink into the trash.

It looked like she wanted to see me. Heading toward the elevator, I spotted someone familiar waiting for it.

Why is he so fucking heavy?

The memory came back like a flash from the past. I quickly moved to hide behind a large pillar. The man was tall and wearing a beige suit.

I zeroed my gaze in on the name tag that swung from his neck, Bradley Jones. I dodged back behind the pillar when he glanced over his shoulder. Breathing heavy, I leaned forward to see him entering the elevator.

The door began to close, I ran past, spotting the button that was lit in the reflection of the car's mirror.

"Fourth floor."

I took the entrance to the stairwell. Seeing the amount of stairs I had to run up, I smacked my cheeks. "Let's go, Jazz."

Racing up the steps, I didn't let myself think about what floor I was on until I saw the sign with the big red four. I shoved the exit door open in time to see him walk around the corner away from me. Chasing after him, I barely avoided a random worker who stepped out into the hallway.

My sneakers squeaked against the floor as I came to a stop at the end of the hallway. Searching, I looked right and left. Nothing.

Taking a chance, I turned right and ran down the corridor, looking through the glass walls of the many offices. Not seeing him, I felt a wave of disappointment. Shit, I shouldn't have hesitated.

I should have walked toward him boldly. It wasn't like he'd seen me that night. I stopped, searching for what else I could do to find him.

"Ms. Ryland?" I turned around to see the man who had shown up at Tak's house with Mr. Kole this morning. He walked toward me. "Are you okay? I spotted you running."

"Sorry, Mr. Danny." I rested a hand sheepishly on the back of my head. "I was sort of lost. I was told to report to Ms. Chelsea's office ASAP."

He nodded. "I can show you the way. This building can be confusing to new people."

I laughed. "I'm definitely confused."

He stepped aside and motioned forward. "This way."

With little choice, I was forced to follow him. As we walked in silence, I thought over what I'd seen. One of the culprits worked here at the label.

That's not surprising. I could think of at least five people that worked with him who wanted to place Tak's head in a meat cutter. However, what was Bradley Jones's motive?

"How is it working out with our favorite singer?"

Confused by the sudden question from Danny, I eyed him. The tone he used had been filled with sarcasm. I didn't like it.

Tak maybe a jerk but he wasn't that cruel. Half the stuff he said could be ignored. No matter how I felt about his annoying focus on getting on my nerves, I wasn't going to talk behind his back.

"Well, it's been pretty boring."

He chuckled, side-eyeing me. Clearly not getting that I wasn't going to talk about Tak.

"You don't have to watch your words with me, Ms. Ryland. I'm sure it's been difficult. Tak's always done whatever he wants and there's little that's done because he's the moneymaker."

"Mr. Danny, I'd prefer it if we didn't discuss my VIP."

At my words, he immediately lost his smile. He remained silent until we reached Chelsea.

"Here we are. Enjoy the rest of your day, Ms. Ryland," he said as he walked away. I watched him go, my suspicion stirring before my thoughts were rudely cut short by the door bursting open.

"Jazz, get in here," Chelsea yelled, her face red.

She grabbed my arm and tugged me inside. I was greeted by the weary expressions of the band's members. Tak winked at me, though he looked just as haggard.

I caught myself before I made a catching gesture and pulled it to my chest. I was getting better at this. Releasing my arm, Chelsea closed the space between us to an uncomfortable degree.

"Explain to me why I'm organizing a benefit concert in a small ass bar, hmm?"

I warily looked from her to the others, but they all looked away. I returned my gaze to her angry face and swallowed. "Because Tak announced one."

"Why?" I flinched. She released a heavy sigh, before inhaling deeply. "Why didn't you stop him?"

"I... I sort of wanted it to happen," I whispered.

"I'm sorry, I didn't hear you." She turned her head, so her left ear was facing me. "You what?"

I squeezed my eyes shut. "I wanted the concert to happen after all that Haines guy said."

"Wow, and you said you weren't a fan," she exclaimed cynically, giving me some space. "I'm surrounded by nothing but troublemakers and traitors. Fine."

She threw her hands up. She focused her next response on Tak. "I'll do it. I'll sell it to Kole and get the marketing on it, *but* you are going to put Nakamura out of their misery. You're going to sign that damn contract Kole brought you this morning or I'll let this shit fall on its face."

Tak's face turned dark. For a beat, I was sure he'd tell Chelsea to fuck off, but instead he gave a bob of his head. "Fine, but on one condition."

Crossing her arms, Chelsea exhaled slowly. "And what's that?"

"No one with the last name Nakamura is there," he said, his voice brokering no disagreement. "The minute I see anyone from that family, I'm out."

Chelsea seemed to weigh his words before she gave a quick nod. "Usually, those people like to take photos with the celebrities, but I'll send Kole to kiss ass." She clapped her hands together. "Then we have a deal. You get a concert, and we get a percentage of four million. Life's good," she crooned.

CHAPTER NINETEEN

Nakamura

Tak

The minute I was able to pull myself away from that damn Chelsea and get back in my car, I was on edge. Shit, I'd agreed to do the commercial with Nakamura. I felt the pressure building in my chest. I pressed a hand against it, rubbing as if I could physically alleviate it.

The Nakamuras were one thing, but that one thing was adding to the overwhelming feeling of drowning I was experiencing. Chelsea still hadn't brought me any information about that night in Vegas. I'd gone to her because I knew she'd look into it quietly, but now I wished I'd gone to Pit. At least he'd have already brought me something, anything to look at.

No, the same reason I couldn't go to Pit was the same reason I hadn't gone to the other four or Skittles. I didn't want them to look at me with pity or disappointment.

"Are you okay?" Jazz asked.

"Fuck no." Immediately, I felt bad. She didn't deserve my anger. "Sorry, you're not the one I'm angry with."

"You're on edge, I get it. You had to say something back to Haines and now you're stuck doing a commercial you didn't want to."

I looked at her, really looked at her and noticed the slight flush to her cheeks and the hard look in her eyes. "Oh, is my bodyguard angry on my behalf?"

"Of course I am. He was just being a dick because of what you said," she blurted before she released a breath. "Then again, you're good at making people hate you."

"The best, but you don't hate me," I said, unsure of why I cared to hear what she thought of me.

Her expression turned thoughtful. "I hated you when you had those dicks toss me into the pool." She hummed. It was a soft sound that immediately caught my ear. "But then you also apologized for it, so I guess my hate dropped to dislike? We're even now." She offered me a smile.

I had debated whether or not I would make a move. Sure, I still wanted her gone. Fired actually, but when I leaned over and pressed my lips against hers it wasn't because of that. Nah, I just fucking wanted to taste her smile. She stiffened as I nipped her bottom lip.

"You're sweet, bodyguard of mine."

As I settled back into my seat, I waited to see her reaction. She didn't move for a second. When she finally did, she pressed her fingertips to her lips and her eyes slowly widened and then... she burst into tears.

***

I shouldn't have kissed her.

That's what I couldn't stop thinking as I entered the house and watched her quickly leave my side. She had shown me such an open grin. It wasn't like the smile she had worn the few times I'd pissed her off.

I ran a hand through my hair and made my way toward my wing. I stopped short at the sight of the large envelope that sat on the coffee table in my living room. Staring at it, I sneered. Maybe she was disgusted by me.

I couldn't tell though, since she'd avoided looking at me the entire ride. I knew she was capable of knocking the shit out of me, but she hadn't. And the following silence had been worse than if she had exploded on me. This was new to me, feeling guilt.

I walked toward the envelope. I picked it up and flipped it over. I stared hard at the embossing there.

I let my head drop. I was really doing this. The last time I'd been anywhere near these people, I'd been tossing my shit into the trunk of my car and going on the road. I'd never gone back, and I'd never planned on it.

Hearing the familiar ringtone of my phone, I pulled it out. Seeing the skull emoji, I immediately knew who it was.

"What do you want?"

"Hey, it's your boy Richie. It's been too long."

"It's been exactly two weeks, two days and forty-five minutes since your last text. I'll assume you've found better clientele, buh-bye now," I said. Deciding to hang up since I wasn't in the mood for Richie's shit.

"Wait, wait, you can't blame me. After that shit about you in the news popped up, I wasn't willing to get another visit from your brother, Deacon. He's not exactly my best friend."

Richie's voice was filled with weary amusement. I lifted the phone and squinted at it as if I could see the short and greasy drug dealer.

"So?"

"So, I figured since you have a concert coming soon, you'd recovered and were ready for your usual order."

"It's amazing how quick you are. When you say order, what are we talking?" I drawled.

"Five blue ones, and a bag of green with no tampering. The clean shit for my best customer."

I chuckled. "Are you sure? I had to break your man's hand for giving me laced green and selling to my label's artists. Didn't your mother teach you not to shit where you eat?"

"Never met her, but I got your point. We won't fuck with the people at your label. Do you want the delivery or—"

"Mail it."

"Wait."

"What?"

I was getting irritated with this clingy shit. What did Richie want from me? I was sick and tired of dealing with people wanting something from me all the fucking time.

"We set up a race tonight. I heard you've been cooped up at your house. Figured I could invite you out to celebrate your second chance at life." His tone turned cajoling. "Trust me, it's going to be big."

I didn't respond right away. The urge to do the right thing and ignore Richie was there, but what would hard-ass Tak do? The person I'd worked so hard to build from the trembling kid I'd been. Shit, what would the assholes do? They weren't the type to meekly listen to anyone.

"Tak?"

"Yeah, I'll be there. Usual spot?"

"Yeah."

Hanging up, I walked to my bedroom. I would go out, get high, and enjoy some racing. Shit, maybe I'd even get my dick wet.

CHAPTER TWENTY

Run Away

Jazz

"You what?"

"I cried."

The wealth of shame I felt was only outweighed by the humiliation I experienced when Trisha burst into laughter on the other side of the phone. I should have called Dutch directly and asked for him to look up Bradley's home address rather than endure this.

The only thing I could say for myself was, the shock of being kissed by Tak had short-circuited my rational thinking. Leaving only the fangirl behind who had realized (a) who was kissing her, and (b) she'd violated one of the golden rules. It had been a big moment. Call me stupid and yeah, fuck me, I was twenty-nine and I had busted into tears after my favorite singer kissed me.

"Oh my God. I can't stop laughing. Jesus, Jazz, what happened after that?" Trisha asked, after her complete disrespect of me. I shouldn't tell her anything, but I did because she was the only person I could talk about this with.

"Well, it was awkward, and I wouldn't be shocked if he keeps his distance from me from now on." I was hit by another wave of embarrassment. "I should have never applied for this stupid job. I should have stalked him and then secretly taken out his would-be killers."

"And miss out on being squashed between him and Omar, no. The best thing you've ever done was become Tak's bodyguard," she near purred. "Girl, Omar is legit my dream one-night bang. He's the only guy I'd willingly play the role of baby mama for."

"Well, get in line. It looks like he's taking auditions."

"Are you serious? I thought he was with that actress. Dammit, why are men such hoes?" she complained.

"I know, right. If they have a dick and there's a moist hole, they'll stick it in."

"You ain't never lied."

"Hold on, I think I hear something," I said.

I stilled, lowering the phone when I heard something outside of my door. Placing my phone face down on the bed, I slowly got up and grabbed the collapsible baton that sat on my dresser. I walked over to my door and pressed my ear against it.

Listening for a few seconds, I heard the sound of shuffling once more, followed by a curse. I snatched the door opened and lifted my baton up.

"It's me," Ark cried, lifting his hands up in surrender.

I frowned, looking at him in confusion. "What are you doing sneaking around here?"

He didn't answer right away. I glared at him.

"Who let you in?" I asked, filled with fear he had heard my statement earlier about looking for killers.

He shook his right hand. I spotted a ring of keys.

"I have a key."

I lowered my baton. "Okay, you still didn't say why you're here."

Ark released a relieved breath, lowering his arms. "I came here to drop off the key to Tak's car, since he told me he'd be staying home tonight. I figured we could also talk about the music for the concert, but I didn't see him in the studio or his room. I was hoping you could tell me where he went."

I stilled, an ominous feeling filling me. "He didn't mention going anywhere else tonight?"

"No," Ark said, taking out his phone. "And he hasn't answered any of my texts either."

Shit, I'd been too busy worrying about my reaction to his kiss. I knew he'd been too quiet.

"You don't think he went out to cause trouble, do you?" Ark asked, clearly worried.

I walked back into my room, grabbed up my phone and hung up on Trisha. I brought up the tracking app I'd gotten specifically for Tak.

"He could try, but there isn't a place he can go I won't find him." A black dot moved on the map of the city. "Bingo."

Ark came to my side and looked at my phone. "Is that him?"

I quickly shoved my feet into my sneakers and grabbed a small hand-sized case and a track jacket. "Let's go, it's better we go after him before he does something to get us all in trouble."

"Yes." Ark chased after me.

If I was a normal bodyguard, I probably would have panicked but as a superfan and car thief, there wasn't anywhere Tak could go where I couldn't find him. And when I did find him, I would ask him what the fuck he thought he was doing.

***

"Slow down."

I ignored Ark's scream. I didn't have the luxury of driving slowly. Turning the wheel right, the tires squealed as we turned

another corner. Damnit. I'd let my guard down and Tak slipped
right out of the house.

Ark gripped his seat belt for dear life. Sadly, I didn't have the
time to placate him. I needed to find Tak before someone tried to
take his life again. Glancing at the phone, I saw he had finally
come to a stop somewhere in the outer limits of the city.

"Woah, woah, car," Ark yelled.

Looking back up, my eyes widened a fraction at the sight of a
car that had come to a stop at the stop light. Swerving hard, I
drove around them, my car jumping over the train tracks that ran
through the city.

"Are you smiling?" Ark's voice trembled.

"Maybe." I probably was. After all, there was nothing like
driving a car at its fastest speed. I glanced at the GPS. "We're
close."

The city sight fell away and soon we were driving through
what looked like a small forest. I came to a stop when I spotted a
barricade ahead. Seeing the four men who stood on either side of
it, I ordered Ark to stay in the car. Putting the car in park, I picked
up the small case and took out my short baton and got out.

"W… wait, you can't go—" The door slammed shut on
whatever else Ark was going to say.

My shoes crunched on the gravel of the road as I approached
the one closest to me on my right. "Hey, can I speak with—"

"Leave, you don't belong here." The guard cut me off, his
posture unwelcoming.

I paused the hand in the air I'd lifted up in a friendly greeting.
"Um, you could at least—"

"I said leave." He moved forward, lifting his chin. He stared
down at me in a threatening way, moving his eyes from me to the
car. "This is an invite-only party. Your car doesn't have the right
decal, so I suggest you leave now. Argh."

Life isn't easy for women. Men really love being disrespectful
when there's no reason to be. He fell to his knees. I lowered my
hand holding my baton.

He grabbed his throat, a look of awe on his face. I used the tip of the baton to lift his chin.

"I don't appreciate being interrupted." I offered him a smile of apology. "I want to know if Tak is here. Is he?"

He pulled his head away. "What are y'all doing?" he yelled at the others, who'd apparently been too shocked to move.

Getting over their surprise, they ran at me. Trisha was right, I did have anger management issues and in that moment, I was pissed.

The one who stood behind the dick on his knees reached out first. Retreating a step, I avoided his first grab. I stepped aside, dodging an attempt to grab me from behind by the other guard. I flipped my baton and slammed it into his side.

He staggered backward. I turned my attention to the third one who attacked me from my front and cracked my baton across his face. He hit the ground hard.

Turning around, I faced the one who'd recovered from my first hit. I spun and hooked my foot behind his neck. Bringing my leg down, I forced him off balance, pulling his body forward and down. His face hit the ground with a hollow thud.

"Bitch." The last guy standing took out a knife from his pocket. He looked both afraid and reckless. "I'm going to enjoy cutting you open."

"Oh, you can try," I said, pressing the button on the bottom of the baton. It clicked as it extended. With a roar of rage, he ran at me. "Sloppy," I muttered, moving back.

As he thrust forward, I knocked his hand up, simultaneously bringing up my hand holding the baton. I brought it down hard against his head before flipping it and jamming it into his gut. Releasing him, I quickly stepped back, leaving him to fall to the ground.

I released a breath and glanced over my shoulder, giving a wave to Ark before I collapsed my weapon and made my way forward.

Whatever the fuck Tak was doing, if it warranted having thugs at the entrance to keep watch, it couldn't be good.

I went ahead and left Ark as someone who could call the cops if we took too long. Brushing the sweat off my brow, I hoped Tak was lucid enough that I didn't have to carry him. I tightened my hand on my baton.

If someone had hurt him… *I'd kill them.*

CHAPTER TWENTY-ONE

Chicken

Tak

The loud sound of music cut through the noise of the milling crowd. I'd picked a spot on the balcony on the second floor of the wood cabin where a few others were chilling and talking. Setting down my beer and a stack of little papers with phone numbers written on them, I took a moment to take it all in.

The bright lights giving a clear view of the lane that was often used for racing. The cars were parked haphazardly along the long curvy road. The party hadn't had one hiccup. Richie wasn't sloppy, he enjoyed his money too much for that.

Turning to face the pool down below, I took in the crowd of scantily dressed models. I took a deep inhale of the blunt between my lips, an odd feeling of rightness coming over me. I felt like this was where I belonged.

The scent of weed would never get old, nor would the sensation of my thoughts becoming like smoke. It was refreshing.

I started going through the numbers that had been stuffed in my pockets by the lovely selection of eager-to-be-fucked ladies below.

"No to you," I said and flicked down one of the many numbers to the floor. "Your area code is Bridge Lake."

Picking up another, I squinted at the name. "Jessica? I don't fuck Jessica's." I tossed it over my shoulder.

"Tak."

I turned around. "Shit, when did they start letting in trash?" I asked, taking another hit.

"I don't know why Kole keeps treating you like a commodity. Isn't it about time you retired? Why not just admit you're washed up?"

I squinted at him, removing the blunt from between my lips. "Little Timothy, I don't know why your mom keeps letting you come to adult parties, but if you keep mouthing off, it will be my duty as an adult to beat the shit out of you."

Fuck, I didn't need this. I was trying to relax, not be stressed out. Why the fuck had Richie invited this kid?

"Humph, whatever, old man," he sneered, flicking his obnoxiously gray dyed hair out of his face. "And call me by my real name one more time and I'll gladly show you the difference between us. It's Tobi."

The level of disgust I felt for the kid before me wasn't because he was a little shit, who'd gotten signed by my label because his father happened to be a sponsor. And it wasn't because he dressed like a twink who'd been poisoned—Jay's words, not mine. No, it was because he'd been the one who fucked with Mira and then denied it, leaving her alone with a baby.

Which resulted in her killing herself. There weren't a lot of people I hated in this world, but this little shit was definitely on the list.

Kole had convinced me to ignore him and not beat his teeth into his skull. It would be bad for business, Kole had said, and yet... I still wanted to break this kid's neck.

Pressing the blunt back to my lips, I looked at him and contemplated how I would deal with Little Timmy. I wanted to relax, I needed to fuck. The last thing I wanted to do was teach this little shit a lesson in manners.

I glanced at the stairs behind him. If he fell, no one would think anything of it, right? A tragic accident is what they would call it.

"Timmy, you're a little shit who's nothing without your daddy. So, I'll take pity on you. Turn around and walk away before I humiliate you more than those clothes are already doing."

The others around us on the large balcony all chuckled at my insult. His face turned red as the hate in his glare grew hotter.

"Fuck you, how dare you?"

I shrugged. "I dare a lot of shit these days. You're not a threat to me and never will be."

I turned, grabbed up my beer, and scooped up my stack of scrap papers. If I couldn't beat the shit out of him or kill him. It was time to move down to the pool side.

"How's that whore Mira?" he asked slyly as he took another step toward me, blocking my path.

I stopped short, feeling rage tickle at my neck. I knew he'd said it to get a rise out of me, but I couldn't ignore him. "What?"

"Oh, my bad," he released a phony gasp. "I forgot, she's dead isn't she?"

I could feel the heat of my anger climbing up my back.

"It's really too bad, she was a decent fuck," he cackled. "Too bad she got clingy. I would have loved riding her a little longer."

In two steps I was on the little shit eater. "Shut up."

I held him up by the collar, the small papers scattered on the ground and the beer bottle that had been in my hand smashed. With the broken edges pressed against his throat, I stared into his eyes.

"One more word and I'll end you right here, right now." I figured I'd go with the direct approach.

He nervously laughed. "You... you wouldn't, not over that dead whore." I brought the bottle up and pressed it into his cheek, a scarlet drop of blood slid down.

I'll kill him now and have Pit's boys cover it up.

"What's going on here?" Richie interrupted. I guess he'd spotted us from below because the next thing I knew his hands were on my shoulders and he had his goons remove Tobi from my grip. "Now, let's calm down. What happened here?"

I tossed the bottle so that it smashed into the wall of the cabin. "He knows."

He looked me over before he nodded and looked at Tobi. "And you?"

Tobi glared at me. "He can't handle that I'm better than him." I didn't bother to respond to that childish bit of crap.

"All right." Richie grimaced. I saw the greedy wheels spinning in his head. "Well, there's one way to do this. We could play a game."

I gave Richie a hard look.

"Look, hear me out," Richie said, quickly seeing I wasn't in the mood for his shit. "If I let you beat his ass right under my nose, my clients will think I don't have any control over what goes on here and that would be bad for business. Trust me, my game choice will make you very happy."

"I doubt it, what game are you thinking of?"

He gave me a look of amusement. I should have known better than to ask. "Why, chicken of course. Don't you remember? It used to be your favorite."

Right, the game I'd played when the music disappeared and the darkness became cloying. Fuck yes, this little bitch needed to be put in his place and I was more than happy to do it. I glanced at Tobi.

"Fine, are you down?"

He snatched his arm out of Richie's goons' hold. "Of course, and the loser has to kneel and lick the winner's shoes."

"Done."

Richie clapped his hands together. "We have us a game." His shout stirred up the people around us who released a cheer.

Walking around a pissed Tobi, I made my way down the steps only to stop at the sight of Jazz coming up them.

"Tak, thank God," she called. Her voice lilting in just the way that made me think of a smooth jazz song. She ran up the rest of the steps toward me, staring at me with a gaze full of worry. "Do you know how worried I was when I realized you'd left without saying anything?"

"For me or your check?"

She squinted her eyes in confusion. "What?"

I didn't want her here. I didn't want her to see this side of me. Reckless and on edge, the hidden parts I buried and only let out when Richie drew me to the underground.

Tak wouldn't give a shit, but Takuya, he cared way too much. I gritted my teeth. I hated the way she made me feel.

"If it's because of that, don't worry, you'll get paid either way," I said as I continued to descend the stairs.

"Tak."

"I've got to go."

I didn't wait for her. I wasn't interested in hearing her confirm my thoughts. At some point, all good things come to an end and I was tired of pretending otherwise. Humans were selfish creatures and families didn't stay together forever.

My life was the only thing that was assured as well as my death. The end was the surest thing in the world. So, playing with my life and holding it up to the gods to judge whether I should keep it or give it away was the most exciting thing I could do. I didn't need anything else.

I leaned back against my car, watching as Richie had his guys rearrange the other vehicles so that the lane was open. Chicken could be played two ways. The two people drove as fast as they could to the end of a cliff or they could drive as fast as they wanted toward each other, with hopes that the other person gave in first.

I felt a bit of nostalgia remembering the last time I'd played chicken. I had gotten busted by Pit who'd been more than a little pissed I'd been high and drunk playing the game. However, this time I was stone-cold sober thanks to that little shit Tobi. A few beers and a blunt weren't enough to take me down.

"I hope you brought a change of underwear. I heard at your age your bowels loosen," Tobi said, laughing at his own joke from where he stood, mirroring me in waiting for the cars to be moved.

I ignored Tobi's shit and walked toward Richie, meeting him in the now opened road. "You guys can move your cars to the starting lines," he said.

"You remember what happens if I die, right?"

He gave a nod. "I assure you we will take care of the corpses and aftermath for all of our racers. We don't want to have rumors going around that we don't handle crashes. It's bad for my dollars."

"I bet," I said.

"Hey, don't ignore me." I glanced at Tobi. "Are you serious about doing this?" His voice shook.

Poor baby was scared.

"Didn't you say you wanted to settle this? Don't tell me you are nothing but talk." I released a bark of laughter. "Here, you race me or let me beat the shit out of you. Which do you want, Lil' Timothy?"

"Fuck you." He turned around and got in his car and drove to the starting point.

"You're serious?" Richie said, for once his dark eyes holding something other than greed as he looked at me. "Your crew won't like you chasing the cross again."

I rolled my eyes. "Richie, I suggest you worry more about how you're going to clean up that fuckers body than what my sister and brothers won't like," I said as I turned around and paused.

Jazz was sitting in the driver's seat of my car. Not believing what I was seeing, I walked over to the driver's side and reached out to open the door, but it was locked.

"Hey, what are you doing?"

She didn't look at me. I felt my confusion and panic spin. "Jazz, Jazz." She turned the key. I shook my head, frantically banging on the glass. "Hey, whatever you're thinking, stop."

She didn't respond to me at all as she took off toward the starting line. I ran after her hoping I could get to her before they started, but before I could reach her, she'd skillfully turned the car around to face my direction. I moved to the middle of the street and waved my arms, but she completely ignored me.

She revved the engine. I turned to say something to Richie, but my voice was drowned out by the sound of a gun going off and a loud yell. The next thing I knew the tires of my car squealed as she raced right toward me.

"Fuck."

I threw myself to the side, hitting the ground, covering my face as dirt and gravel kicked up as she raced past me. I immediately brought my arms down when the smoke cleared. I rolled over and watched my car as it flew toward Tobi's. Like everyone else my eyes were glued to the sight. Before I knew it, I was up and running after the car.

No.

No.

I was supposed to be in that car. A fear I hadn't felt before grasped me. I imagined the sound of steel crashing together and echoing out, the smell of gasoline as it filled the air, and the bright burst of light as the fire ripped through the cars.

I was eighteen once more, my hands and legs trembling as a burning sensation ran up my back. The smell of flesh and the cries of the ambulance rang in my head. I squeezed my eyes shut for a second. The image from the past faded and I opened them again to see the present.

Shit, if she made one wrong move it would be over. I shouted as I ran. My heart was in my throat.

As the two cars drew closer and closer, I prayed that nothing happened. That she'd turn the car, that she'd chicken out. I didn't care. Fuck, I'd lick the boots of anyone if Jazz came out of this unscathed.

The two cars were a breath's distance away. I shut my eyes again as I waited for the inevitable crash, but there was only the loud scream of brakes, followed by cheers intermixed with shouts of warning. I popped my eyes back open. Tobi had turned his car and people were running in every direction away from it.

I moved my gaze back to my car and found Jazz hopping out. A victorious smile graced her face. I ran toward her.

She turned to me. "Tak, I beat him."

I crushed her body to mine, squeezing her to my chest. My heart raced. My ears were filled with the sound of my pounding heart. I closed my eyes as an image of her burning body appeared in my mind's eye.

"Tak?"

I pulled back and grabbed her by her arms. "What the fuck were you thinking?" I shook her. "You could have died."

"You could have too," she said. "Why is it okay for you to put your life on the line, but not me? I'm your bodyguard, if you want to risk a life, risk mine."

I stared at her, completely speechless. Was she crazy? What bodyguard would play a game of chicken for their charge.

"Besides, I won," she said. She glanced behind herself at Tobi who was being helped out of his car since he'd passed out. "He doesn't look like the type to put his life on the line. I wonder what he thought he was doing playing this game."

She turned her head back and looked up at me. "And yes, I keep up with you for my work, but I care about you. I told you already, I don't hate you.'"

I leaned down and took her lips with mine. I needed to confirm she was alive and breathing. Didn't think too much about the why of it, only that moment. I needed her lips against mine.

Her mouth trembled beneath mine before she parted her lips, silently giving me her permission. Like the piece of shit I am, I took full advantage of it and pulled her closer, letting my hands roam over her body. Soft, hard, and delicious, she was the perfect match for my height. The way she fit against my body made me want to see if we fit together in other ways.

The soft pressure of our lips pressed together eventually had to end. I broke the kiss and bit back a curse. Her eyes were glazed over with lust and her lips looked puffed from my kisses. She held loosely to my wrists with her hands.

I couldn't help but to ask. "No tears this time?"

The dazed look in her eyes disappeared, replaced by what looked to be embarrassment. "Shut up."

She went to walk away, but I grabbed her arm, stopping her from leaving and playfully pulled her back to my side.

"Ut-uh, I'm not done with you yet," I teased.

She glared up at me. "But I am done with you and if you don't want to be on your knees, you'll come back home with me. Now."

I contemplated arguing with her, but a simple look around told me the party was over. "Fine, I'll go with you, but you have to agree to do one thing for me."

She gave me a suspicious look. "And what's that?"

I chuckled. "You're not allowed to put yourself in danger like that again."

She squinted at me. "I'm your bodyguard, it's my job to be in danger."

"I'll tell Kole to replace you then," I threatened.

She rolled her eyes. "Fine, whatever you say. Let's hurry. I left Ark in the car alone."

I was about to celebrate until the last thing she said hit me. "Ark, why's he here?"

She pulled away from me, walking away. "He came by to drop off your car."

"Shit, I forgot."

She laughed. "Well, you'll pay for it with a hug, I'm sure."

I cringed. I needed to talk to Jay about finding a new drummer. Seriously.

CHAPTER TWENTY-TWO

Caught

Jazz

A few days had passed since the race and I still couldn't calm down. My skin felt alive. I had lain in bed, trying everything I could think of to sleep, only for my mind to go back to the kiss.

Tak's body crushed to mine. The pure strength he'd shown had taken my breath away. Reaching up, I brushed a finger along my bottom lip.

This was wrong, but I couldn't stop the soft sigh that left my mouth. My phone buzzed on my side table. Distractedly, I reached over and picked it up to read the text.

"I saw you."

I sat up and unlocked my phone to see a picture of me next to Tak's car. It was the moment I'd gotten out after winning. Frowning, I called the sender right away.

"Well, hello, big sister."

"What do you want, Aaron?" I asked, irritated.

"I think we should meet tomorrow for a small chat. I'll send you the address."

He hung up. I dropped my hand to my lap. I should have been more careful.

I'd forgotten the wealthy ran in the same circles as celebrities. I'd thought I was safe because I'd worn contacts and cut my hair. Not to mention I'd gone from wearing top fashions to sweats and T-shirts.

Shit, I had little desire to see one of the children of my father's mistress, but I had no choice. While I lived independent of my father and had my own wealth, I didn't want to give my father anything he could use against me.

Racing at an event ran by a known drug dealer would be an issue. Especially since I was the poster child for his power. I grimaced. I'd try to get some sleep and meet Aaron in the morning.

CHAPTER TWENTY-THREE

Family

Jazz

The morning sunlight filled the ritzy rooftop restaurant Aaron had sent me the address for. I should have known he'd make a show out of this.

"You wanted to meet," I said as I plopped down in the chair across from my half brother. I had to call Chelsea and let her know I'd be late to Tak's shoot because of my appointment.

I flushed, thinking about that kiss again. Tak had dragged me out of bed to run with him. Once again, I returned triumphant. He, however, returned half dead.

"Dear sister, it's been too long," Aaron said as he took a sip from his coffee cup. "It's been what, seven years since the last time you ate dinner with the family."

Aaron had his mother's aquiline nose and my father's handsome features. His gray eyes were described by most as being soulful and his looks made girls lose their heads. Which is why he modeled and had an exclusive contract with a well-known designer.

"I like to keep my food down," I said, waving off the waiter's offer to order. "If I had to eat with you all, I'd be sick for three days after. Get to the point already. You saw me, now what do you want?"

He set his cup down and cleared his throat, giving me a cold smile. "And why do you think I want something from you?"

"Aaron, we're not close. I hate your father and mother, so there's little reason for you or your sister to contact me unless it's an emergency. Which if you called me to tell me Dad is dead… you could've texted." I cheered, ignoring the souring of his mouth. "What is it you want?"

"I'll tell dad where you were if you don't let me borrow the Roarke Mansion in Bridge lake."

"No," I said without blinking.

He flinched, moving his gaze away. "I was joking, you don't have to look at me like that."

My jaw tightened. "It wasn't a funny joke," I said, my voice stiff with anger.

I would never allow anyone from his blood into the place my mother and I called home. The staff and everyone who lived and worked on the estate knew never to allow my father within a mile of the place. I couldn't be responsible for what I would do if I returned and saw him standing within its walls.

Even if I couldn't stop him from buying a home near the Roarke mansion. Which was another reason I lived in Vander City. Less chance of running into him here.

"What is it you really want?"

"Come to this charity event," he said, pushing both a copy of the picture from the race and an invitation across the table toward me. He shot me a sly look. "Father's been bitching about how you've refused all the invitations he's sent over to your office."

"And why do you care whether or not I accept his invitations?"

Aaron usually stayed out of anything dealing with my father and me. Not that a bastard child like him had any right to get involved in the first place.

"I'm trying to earn a few brownie points with father, and I figured this would be the best way. That senator really, really wants his son and you to meet. Apparently, he's under the impression you're the key to something big for his future."

"If I manage to bring you to this event, father will loosen his reigns on the cash flow to my pockets." He leaned forward. "It's the least you can do as my sister."

I glanced down at the invitation. I would have to spend time with my fake family again. I'd already reached my max with seeing my father more than once this year.

I'd been forced to do that for at least four years after my mother died. Forced to play the perfect daughter because of my singular goal to gain information. I knew that one day he'd slip up and give me just the thing I needed to put the final nail in his coffin.

If it hadn't been for that, I'd never even breathe the same air as Clark Bennington. I'd sooner throw my body into a volcano. I bit the inside of my mouth, hard.

The memories rushing back to me. The chair scraped back as I stood. Aaron jumped, taken aback. I picked up the invitation and the picture.

"I'll go, but..." His expression darkened as my eyes bored into him. "I'll make your life miserable if anything comes out about me racing."

He gave me a nod. "There are other copies."

This I was sure of. Not saying another word, I left. I couldn't stomach being in the same vicinity as any of my father's progeny. I laughed at myself, I could barely stomach looking at my own face.

Stepping outside, I took in a deep inhale of fresh air, the nausea abating. Walking along the street, I briskly made my way to the bus stop.

I'd texted Leonard to pick me up from here to ensure Aaron wasn't following me. I had to hurry and get back to Tak. Stopping at the end of the street, the loud riff of a guitar flowed into a melody and a gruff voice floated out from the radio of a car that had stopped across from me.

I lifted my hand, brushing a tear away. The familiar song filled my head and heart as it had done all those years ago. My mind filled with his voice, wrenching emotions out of me as my mind returned to the past.

The smell of despair surrounded me, no matter how I tried to escape from my living nightmare, I couldn't. The window to my room was open and the white curtains swayed in the wind. I lay in bed as I'd done every day over those few months.

The sound of the TV was a low hum in the background. As the IV attached to my arm continued pumping me full of whatever was supposed to be keeping me sane. At least that's what my father said when the doctor had set it up, that it would help.

The door opened as the maid entered with cleaning supplies. Walking over to my window, she closed it and turned to me.

"This morning Mr. Bennington said he'd have Abrams take you out to the garden. Won't that be nice?" she asked.

And as usual I didn't respond, keeping my eyes firmly on the window.

"Well, I think it would be nice," she said, walking over to my bedside to gather the food that had been placed on the side table. She released a sigh, seeing that I hadn't eaten much. "Miss, you have to start eating. At this point, you're going to start wasting away."

And wouldn't that make that bastard called my father happy. Since he'd placed me in this room, I'd slowly started drowning in the sea of dark thoughts in my mind. Becoming more and more comfortable with the idea of floating away into nothingness.

She turned to walk away, and a loud guitar rift filled the room followed by a husky croon.

Darkness spirals around me, taking me from the light, I've found comfort in crying out. But nobody can hear me. Can someone save me? Can someone take me out of the dark?

My maid quickly set the tray of food down and scrambled for her back pocket and muttered loudly. "Shit, I forgot to turn my phone on silent."

The haunting words rang loudly in my head, drawing me out of the thick fog. Weakly, I pushed up and asked.

"Who is that?"

As if startled, she whipped around and looked at me. "What?"

I swallowed, my mouth feeling weird from months of not talking. "Who was that singing?"

Still looking confused, she answered, "It's "Mother's Lament" from a band that just recently released its first single. They're called Rejected One. The lead singer is a freshman in college. And he already has a pretty good-sized fan base. I think his name is Tak something," She added excitedly.

Then, as if catching herself she asked, "Miss, are you feeling better?"

I didn't answer her, instead my mind was occupied with finding out more about Tak and his music. I wanted to know about the person who understood the despair I was currently experiencing.

I smiled at the memory just as a familiar car pulled up. Leonard stepped out of the car and opened the door for me. Getting up, I walked over and got in. The door shut and I waited for him to get in and pull off before I spoke up.

"Take me to Cerion Studio but drop me at the corner."

"Yes, Ms. Ryland," Leonard said. "I placed two contracts in the back for you to review."

I released an exasperated smile, reached for the folders, and picked them up. I briefly wondered how Tak was doing so far.

Since a few days ago when we kissed, he has tittered between teasing me about it or acting like it didn't happen.

My heart kicked up as I remembered the kiss. I ruthlessly squashed down those feelings and thoughts. I couldn't allow myself to feel anything but admiration and loyalty to Tak.

I couldn't pretend we were the same people who'd gone to Bridge Lake High. I wasn't the awkward nerd anymore and he wasn't the weird kid next door. We'd grown up and changed, for better or worse. I'd see this as destinies gift and repay him for saving me.

CHAPTER TWENTY-FOUR

Say Hello

Tak

Jazz entered my dressing room, but her usual air of determination was gone, replaced with a gloominess that perplexed me. She seemed lost in thought as she walked over to Chelsea who stood in the corner tapping away on her cell phone. I couldn't focus on what they were saying as the makeup artist kept chattering around my head to the stylist who arranged my costumes on the hanger on the opposite side of the room.

"It looks like you two didn't have a meeting about this earlier. It also looks like you enjoy talking about work around your client's head. I wonder if your boss knows how unprofessional you are?"

They both sucked in a breath before they lowered their heads and continued their jobs in silence. Pleased, I turned my attention to Jazz's reflection in the mirror. She still hadn't looked my way.

Irritated, I spoke up. "My bodyguard doesn't seem to remember who her boss is. It's not like I'm the reason she's able to work or anything."

She glanced at me and pursed her lips. "I wasn't ignoring you, I just wanted to thank Chelsea for covering for me."

"You don't have to thank her. She's paid to do it."

Jazz's brow creased and she looked like she wanted to argue, but Chelsea set a hand on her shoulder. "Don't mind him, he's being a brat because he didn't get his daily dose of sugar."

I glared at Chelsea. I'd been enjoying myself. Why was she so set on ruining my fun?

"Don't you need to talk to Clint about the set?"

"Nope, I'm all yours," Chelsea said.

Pulling my face away from the makeup artist, I stood up, brushing off her attempts to continue powdering my face.

"I think it's time to switch out managers," I said, avoiding the finicky stylist's hands.

Chelsea walked over to my side and gave me a long look. "No one wants to work with you except for me."

I ignored what she said and walked over to Jazz. "I'm waiting."

"Waiting for what?" she inquired, not meeting my gaze.

I flicked her chin. She looked up at me indignantly. "For you to say hello."

She snorted. "Fine, hello, Tak."

I smiled. "Good girl."

Her eyes glinted in warning, but I was too pleased to say anything. The door to the dressing room opened and one of Clint's assistants told us the set was ready. Hearing this, I left Jazz's side and headed out with Chelsea into the hall to make our way to the set.

Feeling Chelsea's eyes cut into the side of my face, I finally asked, "What?"

"You know, I don't want to believe it, but did something happen between you and Jazz?"

"Yes, I fucked her silly," I answered.

She pursed her lips and glanced behind us at the few people who were moving here and there.

"Watch it, I don't want to have to clean up another scandal."

"Then don't ask, if you don't want a scandalous answer." I gave her a jeering smile.

She rolled her eyes. "Don't shit me. She's not even your type."

"And what makes you think I have a type? A pussy is a pussy."

Chelsea gave me a look. "You say that, but I can tell you what your type usually looks like. From their blonde hair to their long legs, every single one of them were so similar I thought they were quintuplets."

I looked away. "Tell me how you really feel," I said. "And before you go running to Kole. Nothing happened between us."

She made a humming sound. "For now, I won't, but don't forget getting too close to your bodyguard will make things harder for her and not you."

"And who said I didn't want to make things hard for her?"

"You're really fucked up," she said, right before we entered the set area.

I wouldn't deny it. A part of me wanted to see just how far I could push Jazz before she snapped. The night she'd driven my car toward another, without a bit of fear, was seared into my mind.

Something about her eagerness reminded me a bit of myself. The person I'd been before Skittles had shown me not everyone wanted something in repayment for a good deed.

Though I couldn't say if Skittle saving me then had actually done anything good for the world. As I walked over to Clint, who directed the lighting crew while adjusting his camera, I decided I would think about it later. It was time to get to work.

Jazz

I didn't leave the dressing room until I'd managed to tamp down my temper. Every time Tak said good girl, I wanted to punch him, but he was my charge, so I held back. Quickly leaving the dressing room, I followed the masculine shouts coming from the set.

Entering the studio area, I could see everyone's eyes were focused on the two men who were moving around in front of the all-white backdrop. Stopping next to one of the crew, I overheard them speaking to another person.

"I'm surprised Tak's able to keep up with Clint. Usually, Tak would be frustrated and ready to stomp out."

Hearing this, I focused my attention on the white backdrop. The one I assumed to be Clint knelt, his hands steady as he continued to take pictures of Tak, who moved here and there. Tak's energy not once diminishing as he moved from pose to pose under Clint's harsh direction. Standing up to change his position, Clint then checked the picture on his camera.

"Good, once more."

I couldn't help my fascination with how amazing Tak looked with the small pearls of sweat that sparkled on his exposed arms and forehead. I had to give it to the stylist. Tak looked like a fallen angel. I could almost believe at any moment his back would sprout feathery wings and he'd attack Clint for being so arrogant as to demand Tak pose for him.

By this point, I had completely forgotten about Aaron. I moved closer while at the same time the stagehands moved a large gothic themed throne on the set. Tak tossed his large body down into it, breathing heavily as the crew rushed forward and patted at his skin and offered him water. His eyes were on Clint, who stood behind the screen looking over the pictures.

I bit my lip. Sweaty-looking Tak was a delicious Tak.

"I think we got enough for this outfit, we'll change and have you take pictures on the throne next," Clint said as he finally looked back at Tak and smirked. "You're really giving me a run for my money."

"Of course, I'm the star," Tak said, rising.

His clothes were changed right there. I flushed as more and more of his lightly tanned skin was exposed. My cheeks were hot, and I was caught between turning around or boldly watching.

I decided to watch, he owed me for playing chicken for him. This was a perfect repayment. Again, I felt like I could die right then and there.

"Bring the female model in," Clint said to a person standing with a walkie-talkie near the exit.

I tensed at that. A female model? I couldn't be jealous.

It went against the rules of a number one fan. It wasn't healthy to feel jealousy for a professional who was only doing their job.

"Melissa's here," someone announced.

I turned around, eager to see who the model was and felt my stomach sink. She was pretty in a *distraught damsel* sort of way. I was nothing like the girl who daintily walked in, drawing the eyes of all the males working in the studio.

Lithe and graceful, they had given her a silvery wig and dressed her in a diaphanous white gown. I wanted to scream. She was the perfect contrast to Tak's dark god look. And damn me, if I wasn't planning then and there to buy the poster and three copies of the magazine when it came out.

This was the pits, but the wound was healed when I remembered I was the only person to see this live. Crushing my feelings of jealousy and annoyance at the tinkling laughter she released at a compliment from Clint, I looked away and spotted something off.

The light right above Tak swayed. I shifted as the swaying grew more violent. It was going to fall.

The minute the thought came, the light released, and I ran. I ignored the petrified screams from the women who'd been helping Tak change near the chair and the shout from Clint as I slammed into Tak's body, taking him down. The stage light hit the ground with a loud crash.

For a long second, silence permeated the studio. Pushing up, I looked up in time to see someone run. Coming to my feet, I took off after them before anyone said a word.

"Jazz."

I ignored the calling of my name as I ran toward the stairwell that led upstairs to the technical and service area of the studio. I climbed up the iron steps, my adrenaline pumping as I reached the landing. I saw the door on the other side of the catwalk close.

I raced across and slammed the door open only for something large and red to hit me square in the forehead. I hit the ground hard, everything going quiet.

Tak

Chasing after Jazz, I ran across the catwalk and pushed the door open to another stairwell in time to see her get hit with a fire extinguisher. Anger hit me so fast I didn't give the fucker a chance to recover and swung again. I slammed my fist into his chin.

The fire extinguisher slipped from his hand, hitting the floor with a bang. I grabbed him by the collar and lifted him up, walking him back out to the catwalk. I pushed him so his body hung over the railing.

He frantically grabbed my wrist. "Let go."

"Sure." I loosened my hold. He cried out in fear as he fell back.

"Wait, wait," he frantically yelled, reaching to grasp me before he took the spill. His skin was covered with sweat as he nervously pleaded. "Please, please let me up. I'll talk."

"I'm sorry, do I look like a cop to you? I don't need you to talk, just die," I said.

His eyes widened in terror and a terrified scream escaped his mouth. The doors to the stairwell opened behind me. The building's security finally showed up.

I debated on whether to drop him or not but decided against it. Yanking him forward, I threw him down. Turning around, I faced security with an easy smile.

"That's him."

They looked from me to the man who trembled on the floor. Once they had overcome their shock, they were on him. I walked around them and went to Jazz who remained lying on the floor. Chelsea knelt down beside her, running a hand over Jazz's head and winced.

"We're going to have to call an ambulance. Can you drive yourself home?"

"I'll go with her."

She looked away from Jazz's face to me. "What? Are you sure?"

I nodded and bent to reach under Jazz's body to lift her up. "Yeah, lead the way."

Chelsea eyed me. I guess she saw there was no fucking way I was going to leave Jazz's side. Sighing, she nodded and we walked downstairs to meet the ambulance.

I spotted the staff talking to the police. I looked down at Jazz's sleeping face. Apparently, she didn't understand my orders.

I'd told her not to put herself in danger after she'd recklessly raced my car and she'd hopped up and went right back to doing it. I still couldn't believe she'd pushed me out of the way. Luckily, we'd both hit the ground a few feet from where the light landed, but what if she'd stopped short after pushing me. Then she would have been hit by the stage light.

I wasn't concerned with the crowd that grew outside the studio. I was sure the paparazzi and journalists would have a field day with this one. I didn't care.

I was more concerned with the woman in my arms who'd put her life on the line for me. I climbed into the back of the ambulance that pulled into the large parking lot.

"I'll do some crowd control and meet you at the hospital," Chelsea said before she left.

It wasn't long before the ambulance was on its way. It hadn't been lost on me this had been an attempt on my life and if the light had fallen on my head, I'd be dead.

I watched Jazz sleep and finally came to a decision. Originally, I'd been planning to take my time looking into what happened in Vegas, but it looked like what ever happened there wasn't a onetime thing. And if I ignored it for too long, it would affect those around me.

Shit, I had to think long and hard before I made my next move.

CHAPTER TWENTY-FIVE

Health Check

Jazz

I opened my eyes to the sound of a loud beep. A sharp pain radiated through my head. I winced, pressing the palm of my hand to my forehead.

Where was I?

It didn't take me long to realize I was lying in a hospital bed in a private room. Sitting up, I felt a slight panic. Beginning and ending with the fact I was here and the criminal who'd tried to kill Tak wasn't. I needed to know what had happened to him.

I pulled the blanket off and tried to get out of the bed, wincing as the tubes in my arm pulled on my skin. Impatient, I quickly took them out and hopped out of bed. A wave of dizziness hit me. I ignored it.

Reaching the door, I pulled it open. My arm slightly trembled at the weight of it even though it wasn't that heavy. Running out,

I slammed right into someone's chest. Pain radiated through my nose. I looked up and met the irritated glare of Tak.

"What are you doing out of bed?"

Rubbing my nose, I asked, "The guy, what happened to him?"

He ignored my question and placed his hands on my waist. He turned me around and marched me back to the bed. "Bed, now."

I wriggled out of his hold and turned around to face him. "What happened to the criminal?"

"What happened to what criminal?" he asked. Crowding me back to the bed until my legs bumped against it.

"The guy," I said with gritted teeth at his obvious motive. "The one who dropped the stage light. Where is he? Were they able to capture him?"

Looking hesitant, he nodded. "Yeah, they caught him."

"Yes," I said, moving to walk around him. "I bet they need my statement, let's go quickly and ask them who he is."

"No, you're going to lay down and let the doctor look over you."

I waved him off. "I'm fine."

He grabbed the hand I'd lifted to wave him off in midair. I winced, looking up at him in confusion. "Tak?"

"I already told you once, I don't want to see you endanger yourself because of me, didn't I?"

I didn't have time for his tantrum. "I'm your bodyguard. My job is all about putting myself in danger. How can you ask me to not do my job?"

"Then I'll fire you," he said coolly.

He'd what?

My anger grew. I snatched my wrist from his hold.

"No, you won't. I won't quit and I won't let you fire me," I declared defiantly.

He looked down at me in amusement. "And how exactly would you stay hired after I fire you?"

"Mr. Kole wouldn't let you fire me for doing my job," I said as I crossed my arms. Daring him to say I was wrong. "I'm not weak. I've been hit before. You can't really believe this is my first time ending up in a hospital?"

He lost his look of amusement as his eyes hardened on me, but I would finish what I had to say.

"I get it. You see me." I motioned to my body. "And think I need protection, but this body is strong and capable. I can handle a lot more than you think."

I softened my voice and reached out, pressing the flat of my hand on his chest. "Let me protect you, please. Let me do my job."

He looked away from me, his jaw ticking. "I can take care of myself. I don't want to see you get hurt."

Stunned, I wasn't sure I'd heard him correctly. "What did you say?"

He side-eyed me, before turning to face me fully. "I'm not doubting your strength, but that doesn't mean I want to see you get hurt. I'm not weak." He scowled, moving my hand off his chest. "I'm not someone who needs another to be put in danger for them."

"But it's my job to protect you."

"I know and I know you're not going to back down on this." He shook his head. "So, let's put that on the back burner for now. What I want right now is for you to get back in that bed. If you don't, I'm warning you…"

He leaned down until his lips were an inch away and those warm brown eyes stared into mine. "I'll kiss you if you don't behave."

Flushing, I turned my head, pulling away from him. "You're playing dirty." Muttering about spoiled rock stars, I got back into the bed.

He pouted. "Actually, I'm kind of hurt. I was hoping you'd be a bit more stubborn so I could kiss you."

"Asshole," I whispered, clamping my mouth closed when Chelsea entered with a doctor next to her.

I endured being poked and prodded under the watchful eyes of both Chelsea and Tak. One would think I was the musician.

"Has anyone looked Tak over?" I asked.

Chelsea gave me a nod. "He's been checked over. They did it before he changed."

With that, I was forced the deal with the doctor until he finally gave me a clean bill to leave. Tak and Chelsea tried to get me to stay another night, but I couldn't. I wanted to get home and see if Dutch had managed to get Bradley's address for me.

If Bradley and his partners hadn't given up on killing Tak, then I couldn't waste time lazing around in a hospital bed. It was time I got more into this search for answers. I couldn't let this chance slide by.

Tak

Back home, I sat in the study I rarely used. I met Chelsea's worried gaze from where she sat across from me. She'd just gotten off the phone with the police and came to tell me what they reported.

"Well, what did they say?" I asked.

Her expression was troubled. "They said he's no longer in custody. They didn't even get his motive for trying to kill you out of him. The fucker must have connections because he was able to have his bail set at a measly five thousand and was out before the ink dried on his paperwork."

I released an incredulous laugh. "I should have fucking known."

"Tak."

"No, it's fine. Hasn't this city always been like this? Never mind, at least it's obvious someone with money is behind him. Now there's the question of how I can get my hands on him and make him disappear for trying to kill me."

"I'm going to pretend I didn't hear that," Chelsea said.

"Whatever makes you feel better," I replied. "Did you look into what I asked for?"

She shook her head. "I wasn't able to find out anything from the hotel. Management said the camera on the floor of your hotel room had been broken and when they asked their staff, no one remembered anything weird from that night."

I grimaced. "But there's also no footage of me arriving at the hotel."

"They said they could only assume you entered through the back door since the cameras were broken back there as well. They also mentioned that not only were the back door and the eleventh floor cameras not working, but two of their elevator cameras didn't work that night either. Apparently, they were to be fixed the next day."

I squinted. Something smelled heavily of bullshit and it wasn't Chelsea's cloying perfume. The husky sound of my own voice filled the air interrupting my thoughts.

Hold me down as I scream out. My broken dreams are endless. So, I curse you with my hatred.

Chelsea smiled tauntingly. "You actually soberly made your own song your ringtone?"

"You soberly picked out that vomit-colored dress to wear today. You don't see me judging you for it," I said right before I answered my phone.

"Dick," she muttered as she stood up and walked out.

"Hello?"

Kole's voice entered my ears. "I heard from Chelsea what happened."

"You also heard that fucker actually got out on bail, right?"

"I'll get our people to look into it," he said, sounding colder than usual.

"Kole had always been protective of his artists. Most people saw him as the opposite of me. He wasn't reckless or likely to go back on his word. If someone wanted to stretch it, they could call him *kind*, but when it came to protecting his musicians, he could be as ruthless as Jeff.

"Finally. I can see you actually doing your job."

"Tak."

I grimaced. "Don't, I'm fine. You should be thanking your new hire. She's the reason my head wasn't smashed in."

There was a beat of silence before Kole asked, "So… I'm starting to believe I may owe you an apology. What happened in Vegas?"

"I don't know, I keep telling you," I say in frustration. "There's a big fucking gap in my memory."

"Okay, okay. I'll beef up your security some more."

"The fuck you will. Jazz is enough, she's been doing her job."

"Are you actually saying something nice about your bodyguard?"

"That doesn't mean I won't try to sleep with her. I have every intention of fucking her out of her job." Just imagining Jazz under me, screaming as I pounded her into a wall, bed, or maybe even the pool, sent zings straight to my dick.

"I'm going to ask that you not talk like that to me or anyone else. I have enough problems without having to deal with a sexual harassment charge being filed against you."

Immediately my dick deflated. "I take offense to that. I've only ever had beautiful consensual sexual encounters. Maybe if you acted like me the number of interns you go through wouldn't be so high. Speaking of which, is the one with the perky breast still there?"

"Goodbye, Tak."

Before I could tell him goodbye, he hung up on me. I laughed. The fucker was so sensitive about his harem of interns.

My smile dropped when I thought about what Chelsea said. Something didn't sound right. It looks like I had no other choice but to reach out to Pit or Deacon to get this situation looked into.

The only problem with that was I didn't want to call them. No matter how much I knew I should, I needed some more time to think it over.

And I wasn't completely sure if the dumbass who'd tried to smash my head in was related to what happened in Vegas. He could have been one of millions of people who hated me for being Tak Jensei. I released a humorless laugh at that thought.

No one could hate me as much as I hated myself.

CHAPTER TWENTY-SIX

Blue Pill

Jazz

"Do we really have to do this?" I asked for like the third time.

Chelsea stopped typing as she looked at me. We sat in Tak's living room across from each other. "Every time an employee is injured, we have to write a report and since you're an onsite worker it needs to be done immediately."

I squeezed the pillow in my lap. "I understand, but was it really okay to let Tak go alone to the premiere tonight after what happened today?"

She shrugged. "I didn't send him alone. The security team loaned us a few guys who can play his babysitters until you're feeling better."

"I'm feeling better now," I insisted as I tapped my forehead. "Not a trace of dizziness."

"Well, Tak said he'd feel safer if you rested tonight."

I frowned. "I don't think he trusts me to do my job."

"That isn't true," she said. She didn't look at me as her fingers continued to fly over her phone. "In fact, it's because he trusts you, he's not comfortable with putting you in danger." Coming from Chelsea it sounded far less like fake flattery.

"Isn't that kind of my job?"

"Right, which is why I feel the need to warn you once more." She paused her typing and met my stare with a calm one of her own. "You cannot get in any sort of relationship with him. It would automatically terminate your employment here."

I immediately thought about the few kisses we'd shared. I knew I couldn't have sex with him and those kisses had definitely already crossed a line. I couldn't allow anymore forms of intimacy between us.

"I understand that all too well. I have not once entertained becoming something more than a comrade and friend to him," I said.

"Good to know. It's easy to spin some sort of romantic dream when dealing with Tak and his interest."

"Trust me, I'm not the type to build castles out of moonbeams. I'm well aware of the rules of the world. I can't become irreplaceable in his life. My beginning and end have to be seamless."

I had come here to help Tak, but I had never once thought of becoming a permanent fixture in his life.

"End?" she repeated, her tone curious. "Are you thinking about quitting?"

Catching myself, I laughed. "No, not anytime soon. Besides, I wouldn't make it that easy for him."

"Don't."

I couldn't stop the sadness I felt at the inevitability of my leaving his side one day.

Tak

I'd recently become very fond of balconies. It was the best place to hide away from unwanted company. At least it used to be. After the past few days, I was starting to think I had a bad fate when it came to them.

I looked down at the crowd of stars below in the ballroom. Every one of them falling all over themselves to get to know the producers and directors who were smiling. The band had been invited to the premiere of the movie we'd done the soundtrack for.

"Kole finally let you out." I didn't bother to turn to look at Omar. Of course, here he was to ruin my night. "I thought you'd be on lockdown forever."

"Is this number twenty-six or seven? I can't keep up," I asked as I turned away from the crowd below.

He glared at me the minute I turned around to look at him. Standing next to him wasn't one of the gross amounts of lovers he had, but his actual longtime fiancée.

"Ah, it's number one." I gave a slight bow of the head. "Hello, Risa."

She gave me a smile, but the warmth wasn't there. Not that I expected it. I'd stopped caring about her feelings when it became clear she was fine with pulling others into her and Omar's dramatic as fuck relationship.

I could abide many things, but disloyalty wasn't one of them. Two people made vows to each other and if they didn't intend to keep them, they should keep it basic. Instead, Risa had dragged Ark into her petty lovers game with Omar.

Giving the idiot hope only to turn around and act like she'd never wagged her tail in his direction. Every time I saw her, I automatically thanked God I kept my relationships simple.

Fuck 'em and leave 'em.

"It looks like you haven't changed much, Tak, and here I thought a near death experience would change you." Her voice was soft, but the scathing tone was clear as day. She brushed her raven-colored hair back.

"You thought wrong. I decided I'd give a big fuck you to the angels for bringing me back and be as bad as I can be. Nothing worse than being too good." I turned my ugly smile on Omar. "But I'm sure with your cheating habits Hell would welcome you with open arms."

"Tak," he growled, taking a step forward.

A part of me wanted him to put his hands on me. If he took one more fucking step, I could cause a scene and leave this stupid event and go home. I wasn't going to examine too closely why I'd rather be home than here. I squinted, more than ready for a fight.

"No." Risa stepped in front of him, blocking Omar from reaching me. "He's not worth it."

I laughed at that because if that came from anyone else it would have caused a very, very small feeling of pain. Luckily, I knew her dirty secret. She fucked Ark while she and Omar were taking a break.

"Right, I don't think you're the one who should talk about *worth*," I said to her back. "I know it's hard to choose sometimes, but I can't say you picked well."

I shrugged, ignoring the way her back tensed. "Ark, the sweetheart or the cheating Omar, who can't stay loyal to a single woman to save his life. Hmm, so many choices."

I walked past them.

"What the fuck are you trying to say?" He placed a restraining hand on my shoulder. Smiling, I placed my hand over his.

"Do you really want to know?" *Please, fucking want to so we can fight and I can go the fuck home.*

"Omar, let him go," Risa said, walking up to his side and placing a hand on his arm. "He's trying to piss you off on purpose."

"Oh shit, look at little Risa using her head," I taunted knowing she was trying to stop me from revealing her little secret.

"Fuck." Omar pushed me away and glared at me. "One of these days I'll punch that damn ass-eating smirk off your face."

I brushed the invisible dust off my shoulder and straightened my suit jacket. "You had your chance, but your girl stopped you. Don't get pissed at me because you can't deal with your own shit," I said as I walked around them and headed downstairs.

"Son of a bitch." It felt like my head was being crushed. The bright lights and the smell of perfume was getting to me.

I was sick of this feeling. The world was too real and so much was happening. I felt like I was drowning under the number of eyes on me.

My breathing grew harsh as I searched for something, anything to relieve the tension running through me. I walked over to the bar and pulled out a little plastic bag from my pocket. It held a few blue pills from Richie I still hadn't used.

I wondered how long it had been since I'd had the hard shit. It was time to break the drought. This night was over and quite frankly, I was over playing a good boy.

Two pills and a shot and suddenly the world felt a whole lot better. The colors dimmed and the music roared to life.

Jazz

After saying good night to Chelsea, I texted Dutch back a quick thank you for sending me Bradley's address and asked him to look into the guy who'd been arrested. After I got comfortable in bed, I wasn't sure how much time had passed before I heard it. A loud masculine yell.

I got up, breathing harshly. I grabbed my cell and pulled the side table drawer open and grabbed the gun that I kept there. I usually kept it locked away in its case, but with the incident at the studio, I felt the need to have it out and ready to use. Tak's enemies could try to attack him in his own home one night.

Crossing my arms, I then turned on the light on my cell phone and rested it over the top of my gun. I only uncrossed them to open the door and took up the same pose once more. I turned the light to the right and left to ensure there was no one attempting to hide in the hall.

Another yell caused me to run down the corridor. Stopping at the opening into the living room, I backed up and pressed my back against the wall, slowly shifting to the edge. I leaned forward. My hold on my phone loosened and my shoulders slumped as shock invaded my mind.

Tak stood in the center of the room, his hands pressed to his head. He shook it frantically back and forth.

"Shut up, shut up," he yelled. "Stop it." He pleaded to no one.

My heart broke as I watched him. It took me a minute to realize he held a gun in his hand. Fear quickly took the place of the shock. I turned my gun on safety and laid it down on the floor as well as my phone.

I paused as he turned, lashing out with the gun, smacking it into one of the intricate glass statues that sat on one of the three high pedestals in the living room. The figure wobbled before it tilted over and slammed onto the ground, shattering into pieces. He stared at it, a stark look of loss taking over his features.

"Fuck," he said, before he released a breathless laugh that held a bit of grief.

"Look, one day it's perfect and the next..." His muttering trailed off, before he shook his head. "Fuck it, I'm so tired."

He lifted the gun to his head. It wasn't wise, but I ran toward him praying my speed was faster than he was at pulling the trigger.

"Tak," I shouted his name.

He didn't turn around when I called out to him. I wrapped my arms around his waist as my body hit his back. His body trembled. I tightened my arms around him.

"Tak, put it down," I desperately ordered, trying to speak over the sorrow in my throat. "Please, put it down."

He stiffened and became as still as a statue. His breathing harsh before the hand that held the gun fell to his side. He laughed, but it was empty of any joy.

"It stopped," he whispered, before his body suddenly went slack and he fell backward.

I cried out in surprise as I landed on my butt when he landed on top of me. The gun clattered to the floor. I sat there dumbfounded.

The adrenaline running through my body slowly draining away. I pushed him off me and stared down at his unconscious face and then looked at the gun that was a few inches from his hand. I'd seen despair before.

Felt the aching feeling of being swept away. The paralyzing sensation of your world falling apart and knowing you're too weak to do anything about it. I'd found my savior in Tak's songs.

His voice telling me it was okay to lose hope, soothing the choking numbness I couldn't escape without his music. And now, I could see where those words came from. Demons had plenty of shapes and everyone had them somewhere in their lives.

I reached out and gently brushed my fingers against his cheeks. The tears that fell from my eyes, falling onto his skin. A part of me wished they had the power to heal, but they didn't.

I could only weep for him. Silently and in the shadows, I could only pray and make wishes that the man before me would someday heal from the things that haunted him. If the only thing I could do was save his life, then I would do that.

I owed it to him. He had saved mine. The girl who'd seen the worst of human nature, greed, betrayal, and obsession.

I wanted to do something, at least one thing for him. Then, I swore I would leave and take my lies with me. I was determined to stay by his side.

If I had to stop these growing feelings inside me, I would do it. Brushing the tears from my face, I managed to slip out from under him and walked over to his gun and picked it up. I continued into the hallway to gather my phone and weapon.

I returned to my room and locked them both away in there. After pulling my hair back into a ponytail, I went in search of a dustpan and broom. I'd clean up and then somehow get Tak back to his bedroom. I would think about everything I'd seen tomorrow.

CHAPTER TWENTY-SEVEN

Shame

Tak

"Are you going to take him?"

I was being discussed by my parents like I wasn't in the room once again.

"I can't, I have to go on a business trip to Hawaii." My mother was always focused ahead, her eyes on the next possible deal. "Can't you just leave him with his grandmother this time?"

"You know she's gotten too old to watch him. Aren't you his mother, shouldn't you be more caring toward your son?" My dad demanded in a harsh voice. The smell of his cigarette always made my throat burn. "I've been lenient so far, ignoring you're "trips" when I know damn well what you've been up to this whole time."

"Ha." My mother's face changed before my eyes. "That's funny coming from you, I don't think you have any place to talk. You started this. Did you think I'd just be miserable and continue to love you?

Don't be so arrogant, I'll never be a desperate woman, not even for you."

I wondered why they didn't want to stay.

Mom nor Dad.

"Please stay." I sat up. My hand held out to no one.

Only my TV looked back at me. I dropped my hand to my side and squinted from the pain radiating behind my eyes. I had a bad high the previous night. Covering my face with both my hands, I tried to remember past the pain, but it was impossible. I shouldn't have taken those two pills.

I reached out to my side, searching for the familiar feeling of steel only not to find it. I frantically searched the bed covers, still not finding what I was looking for at all. Panic began to set in. What if one of the morning cleaning staff found it?

Shit, I needed to find it. I went to get out of bed only for the click of my bedroom door opening to stop me short. The scent of food filled the room. Jazz came into view, her eyes bright and her smile wide as she carried in a tray with what looked like porridge on it.

"You're up," she said. She walked to the side of my bed and set the tray down on the side table. "Are you feeling better?" She reached over and pressed her cool hand against my forehead. With a sigh, she pulled back and grabbed up the two Tylenol tablets that sat next to the bowl of porridge. "I know you shouldn't take medicine on an empty stomach, but you can take these and then eat. Here."

I looked from her to the medicine in her hand. "What happened last night?"

I almost missed the shadow that past over her eyes. Her smile softened. "As far as I'm concerned, you got very, very drunk and fell asleep. So now you're suffering from it. That's also what Chelsea thinks. If you want to talk about something else, I think it would be better to do so after you've gotten some rest."

She'd seen me at my worse. I could see it. I was hit with a truck load of embarrassment and shame. And like a coward, I took the glass and medicine from her without another word.

Hell, I was grateful she was still here. I knew how I could get when I had a bad high.

"Thank you," I said, not looking at her, feeling too exposed.

She took the glass from me and placed it on the tray. "You're welcome," she said simply before she left the room, closing the door behind her.

I bent forward and pressed my hands to my face, trying to muffle the breakdown as I cried.

CHAPTER TWENTY-EIGHT

Second Try

Jazz

"Did something happen between you and Tak?" Chelsea asked thoughtfully as we stood outside, watching Tak being filmed on the walkway below near a scenic lake view, where a few ducks quacked in excitement. The weather was still warm, despite the light mist that covered the ground.

"No, why?" I asked, feigning ignorance.

It had been almost a week since the night I'd dragged Tak to his bed and cleaned up the mess that had remained after he'd lost control. There had been a weird tension between us ever since. He seemed to be eager to tell me something but every time our eyes met, he'd turn away.

"Because you two haven't looked each other in the eyes this entire time. Every time you two talk, he looks away and you look to the side." She eyed me with suspicion. "You can tell me, did you two sleep together?"

I watched below as the female model grabbed onto Tak's arm. They seemed a little bit too close, but I decided not to intercede. Wouldn't his manager intrude if she thought it was too much?

"No, we didn't." I sent her a look. "And is that really something you should ask out in the open?"

She shrugged, turning her attention back to Tak who smiled down at the model while putting a firm hand on her shoulder to keep her back. "They're all down there. No one can hear us."

"Well, there isn't any affair," I said. "So, there's no need to worry."

"Are you sure?" she asked again. And for some reason I found myself irritated.

"Yes, I am," I harshly whispered.

Pursing my lips together, I averted my eyes from Chelsea. She didn't deserve all of my irritation. Sure, she was getting on my nerves, but she wasn't the source of it.

I glanced at Tak—he was. I was frustrated with his mixed messages.

"Cut. Let's take a break," the director announced, using his mic.

"Don't worry, I'll make sure my contract isn't broken," I said as I watched Tak walk toward us, having managed to shake off the clingy model.

Chelsea released a humming sound. "Whatever you say, I'm going to go talk with the director and see how much longer this shoot will be." She walked away just as Tak reached my side.

"God, it's hot," he exclaimed, pulling off the thick fur-lined coat he wore and tossed it over the bench that was next to where I stood. "Whose plan was it to shoot a commercial for winter during the summer?"

I couldn't help smiling as I reached down and picked up the towel off the bench and handed it to him. Quickly, he got rid of the sweat gathering at his neck and brow before tossing it back on the bench.

"You're handling everything fine so far, even the aggressive flirting from your co-star…" I trailed off, my attention falling on the girl who excitedly chatted with her manager. "I have to say it's going pretty well," I said and looked back at him.

An intern who'd been running around stopped by Tak's side and handed him a bottle of water before heading over to serve the rest of the film crew.

Tak's expression turned thoughtful. "You know, we still haven't talked."

"What exactly should we talk about?" I asked, feeling the nervous ball in my stomach tighten.

"That night, I think I'm ready to talk about it. At least with you," he said, I could hear the tone of nervousness in his voice.

I moved my gaze to his face. I tried to read him only to be left as clueless as before. "Why? I'm no one special."

The corners of his mouth kicked up as he lifted a single brow. "Well, aren't you?"

I frowned. "I'm not. I just don't want you to feel like you have to explain anything."

"I don't have to," he said. "I want to."

I weighed his words. I could push him away here and now. We could continue this cold and awkward relationship—me being treated strictly as his bodyguard—or I could let him open up to me and lose a few of the shadows behind his gaze.

"Okay."

"Thanks." He held the water bottle out to me. "I'm going to makeup."

I wasn't sure what he was thanking me for, but I quietly accepted the bottle back. He walked around me and headed to where the stylist and makeup artist were waiting near one of the trailers. They eagerly waited to touch him up.

I followed him with my gaze, feeling an odd sense of déjà vu. A vision of him in a beaten leather coat, torn blue jeans, and earphones plugged deep in his ears popped into my head. His black hair a wild mess on his head and his gaze holding dark secrets that had made my young heart ache.

I sighed as a fond smile came to my lips. I wondered sometimes had there ever been anyone else who'd drawn my eyes as he did? I couldn't remember.

My greatest and worse moments were tied to him, always. I only wish he knew or remembered, but if he did he'd know Jazz didn't exist. Everything would unravel and I'd be forced to part with him.

I tightened my hand on the bottle on reflex. Tak was my world, whether he knew it or not. Some would call me crazy and maybe even a stalker, but if they had loved someone as I did.

If they had found salvation because of another as I had, they would understand. If he wanted to talk. I'd hear what he had to say.

CHAPTER TWENTY-NINE

My Crew

Tak

"You're a fucking prick."

I winced, trying not to wilt under the onslaught of curse words Deacon had for me. "It's been what... a few weeks and you're calling me now? If it wasn't for Luke saying you needed some space and your little tantrum with Skittles and Pit, me and everyone else would have kicked your door in and beat the shit out of you."

I nodded, knowing he couldn't see me. "What the fuck were you thinking? Huh? You're just going to off yourself and not say shit to us about it? Did you even think of us as your brothers or about Skittles? Tak? Tak, you better not have hung up. If you did, I swear to God—"

"I know I was wrong."

He inhaled sharply. I could imagine him now, gaze sharp and his posture hunched as he thought over how he wanted to beat the shit out of me. "Tell me exactly what you did wrong."

I gritted my teeth before saying the first thing that popped into my head. "Trying to kill myself?"

"Wrong."

Huh? That was what I'd done or at least that's what the public believed. "I didn't let you all visit me in the hospital?"

"No." His voice was harder this time. "Try again."

I frowned. "What the fuck, Deacon? There's plenty of shit I've done and unless you're trying to have me do some twisted fucking version of a confession, you should stop wasting both of our time and tell me what you think I did wrong."

He was silent for a long time. "First of all, check your fucking tone. Don't ever come at me like that. And since you're an idiot, I'll spell it out for you. You didn't believe in us."

Huh? I'm sorry, was this the fucking Deacon I knew? Mister hard knuckles, who only cared about his shop and coin?

"What does my belief in you guys have to do with me offing myself?" I ask more out of curiosity because again, I didn't actually do it to myself.

"If you believed in us and our crew, you wouldn't have done something like this. You've been acting like a little bitch since Pit and Skittles started dating. If I noticed, everyone fucking did.

"We're not the type to sit around pissing away and crying about our feelings, but did you ever think of coming to us? Trusting us with your thoughts, shit."

"That's the most I've ever heard you say in my entire life," I said, feeling more than shocked by his words.

"Shut up, if it wasn't for this dumb shit, I'd still be quiet, I'd stay quiet," he snapped back.

I laughed but it was empty. I couldn't bring myself to explain to him my mind's inner workings. I couldn't yet find the courage in myself to share my weak self with my friends. It was funny and sad as shit. I wasn't able to be the real me around the men I'd been friends with since I finished high school.

What could I say?

I was still having a hard time dealing with my sobriety and my own thoughts. Digging into my pocket, I pulled out a perfectly rolled blunt. A man had to enjoy the simple things in life.

I'd flushed the blue pills down the drain. Shit was the main reason I'd been avoiding Jazz and had finally called Deacon.

"Listen, what if I told you I didn't try to off myself?" I asked, grabbing my lighter out of the basket on my desk and lighting the end of my blunt. I set the delicate thing between my lips and took a deep inhale before taking it out and continued to talk.

"I'd say explain."

I took another hit. "Here's the thing. I was chasing some fucker who decided my car was his."

"You're shitting me."

"Nope," I said. "And during chasing this damn thief down— somewhere in there—I got knocked out and ended up back at my hotel room with slit wrists. Luckily, I was saved by the EMTs."

"*Tak*," he drew out my name in a quiet hiss that made me aware I'd pushed him to the edge. We all knew in our crew that sound meant pain for others. "I'm really starting to regret not kicking your door open."

"Wait, it gets even better," I said, the lovely high making me chuckle. "Someone tried to smash my head in with a stage light. The perpetrator was released on bail and has disappeared."

"Son of a bitch. When I get there, I'm ripping you a new one," he threatened.

"Stand in line," I said, exhaling a perfect string of smoke. "Anyway, can you look into it for me? I can't get the legal routes to get me the information I need. Honestly, I've been thinking of calling for a while."

"Why didn't you?" Deacon asked.

I shrugged. "Didn't feel like it."

"Tak."

"I'll see you later."

I hung up the phone, knowing the following two dings were from Deacon, telling me off. I leaned back against my chair and stared at the wall blankly.

"That was one," I said aloud before taking another hit. "Now on to the next task."

This time I decided to text Pit and Skittles that I needed their help. I figured it would save me going through the same shit I'd gone through with Deacon.

A few minutes later Skittles texted back.

Skittles: Who am I about to fuck up?

Followed by Pit's.

Pit: Deacon called. You fucked up, kid. You should have come straight to me. I've got this.

CHAPTER THIRTY

Let's Talk

Tak

Jazz sat across from me in my living room. It had been a few hours since the end of the photo shoot and since I'd told her we'd talk. The air between us buzzed with something I couldn't put my finger on.

Even with the stress of speaking to her about *that* night, I couldn't stop my mind from thinking about fucking her. I had a thing for sweets. From the few times I'd stolen kisses from her, each one had been sweeter then the last.

Her eyes were filled with determination as she met my gaze head-on. I couldn't help thinking about my attraction to her. She was shorter than me, I liked them taller.

She was curvy and while I was never a man who denied himself variety, the women who normally ended up in my bed weren't curvy. However, every curve on her caused my hands to itch with the desire to touch them.

She had an almost pixie look about her. Where you first thought she was weak and easy to bend, you soon learned there was a fiery passion that ran in her and it was as hard as steel. She tilted her head.

"Have you finished looking me over?" she asked, her voice holding only amusement.

Her voice always sounded like a smooth lullaby. Something told me the first time I heard her cry out during sex it would be my favorite sound from then on.

"No," I said and enjoyed the weird way she worked her mouth when she couldn't find a word to say back.

She fluttered her fingers together as she shifted. She was odd. At some moments, she was like a fan, watching me with shiny eyes and her expression as bashful as a woman who'd never touched a man.

Other times, she was bold and reckless. I immediately remembered her taking my car and playing chicken and my amusement disappeared.

"That night, I took two pills. Normally, when I do blue it doesn't hit me so hard. I don't fall so deep. But since I've been avoiding the heavy shit for so fucking long, it looks like I've lost my resistance to the stuff. That night was the result," I explained.

"I… My childhood wasn't the best. I grew up more alone than the average kid and, uh, someone in my life took advantage of that. I got beat up a lot and I've never really dealt with it like I should have, I guess.

"Sometimes I'm okay, and then, I'm… just not." I swallowed, trying to face one of my demons was like climbing over a mountain made of glass. "Anyway, I've been using for so long that when my thoughts and emotions get a bit too overwhelming, I tend to lean on a few pills and the occasional blunt to get through it."

"To be honest, I know I fucked up, but I'm usually alone when I'm dealing with both my highs and lows. That night, for some reason I was low, real low. I hope we can move on from this and know that will be the last time it happens."

She stiffened, her eyes growing dark. It was at moments like these I realized she wasn't just someone who worked for me. She wasn't another fan. She was a comrade in pain. She looked at me not with pity but with understanding and acceptance.

I felt my heart clench. Fighting the urge to reach across and drag her into my arms was killing me.

"I lost my mother when I was in high school," she suddenly announced.

Her words took me aback. "Huh, repeat that?"

She smiled at me, but it held a ting of sadness to it. "I lost my mother when I was in high school." She didn't lose her smile, nor did she look away from me. "I found her the same night my date for prom stood me up.

"I walked back from my school because I was too embarrassed to call the limo back for only me. I walked home and opened the doors and found her at the bottom of the steps, dead. They said she'd taken a few too many sleeping pills. It must have made her drowsy and she fell. The officers told me with the amount she took, it was possible she was trying to kill herself." Her smile was gone and her eyes were empty.

"Stop." I stood. "You don't have to tell me. Shit, I didn't tell you so you would tell me something traumatic about your past."

"It's only fair," she said, standing as well. "I just don't want you to think I think of you any differently. We all have demons, I shared one of mine with you."

"Don't you hate her?" I asked.

She looked away from me. "And what would my hate do?" she asked, shrugging. "I don't, there isn't any point when she's already dead. Anyway, now you know one of my secrets. And I know yours. Is there anything else you need to get off your chest?"

I stared at her. For the longest I'd hated my family and everything about them. I still couldn't stomach even hearing their name.

"No."

"So, with this, we can go back to normal," she concluded, giving me a small smile.

"Actually, I think there is one more thing we should talk about."

"And what's that?"

"When are you going to admit you're attracted to me?"

Call me a dick, but this emotional shit had a time limit. Now it was time to see just how close I could get to getting in her pants because I couldn't think of anything else except using this moment as an opportunity to fuck our brains out.

Jazz shook her head. "Your timing sucks."

"So, you are attracted to me."

"I didn't say that. Do you even listen when I talk?"

I grabbed her wrist, pulled her over, and leaned in close. "No, not really."

She slapped my shoulder, glaring up at me. "Let go."

"Sure, as soon as we have our make-up kiss," I teased.

"Tak," her angry words were cut off by my lips.

Delicious, she tasted like pure sugar on my tongue. I took her lips in the way I'd been dreaming about, hungrily. She was like a sweet and sour candy I could suck on all day.

Her moans were added perks. My lips craved more of her, even as I kissed her. She smelled like a cupcake.

I wanted to open up her pussy and lick the cream from between her legs. Groaning, I pulled her closer. She let out another moan and pressed her hands against my chest. I abruptly broke the kiss, otherwise I'd have her stripped and panting under me on the couch behind her.

She gasped, falling back to plop down on the couch. With eyes glazed with lust, she looked up at me, dazed.

"Now we've made up," I panted out.

She peeked her tongue out to lick her bottom lip. Eventually her eyes regained focus as she stood up. "Mmm," she hummed before beating a quick retreat.

"Shit." I looked down at my hard friend. "Soon, I fucking swear, you'll get some."

It was time for a cold shower.

Jazz

I really needed to stop those kisses between me and Tak. I really, really should. Yet, I didn't want them to stop. Shutting the door to my room, I walked over to my desk and stared down at it.

My mother died when I was in high school.

Remembering my earlier words, I cringed. I'd only wished to share something that would make what he had said worth it. Since he'd shared with me one of his demons, it was only right for me to do the same.

I rubbed my hot cheeks. I couldn't shake the feel of his lips against mine. What was wrong with me?

A stalker fan infiltrates her favorite artist's staff and steals kisses from him. That would be the headline once I was caught. Being an heiress would be second in the entire story of how I lied to him.

However, I couldn't get rid of his words that kept ringing over and over in my head.

I didn't know how to deal with him and yet, I couldn't get enough of being around him. I wanted more of his blunt words and his teasing tone.

I wanted to see his darkest moments and I also wanted to be there for when he found the light at the end of the tunnel. Nothing about Tak disgusted me, nothing about him could push me away. I leaned forward and pressed my hands flat against the desk.

Was I crazy?

CHAPTER THIRTY-ONE

Break In

Jazz

Only I would be spending my day off like this. *Happy Monday*, I think with a snort to myself. I wriggled two lock picks into the lock of Bradley's house.

I had known Tak would have a few enemies close to him, but to find out both his attackers worked at the label had still been a little startling. And one of them even worked in the HR department. Dutch had kept an eye on everything related to Bradley since IDing him which is why we'd learned he'd be out of town this weekend. Giving me a chance to snoop around his place.

"Dutch, were you able to find anything in his phone records that's suspicious," I whispered, my voice muffled behind my face mask.

I released a sigh when the lock clicked. I quickly removed the picks and placed them in my back pocket. Dutch's voice came over the earphone in my right ear.

"No, at least nothing too obvious. He has a few calls from a random number, but I can't find anything else."

"Could he have used a burner phone?" I asked as I opened the door slowly.

"Sure, after I check Bradley's security cameras, I'll check his bank accounts."

"Thanks," I said.

I leaned forward to listen with the ear that didn't have an earphone. Hearing nothing, I snuck in, remaining low. I entered the kitchen and crawled across the floor. When I reached the other side, I turned and sat down on the floor, my back pressed against the bottom cabinets.

"See anything?"

"No, it's all clear," Dutch answered.

"Got it. Where is the office?" I asked as I slowly rose to my feet.

"The door you entered through is to the kitchen. The living room is right around the corner from it and the office is across from there," he said.

I pursed my lips together and walked around the corner with my back pressed against the wall. Leaning forward, I investigated the dark living room before turning for the room I intended to head into. An ominous chill ran down my back. I swallowed, suddenly feeling the sensation of being watched.

"Jazz, watch out," Dutch shouted.

Before I could answer, someone shot toward me from the dark living room.

"Shit," I retreated.

"Come here," the person ordered in a harsh voice.

They grabbed the backpack on my back in one hand. I spun completely around, escaping the shoulder straps. Grabbing a knife from the knife block, I then straightened and stood with it in my hand.

I stared the person down. It was clear he was the one up to no good. He was dressed from top to bottom in black. He carelessly let my backpack drop to the floor.

"Who sent you?" he gruffly demanded, pulling something from his back pocket, black gloves. He slipped them on. "You should tell me voluntarily."

I laughed. "And why would I do that?"

"Okay, the hard way it is."

The space was small, but I moved forward. The knife made its mark in his shoulder. However, he didn't flinch. Taking a bold step forward, he reached out to grab at my arm.

I dodged, stepping sideways and pulled the knife out of his shoulder. I spun it as I lowered myself and brought it across his stomach. His shirt tore, revealing the Kevlar vest beneath it.

His hands landed on my shoulders and he grabbed me up. He pulled back his right hand and he made a fist, plowing it into my stomach. I gasped, my eyes watering.

I smacked his hand off my shoulder and grabbed the rack of dishes. I pulled hard to make sure it hit him, then I turned to run.

"Stop," he yelled.

I ignored him, grabbing my backpack up. I ran deeper into the house, past the living room into the hallway. There was a hard yank on my backpack as he caught me and pulled me back.

I turned, twisted my hip, and lashed out with my foot, hitting him square in the chest. He released a grunt. Not waiting for him to recover, I ran for the front door and pulled it open.

Running out into the street, I noticed almost instantly he didn't chase after me. Breathing hard, I continued running until I couldn't see the house. Stopping, I took a deep breath, the sound of my heart pounding in my ears.

"Don't cover my mouth, something's happening to Jazz. Jazz, are you there? What happened? It sounded like a war was going on over there. I could hear it in my apartment and came over to check."

"There was someone else in the house," I answered, taking a look around and realizing I'd ran in the opposite direction of the neighborhood's entrance. "Dutch, I thought you said it was clear."

"The fucker must've been standing in a blind spot. It was like he jumped out from behind the damn camera," Dutch explained.

"Is he still there?"

There was a beat of silence. I found myself saying, "Dutch, Trisha… Why did you guys go silent all of a sudden?"

It was Dutch who answered. "Bradley pulled in and entered the house right after you ran out."

"What, isn't that other guy still there?"

"Yeah, and…" He stopped talking, but I could still hear Trisha yelling something in the back.

"And, what? Dutch, tell me what's going on," I demanded.

"He killed him, the guy who attacked you killed Bradley just now."

My body went cold at his words. I stood there staring numbly at my feet. When the shock finally wore off, the sound of sirens filled the air.

I looked up to see the lights of the police cars that were approaching, I assumed they were heading to Bradley's house, where I'd just run from. I needed to get as far as I could from the scene.

"Dutch, I'm going to hang up. I'll call you once I'm back at Tak's place."

"Okay, be safe."

I hung up and started making my way toward the neighborhood exit. Bradley was killed by the man I'd run into when I'd broke in. Which only left me with one conclusion. I was going in the right direction in searching for the people who'd attempted to kill Tak.

CHAPTER THIRTY-TWO

Practice

Jazz

The hard sound of a guitar poured out of the speakers as Tak sung. His voice filling the studio room. The band continued playing into another track from their last album, *Disfunction*.

It had already been a few hours since they'd started practicing and it didn't look like they had any intention of stopping soon. I had already been blessed once to see a shirtless Tak. Yet, I was being blessed again with a front-row seat to a live performance from Rejected One.

I could have died happy. My heart nearly exploded as I repeatedly told myself I couldn't dance or sing along. I remained seated in the corner, watching as Jay smoothly revved up to the song's climax with his skillful guitar playing.

Omar stood with his dreads held back with a hair band, plucking the strings of his bass. He smiled like a Cheshire cat as his eyes flicked every once in a while to Ark who kept the whole thing together with his continuous drum playing.

I wanted to scream along, but I was in the room with Chelsea and a few others I decided to call the entourage. I wasn't sure what they all did, but they'd all been welcomed into the studio.

I focused completely on Tak as they moved to the next song, last night's debacle totally forgotten in the moment. Tak hopped up and down. His energy was obviously through the roof. He demonstrated this by stopping and releasing a familiar smooth run into the mic.

"You must like their music." I looked over at one of the people who I'd grouped together in the entourage, who had finally deigned to speak to me. She had raven hair and smiled softly at me. "This is actually one of my favorite songs."

I dropped my gaze and forced myself to stop tapping my foot. Meeting her eyes once more, I nodded.

"I'm not a big fan, but I can appreciate the music they make."

I released an inner scream of a dying animal. Every fiber of my being wanted me to take back the words I'd just said. However, I couldn't let them know how much of a hard-core fan I was.

"I assumed from the way you were swaying to the music you were a big fan," she said.

I hadn't realized I was swaying. I honestly wanted to scream. *Yes. Yes, I am. I've been here since "Descension".*

I couldn't say that though. It was painful. If I had to choose between this or being stabbed a thousand times with needles, I'd much rather the needles. Taking a deep breath, I forced out a Mona Lisa smile.

"It's more like I can't help it since this song is really good. I'm still learning who's who. What's your name?"

The girl released a laugh. "No problem, I'm Risa. I'm engaged to Omar." She motioned toward the window. "He's the one with the dreads."

I glanced back at the glass window that separated us from the band. I felt a mix of offense and amusement. Did she think I didn't know who Omar was? Besides, I still remembered when Tak called him out for cheating.

Thinking this, I only said, "Oh, okay."

She chuckled. "You're the new bodyguard for Tak, right? He must be a handful."

That statement was something I'd heard way too much. I knew there were those who didn't like Tak, but I never knew they were this comfortable expressing it. I'd honestly grown tired of hearing it.

"No, not really," I said.

I wasn't expecting her welcoming expression to turn cold.

"Hmm, I guess you're actually more of a fan than you thought." With that said, she turned her attention to those next to her.

Taken aback by her sudden coldness, I stared at her, thinking over her reaction. The door to the booth opened, catching my attention. The band came into the control room.

All of their shirts were drenched in sweat. Before I realized what I was doing, I'd picked up Tak's black towel from the chair he'd left it on and taken it to him.

He smiled down at me and winked. "Thanks, Jazzy."

My heart skipped a beat. I quickly looked away out of embarrassment and said, "You've got one more round of practice you can do before we have to leave for your next appointment."

"Shit, do we really have to do it today?"

"Yep." Chelsea cut in and as usual, her eyes were on her phone. "PR for this last-minute concert is important. Unless you're saying you're not interested in doing it? I could always cancel it."

"Don't lie." He glared at her with no heat. "You'd kill me if I canceled."

"No, we would kill you," Jay cut in. "Besides, Conner said he'd pay money to see you back in a dive bar."

"He could pay to see me fuck you—"

"Tak." Jay's face turned red as he glared at him. "Finish that sentence and I swear to god I'll sell your number on eBay."

The bodyguard in me said, no, but the stalker in me said yes. I couldn't believe I'd reached such a new low as a fan.

Tak turned his attention on me. "Ready for the last round?"

"Yeah, go ahead," I answered. More than excited to hear them play some more.

A mischievous look entered his eyes before he bent down and brushed his lips against my cheek. The following silence after Tak's bold move could be cut with a knife. I stood stiff and tense as he tossed his towel into my hands and went back into the studio room.

I could feel the sting of everyone's eyes on me. I turned around and found myself stared at by everyone in the room. All of them wore different expressions of shock.

Ark looked at me as he walked back into the studio. Followed by a wide-eyed Jay and a head-shaking Omar.

I dropped my eyes to my feet and walked over to the corner, retaking my seat. Ignoring the fiery glare from Chelsea. I wasn't in a relationship with Tak.

I wasn't.

Tak

"How long are you going to bully the poor girl?" Chelsea asked as she followed me into my bedroom.

I tossed my sweaty shirt into the laundry basket.

"I don't know what you mean," I said, feigning ignorance as I walked into my bathroom.

The session had been longer than usual. It'd been too long since the last time we'd rehearsed. And for once, there hadn't been any drama to make it tense.

"I wasn't born yesterday," Chelsea said.

I stuck my head out of the bathroom. "It's not bullying if she likes it."

She shot me a look. "Does she? You're willing to threaten her contract with you?"

"What makes you think I care about that?" I asked. Stepping out of the bathroom with a towel around my waist. "I've never ignored a woman's open arms, but if you're afraid I'll jump her. I won't."

"I know, but kissing, touching, and giving her those hot looks. You're not fooling anyone, you like her." She shot me a curious look. "Not that I can think of why. What changed between you two?"

I shrugged. It wasn't really any of her business. I mean, no matter what I said it wouldn't make sense. Jazz had this air about her like an R & B song that rocked me to sleep.

Her presence calmed me. Even when my hands itched to try another pill, I'd hold back imagining her face. Sure, I didn't want to grow attached, but something told me I already was.

It was hard as fuck trying to balance my own nature with the desire I had for Jazz, but either way I didn't want her to go anywhere. The idea of losing her brought forth this uncomfortable sensation in my chest, like something was pressing on it. However, I also didn't want a babysitter.

"Nothing, I'm just enjoying Kole's gift. What's the problem?"

Chelsea glowered at me. "You've broken a lot of hearts and I usually don't care, but I like Jazz. She's a good kid, so if you're going to do anything make sure you don't force me to play the bad guy again."

"I promise not to make you play the bad guy. If it gets out of hand, I'll end it on my own."

She weighed me with her hard stare before she turned to walk out of my room. "Good, because if you do, I'll have your ass and you'll have my two weeks' notice. Now hurry up and get ready."

I watched her go, thinking over what she'd said. Hearing my phone buzzing on my dresser, I walked over and picked it up. "Hello?"

"Yo, good news is, we got a lead. Bad news is, he's dead," Pit answered on the other line.

"Dammit." The fuck was it with my luck lately.

"Yeah, and get this. He worked for your label."

I wanted to be surprised, but I wasn't. "What was his name?"

"Bradley Jones, he worked in your HR department. They paid his ass a grip to come for you," Pit said.

I closed my eyes briefly and pinched my brow. "Was he the only one?"

"The cameras showed two others, but it's been a bitch trying to get info on them. So far, only got information on the one," he started to say when he was interrupted by something crashing in the background, followed by a man's scream. "Shut that shit up," Pit shouted before turning his attention back to me.

He quickly relayed all the information I'd learned from Chelsea before telling me something I didn't know. "From everything I've found this is starting to smell more and more like a professional hit. Someone with some money wants you gone. Whose Cheerios did you shit in?"

"Fuck if I know, I've been living a peacefully high existence. Shit, I haven't even fucked since before Vegas."

I wasn't lying, I'd kept to myself over the last two years. Aside from spending time with the crew and Skittles, I'd been pretty quiet.

"Right, well, I'm going to look into the other dude. I have Roman looking into the money trail and once I find something, I'll contact you."

"Got it."

The line went dead. Thinking over what Pit told me, I decided to grab a shower and figure out what my next step would be to get my hands on the fucker after my life.

CHAPTER THIRTY-THREE

The Past

Jazz

I stared at myself in the mirror. My human-hair wig had been done in wavy curls that reached the middle of my back. The makeup was elegant and highlighted my gray eyes.

Only three days ago, I'd been basking in Rejected One. After that I hadn't thought it would be so easy to sit back in this chair and go back to being an heiress.

"You look good as always," Aaron said from the doorway behind me.

I turned around in my vanity chair and watched as he swaggered into my dressing room. He wore a tailored suit and leather shoes that had been polished to perfection and his hair had been freshly cut. I stood up, the Dolce and Gabbana black-lace heels holding my feet comfortably. I gently straightened my black cocktail dress, avoiding the row of gold buttons running down the front of it.

"Forgive me for not thanking you for your compliment." I made my way toward the door, stopping by his side on the way I gave him a dirty look. "Make sure you remember I'm only giving into you because of that picture. The minute you misplace it, I'll make you regret threatening me."

"Oh, that's a scary look. Don't worry," Aaron said. "I wouldn't ruin the only thing I have to put a leash on you."

I offered him an unfriendly smile and looked at the breast pocket of his coat. "Don't get too cocky. I know a bit more about you than you think. Maybe you should start thinking about the things in your life you don't want anyone to know."

I walked past him and into the hallway of the house I'd sworn never to return to. The mansion was a visual representation of my father's desire for attention. Garish and over the top.

A display of his self-conscious need to show off his money. As I walked down the hallway, I passed overpriced paintings and ornate statues with missing limbs. For my father and his wife, everything they stuffed into their home was a show of wealth and power.

I saw it for what it was. A desperate ploy to demonstrate their wealth to the top one percent. The entire house smelled of nouveau riche desires.

They were frantic to stay in this world of gilded gold and money. Sadly, they didn't know they'd already lost the game from the beginning.

I reached the top of the steps and immediately felt the wave of attention from the people below. The look in their eyes a little too much like a starving hyena. I lifted a hand and thoughtfully flicked the end of one of the heavy gold earrings. I descended the staircase and spotted my father surrounded by his usual sycophants.

He stood near the back by the refreshment table with my stepmother. She was lovely as usual, wearing the latest Siriano creation. Her figure was slim and tight.

Upon first meeting her, it was hard for others to believe she'd given birth to two kids and was swiftly approaching her fiftieth birthday. When her gaze landed on me, she smiled. I didn't bother hiding my own distaste when she grabbed my wrist. After all, if a family wasn't dysfunctional, could it call itself normal in this circle?

"My dear, Alicia. We were just talking about you?"

The only reason I didn't shake off her hand was because of the people around us. She drew me closer to the circle. The few people that had been huddling around had already scurried off and it was only Senator Harrison, his son and a man I didn't recognize still there.

"I'll be in touch with you at a later date," the stranger said, handing my father a card. I barely got a glance of it before my father took it and placed it inside his suit pocket.

"I'm sure," my father, Clark said with a slight frown.

Without another word, the man left. For a moment, I watched him go, wondering who he was. My focus moved away from his retreating form when my stepmother's voice drew my attention back to Senator Harrison and his son.

I only remembered him due to my father's constant push for me to meet him. "This is Gerald. Your father was telling him about your time as an exchange student in Spain."

Spain? Right, I'd gone there for a month when my father had started pushing for me to move back in with him. After realizing I had no intention of playing nice with his bastards and whore wife, he stopped. Unfortunately for Gerald, my stepmother had lied to him about why I went to Spain.

"Yes, and what did you tell him?" I asked. "I hope none of my embarrassing stories."

"She told me you spent more time on the beach than in the classroom. There's nothing embarrassing about that," Gerald cut in.

I finally gave him my full attention and in response he offered me a smile. It was one filled with privilege and probably the cocky belief he was the most handsome man in the room. It was a smile that stirred up an old memory of mine.

"Did you use to go to Bridge Lake High?"

Gerald's expression turned thoughtful. "Yeah, how'd you know?"

I managed to keep my expression pleasant as I asked, "Did you go to prom?"

He laughed, shaking his head. "No, actually at that time me and a few of my idiot friends decided to prank a few girls. Instead of meeting them at the dance we all skipped and went to Ol' Ren's to bowl and hang out. I sometimes wonder whether they went or not."

"Well, I can clear that up for you. I did go to the prom. Of course, once I realized that you asking me was nothing more than a prank, I left," I said and enjoyed watching the confusion take over his face.

"What?"

"You said you wondered if the girls you asked to go to prom actually went," I explained as his face slowly drained of color.

"You must've forgotten my name, Alicia Roarke. At the time most people called me Alice or Weirdo Alice. I liked coloring my hair a variety of shades then and I wore thick glasses. Probably why your crew thought I'd be an easy target to prank."

Gerald looked from me to his father, who looked like he'd just eaten a bitter fruit.

"This must be destiny. If I'd known you and Gerald knew each other, I would have sent you an invitation for his return party. He just got back from closing a major deal with a large production company in China," Senator Harrison said, his smile tense. "Maybe the two of you can catch up with each other. Seeing as how you used to be classmates."

"Yes, it's been almost fourteen years since you guys went to school together. Why don't the two of you go off and talk some more," my father added, sending me a warning look. It was clear he wanted me to stop talking and kiss ass already. I wasn't interested.

"No, I think it'd be better for me to get some air. It feels a bit stuffy."

Without another word, I walked away. I zeroed in on the farthest corner of the ballroom. I was halfway there when someone grabbed my arm, stopping my escape.

"Whoa there. You're not planning on running away, are you?" Aaron said as he walked around me to block my path. I curled my fingers into a fist, trying to control the urge to punch him.

"Let go."

Apparently, seeing the anger on my face, he released my arm. "Okay, okay, but you can't leave yet."

"And why can't I?"

"Because he made a bet with his loser friends that you would come. If you leave now, he'll lose money," Gloria, my half sister said as she approached us.

She wore a green gown that was slit high on her right thigh. Her light golden skin matched perfectly with her gold jewelry and gold heels. Aaron shot her an annoyed look.

Gloria ignored it as she continued. "I told him it was a stupid idea and a waste of time."

"And I told you to mind your business," Aaron retorted.

"What you're doing is my business." Gloria looked from him to me. "I think we're the only two who can see just how ridiculous our family is. Right, sister?"

"I would first have to think of us as a family."

A cool look of amusement covered Glorias face. "Is that so? Well, I guess I shouldn't be surprised. It's not like I don't already know how you think. You're the real thing and we're nothing more than fakes, dressed up to look rich in the eyes of the people here."

"I don't think your fake," I said. "I actually don't spend too much time thinking about you two at all."

And it was the truth. I'd much rather spend my time thinking about my cousins or Rejected One. I held little interest in my two half-siblings.

Aaron liked flaunting his father's money around. Nothing but greed and the fear of it all ending filled him. He had no talents— and if he had them—living in his father's shadow had choked them out.

Gloria was different. She was shrewd enough to build her own business and join a circle of like-minded women business owners.

"You're both nothing more than the result of a man who can't keep his word." I looked from them to their parents. "I know where to place my hate, trust me."

"You should really move on," Gloria said. "Isn't it time you let it go. It isn't like Dad killed your mom. She had an accident and honestly holding this grudge against him won't get you anything except disappointment."

I didn't say anything, only looked at her. I made sure she could see all the hate and anger inside of me. She blanched and Aaron stepped in front of her as if to protect her. Seeing this, I looked away.

I spoke softly, so only they could hear me. "Those who are uninvolved should keep their opinions to themselves." My stomach tightened from the amount of bitter bile that filled it. "This is more than hate. I don't need the children of an adulterer to tell me how to feel. My kindness is the only reason you have what you have."

I turned on my heels and walked away. I didn't stop until I reached the veranda doors. I pushed them open and the minute I stepped outside, I felt like I could breathe again.

The black sky spilled out before me and the lights of Vander City lit the world at my feet. I focused on breathing through the swirling mass of anger and hate pulsing inside me.

"Let it go?" I repeated in disbelief.

I stared down into the yard of this lavish house my father had bought for his whore. He'd taken money my mother had given him out of love and thrown pearls before swine. While treating his actual family like they were maggots at his feet.

Yelling and arguing with my mother to release him from their marriage as if she'd been the one who'd asked to marry him. He'd pushed and pushed her until she ended up nothing more than a broken doll at the bottom of the steps of our home.

I would never forgive him. One day, I would rip everything he loved from his hands and laugh. I would drag the entire Bennington family down to Hell, but it wasn't time yet.

I needed to first finish dealing with Tak's problem. Once I'd finished with that then I'd turn my attention back to my father. For now, I would let Clark Bennington roll in his arrogance and false pride like a pig, before I took it all away.

I calmed down and fixed my dress. Soon my father would pay for everything he'd done and more. I just needed to bide my time and patiently wait for the chance to reveal everything about him to the public and put a final nail in his coffin.

CHAPTER THIRTY-FOUR

Pleasant Vibe

Tak

The sound of the door opening reached me from my seat on the couch. I'd spent my time thinking over who could hate me enough to want to kill me. I soon realized the list was fucking long.

At some point, I'd gotten up to get a beer, hoping it would dull the oncoming headache. It didn't. After a few minutes passed and I hadn't written down another name to my list, I realized I was waiting for Jazz.

The mansion felt empty without her there. Jazz had asked for this Friday off from Chelsea and I hadn't thought anything of it. However, I wished I'd told her ass to stay home.

I'd told myself I wasn't growing attached, but knowing Jazz was about to come through the door filled me with relief. She entered the living room, her short curly hair a mess around her head as she snuck in. I watched in amusement as she stopped to undo her heels and take them off.

Seeing the high heels in her hands caught me off guard. I'd only ever seen her wear those ugly flat sensible shoes. I was irritated that I'd missed the sight of her lovely ass swaying back and forth above those tall daggers.

She released a low moan of relief as she rolled her ankles. Her tight black cocktail dress was pretty nice and hugged her curves. Immediately, I wondered who'd she'd met in such a nice dress. I felt like I'd eaten shit.

"Looks like you had fun."

She jumped and whipped around. "Shit, Tak." She pressed her hand against her chest. "What are you doing hiding in the dark?"

I covered my mouth so she wouldn't see the shit eating grin I wore. Some of my earlier annoyance melted away seeing her disgruntled face.

"I wanted to test my bodyguard's reflexes."

She rolled her eyes, walking toward her wing. "I don't know how you say half the shit you do with a straight face."

"Practice," I said, following her. "I've been talking shit since I was young."

"I can believe it," she said, not bothering to look at me. "Are you planning on following me to my room?"

"Your room, but my house," I said with no shame.

She stopped suddenly and turned around, giving me a curious look. "Were you waiting for me this entire time?"

My brain stalled.

"What? No."

Shit, that wasn't what I'd been planning to say.

Jazz looked me up and down, her eyes squinted. "Are you sure because you're following me like one of my cousin's nephews does her. He'll usually follow her around like a little duck after she gets home from a long business trip."

"Don't flatter yourself," I said, reaching out and flicking her forehead. "I'm just making sure you don't pass out drunk on your way to your room."

She lightly smacked my hand away. "I didn't drink that much. I actually could go for more."

I wanted to spend more time with her, so before I could think it over, I said, "Fine, go change and we can drink together."

Her expression turned thoughtful.

"What are you thinking about now?" I asked.

"I'm thinking about whether or not it's professional to drink with my VIP." I swear this woman spent more time thinking about our regulations than anybody else who worked for JS Records.

"Aren't you off? Just count it as having a drink with your co-worker after work. Besides, you've already drunk around me before."

"Okay, I will. Let me go change."

This time I didn't follow her. I didn't need her accusing me of being a fucking baby duck again.

When she joined me after changing, I pretended not to be disappointed. The woman should have read the mood and worn a slinky piece. Instead, she'd gone with an oversized black T-shirt and large gray sweats.

"I'm going to be honest. Your idea of sexy nightwear is horrible."

Jazz rolled her eyes and walked past me. "Too bad I have no interest in being sexy."

"Don't worry, I can be sexy enough for both of us," I said as I followed her. I wanted to be near her. The smell of her and sound of her voice drew me along like a puppy. Fuck it, call me a damn duck. "How was your night out?"

"No comment."

She opened the fridge and took out a beer and slammed the door shut.

"Who did you go to meet?" I ignored the sting of jealousy I experienced thinking she may have met with a man.

She shot me a look. "Family."

My lips twitched. "I'm guessing it wasn't a fun family gathering."

Turning around, she pressed the side of her beer top against the counter edge and hit it. The top flew off, hitting the floor with a pinging sound, while beer foam spilled out covering the floor and counter. She took a quick swig and then set the bottle down on the counter as she wiped her mouth.

"It's not like I expected it to be a harmonious get together, but I remembered why I don't like being around them. They make me remember things I don't want to."

I understood her more than she knew. "Well, at least now you can relax."

She tossed me a look. "I'm not being professional at all."

"We already talked about this." I walked over to her side and picked up her beer. "Besides, there's no point in saying anything about professionalism when you've already used my thirty-thousand-dollar kitchen counter to open your beer."

She glanced from me to the counter. "God, you would point that out."

I smirked. "Of course, but I'm a generous boss. If you give me something in exchange for your horrible treatment of my counter. I'll let it go."

"And what exactly do you want?"

I took a drink from her beer. "What do you think I want from you?"

"Sex."

Laughing, I set her bottle down and leaned in close to her. I settled my chin on her shoulder and spoke into her ear. "That's only one of the things I want from you. Can't you think of anything else?"

Both of us wore surprised expressions when she released a deep throated moan. She cupped her hands over her ears as she turned and faced me, her eyes bright with lust and her face flushed.

"D... don't do that," she stuttered.

She eyed me as she took a step back. "Let's hold off on me paying you back for the counter for now. I... I'm actually sort of hungry."

Hungry? That was the last reason I'd expect her to use to avoid me. I straightened up and seriously thought over all my life choices. When had I come to the point where a woman would rather eat than fuck me?

"Tak?"

I looked down into her brown eyes and felt the plethora of words I wanted to say get stuck in my throat. I noticed the dark circles under her eyes and a bit of redness around the rim of them. I realized then, I didn't know a lot about Jazz and that irritated me.

"If you're going to cook, cook something for me as well."

Her expression brightened and she laughed. "Sure, better yet how about you help me. Something needs to go along with this nasty ass beer of yours."

Insulted, I playfully glared at her. "I'll have you know Blue Moon is amazing."

"Yeah, right."

She walked over to the fridge and opened it. "How do you feel about mushrooms?"

I grimaced. "Am I supposed to have certain feelings about fungus?"

"So, mushrooms it is," she said as she reached inside and pulled out a container of them and placed it on the counter behind her. "Now, how do you feel about chicken skewers?"

"Sounds good."

I watched her get to work. Occasionally she'd ask me to grab things for her here and there. A few minutes had passed when I asked, "So why did you have to meet with your family?"

"My dad wanted to see me," she said as she cut the onion in front of her.

"Your dad?" My brow creased. "I thought you lived with your uncle and aunt?"

"I did, but that was only for a short while after my mom passed away," she said. Finished cutting the onion, she placed the knife aside. "My dad and I don't really get along."

"Well, I can relate. I think the last time I saw my father was when I was in elementary school." He'd never bothered to show his face again since then.

She offered me a soft smile. "Looks like we have more in common than we thought."

I returned her smile and walked over to her side. "Here, show me what you need me to do."

***

"This is good," I found myself saying a while later. As I smeared some more of the mushroom sauce Jazz made on the toast in my hand before taking another bite. Her eyes crinkled in the corners with pleasure at my compliment.

"Thank you."

She cheerfully took another bite of her own food. We were sitting on the marble floor in front of the doors that led out to my veranda. A full moon hung, giving us a pretty nice view of the backyard and pool.

"I'm kind of impressed with myself. I didn't expect it to turn out so well." She reached for another chicken skewer on our shared plate.

"Neither did I," I teased. "Where did you learn how to cook?"

"I'm going to pretend you thought I was a great cook. And I'll have you know, I taught myself," she said, reaching for her glass of white wine. "I'll forgive you for your doubt in my skills because you brought out the good alcohol. I knew it was weird when I didn't find a single bottle of wine or brandy in this place."

"I don't share well, especially not with the random people Kole might send here for business. Why should I share my good liquor with people that annoy me?"

"Aren't you worried I'll go searching for the rest of your stash?" she asked, giving me a mischievous look.

"You don't have to search hard. It's inside a safe in the basement. It requires a fingerprint and retina scan to open."

"Are you serious?"

"If it's mine, I protect it at all costs."

Just how I would protect her from the piece of shit after me. I couldn't remember when I'd started considering her as mine. I had a very small list of people I considered friends and an even smaller list of people I had the desire to get closer with.

I reached for my beer and took another long drink, trying to cool myself down as my thoughts turned to claiming Jazz. Yet I still felt the terrible urge to ruin this cute moment just for a taste of her lips. She finished her skewer with a pleased hum and gave me a cheeky look.

"Aren't you lucky your bodyguard can toss annoying people on their ass and cook for you."

Unable to hold back, I reached out and placed my hand behind her head. I leaned forward, ignoring the platter between us. I hovered my lips over hers.

"Aren't you going to stop me?"

"Do you want me to?" she asked.

I didn't pull back and she didn't retreat. The space between us crackled with a heady tension. I wanted to selfishly take her lips and remove those baggy clothes from her body so I could explore it. Still, I didn't make a single move to actually do it.

"Tak, are you going to kiss me or not?"

I pulled back. "No, I don't think I will this time. We should change up the rules."

Confusion colored her voice. "Rules? What are you talking about?"

I dropped my hand from the back of her head and stood. "I've decided I won't kiss you. This time I want you to kiss me. I can't always be the one making the first move."

There was a beat of silence before she burst out into laughter. "You're kidding, what makes you think I even want to kiss you?" she asked as she got to her feet and started gathering up our dishes.

"If you didn't want my kisses, why did you let me take so many already?" I enjoyed the look of embarrassment she wore as she turned her back to me.

"Because I can't knock my boss into next week," she tossed over her shoulder.

"Don't lie, we both know I'm good at making your knees weak."

I ignored the loud snort she released before she disappeared into the kitchen. I grimaced the minute she was out of sight. I was hard as a rock and I'd just told the single woman I wanted to fuck I wouldn't touch her until she made the first move.

I beat a hasty retreat to take a cold shower. Fucking around with Jazz was going to give me blue balls, but it was worth it.

CHAPTER THIRTY-FIVE

Talk Show

Jazz

I escorted Tak to the broadcasting studio the next day. He'd been scheduled to appear on a talk show to promote his band's upcoming concert. The lights flashed as journalists and paparazzi attempted to get his picture, while fans who'd learned about his appearance screamed out their love from behind yellow barriers.

I felt a bit nostalgic for the days I spent doing the exact same thing. Once we entered the building, the noise and lights immediately came to an abrupt stop. Releasing a relieved sigh, I felt someone tap the back of my head and turned around. Tak looked down at me with a smug expression.

"You're not feeling tired yet, are you? That was just a small piece of what happens when I come out."

I rolled my eyes. "Yes, yes, I know you're Mr. World Star."

He clicked his tongue. Completely ignoring the people around us, he tugged on my right ear. "You're being rude, Ms.

Bodyguard. Shouldn't you be nicer to me? Especially since I'm always *so* genuinely nice to you."

If I noticed the naughty lilt to his voice, I was sure everyone else around us heard it. I took a deliberate step away and turned from him, spotting Chelsea who walked toward us with an unknown man by her side. Together with Tak and his entourage, we met them halfway.

"Tak, this is Steve Gross, the host of Radio 2."

As usual, Chelsea got right down to business. I took this chance to fall back as she spoke with Tak about the show and what he needed to do as we walked upstairs to the dressing room. Listening to them, I allowed myself to enjoy Tak's serious work face. Something I hadn't seen a lot since I started this job. It was nice.

"Here is the script, just skim over it a bit. It's not too rigid, but it gives you an idea of what we'll be talking about," Steve said as he handed over a rolled booklet to Tak.

"That's good because I don't like rigid shit. It makes me sensitive," Tak said.

"Tak," Chelsea chided, before she turned to Steve. "Don't mind him."

Steve laughed good naturedly. "It's fine." With that, he left us.

"Didn't you say you were going to behave?" Chelsea turned to face Tak.

He gave her a confused look. "Wasn't I? I think I've been acting pretty well." He turned to me. "Jazz, what do you think, was I bad?"

The only reason I didn't roll my eyes was because everyone looked at me. I held back the curse words tickling at the back of my throat, I should have known his seriousness would last only so long. "I'm just going to say yes to keep the peace."

Lucky for me the two decided to take my answer and entered the dressing room together. I chose to stay outside and took a seat in one of the chairs that lined the hallway wall. That way I could keep an eye on who came and went.

There was also another reason. I needed to touch base with Dutch. Pulling out my phone, I dialed his number and patiently waited for him to pick up. The phone clicked as it was answered.

"Hey, have you found any trace of the guy who murdered Bradley yet?"

"Didn't I tell you to keep a low profile?" Zeno's voice held anger.

Pulling the phone away from my ear, I stared at it. The number I'd dialed was Dutch's, but Zeno had answered. I could hear someone arguing in the background.

I took a deep breath and asked, "Why do you have Dutch's phone?"

"Answer my question first. You're following that singer again. Didn't I tell you to leave him alone?"

"Yes, but I decided not to." I tightened my hold on my phone in reaction to his low chuckle. "How'd you find out?"

"One of my informants saw you at the Bennington ball and followed you to his house. He acted like he was doing me a favor, but you and I both know he thought following you would give him some dirt to sell. Lucky for you, I bought the info and paid for him to keep his mouth shut. So, I suggest you give me one good reason why I shouldn't come and pick your ass up right this minute."

I bit my bottom lip. I very rarely went against my eldest cousin. Zeno had taught me how to survive off the grid so I could have some semblance of life away from my father's influence when I was younger.

He understood more than anyone just how far my father was willing to go to have me under his control. He'd watched as I'd painfully weaned myself off the drug my father had the doctor put me on to keep me trapped in that dark depression.

"Because you know how important he is to me, he's the reason I'm able to sit here and talk to you right now," I said, giving a look around the hall.

I couldn't leave, I'd have to wait for Tak to enter the studio before I could go somewhere private. Zeno made a frustrated sound.

"Jazz, come on. He doesn't even remember you."

"That's okay, he doesn't have to. It actually works out better for me if he doesn't." I spotted someone coming down the hall. "Look, I'll call you back once I get somewhere more private. Tell Dutch to give me a heads-up if he finds something else. I really need to know who attacked me that night when I went to Bradley's."

"Wait."

I hung up and stood to check to see who it was approaching. Seeing it was an intern that'd been sent to let us know Steve was ready, I knocked on the door. Chelsea opened it.

"They're ready for him now."

She nodded and called back to Tak. "It's time."

Chelsea faced forward and stepped out followed by Tak's tall frame. I couldn't help replaying Zeno's words in my head. He was right.

Even though we'd lived next door to each other as children and we'd waited for the bus together as teens, there wasn't even a sparkle of recognition in Tak's eyes. Still, like I'd told Zeno, I was okay with that.

I didn't want Tak to remember the little girl who'd watched him through the iron gate as he'd sat in the yard pulling grass. I don't think he, or I, had many good memories of Bridge Lake.

"Hey, are you okay?" Tak asked, tapping me on my forehead.

I leaned away. "I'm fine. Just thinking about something." Avoiding his probing stare, I walked ahead of him. "Let's go."

Once at the studio, I watched as Tak walked in. Seeing he was safely inside, I decided to take a bathroom break. I let Chelsea know before I left the control room.

She gave me an absentminded wave, her focus completely on Tak. I headed to the bathroom down the hall. I'd told Zeno I'd call him back, but I wasn't in the mood to.

After our conversation, I couldn't help asking myself if what I was doing would really help Tak. I could easily have handed all the evidence over to the proper authorities and let them deal with it, but the minute I thought this, my mind rebelled against it.

I didn't want to hand Tak over to anyone else. I knew I was being selfish and foolish but being with Tak was one of the few things in life I'd desired. How could I just give up seeing and being teased by him every day? What was wrong with wanting to be the person who saved him?

Thinking this, I took my time in the bathroom. Once I'd finished, I decided to hang out in the waiting area. I could watch the live recording of Tak on the flat screens that decorated one of the walls. I checked my wristwatch, seeing about an hour had passed. The show itself only lasted an hour and a half.

Getting up, I headed back toward the recording studio.

"Alicia." Hearing my name, I turned around without thinking. I widened my eyes at the sight of Gerald, who stood with a few people near the elevator. Recovering quickly, I turned away.

"Wait, Alicia."

I ignored him. How could I have turned around when he called my real name? I'd really been in my head. I quickly walked around the corner to lose him, but he obviously was determined to stick to me.

He placed a hand on my arm. "Alicia, wait. I wanted to apologize."

I turned around and pushed his hand off me. "I'm sorry, but you've got the wrong person."

His brow crinkled as he looked me over. "You're lying, your eyes and hair aren't the same, but I already heard from your brother you liked keeping a low-key presence. I get it, it's hard being someone like us. We have to do anything we can to maintain our private lives."

I gritted my teeth as I gave a look around. I needed to get rid of him. "If you're aware of that, then do me the favor of acting like you don't know me."

Once again, I tried to shake him off. This time he grabbed my wrist. "Look, I'll let you go once you listen to my apology. My dad's eager to see us get together, so I wanted to invite you out for dinner as an apology."

Tired of his persistence, I took a step closer. "I don't want to have dinner with you, and I have no interest in accepting your apology. Now, since I've made that clear, I'm going to ask you once more to let me go before I make you."

I should have known Gerald was human trash. He smiled down at me. "Don't act so cocky. It isn't like I'm doing this because I want to. Just come to dinner with me and stop throwing a tantrum."

I curled the fingers of my free hand into a fist. One punch would not only make him less of a problem, but also teach the arrogant fuck a lesson.

"Jazz?"

Knowing who it was who called my name, I no longer hesitated and lashed out with my foot. Gerald released a pained cry and fell to one knee, which resulted in him losing his hold on my wrist. I leaned down and whispered in his ear.

"I'm not cocky, you're just not worth my time."

I patted his shoulder before I left his side and walked toward Tak who stood at the end of the hallway. He looked from me to Gerald who was on his knees.

"Who is that?"

"Someone who doesn't know how to take no for an answer," I said, holding my hand out. "Are you done?"

Tak wordlessly walked past me, ignoring my hand. "Wait, I already dealt with him."

"But I haven't," he said savagely.

Gerald slowly stood. He'd barely straightened when Tak reached him and with no hesitation swung, hitting Gerald square in the jaw. He grabbed his collar, keeping him from falling.

"Wait, you can't pass out yet," Tak said, his voice sounding almost excited. He punched Gerald once more.

"I know a lot of scumbags like you, you're always looking for girls you think don't have any backing. You fucked around and messed with the wrong girl." He punched him again and shoved Gerald so hard his back hit the wall with a thud sound.

The loud bang pulled me out of my shock. I ran over to Tak. "Stop, that's enough."

I grabbed his arm, knowing if I didn't stop him this would turn into a bigger issue. He acted like he couldn't hear me as he fought my hold and pulled his leg back to kick Gerald who was knocked out.

"Tak," I shouted. Seeing he wasn't going to stop, I grabbed his collar and yanked him so his head turned toward me and kissed him, open-eyed. I watched as the anger in his eyes cooled. Ending the kiss, I turned and pulled him behind me. "Come on."

He quietly followed me out of the hall, both of us paused when we saw Chelsea, who looked from me to the scene behind us. I expected her to yell, but instead she said, "Why?"

"The fucker was harassing Jazz, so I taught him a lesson," Tak answered with his usual cockiness.

She sighed and pulled out her cell phone from her coat pocket. "Got it, I'll take care of it, but don't be shocked if Kole calls you to the office if the victim presses charges."

Tak walked forward and glared down at Chelsea. "Tell him to make sure he thinks twice about it. And as for that fucker, just find out who he is and make sure he doesn't stir up trouble. It wasn't like I beat the shit out of him for myself."

"So, you want to go from rebellious rock star to heroic dark angel," Chelsea said as she started tapping away on her phone. "I'll get PR on it."

"Finally, you're fucking doing your job. Sounds like it's time for you to get another raise," Tak chortled as we walked back to his dressing room.

I followed him silently. I needed to contact one of the Roarke family's lawyers and get them to reach out to Gerald. I couldn't let this situation get out of control. This was the last thing Tak needed in his life.

"Tak?"

He didn't answer me as he dragged me into his dressing room and shut the door. Letting go of my hand, he then took off his leather coat and tossed it on the couch. I gave a quick look around the modest dressing room.

It was clean and bright. When I refocused on Tak, his back faced me. A memory from when we were in school came to me.

Tak standing over the school's bully he'd beaten to a pulp when the bully pushed one of the other kids down the stairs. Tak had always been the only one willing to defend the kids who'd been labeled as different back then. Like everyone else, I'd thought he was just a troublemaker and one of the cool kids.

Until that day when he proved that he had a ferociously protective side for those weaker than him. The teachers had to drag him off the bully, but like a lot of the kids at our school, Tak was from a wealthy family. He was only suspended for a week.

Overwhelmed with my memories from back then, I walked over to him and hugged him from behind. "Thank you." I pressed my face to his back.

He stiffened and turned to look over his shoulder. "I don't need you to thank me."

Finally gaining control of my emotions, I looked up at him. "But I want to thank you and I want to kiss you."

He turned around fully and picked me up. Taken aback, I wrapped my arms around his shoulders.

"I've been waiting to hear those magical words since last night."

He walked over to the vanity counter and set me down. Deciding to take control, I pulled him down and took his lips with mine. He played along the seam of my lips with his tongue.

I opened them, tasting his delicious flavor. The addictive smell of his cologne filled my nose as I fell deeper into his kiss. I allowed my hands to wander up to his hair, drawing him in closer.

He moaned. I widened my legs so he could step between them. With a groan of pleasure, he pulled back and kissed along my cheek and neck.

"Fuck, I want to fuck you right here."

His voice was like liquor, it entered my soul and made me drunk and foolish to his desires. Without a word, I let go of him and pulled off my jacket and unbuttoned my shirt.

"Then do it."

His brown eyes deepened to black, the heat in them seared my skin as he moved one of his hands to my chest and tugged my bra down, then gently grabbed my breast. He leaned down and took my nipple into his mouth.

My stomach tightened as he sucked, while he pushed his other hand down into my pants. I panted as he entered my underwear with his long fingers, and he found the seam of my pussy. He wriggled his fingers, asking for entry.

I widened my legs a bit more and bit my bottom lip when he found my nub with astonishing precision. He pulled back, my nipple popping from his mouth. He leaned forward so his lips rested near my ear.

"Looks like Ms. Bodyguard has been drooling for my dick this entire time." He curled his fingers up. I cried out, pressing my chest against his. "Not only are you soaking my fingers, but you're already so swollen. Fuck, don't regret this, love."

He licked the outer shell of my ear and continued whispering naughty things into it. Tak played me just like he did the guitar, thrusting and stroking, taunting me to move my hips against his hand.

"Shit, Jazz. I'm going to need your help." I could barely hear past the sound of my throbbing heart when he unzipped his pants. "Here, give me some love too."

He took my hand and placed it over his warm dick. It was soft and throbbed in my grasp. He pressed a kiss to my forehead. "Don't be shy and stroke him."

He twisted his fingers inside me. I closed my eyes and stroked, unable to focus as he fiddled with me like I was his personal plaything. In that moment, he could order me to do anything and I would do it.

"Good girl."

The room was filled with his low murmurs and my small cries of pleasure. After a few minutes, I felt the first ripple of my orgasm come over me and greedily lifted my chin for more of his breathtaking kisses.

Squinting his eyes in pleasure, he leaned down and filled my mouth with his tongue.

His body tensed against mine as he came all over my hand. A deep groan coming from his chest. "Shit, Jazz."

I enjoyed the afterglow as he leaned his body against mine. After a few minutes, we finally pulled apart. He took a step back and stuffed his dick back into his pants. I looked down curiously at the semen that coated my hand.

"Let me get you a towel," he offered.

"No need." I lifted my cum-covered hand and licked it off, not looking away from him.

I watched surprise flicker across his face before something dark entered his eyes.

"Jazz." He took a step toward me, but the sound of his phone interrupted whatever he'd been thinking about doing.

I dropped my hand and hopped off the counter to go to the bathroom that was in the dressing room. I'd needed to straighten myself up and think over what I'd just done. The line I told myself not to cross, I'd crossed.

Shit, Tak really had a habit of destroying my plans.

CHAPTER THIRTY-SIX

Long Time, No See

Tak

The next day I waited in the photography studio for them to change the background scene from white to black. The memory of Jazz's bold expression when she licked my cum off her fingers played over and over in my head. The photographer and Chelsea stood near a table covered with monitors, both going over the pictures I'd already taken.

Meanwhile, Jazz stood next to the exit, her gaze constantly scanning the room. I wondered if she thought she looked fierce because to me she looked cute. I enjoyed the fact that I could watch her at my leisure.

I frowned when I heard a familiar voice. "How many more shoots before he's done?" Kole asked as he walked in.

The good mood I'd had washed away the minute I saw him. Chelsea turned away from the monitors.

"Just a few more, he should be done in the next half hour."

"What brings you here?" I asked when he stopped in front of me.

"Chelsea called me about what you did at the broadcast station."

"And?"

"You're fucking lucky the guy decided not to press charges. For some reason he wanted it all to be pushed under the rug," Kole said, frowning. "Actually, he seemed more than a little bit desperate for us to not share it with the media."

"Good." I laughed. "And here I thought he'd try to spin it in his favor. Apparently, the little shit cares about his image."

He released a sigh. "Whether he does or not, you have to stop being so reckless. I told you, keep a low profile and stay out of trouble."

"Fuck that, if someone in my circle is being mistreated, I'm going to do what I have to. And if that mean's beating some little shit to a pulp, that's just what's going to happen."

He glared at me. "We're going to have to do something about your mouth."

I licked my bottom lip suggestively. "But I'm so good at using it."

Seeing as that didn't get him to leave, I asked. "Why are you still here? You're causing my limbs to freeze. Don't you have some intern to harass?"

He ignored me and said, "The Nakamuras called, one of them wants to have a one-on-one meeting with you. They said they'll increase the pay if you do it."

"Kole, you know better than anyone, I don't like repeating myself. I won't meet with them. The only way I'm going to do any advertisement with their company is if they keep their fucking owners away from me. If they can't do that one thing, then like I said before, I won't do it."

His jaw ticked. Good, I hope the fucker was stressed. I told him no to begin with and the one card he had he'd used to get Jazzy in my house.

The only reason I was doing the fucking commercial was because of Chelsea's annoying ass. On this, there was nothing else he could do but deal with it.

"Listen, think of it as paying me back for dealing with the near shitstorm you almost started. This is the last thing I'm going to ask you to do."

"Ready on the set," the photographer that had been talking to Chelsea announced.

I looked away from Kole and said, "Look, they're calling me."

I was pleased as I felt his eyes boring into my back as I walked away. He should feel a bit of the gnawing irritation I'd felt every time he'd approached me with the Nakamuras' name. Kole needed to drop it and fucking go work on something other than me.

I'm sure there's some girl group waiting to be signed out there.

***

"Fuck, I'm starting to think it's time to leave JS Records," I said after finding Kole outside of my dressing room as I exited. Jazz followed quietly behind me.

He leaned against the wall across from the door and held out a card. "This is the amount we lose if you don't go."

I took the card from him and dropped it on the floor. "I don't care how much it is, I'm not doing it. I already agreed to do the damn advertisement, this is where I draw the line."

I stomped off, making sure I stepped on the card as I left. My schedule for the day was done anyway. All I wanted to do was get as far away from Kole as possible.

"Tak."

I ignored Jazz calling after me as I nearly ran to where my car was parked. I was sick and tired of everyone pushing me to meet with the Nakamuras.

I slammed out of a random door I assumed to be the exit and found myself in an outdoor break area. "Shit." I kicked the trash can that stood next to the door, before shoving another door open and finally getting outside.

Taking a deep breath, I pulled at the collar of my shirt. It felt like I was being strangled.

"Tak."

"Back off," I yelled, turning on Jazz who'd followed me outside.

Looking startled she took a step back.

Seeing this, I quickly apologized. "Sorry, you're not the one pissing me the fuck off."

She averted her eyes. "No, I get it. I should have let you blow some steam off first."

I rolled my eyes. "You got a pack of edibles or a number for a hitman?"

Her brow wrinkled. "No to both, fortunately."

I laughed. "No, it's actually unfortunate. I need something, anything to take this edge off."

She shook her head. "There are other ways to take the *edge* off."

I shot her a look. "Well, the last time I went out to burn it off someone took my place."

"You don't need to put your life on the line to get relief from stress." Her eyes turned fiery with anger. "First, I should ask why you feel so strongly about not working with the Nakamura company?"

I took a look around before I met her gaze again. "Can't I just not fucking want to do it? I don't fucking get this fame shit. I thought I'd be living more freely, not pushed to do something someone else wants," I whined, knowing I sounded childish. "I had more freedom as a drugged-up high schooler, shit."

"Then why do you keep doing it?" she asked, her voice soft.

I released a frustrated breath and covered my face with one hand, thinking it over. I finally dropped my hand to my side and asked her.

"Tell me, what are you good at?" Her expression turned thoughtful. "Like the talent you have that could make you money," I added after a quick thought.

"Well, I speak two languages and I can cook. I have an MBA in business, a black belt, and I am certified in fitness training..." She trailed off when she saw my incredulous expression. Releasing a nervous laugh, she then said, "I had a lot of time on my hands at some point. So, I went after a lot of things."

"Well, I'd always been considered a disappointment when I was younger. Nothing more than an annoyance to the people who called me son." I waved off the sympathy in her eyes.

"Nah, don't feel sorry for me. Anyway, the one thing that's always been with me is music." I closed my eyes and immediately my head was filled with the soft strings of a violin and the loud rumble of drums. "All my life, it's either been in my ears or playing in my head."

When I opened my eyes, she hadn't looked at me with sympathy but possessiveness. And it probably pointed out some sick desire in me because I found the idea of a possessive Jazzy hot as fuck. In the blink of an eye, it was gone, and she was once more back to an intent stare.

"I can't breathe without a mic or a stage. Music is all I have. It's both my prison and a form of freedom."

I struggled for a moment before I continued. "And Kole is the one who took my investment and my music and made my barely-there dream come to life, but this shit is starting to feel more and more like a cage. It's ironic that the single thing in this world I love the most is the reason I have to meet with the people that I hate the most."

I turned away from her. "Shit."

"Come on. Stand up," my cousin taunted.

My small hands scraped against the rocks as tears slipped down my face. I forced myself to stand, even though my knees shook. I tried to endure another punch from him, only to fall right back to my knees.

"I'm so glad aunty lets us play together," he crooned.

"Tak?"

Coming back from the past, I looked down to find my hand held by Jazz. She looked up at me so earnestly I almost forgot she was there.

"I promise, I'll protect you."

"Huh?" I'd been completely lost in my memories of the past.

"I'm saying that I'll go with you. Since Mr. Kole is intent on having you meet with them. You can bring me, and I can make sure nothing stupid happens." My nose wrinkled at what she called Kole. He wasn't Mr. anything. He should be called snake. "I'll make sure they don't cross the line."

If they crossed the line, I wouldn't need her to do anything. I'd take care of them myself.

I had avoided thinking about it but seeing how they kept pushing Kole to have me meet with them, it looked like they no longer wished to ignore me and weren't interested in letting me ignore them. Suddenly, I lost my bravado and fear grew inside of me. A fear I'd ignored since I'd left Bridge Lake.

I tightened my hold on her hand as she continued to stare up at me. I couldn't stand it if she looked at me and saw the weak kid I'd been fighting to hide all this time. Then again, she'd already seen me at my worst.

Maybe I could actually meet them and prove to myself I wasn't that scared of them anymore. I could finally be free from Takuya Nakamura—who'd prayed by his bedside for his parents to come home and that someone would believe him when he told them what happened to him.

"I'll do it."

She seemed startled. "What?"

"I said, I'll do it." I gripped her hand tighter. "You're the one to blame if I cause trouble, right?"

She fluttered her lashes. "O... Okay." I pulled her along behind me and reentered the building. "Where are we going?"

I didn't answer her, dragging her along as I walked back to where I'd left Kole. He quietly talked to Chelsea, the two of them looking over her tablet.

"I'll do it."

Both of them looked up at me in confusion. I lifted my hand that held Jazzy's.

"I'll do the fucking dinner with the Nakamuras, but only if Jazzy comes. She said she'd be responsible for me."

The two of them looked from me to Jazz, who'd been trying to pull her hand from mine. I refused to let go, so she pulled at the back of my shirt with low hissed threats.

"Is that true, Ms. Ryland?" Kole asked. I could see his doubt, not many could control me. "Are you willing to keep an eye on our singer, so he doesn't do anything stupid?"

"Yes." Jazzy moved from around me and offered Kole a confident smile. "Yes, I believe it's best someone accompanies Mr. Jensei, especially considering his clear dislike of their company. I can go as a *date* so that he's not alone, and if they cross the line, I can stop them in their tracks."

I couldn't help the excitement of the idea of seeing her in a dress. Fuck, and then I would have the pleasure of taking it off her.

"And this works for you, Tak?" Kole asked me.

"Why wouldn't it?"

Damn right, I was going to use this chance to go on a date with Jazz. And there wasn't a damn thing he could do about it. I ignored the look of suspicion Chelsea shot me.

I'm going to meet with the Nakamuras and tell them to stay the fuck out of my life. And once I was finished with that, I was going to celebrate by dragging Jazz home and fucking her into a coma. I mentally salivated at the thought of being balls deep inside her, with her sexy legs wrapped around my waist as I made her sing from taking my dick.

Kole gave me a hard look before he finally seemed to get the fucking picture. This is my price for going to the damn dinner and for him not believing me about the attempted suicide from the beginning.

"Fine, the dinner is tomorrow night." He looked from me to Jazz. "I'll be sending the limo by at nine thirty. Don't be late."

"I'll make sure we're on time," Jazz said respectfully. I would fuck that out of her. She'd be calling Kole a snake bastard before tomorrow night was over. I put my sex drive on that shit.

"Good." Kole turned his attention to Chelsea. "Make sure it's done and make sure they're both dressed appropriately for it."

"Got it," Chelsea said, her eyes going back to her tablet.

Kole didn't say anything else, leaving with Chelsea.

"Well, that went better than I thought it would," Jazz said as she pulled her hand out of mine.

"Really, I thought for sure Chelsea would say no," I said thoughtfully.

"Why?" she asked.

I decided against mincing my words. "Because she knows I want to fuck you and they basically gave me the green light. I mean, think about it, it's our first date," I said as I threw an arm around her shoulders and rubbed my chin against the top of her head. "I can't wait for the meeting with the Nakamuras to end, then we'll really have fun, love."

"Shut up," she snapped, throwing off my arm before she walked off.

I watched her go, noticing the flush at the tip of her ears. I didn't know what was cuter, her trying to act professional after jerking me or the fact she thought she needed to protect me. Either way, it was nice having someone I didn't have to share with anyone else.

My smile dropped as I straightened and slowly followed after her.

Yeah, it was nice.

CHAPTER THIRTY-SEVEN

Who

Jazz

"It's a date," Trisha said, sounding excited.

"It's not a date," I said, killing her delusions. Chelsea had sent me a few dress options and I was going through them. "It's an assignment, I have to keep him safe while he eats food with the family he apparently hates."

"Right, did you ever figure out why he hates his own family so much?" Trisha asked as she started loudly chewing her chips in my ear.

"No, I've been a bit too occupied with trying to figure out who's trying to kill him. Oh, that's right, did Dutch get anything about that guy I ran into at Bradley's place?"

There was more crunching noise before Trisha answered. "Yeah, he found someone who closely resembled your attacker's description. Also, note the guy who tried to smash Tak's head in got bailed the same day he got arrested."

I tossed the third dress choice down on the bed. "And you waited till now to tell me?"

"Well, Dutch wanted to make sure he wasn't missing anything. With Bradley's murder, he wants to make sure he checks everything thoroughly before he sends it," she said.

"Fine, send me the pictures of both of them."

"Okay. Hey, Dutch, Jazzy said email her both of their profiles."

I picked up my tablet, going straight to my email.

"Did you get it?" she asked.

"Yeah, just did." Opening the email, I immediately recognized the two men. "This guy is one of the guys who knocked Tak out in Vegas." The one who had the scar on his chin. I remembered because the light from his phone had highlighted it.

I read his name aloud. "Tony Enson. Wait, he used to work for the label's building security."

What sounded like a struggle reached my ear before Dutch came on the line. "Yeah, and get this, Bradley is the one who fired him."

"So, Bradley was over Tony. Bradley fires him and then Tony kills him. Something's not adding up." I walked back and forth in my room. "Was there a report written about why Bradley fired him?"

"Yeah, it's on the last page," Dutch said.

I scrolled down to the last page. "He was stealing and reselling the artists' property?"

"Apparently, but it didn't feel right to me. So, I looked into it and found out something interesting. JS Records splits their security teams by floors, depending on their clearance.

"So, for instance, floor one and two has your usual mall-type security guards. In fact, they aren't allowed to go above floor two. And all the rehearsal rooms are located on the third and fourth floors.

"How could a level-one security guard have access to the stars' items on the third floor?" I asked.

"The only way he could get access is if someone was helping him," Dutch explained.

I frowned. "How do you know what floor his clearance was on?"

"I got my hands on the company's personnel list and schedule for the workers. It took some digging since he'd been fired for a while, but I found out that Tony was a security guard on the first floor of JS Records. But his clearance never went above a level one. On the other hand, Bradley worked on the fourth floor in HR."

I chewed my bottom lip. "So, you think Bradley was the one stealing the items and giving them to Tony to resell? But it doesn't give him motive to go after Tak."

I scrolled to the next file. "Mitchell Rendon." I was taken aback by how little information there was under this profile. "Why is there so little about him?"

"I tried to find information on him, but there wasn't a lot. I'm fairly sure he's using a false identity like yours," Dutch said.

I thought over what he said, it was confirmed that Tony was the killer. The only problem I had was I couldn't figure out why.

"Okay, then let's see if there are phone records or maybe bank statements that give us some clue as to why Tony decided to kill Bradley. I still can't believe how fast Mitchell was bailed out."

The Vander City justice system left a lot to be desired. If one had the money, they could get away with a lot more than the average person. My dealings with my father had taught me that.

I set my tablet on the side table and continued. "Let's keep an ear out for them for now and do me a favor, Dutch. Find out what Julius has found so far. Clark has been desperately emailing me about coming to another meeting with the senator's son. It's getting to be a little much."

Dutch's voice turned cold. "Is he up to his old tricks again?"

"I think so, one way or another he's always trying to take advantage of my family's name."

"He should be grateful your mother's name got him the money he needed to be where he is today. Dick should kiss your ass in thankfulness," Dutch said.

"I agree, but let's put that aside for now. I'll call you back if I need anything else."

"Got it, bye."

Once I was done with Tak's business I would focus my attention on Clark Bennington since he wanted it so bad.

Clark Bennington

"Dammit, it shouldn't be this hard to meet with my damn daughter," I shouted as I threw the file in my hands at the idiot standing in front of me.

"How many times is she going to ignore my calls? Disrespectful bitch, just like her fucking mother," I yelled, drawing in a harsh breath.

"C... calm down sir," Dilbert said desperately as he wiped his disgusting balding scalp with his handkerchief. "I've already arranged for some men to follow her to see where it is she's been going."

"And you think that will work?" I said, my voice dangerously thin. "It won't. Not with that fucking Liberiu in the picture. He might not be able to destroy me because of that little bit of blackmail we have on him, but don't think that makes him any less a threat."

This shouldn't be so fucking hard. I curse the day I had been late on doping her mother with the pregnancy pills. I'd hoped the child would be like me, but she'd come out like her mother. The only thing of mine that damn bitch had was my eyes. Which she enjoyed using to look down on me with.

"Get out."

"Yes, sir," he said, quickly backing out of my office.

The phone rang. I flinched, feeling a cold sweat building on my back when I saw the number calling. "Fuck." I reached down and picked up the phone. "Hello?"

"Your daughter handed you an ace in the hole, have you thought about our offer?" The person on the other end said in a cold voice.

"I've already told you to tell your client I'm not interested in your services."

I had no intention of working with the bastard on the other end. I'd rather put all my chips on Senator Harrison than some no-name stranger.

"Are you sure you won't regret this? Delivering Takuya Nakamura would be the answer to all your problems. Your company is already in the red and it's only a matter of time until the Feds discover you've been embezzling money from the Roarke Foundation to keep it afloat."

"I'm sure," I said.

"Then I wish you luck, Mr. Bennington." He hung up.

I released a sigh of relief, placing my phone down on my desk. There were some monsters in Vander City that were better left alone.

CHAPTER THIRTY-EIGHT

Date

Tak

Looking at the clock on the wall, I pressed a hand to my stomach. I hadn't felt this nervous since our band had won its first music award. Chelsea continued her annoying lecture about how I should act.

Pretending to listen, I focused my mind on all the things I would do to my bodyguard after the dinner. I submerged myself in my daydream so that all the annoying thoughts about the Nakamuras fell to the back of my mind. Checking the time, I wondered what was taking Jazz so long.

"Okay, I'm ready to go." She sounded just as jittery as I felt.

I couldn't stop the happiness that came from knowing she seemed nervous about going out with me. As she entered the hall, I completely ignored the reason we were going out. I had to bite the inside of my mouth to keep in all the dirty words I wanted to say to her.

She wore a slinky gold number that the light bounced off with every step she took. A slit on the right side exposed her leg. It was a glorious sight, especially in the black strappy heels she wore. I whistled, ignoring the look Chelsea shot me.

I wondered how Jazz made her skin look so smooth, it looked like it had been kissed by light. Her hips swayed, the heels forcing her strides to be long and seductive. Completely different from her athletic stride.

Naturally, I had the urge to kiss her. Her lips looked so inviting. I could feel Chelsea's eyes boring into the side of my face.

"How do I look?" Jazz asked, completely unaware she'd turned my dick to stone. She turned in a circle. Her dressed revealed the top half of her back. I wanted to lick it. "Is this good enough?"

"Yes, and fuck yes," I nearly shouted.

She bit her lip at my praise. Glancing at Chelsea, she asked, "What do you think?"

"You look good, are you interested in modeling?" Chelsea queried thoughtfully.

"Okay, let's not get ahead of ourselves," I said. Blocking Jazz from Chelsea's shark eyes. "It's time we got on our way."

Chelsea smiled at me with a knowing look. "I can take a hint, I'll let it go for now." She gave Jazz a meaningful look. "We can talk later."

I gave her a tight smile. "No, you won't. Jazz?"

Jazz looked up from where she'd been fussing with her dress. "Yes?"

"Time to go." I grabbed her hand and pulled her along behind me. "We don't want to keep the lounge of lizards waiting."

"W… wait, Tak," she called to me as she followed me. "Bye, Ms. Chelsea, I'll text you when we get there."

We quickly left the house and approached the limo that was parked outside. I waved away the driver who stood by the door. I gently slung Jazz forward, moving her so she stood in front of me and grabbed her waist.

Reaching around her, I then opened the car door. Completely ignoring her protest, I smoothly guided her inside.

"Tak, stop. Wait."

I waited until she'd situated herself and the end of her dress was inside the limo before I shut the door. Turning around, I gave Chelsea the finger before moving to the other side and getting in. That witch was trying to get my bodyguard to show off her beautiful body to the masses.

The very idea of some fucker panting over a picture of my Jazzy made me violent. No, we wouldn't be letting that happen. Fuck no.

Even as she lectured me for not letting her speak to Chelsea I couldn't take my eyes off the globes of her breasts. They looked swollen, like they needed me to rub them better.

My fingers weren't only good at strumming a guitar. I could tease and flick her nipples until they were little peaks. Then I would suck on them until both were swollen and ripe.

Surely a woman who could make her skin glow would taste as delicious as she looked. Thinking about her caused a pop song to fill my head, I grimaced.

"Tak, are you listening to me?" she asked.

"Absolutely not."

She poked out her bottom lip as she moved back. I had this theory that she did it on purpose. She purposely showed up looking like my favorite treat to torment me.

This was all her devious plot to have me ruin her contract and then I'd be forced to keep her and treat her like the goddess she was. I needed to think over why the idea didn't bother me. She released a small huff of annoyance and turned her attention to the window of the limo.

Which gave me a delightful view of her long neck and beautiful collarbone. I never once thought a fucking collarbone was sexy, but here I was getting turned on at the idea of my tongue tracing it.

"Could you at least tell me where it is we are going to eat?"

I averted my eyes. I wouldn't be able to think straight if I met her gaze head-on.

"It's a small spot in the hills, it's called *Farmer*," I managed to say through the cloud of lust clouding my mind.

"Farmer?" she repeated, sounding alarmed.

Curious, I looked at her. "Have you heard of it? It's a pretty exclusive spot with private rooms. They don't have a main chef there but switch them out every month. They always run out of reservations pretty quickly."

"Ah, is that so," she said with a forced smile. I could tell immediately something was wrong.

"Do you not want to go?" I asked, praying that she'd say no, so I could take us to a nice hotel where we could fuck each other's brains out until we couldn't move.

Please put me out of my fucking misery already, I mentally begged.

She shook her head, offering me a small smile. "No, I'm fine. I was thinking about how different my life would be if I hadn't applied to be a security guard. I wouldn't be on a fake date with a rock star or eating at such an exclusive restaurant."

And I wouldn't be suffering from blue balls.

I kept those words inside for two reasons only. One, I was sure Jazz had a knife in her little gold purse and two, I didn't want to ruin the mood.

"Well, good thing you did apply. If you hadn't gotten the job, I wouldn't get to share this nice limo with such a beautiful woman."

Her expression turned coy and fuck me if I didn't want to jump her and eat her.

"I'm sure you've shared a limo with a lot of beautiful women."

"And yet, I can't remember a single one of them when I look at you." I was amazed to realize I really meant it. I couldn't remember the faces of any of the other women I'd slept with. "Shit, that's actually true."

She burst out into laughter. "You're really an ass sometimes. How could you say that like you're shocked?"

I found myself laughing along with her. "But it's true."

She shook her head, her laughter dying as she gave me a look filled with a mischievous light. "I would have given your compliment five stars, but I'm now going to have to make it four stars."

"Well, I can't win them all," I said as I took her hand in mine. "But I'll keep trying for those five stars though. I'm not a quitter."

"You can, but be forewarned, I'm a tough critic," she said, letting me entwine my fingers with hers.

"I'm a musician, I'm used to being critiqued."

I leaned forward and ignored the common sense God gave me and claimed her lips in a heated kiss. And dammit if it wasn't the best reckless thing I'd done lately. They tasted like strawberries and I had a sweet tooth.

When she tried to pull away, I chased after, taking a taste of those pouty lips once more. She lifted her hand to push me back, but I wasn't going to let this close space go to waste. I grasped her hands.

"Please Jazzy, don't push me away," I whispered, giving her a little space.

Her lashes lifted and again she gave me an unreadable look. "Don't make me have to choose."

"Choose what?"

"To choose between my job and a single moment."

I smiled. "You don't have to choose anything, just let go."

"If I let go, there isn't any turning back for me," she said, her voice thick with emotion. "Are you willing to accept that?"

"I'll accept anything if you let me kiss you again," I said right before taking her lips in a deep kiss. Quieting her protest and demanding she answer me back with the same passion. The feel of her was perfection and the smell of her was marvelous. I had always been a greedy kid.

Jazz

Tak wasn't fair.

He completely overwhelmed me and suppressed my protest with his kisses. Since the beginning, I should have kept him at arm's length. I wasn't arrogant enough to think he loved me or anything. However, as a person who'd gotten so close to him, there was a singular truth I couldn't deny.

I was lying to him.

Each time I accepted one of his kisses, the amount of damage that could result from him finding out the truth grew. I'd originally entered his life to repay him for the music that had awoken me from a living state of shock. I imagined myself to be his hidden guardian angel, but the reasons for my presence in his life were starting to blur.

I had to remember that none of this was real. Tak didn't even remember me and even if there was a small part of me who wished he'd suddenly recall my face, I was also terrified that one day he would remember.

The car stopped and I tore my lips away from his. "Stop, we have to stop."

Breathing hard, I tried to regain some of my earlier composure.

"Are you sure you want to?"

I looked at his strained expression and felt an odd sort of thrill. His eyes were dark and held both danger and lust. It felt like at any minute he would swallow me whole.

If I let him, he'd absorb me until the only thing I could think of was him and nothing else. I knew if I didn't stop him now my mind would be only filled with my desire for him. I ignored the stark need on his face and said, "Yes, we have to. Otherwise, how will you explain missing the dinner?"

He frowned as if he'd completely forgotten about it. "Ah, I guess we'll have to finish this at a later time."

I scooted back a little to increase the space between us. Turning, he relaxed back into his seat and pulled on his suit jacket. "You get a pass for now, but don't think we're not going to finish this later."

The driver opened Tak's door and he stepped out, leaving his words behind for me to ponder. I sagged against the back of the seat, letting the tips of my fingers run over my bottom lip. If I didn't get out of his house in the next few weeks, something was bound to happen between us.

The door opened on my side, revealing Tak who offered me his hand. I hesitated for a brief second before I took it and got out. My gaze fell on the Farmer restaurant.

The front of it was lit up with low yellow lights, making it stand out amongst the green hills and tall trees. The sun was slowly sinking behind it, giving it a real picturesque look. A few of the other customers got out of their cars and entered the restaurant with expressions of excitement.

Tak escorted me over to the steps at the front of the entrance. As we ascended them, a few of the people waiting in line could be heard speaking in several different languages. Their voices adding to the rich ambience.

Once we reached the entrance, we were greeted by a host in a nice gray suit who politely requested our reservation name. Tak said the Nakamura name, hearing this the hostess called over a waiter to lead us away.

My stomach tightened at the delicious smell of food in the air. As I perused the inside of the restaurant I spotted a familiar face. Trisha stood in an expensive black dress toward the back of the restaurant, talking to one of her staff.

She looked up just in time to see me. I could see the confusion in her eyes before she looked to my left where Tak stood. She gave me a secretive smile before she pretended she hadn't seen me and continued talking to her employee.

I glanced up at Tak to see if he'd seen my small exchange with Trisha only to see the corners of his eyes and mouth were tight. I realized I'd nearly forgotten why we'd come here. Tak was being forced to meet with the family he hated. I was supposed to be the wall between him and the other Nakamuras.

A single kiss from the idiot next to me and I was making moonbeams out of clouds. Sighing, I straightened and focused. The waiter led us passed the open eating area toward the private rooms.

He led us to the last door on the left and opened it. Once the door was opened, we were greeted with the sight of two men and a woman. Their Asian features were handsome and elegant. I could immediately see Tak's resemblance to the two older men.

"I was under the impression there would only be one of the Nakamuras here," Tak said, his voice cold.

I looked at the three and noticed each of them wore a stiff expression. I wondered if they'd known Tak had no interest in meeting them. Someone spoke up from behind us.

"Cousin, you shouldn't be so cold to family. Aunt has been dying to see you after all these years."

Tak and I turned around to find a man standing behind us. And even though he was smiling, it felt fake.

Tak didn't say anything as he took my hand in his. I looked at him, his eyes were filled with visible disgust. The man walked up and placed a hand on Tak's shoulder.

Something flashed in Tak's eyes. My back tensed and I reached out and grabbed the man's wrist in a hard grip. After seeing the brief flash of fear that entered Tak's gaze a moment ago, I could see he didn't like this man one bit.

"Remove your hand," I said. I'd told Tak I would protect him and if that meant I had to throw his relative on his ass, I would. "I'll only repeat myself once, remove your hand."

The man cast me a look. "Takuya, your date's a bit uptight, don't you think? She must not know we're family."

I knew and didn't give a single shit. Instead of waiting for Tak to say anything, I tightened my hold on his wrist until he yelped out in pain.

"Ow, shit." He yanked his hand out of my hold and took a step away. I moved so I stood between him and Tak.

"Fuck, are you crazy?" he angrily shouted.

"I warned you twice and that was me being nice." I glanced over my shoulder at the three people who were still sitting, their expressions filled with worry. "I would assume you wish for this dinner to continue without suffering any injuries, right?"

"Sakai, enough," the man who sat at the head of the table said, standing up. He offered Tak an apologetic look. "We apologize for his behavior. Let's all take our seats and order drinks. And then we can talk about why we wanted to meet with you."

I turned around and gave Tak a questioning look. "What do you want to do?"

Tak didn't answer me right away, his expression dark as he looked down at me.

"Tak?"

He glanced at his cousin and said, "We might as well stay." He turned around and faced the man who'd urged us to sit. "They put in a lot of effort to drag me here. I should at least pretend to listen to their bullshit reason for coming back into my life like unwanted baggage."

I followed him to the free seats that were across from the couple who'd remained quiet since we'd entered the room. Tak reached for my hand once more under the table. I took it and felt it shake.

I looked at him. His smile was taunting, and his eyes held a sardonic light. I don't think anything he was really thinking showed on his face, but from his trembling hand, I could sense this meeting was a lot harder on him then I'd first assumed it would be.

That Sakai bastard took his seat at the end of the table. I secretly wondered what these people had done to Tak to make him hate them so much.

Tak

The people who shared DNA with me had barely changed. My uncle Ayaki Nakamura was still the one who kept Sakai under control. Not that it had helped any when my cousin had visited me alone during the summers.

My uncle shifted his eyes to my father, Daichi Nakamura, who's gaze was firmly focused on the table, a faint look of regret on his face. When he finally looked up at me, he squinted his eyes slightly as if he couldn't quite believe I was sitting right across from him.

"It's been a long time, son."

"I'm amazed you remembered I exist." I didn't have any use for the false politeness they practiced. I leaned back, placing my free hand on the table, tapping out a steady beat.

"I kept telling Kole I'd do anything to not work with your company and yet here I am. For some odd reason, your people kept pushing for me to not only work with you but meet with one of you.

"Something I really, really didn't want to do. I'm interested in knowing why you all were so desperate to meet with the son you abandoned. I thought my letter in college was enough. So, tell me why the people who wanted me gone the most are so very invested in meeting with me now."

"We didn't abandon you," my dad's wife said defensively. "Your father and I were hoping we could get our home settled before he brought you in."

I laughed. I couldn't help it. "And that took you the entirety of my childhood to do? You should have work harder on your bullshit, I'm a little too old to believe such fucked-up reasoning."

"Takuya, watch how you speak to your mother. You will respect her," my father snapped.

"Did you forget, old man, I don't have a mother," I said. "The day you and mom finalized the divorce you told me I no longer had a mother and should forget her. You just failed to mention then that I would also no longer have a father after he met someone else. That he'd find himself a perfectly respectable woman to marry and that he'd take in her kids while completely abandoning his own son to a nanny and a bunch of servants."

I didn't bother to fill in the tense silence left after my harshly spoken words.

Ayaki cleared his throat and spoke up. "We reached out to you because your father is thinking of retiring. Because of this, we have to decide on who will be taking over his seat. Unfortunately, your stepmother's children have been found ineligible as they are not of Nakamura descent—"

"Please tell me you didn't reach out to me because you want me to take over the family business."

The me who'd grown accustomed to being nothing to this family wasn't surprised. I'd been a kid who'd been beaten repeatedly by his cousin and when I begged for help, they pawned it off by telling me it was only child's play.

Yet for some fucked-up reason, I'd actually thought they'd wanted to see me because they'd realized they'd fucked up. I still had that damn child inside of me who held on to hope that his father would come home even when he'd been steadily spending less and less time with him. The kid who'd pretended he didn't mind living in a big house alone in Bridge Lake.

I was still that fucking child who wanted his father's love. I hated myself and that dumb child inside of me.

"This is your family, Takuya. Don't you think it's time you stopped this playing at music and settle down?" My uncle's words flew right over my head.

I released a derisive snort. "First, I have no intention of ever being a part of the Nakamura family." I stood, pushing my chair back. "Second, I won't be doing the commercial and if you or anyone with your filthy last name ever approaches me again, I will gladly have my lawyers deal with you."

Jazz stood up next to me, still holding my hand.

"This has been a waste of a good night." Without another word, I moved to leave.

Rising from his seat, Sakai tried to stop me. "Cousin, wait, don't leave."

Sakai reached out. I released Jazz's hand, turned around, and smashed my fist into his jaw. He staggered back and I caught him by his suit jacket. "Woah, I'm not done yet."

I drew my arm back and slugged him four times, making sure each one made a beautiful meaty sound. His head lolled back. I shoved him away from me. He hit the ground hard, his head hitting the chair he'd stood from.

I squatted in front of him. "Let me make this clear, I'm no longer that little kid you used to beat up. If I ever see you again, I will kill you."

I stood up and turned around and retook Jazz's hand and left. It took a lot of the little control I had not to stomp him into the ground. Walking into the hallway, I tried to tamp down the rage that filled me. It felt like every single emotion I'd ever locked away had been released and they were trying to suffocate me.

"Tak." Jazz pulled me to a stop once we reached the exit of the restaurant. I took a deep breath and looked down at her. "Are you okay?"

Instead of answering, I said, "I want to go somewhere where no one can find me."

Staring into her warm brown eyes calmed me down. She reached up and brushed a few strands of my hair back. "Okay, then where do you want to go?"

"Anywhere is fine."

She smiled. "I think I know a place. Do you trust me?"

"Yes." And I realized I really did.

"Come on, let's see if your driver has enough gas to go to Bridge Lake."

She dragged me behind her, and I gladly followed her. In all honesty, Jazz could lead me to hell, and I'd still follow her.

CHAPTER THIRTY-NINE

Take Me Away

Tak

An hour later, I wasn't sure I could trust her. She'd brought me to the middle of butt-fuck nowhere.

"It's right up ahead," she called back to me as we walked up a driveway that cut through the woods around us that were dense and dark. The driver had dropped us off and had left to go back to Vander City under Jazzy's direction.

"I want you to know it's a lie what they say. Artists aren't worth more dead than alive."

She didn't look back at me when she said, "I thought you said you trusted me?"

"Trusted. Past tense."

She laughed. "Stop being a baby and come on."

I decided I should check my cell phone and see if I had enough power. I did, which made me faintly relieved. I replaced it in my back pocket just as a cabin came into view.

"Is this it?" I asked as she climbed the steps and picked up a flowerpot.

"Yep, it's my very own version of a secret garden." She grabbed the small tree plant and yanked it out along with the dirt. Reaching inside she pulled out a key and after replacing the tree she set the pot back down. She turned around to face me.

"You said you wanted to get away and as your bodyguard it's my job to make my VIP feel safe. I thought this would be a good place to take a break."

I absentmindedly listened to her as I took in her appearance. Her hair was messy and her lipstick smudged. I couldn't think of a more beautiful sight.

I walked up the steps and reached out to pull her into my arms. I rested my chin atop her head and murmured.

"I don't know what I did before you."

"Simply existed," she said as she gave me a coy smile. "Now, you're living."

"You sure have a high opinion of yourself."

She chuckled. "I'm a hot commodity. There are some people out there who'd pay big dollars to be alone with me."

"Is that so?" I'd have to keep an eye out for them. No one else was allowed to enjoy Jazz's company.

"Now, let me go so I can open the door."

Reluctantly, I released her. She gave me her back as she went to unlock the door. I looked away from her and took in the view.

The surrounding area had just enough lights here and there so I could see there was a great distance between Jazz's cabin and the next. It occurred to me that land like this in Bridge Lake had to be pretty high-priced real estate.

"What did you say your parents do again?" I asked out of curiosity, returning my gaze to her back.

She paused in opening the door. "Nothing much, really. My father is in business and my mother, well you already know she passed away when I was in high school."

How the fuck could I have forgotten that? "Sorry."

"You don't have to apologize." She glanced back at me as she opened the door. "This place is actually my inheritance from my grandad. He and I spent a few summers out here when I was younger, it's a nice place to think."

Together we entered the cabin. There were low lights on in the corners of the living room, giving the interior a warm cozy look that screamed Jazz to me.

"How often do you come out here?"

"A lot, especially before I got this job. That's why I tend to keep this place fully stocked."

I walked over to the wall where there were black and white photographs. Not even one was of Jazz, unfortunately. I turned around to take in the entire living room. There was a fireplace and a large brown leather couch that sat opposite it. The wood flooring was covered by a large fall-colored rug.

The kitchen was a few steps behind the large couch. A high kitchen counter separated the living room from the kitchen. Jazz walked into the kitchen and set her key on the counter.

She bent down and removed her heels with a sigh of pleasure and tossed them into the corner of the living room.

"Do you want some tea?"

"Yeah," I answered. The sight of her bending over had derailed my focus.

She walked over to the sink and grabbed up a teakettle off the counter beside it and filled it with water before she set it on the stove top.

She turned on the stove and then faced me. "Shouldn't take too long. In the meantime, do you want to change out of your suit?" she asked as she walked from behind the counter. "I have some clothes in one of the guest room drawers. When my cousins come to visit, they always leave something behind."

It suddenly dawned on me that we were alone. I'd been waiting to have such a moment for so long. I watched as she ran her hands through her messy hair.

I knew then if I didn't take advantage of the situation, I'd never get another chance. Walking across the room, I grabbed her hand.

"You didn't answer my question last time."

She looked up at me in confusion. "What question?"

"I told you I'd accept anything if you let me kiss you again."

"That's not a question. That's a statement." She looked away from me.

"Look at me."

She did and there was reluctance in her eyes. "I want an answer, Jazz. I'm saying I want you and we both know you want me. So why won't you just put us both out of our misery and let me fuck you?"

"Putting you out of *your* misery could cost me my job," she answered.

"Aren't I worth more than a job to you?"

The look in her eyes turned angry. She reached up and grabbed my tie and yanked. I stumbled forward. She raised her chin up so that her lips hovered near mine.

"Let's say I don't give a shit about my job. Let's say I do sleep with you. Can you honestly say it would be worth it? I'm not the type who enjoys one-night stands nor do I enjoy casual sex."

She leaned close, letting my tie go. A possessive look entering her eyes. I wouldn't lie and say it didn't turn me on.

She continued. "If we fuck it's because you're planning on being mine. And I don't let go of things I consider mine easily. So let me ask you once more, are you sure you want me that badly?"

I swear, the minute she started talking all aggressively all my blood went straight to my dick. The only thing that would keep me from fucking her would be her own denial.

I grabbed her chin and stared down into those pretty brown eyes. "You're not the only one who has conditions. You're mine and like you, I don't like to share. I also like to have control." I looked down at her lips, moving my hand from her chin to her throat. "Complete control. If you thought I was obnoxious when I was pursuing you, you're not ready for what I'll become now that you're mine."

"What makes you think I'm afraid of that?"

I flashed her a wicked smile. "That's my girl." I wrapped an arm around her waist and pulled her closer. "Shit, Jazz, I don't think I could want anyone else as much as I want you. Matter of fact, there won't be anyone else. My dick's picky, it doesn't like to share either."

She lowered her lashes. "Don't complain if I beat the shit out of a girl if she comes on to you."

"Back at you. Don't get too angry when I fuck you in a closet because you said something to another guy," I rebutted.

After a beat of silence, she tried to wriggle out of my hold. "Are you going to let me go so I can take my clothes off?"

"Let me think about it. It feels to good holding you in my arms," I teased.

After a few seconds, I reluctantly let her go.

Her lips pursed. "I just want to make it clear. I didn't bring you here for sex," she said as she turned around and gave me her back. "Unzip me."

"Yes, ma'am."

I felt like a fucking kid on my birthday. I grabbed the zipper that started at the middle of her back and pulled it down. I never knew how erotic it was to hear a dress being unzipped.

I parted my lips as I saw the tattoo that graced her spine and ass. It didn't start until the center of her back and moved down around her ass. The mystery of the peek of Ivy I'd seen before was now solved.

The design was of a briar patch of roses with snakes intertwined in it. I released a whistle.

"That's a beautiful piece." I leaned forward and bent to press my lips to the top rose.

She released a small shudder. "Thanks."

Biting my bottom lip, I continued to enjoy unwrapping my prize. What made it even more enticing was that it was for me only. Ah shit, I could feel my own possessive needs stirring.

Her beautiful skin was a warm almond color that complimented my own warm tone. Wordlessly, I continued trailing kisses down her back. My hypotheses had been right.

Jazz was tasty all over. Fuck, I wasn't sure how long I'd last. I should have just said fuck it and pulled her dress up and took her against the kitchen counter, but I wouldn't.

My Jazz deserved the couch because there was no fucking way we'd make it to a bed. Hell, if I'd had the time to plan, I would have built an altar so I could worship her on it.

Once the zipper reached her ass, my heart rate increased. Her ass was perfect. Like perfectly rounded bubbles.

"Damn, I don't think I can take this slow."

She looked over her shoulder. "Who asked you to?"

Jazz turned around fully facing me and removed her hands from her breasts. She pushed her dress down letting it hit the floor. She stepped out of the circle it made, brushing her chest against me, then pushed my suit jacket off.

My jacket slipped from my shoulders and hit the ground. Jazz walked me backward, her nimble fingers undoing my shirt at the same time.

"You're not the only one who's been waiting for this moment," she whispered. She opened my shirt and trailed her fingers down my chest. The back of my legs hit the couch, stopping me in my tracks. She looked up at me. "Since we've decided to do this. Don't make me wait any longer."

I pushed her hand away and picked her up. Her arms automatically wrapped around my neck and her legs around my waist.

"Damn, don't complain later when you can't walk," I warned. I walked her around the couch. Holding her, I fell on it. She laughed as she pressed a kiss to my chin before she whispered in my ear.

"I don't want to be able to even move when you're done."

Triggered, I escaped her arms and pulled my shirt off and released my buckle. Jazz didn't hesitate to unzip my pants. Soon our skin was pressed against each other's and her lips were on mine.

I needed her more than I needed water, air, or even music. The sound of her breathing and the feel of her hands on my skin were more addictive than any drug I'd ever tried. I had never felt as free as I did when she was in my arms.

Her hands brushed along my chest and around to my back, where her nails scraped against the hidden scars there that I earned long ago. Now a bird of prey and an honor to my brothers decorated it. I winced.

She stopped, her eyes filling with worry. "Are you okay?"

I brushed her off. "Old wound, it's nothing."

She frowned. "Are you sure?"

I rubbed my dick against the fabric-covered seam of her underwear. Both of us released sounds of pleasure. "Does that answer your question?"

Before she could say anything, I reached up and grabbed the back of her head and brought her forward for another probing kiss. Our tongues dueled for dominance, but we both fucking knew who would win. I broke the kiss and peppered kisses down her chin to her neck.

She panted as I dragged my freed hand down her chest to her sexy panties. Pushing my hand inside them, I then brushed my fingers along the lips of her sex and felt the juices of her pussy.

I smiled against her neck as I drew them out. "Jazz, I want to taste it."

She pulled back and looked at me. My dick turned to rock at the bashful look she gave me. Shit, that was a hot contrast to her bold actions from earlier.

I lifted my fingers that were still coated with her pussy juices and sucked on them. "This isn't enough, you're not planning on denying me, are you?"

Her lashes fluttered. "What do you want me to do?"

"Get up," I ordered gruffly.

We both moved so Jazz could stand over me, her feet on either side of my thighs on the couch. "Shit, it's beautiful."

Her pussy juices had leaked through her underwear so now the fabric outlined her thick nether lips. I looked up at her and could see she was biting her lip. I lightly brushed my hands up her legs.

"Don't be nervous, love, it's beautiful and it's fucking drooling for my kiss."

With my right hand, I slipped her underwear to the side. With my other hand, I drew her closer and inhaled deeply. "How the fuck does it smell like strawberries? Fuck."

Without waiting for her to answer me, I buried my face in her sweet pussy. The taste coated my tongue and had my dick weeping. She dropped her hands to the back of my head as I licked along the lips of her pussy. I paused to suck her clit just to get her to grind against my face.

"Tak, I… fuck."

She rolled her hips against my face like she was trying to fuck it. I grabbed her ass to pull her closer as I feasted on her delicious pussy.

I'd tasted Twinkies, brownies, cookies and every sweet known to man. Jazz was better than every single one of them. I could hear her breathing growing strained as she tightened her hold on the back of my head.

"Tak, I'm…Tak," she called out my name as she leaned forward, her legs trembled slightly.

I opened my mouth as more of her juices spilled out. I lapped up every drop of her as she orgasmed on my tongue. I drew back panting.

Eating pussy had never felt like a full fuck before, but as she stood over me trembling, I was fully satisfied with my meal. She slowly lifted her leg and moved to the right of me and sat down beside me. Her chest was heaving.

"Shit."

"Jazz, we're not done yet," I said. I stood up in front of her and grabbed my dick through my pants. "You still haven't let him have a taste yet."

I pushed down my pants and stepped out of them, letting my dick free. Her eyes zeroed in on it. "What should we give him first? Your mouth or…" I looked pointedly at her pussy that was probably still rippling from my love and care.

"How about this," she said scooting forward. She placed a hand on my hip, a naughty smile coming to her lips. "Let me see if you're just as sweet as those damn snacks you eat."

Before I could say another word she grabbed my length, opened her mouth wide, and swallowed it. "Shit."

My toes curled as she swallowed my cock down her hot throat. The pressure of her tongue against my tip was magic. She swirled it around and gave love to the slit.

"Jazz, fuck, slow."

I choked on my tongue as she hollowed her cheeks and sucked. If I hadn't seen her smile. I would swear she didn't have any teeth.

She deep-throated my dick like a champ and hummed. I pressed a hand to the back of her head.

"Dammit, fuck. Suck me, shit."

Her mouth worked me up and down until I felt my legs go numb. She slurped as she released me and with a pop, my shaft left her mouth.

"You should keep eating sweets," she said as she licked her bottom lip. She wrapped her soft hand around my dick and started stroking it. "Come in my mouth," she said, staring up at me. She swallowed me whole once more, dropping her hands to my thighs.

I smirked. "As you wish, love."

I placed my hands on both sides of her face and started to fuck her mouth. She didn't blink, her eyes holding only demand and hunger. Fuck, Jazz could never disappoint me.

"Fuck, baby. Swallow every drop. Don't let one fall," I ordered and gritted my teeth as I shot my load into her mouth.

My beautiful Jazz swallowed every bit of my seed like a motherfucking champ. I pulled out of her mouth and watched her smack her lips like she just drank a fucking latte.

"Damn, Jazz."

I leaned down and kissed her, tasting both of us on her tongue. I felt like I could get drunk off our mingling flavors. Breaking the kiss, I knelt down in front of her. I trailed kisses down her neck to her chest and continued my devout journey downward until she released another deep-throated moan.

Lifting my head, I grabbed her right breast and kneaded it, enjoying the silky-smooth texture of her skin. I leaned forward and caught her brown nipple between my teeth. Jazz released a pleasured mewl as she buried her hands in my hair, lifting her chest to my mouth.

Swirling my tongue around it, I tortured the cute little thing until it was standing up. I released it and turned my attention to her left nipple until she pulled at my hair.

"Enough, Tak, stop teasing me," she panted, looking down at me with dazed eyes.

I licked my lips. "Don't tell me my lovely bodyguard can't endure longer than this?"

She glared down at me. I laughed, grabbing her by her waist. I lifted as I kicked off my shoes and joined her on the couch. I moved her so she was on her back. Shifting over her, I moved between her legs.

"Love, you shouldn't rush a masterpiece you know, but if you insist." I leaned down and grabbed the top of the thong she wore and pulled.

She lifted her hips so that I could get it down her shapely legs and off those ankles I planned to kiss later. Once it was fully off, I tossed it over my back not caring where it landed.

"I better be able to find that when we're done."

I ignored her as I grabbed both her legs and lifted them up. "Bring your knees to your chest and hold them there, love."

She frowned, but grabbed her legs, pulling her knees in, exposing everything to me. Her pussy lips glistened like jewels.

"Look how wet you are, Jazzy. You're damn near salivating for my dick. And here I thought you didn't like me, I guess my first taste of it wasn't enough for you," I teased as I looked up to find her glaring at me. "Tsk, let's fix that expression of yours."

I leaned forward and gave her yummy-looking pussy a hard lick. Maybe that's all I would do, eat her pussy until she couldn't tell up from down. She released a small hiss as her head dropped back. I licked my lips, enjoying the taste of her juices on them.

I'd always been the type to have seconds and since she was my new favorite snack there was no way I wasn't going to indulge. I decided to go in for another taste as I pinned her leg with one hand and placed the other against her belly. This time she couldn't grind with her legs pin to her chest, she could only enjoy the torture from my tongue. A thrill filled me from having the little firebrand held captive under my tongue.

Jazz

I'd completely said fuck you to every fan rule I'd ever abided by. And I honestly couldn't find a single fuck to give as I rode Tak's tongue. I'd always wondered if he was good at anything other than singing and looking hot all the time.

I'd just discovered his other talent, eating pussy. He had full control of me as he sucked and stimulated my clit. He released a small hum every once in a while as if he was enjoying one of the sugary snacks he hoarded.

With his long fingers, he tapped out a beat on my stomach. I bit my lip as I felt the first white flames of my orgasm running through.

"Ah," I groaned as the walls of my pussy rippled.

He grabbed my hips and lifted me higher as he continued slurping away at my core. "Shit, I think I'm a pussy eating man now," he said as he set me back down.

His intense stare burned into my skin. I felt like a plate that'd been licked clean. He smirked.

The wings tatted on his chest drew my lazy gaze. He crawled up my body. "Don't tell me your already tapped out, we've got a lot more to enjoy. I only ate you out twice."

Taking a deep breath, I let go of my legs, letting them fall. I pushed myself up. Tak grabbed my face and took my lips in a demanding kiss. He dove his tongue inside. I could taste everything that was Tak and my own essence in his mouth. I didn't care about anything but feeling him some more. He'd become my obsession.

I broke the kiss. "Please, fuck me already."

"So impatient." I could feel the hot press of his dick against my sex.

"Shit, you're so fucking ready for me, love."

He pressed his forehead against mine as he positioned himself and slowly pushed forward. I looked down so I could watch as his hips flexed against mine, his length entered me inch by inch. There was a slight pinch as he pushed in deeper followed by the uncomfortable feeling of my pussy stretching around him.

I saw as his eyes widened at the slight resistance, but I ignored it and proactively lifted my hips to take more of him. I gasped when he flexed his hips forward, fully impaling me. Together we just stilled, breathing as my body adjusted to his size and this new sensation.

At that moment, we were in sync with every inhale and exhale we shared. "Jazzy?"

I knew what he was asking me as the struggle to hold back was clear in his expression.

"Move, Tak. Please, move."

"Shit." He pulled back and thrust into me with his full strength. The feeling was akin to electricity running through my body, bringing all my nerve endings to life.

"Fuck, I knew it would be perfect," he muttered as he covered my neck and chest with kisses.

My heart pounded in my ears. His low worded compliments and dirty words sounded better to me than a Rejected One song. Our skin sliding against each other's became another form of torture I wished would never end.

"More, ah, fuck me, Tak," I yelled as he took me further and further down the rabbit hole.

I wrapped my arms around his neck. My mind stayed somewhere between pain and pleasure. Everything felt too intense. I was swiftly losing my grip on reality.

The sound of my heartbeat matched his. Pretty soon I could barely make out what I was saying.

"I... I... Tak."

He grunted. "Shit, go ahead. I'm there... fuck."

My body tightened like a bow string as I sucked in a tight breath. Tak's grip on my hips tightened until I was sure there would be bruises there. With a shout, he expanded inside me before a sudden warmth filled me.

The edges of my vision darkened as he continued thrusting his hips, filling me to the brim with his cum. I could barely move as he rested on top of me. Funny enough I didn't find it uncomfortable.

I liked his weight on me. Spent and exhausted, the two of us rested against each other without moving.

"So... you're an untapped pussy." I didn't have the strength to hit him.

"Shut up."

He chuckled, rubbing his jaw against my chest. "I miss when you only said *more*."

Deciding to ignore him was the best remedy, I closed my eyes and let myself drift off to sleep.

I wasn't sure how much time had passed when I awoke to him carrying me up the stairs. I tried to stay awake, but soon enough I fell back to sleep.

CHAPTER FORTY

Untouched

Tak

Early the next morning, I sat in a chair in the corner of the bedroom. I watched as Jazz slept. I never thought she'd be a virgin.

In fact, with my head clear enough to think about it, I wondered if she would wake up to regret giving me her first time. Most the women I'd been with had been experienced. I'd never wanted the emotional stress that came with being a woman's first.

Being the fuck 'em and leave 'em type, I never wanted anyone to entrust me with something like that. I felt like I was completely out of my depth. Like what the fuck was I supposed to do the day after?

Should I give her flowers or chocolates? Would Jazz expect me to propose? I brushed a frustrated hand through my hair.

Jazz released a low groan as she shifted under the covers. I stilled and waited for her to wake up. A small part of me expected her to open her eyes, see me, and immediately say she regretted the whole fucking thing, but as usual she managed to act outside of my expectations.

Sitting up, she rubbed her eyes. I was flashed by a bright gray iris. Astonished, I barely took in her small wave, sleepy lover's smile, and her raspy voice when she said, "Morning."

She pushed her blanket aside and gave me a beautiful view of her nude body as she got out of the bed to go to the bathroom. I still hadn't moved from the chair. I was too occupied with thinking about what I'd just seen. Jazz's eyes were gray, I'd never noticed before. I wondered why she covered them with brown contacts.

The door to the bathroom opened, derailing my thoughts as she looked over at me. "Sorry, I didn't ever show you where the extra clothes were, but I see you found them on your own."

"It's fine, it didn't take long to find them in the guest room drawer. I figured it was better to let you sleep a little longer."

So far, so good.

"Thanks," she said as she disappeared back into the bathroom.

This time she didn't close the door and I could hear the shower running. Rising from the chair, I walked to the door and bit my lip at the sight of her standing behind a clear shower curtain. The water ran down between her perky breasts and disappeared between her lovely thighs. I completely forgot about her contacts at the sight of her wet body.

"Jazz?"

She looked over at me through the plastic curtain. "Mm?"

I pulled off the T-shirt I wore and shoved my pants down. "I think I need to shower."

She turned and pulled the curtain aside, giving me a weird look. "Didn't you already take a shower?"

I shook my head. "No, I didn't. Something you'll learn eventually is that all men…" I paused, frowning. "Fuck that, you don't need to know about other men. Just know I prefer to shower with you in the morning."

She laughed as I shoved the curtain fully aside and entered the shower. "Is that so?"

"Yeah, that's so." I wrapped my arms around her and pulled her close. "I like showering, especially after a good night's fuck."

She gave me a naughty smile as she reached down and grabbed my dick boldly. God, I loved a woman who knew how to take action.

"Then what do you think of morning sex?" she asked. "Is that something you prefer or are you more of a night fucker?"

"I like it. I like it a lot. It's my favorite morning workout," I said as I bent down and picked her up. "Shit, this is the best. I knew there was an advantage to you being short."

She wrapped her legs around my waist as I slowly entered her. Jazz slapped my shoulder. "I'm five-eight. I'm not short. You're just too tall… ah." Her moan was music to my ears. From now on, I'd stop all her lecturing with a single stroke.

Pretty soon I gave her more reasons to be loud. The sound of our skin slapping together filled the bathroom. Her body was slick and rubbed against mine. I turned us so her back pressed against the wall and I could thrust deeper into her welcoming pussy.

"Only me." I took her lips in a deep kiss. Breaking the kiss, I said, "Only me, Jazz."

She bit her lip and nodded as she closed her eyes, but it wasn't enough. I needed to hear her say it.

"Say it. Tell me I'm the only one for you."

She opened her eyes, those dark orbs meeting mine. "Only you, no one else," she said, her voice rough and filled with desire. "Now fuck my brains out."

I reached and grabbed her throat. Tightening my hold, I leaned forward and whispered in her ear. "Don't rush." I brushed a kiss against her cheek. "You'll barely feel your toes when I'm done."

Her pussy clamped on my dick. I pulled it out before I slammed back in like it was a battering ram. I fucked her until she screamed my full name.

It was to our advantage that I was physically fit. Otherwise, I wouldn't have been able to beat her pussy until she saw stars. Of course, one round wasn't enough, I needed at least two more before I got my fill. Fucking Jazz was my new favorite pastime, but I wondered when she'd let me see her real eyes.

***

"Do you want chocolate chips on your pancakes?" Jazz asked from where she stood in front of the stove.

I looked up from my cell phone. "Are you insane?" I exclaimed, giving her a look of disbelief. "Of course I want chocolate chips on my pancakes."

I sat on a stool at the kitchen counter with the smell of buttermilk and chocolate surrounding me. As the radio played "Better" by Khalid—someone I had heard about but had never really listened to. When I'd told Jazz this, she'd looked at me like I was a criminal.

I watched her sing along and shake her hips as she walked over to the fridge to pull out a few ingredients. She wore a long T-shirt and shorts that I couldn't help but thank for the occasional flash of her ass. She moved gracefully behind the counter.

"I should have known. I've seen your stash of sweets."

I gave her a deadpan look. "Why are you saying that like there's something wrong with it? I work out. I deserve a Twinkie every once in a while."

She laughed. "I've seen you put not one, but three of them in your satchel and if it wasn't for the fact that Chelsea stopped you, you would have added a chocolate brownie. You have a sugar addiction."

"You know what, I don't need this type of negativity in the morning," I huffed.

She walked over to the counter and leaned forward, pressing a kiss to my cheek. "Does that make you feel better?"

I moved so I could kiss her fully on the mouth before I rubbed our noses together. "I think I need another one to fully feel better."

She gave me another kiss. I smiled against her lips. "Good girl."

"Are you sure you're feeling better now?" she asked. Her voice full of that teasing tone that made me want to take her on the counter.

I shook my head. "You really shouldn't tease me too much. I don't think your newly touched pussy could take it."

"Oh God. How many times are you going to say that?" she asked.

"I'm proud of myself. I was gentle enough so that you could walk." I motioned to her, then spread my arms wide. "Behold, you aren't walking bowlegged."

I dodged the punch she aimed at me and hopped off the stool, grabbing my phone. The screen was filled with missed text messages from Chelsea, Kole, my band members, and surprisingly also from Pit and Skittles. I hadn't thought my disappearance would cause citywide panic. I'd only been off the grid for a night.

I didn't want to respond to any of them but seeing as I'd been accused of trying to commit suicide a month and a half ago, I knew I should. Although, I really didn't want to leave the comfortable cabin yet.

"Okay, okay, I know when I'm not wanted. I'm going out to the porch to make a phone call," I said.

She hummed in acknowledgment of what I said as she turned her attention to cooking breakfast. Leaving the kitchen, I walked outside. I stretched my arms up, breathing in the chilly air.

It felt good to be out here with Jazz. No one fucking demanding I do shit I didn't want to. I was shocked to find such peace in Bridge Lake, a place I'd been avoiding since I left. Deciding to bite the bullet, I called Pit first.

"Where the fuck are you?"

"Well, hello to you too, sunshine. How are you doing on this perfectly sunny morning?" I said cheerfully.

"Eat shit, Tak. Why haven't you been answering my texts?"

"I was busy doing something your old ass probably needs a pill for. Fucking."

"Oh, well, I guess you don't want to know the name of the second guy who's got it out for you."

"Who's the second guy?"

"Tony Enson. I had to go to some dark doors for this. And once again, the fucker worked at your label. I'm starting to think your label needs to do a better job of looking into their employees' backgrounds."

Hearing that both of my attackers had worked at my label was more than a little disturbing to hear.

"Anything else?"

Pit released a heavy breath before he continued. "I'm still looking into the one who dropped the stage light. His ass is gone in the wind at the moment, but we know I catch air."

"Shit, I thought we could at least get some eyes on him," I said just as the door opened behind me and Jazzy stepped outside. I lowered my phone casually.

"Hey, the pancakes are done. Hurry up and come inside before they get cold."

Forcing myself to smile, I said, "I'll be right there."

"Don't blame me if I eat them all," she joked before going back inside.

"All right, when I'm headed back I'll call you and we can continue this then," I said to Pit.

"Again, where the fuck are you?" Pit asked, sounding exasperated with me.

I debated over whether or not I should tell him.

"Tak?"

"Bridge Lake."

"You're fucking kidding me." He burst out in laughter. "Shit, didn't you say you'd never go back?"

I shrugged, though he couldn't see it. "Pussy can make you do some amazing things."

"Point made," Pit said. "Anyway, one last thing. Skittles sent out a mass text for you all to come to the bar. Don't ignore her. She's not playing with you anymore."

I thought it over. Was it time for me to stop avoiding my brothers and sister?

"Yeah, I'll be there."

"Later."

The line went dead, and I went back inside.

I would deal with everything once we got back. For that moment, I enjoyed my morning with the woman who'd given me a haven away from the rest of the world.

CHAPTER FORTY-ONE

Reunion

Tak

Pit's bar was on the other side of Vander City and usually boasted a good-sized crowd. Skittles had asked us to meet up on a night that wasn't a peak night, so the parking lot wasn't filled. I'd given Jazz the day off.

She'd bucked at it at first, but I'd reminded her that she hadn't taken her usual time off on Monday. She'd reluctantly left this morning.

Getting out of my car, I nervously checked my reflection in the window of my truck. Another attempt at stalling before I had to face the others.

"How much longer are you going to check yourself out?" Deacon shouted from the open window of his car as he pulled up.

I turned around to see him get out of his parked car. He wore his usual ensemble of a black T-shirt and black aviator glasses. The tattoos that decorated his arms stood out against his skin.

"Don't sound so bitter, old man. It's rare to have a face worth looking at." I gave him a sympathetic look. "One day someone will love you for your personality, trust this little brother of yours."

He flipped me off.

"Sorry, can't. Would love to but can't," I said as we walked toward Pit's bar.

Entering the bar, I spotted Skittles sitting there, she waved at me. "About time you showed your little ass up."

I walked over to her, keeping a look out for the single person I didn't want to run into. "Well, I know you guys can't live without me. So, I figured I'd grace you losers with my presence."

"Don't play with me, Tak."

"Baby, relax. I got his ass."

I froze a few feet away from Skittles. A chill running down my spine as the familiar voice came from behind me. Forcing a smile to my lips, I whipped around.

Of course, it was Pit. He was the only one in the group who could give me this sort of vibe. He looked me over, his expression empty of emotion.

"Kid, there are so many things I could say right now. You're lucky I didn't show up without Skittles and kick your fucking door in." His voice never raised and he kept a straight face. "If you didn't show up tonight, it would have been a problem. I'm not playing these games with you. You've been rolling in shit, shit I can solve."

I balled my hands at my sides, keeping my strained smile. "Good to know."

Deacon entered the bar along with Luke, who looked like he'd just woken up. "Skittles, you really called everyone in, didn't you?" Luke said giving a big yawn.

Skittles hopped off the stool she'd been sitting on and walked over to my side. She placed a comforting hand on my back. Similar to how she'd done when I'd been nothing more than a snot-nosed kid.

"Tak, I told you a long time ago, I. Will. Fuck. Someone. Up. For. You. Someone signed a check they can't cash. You may be going through a ton of shit, but you have a team of fighters around you. It's time we remind him of that," she said looking at the guys before turning back to me. "You fucked up big time you little shit. This was supposed to come to our door from day one. You're going to stop acting like a little pussy tonight. It's not becoming."

I shot her an annoyed look. "You don't have to keep shooting me when I'm already down, you know."

Pit shook his head. "Come on, Ox will get us drinks and we can get down to business."

"Yes, the main reason I decided to come," Luke said as he followed him to the back room.

"I'm not drinking that disgusting beer Ox keeps trying to get us into. Oh my God, I love him, but that trash is a no for me," Skittles said as she left my side and followed Pit.

Deacon walked over and gave me a knowing look. "We're pretty much know about everything, thanks to Pit. He never stopped keeping an eye on you and your situation. Honestly, we already knew you wouldn't have done something as selfish as kill yourself on Skittles' day. I know Skittles already said this before, but we're family, kid. We're never going to just disappear on you. We're Assholes for life, and that means you're stuck with us for life, okay?"

I looked away from his probing stare and nodded. "I know."

"Good." He grabbed my arm and pulled me along behind him. "Now let's get some free drinks."

Pit, who'd walked toward the back room and paused said, "When did I say this shit was free? All of you motherfuckers are paying."

His words were followed by everyone's groan of pain. Skittles laughed. "Don't worry, it's on him or his dick will be dry tonight."

Pit looked at her and quirked a brow. "I had you by the throat all morning, I'm good."

"Fuck you, Pit."

"You want me to." He winked.

I joined Luke and Deacon in pretending we didn't hear them arguing. Some things just never changed.

Jazz

"Look who decided to come back home," Trisha greeted me as I entered her apartment. She looked behind me. "Where's Leonard, didn't you go by the office?"

"I had him meet me downtown with my car and sent him back to the office. I decided to drive myself around today, I'm tired of being carted everywhere."

"Wow, out of all the times I asked you to let me get a ride in your Lamborghini, you didn't even offer to take me for a joy ride and to add insult to injury, you're off today. I see how you are cousin. When I saw your nappy ass at Farmer, did I snitch? No, but now I don't know what I'll do since I'm so hurt."

"Don't be that person," I said as I hauled my newest purchases of Rejected One merch over to her couch. "Julius texted me yesterday and told me Dutch could fill me in on why my father was pushing for me to get to know Harrison's son. Besides, I was kicked out by my boss last minute. So, I figured I'd come by and check on you and Dutch. See if the brownstone was still standing."

"Well, not only is it standing, but it's also thriving," she said with humor.

"Okay, I was starting to worry since you and Dutch are like vinegar and oil. And there's no one here to keep an eye on you two with Zeno, Julius, and me out."

Trisha sent me an annoyed look as she walked into her kitchen. "I shouldn't offer you anything, but my mother raised me right. Want something to drink?"

"I'm good, do you know if Dutch is busy?"

Trisha opened her freezer and took out a container of vanilla ice cream and placed it on the counter. She gave me a blank look. "Why would I know whether he's busy or not?"

I rolled my eyes. "Oh my God, because you are always in Dutch's business. And you know... you live next door to him."

She frowned. "Hey, I'm not that bad. I've been staying in my apartment and not driving him crazy for at least a week. Besides, with the guys all focused on your dad it's been pretty quiet here."

"So, Zeno hasn't been trying to get you to convince me to leave Tak?" I asked as I walked over to her.

Trisha shrugged. "No, not really. Zeno and Pops probably think it's better for them if you stay with Tak. It's not like you're going to run into anyone you know while you're with him."

Groaning, I covered my face. "You mean, like Gerald Harrison, the son of the man my father seems desperate for me to get to know?"

There was a beat of silence. "How in God's name did you run into him?"

Letting my hand drop from my face, I gave a quick rundown of what happened.

"I had the Roarke lawyers convince him it was in his best interest to let it go. Lucky for me he saw it my way and signed the NDA."

"Well, shit. And you're sure he hasn't told your father?" she asked as she made her concoction of banana, ice cream, and milk.

I wrinkled my brow in thought. "I haven't heard anything about it from him. You didn't answer me earlier. Is Dutch busy?"

"Yeah, he's been holed up all day in his apartment in a *Call of Duty* tournament."

Her expression turned mischievous. I wanted to hit her. Of course Trisha knew what Dutch was doing.

Before I could stop her, she'd already made her way out of the apartment toward Dutch's. The only choice I had was to follow her next door. When I entered his apartment, Dutch stood looking at Trisha like he wanted to toss her out the window. His monitors posted his rank and the sound of bullets flying in the background of the game were a clear indication his game was over, and he was out of the tournament. My guess, thanks to Trisha.

"Trisha, I'm going to count to three and if you don't give me a good reason for interrupting me, I'm going to burn every single Birkin in your closet."

Before Trisha completely riled Dutch up, I stepped forward. "I want to know what Julius, Zeno, and Uncle Carter are up to and why my father wanted me to meet with Senator Harrison's son."

Dutch immediately shot Trisha a dirty look. "You better thank God Julius told me Jazz was coming," he said this as he turned around and sat down at his computer.

With a few clicks of his fingers, the screen changed from Call of Duty to a bunch of numbers and documents I was barely able to keep up with.

Dutch continued. "We've been keeping track over the last two years of your father's business dealings. Originally, we were doing it in an effort to see if we could buy his shares in your family's company and buy his own company out, but last year we noticed a discrepancy in his accounting books. He's spending at a far higher rate than he's been earning. It's not going to take long before he ends up filing for bankruptcy."

I frowned. "Let me guess, the one who found the discrepancy was Julius."

Dutch and Trisha shared a look. Trisha was the one to break the silence first. "Yeah, since he's the one leading the investigation against your father."

"Okay, so what did you guys find out?"

"Well, we wondered how he was keeping his own company a float and we discovered an odd flow of money going from the Roarke Foundation to an offshore account. It didn't take long for us to find out he'd been using money from the foundation to keep his own cash flow in the black," Dutch explained.

"Julius believes your father approached Harrison to prepare for the possible investigation. Or he's hoping Harrison would stop it from happening in the first place. Either way, it's clear the payment for Harrison to do either is you."

A loud alarm completely disrupted the tension in the air. I mentally set aside the information my cousins had given me and turned my attention to the bright red flashing alert that'd popped up on his screen.

"What's that?"

Trisha took a bite of her ice cream as she said, "Since we weren't sure when those two guys would pop again. Dutch put trackers on their accounts and social media, so if there was any activity we would know."

"And by the looks of it, the one called Tony just got a huge amount of money," Dutch added. All three of us looked at the screen.

Trisha released a sharp whistle. "How many zeroes is that?"

"A lot." Suddenly, A chill ran through me. I took out my phone, opening the tracker used on Tak's phone. "Something doesn't feel right. I'm going to go find Tak."

"Now?" Trisha asked looking at me with worry.

I took out my key fob from my back pocket with my free hand. "Yeah." Turning my attention to Dutch, I asked, "Can you track who sent the money to him?"

"I can try, but the person who's been paying them has been using dummy accounts, so it'll be tough."

"Try, if you at least find a trail of any sort that'll be enough."

"Got it." Dutch's fingers flew over his keyboard.

I headed out and heard Trisha call after me. "Be careful, Jazz, don't do anything too reckless."

I rolled my eyes at that. "I'm the best driver in this building aside from Zeno. I'll see you guys later."

I hastily left, heading to the garage. That sudden deposit had me worried. The only reason Tony would have gotten such a huge amount of money out of nowhere is if the same people who'd paid him before had given him another job.

Even though this was all conjecture on my end, I still felt the need to find Tak right away. I ran down the stairs and exited for my black Lamborghini. Unlocking the car, I got in and pressed the start button.

I sped off, following the map on my phone. Silently, I prayed that Tak would be fine.

CHAPTER FORTY-TWO

Shots Fired

Tak

I listened to Deacon and Pit talk as they plotted out exactly what we'd do to catch who ever had it out for me. Personally, I knew I should have come to them right after my scandal and I wished I'd had the balls to admit I'd been too worried about what they'd say when I told them the truth.

Fear of not being believed still remained with me from my childhood. I felt shitty. I'd judged my crew as if they were the Nakamuras.

I watched as Luke said something dickish and got punched in the shoulder by Skittles. The urge to confess about the insecurities that had been haunting me since Pit and Skittle had become a couple rode me, but someone else came to mind when I thought about sharing my worries.

For some reason it felt wrong to tell anyone other than Jazz about them. Oddly, I felt like she'd understand me better than anyone else. I wanted to see her.

"Hey, where did you go?" Luke waved his hand in front of my face. "Earth to Tak."

I smacked his hand away. "I was thinking, so we're going to use my show as bait?"

Deacon and Pit nodded. Pit expression was serious. "As long as you're okay with us setting up a trap at the Ol' Bull. It's the perfect opportunity to create another *accident.* We'll be ready to catch them if they make a move."

"Okay, that makes sense," I agreed.

"If they show, we'll catch them," Skittles said. "Either way, I get beer and a concert. I think we all win here."

Pit shook his head. "I'll get Roman to get us maps and details of the bar and area around it and we'll start planning from there," Pit said to Deacon and Luke. "Depending on how they move, my guys will be ready to adapt immediately. My uncle is on it. Since things have been happening outside of Vander he's casting a wider net to see what we come up with."

My phone vibrated in my back pocket. I was going to ignore it but with the slim chance it could be Jazz, I pulled it out and checked the name only to find it was Kole. I answered it only because I was sure he was calling about my family.

"What happened between you and the Nakamuras?" Kole inquired before I could answer.

Knowing this was going to be a long conversation, I stood up. "I'll be back."

I walked out of the back room and through the casino to the bar.

"What happened?" Kole asked again.

"Simple, they didn't stick to the agreement. When I arrived not only was it more than one person, but Sakai was a little too hands on," I said.

"What, he touched you?"

Sure, he only touched my shoulder but Kole's protective ass didn't need to know that.

"Yep, and I laid his ass out because of it." If I could go back, I would beat him all over again.

There was silence for a moment. When he spoke again his voice was cold. "You no longer have to worry about doing the advertisement for Nakamura. Seeing as how they've violated the agreement; they will be paying us for their companies breach of contract."

"I wonder what should be said in a moment like this. Wait, I know. We shouldn't have accepted their offer in the first place.

"Let me make this clear, Kole. This will be the last time you push something like this on me. If you do this again, no matter how much you're respected in this industry, I'll accept your two weeks' notice with a fucking smile. Our partnership has always been convenient for me, but don't make me start to think it's more trouble than it's worth," I said.

I'd been playing his good artist since he'd discovered me. I never argued with how Kole ran JS Records or bragged about the fact I owned the record company. Back then, when I gave him the demo, I'd been too busy plotting my own demise.

As usual I'd failed at trying to off myself by climbing the tallest tree on campus, only to end up in the newspaper for saving a cat. The next morning, I woke up to a phone call from Kole, begging me to sign with him. At first, I'd told him to fuck off, he'd been working for a bloodsucking label and I wasn't interested in being controlled.

The next thing I knew, he'd quit his job with them and came to me with lint in his pocket and a heavy list of connections in his notebook, still asking for me to work with him. Twelve years later, not many knew it was my money that had created the foundation of JS Records.

"I'll forget to be polite and treat you like the rest of the shitty label execs out there," I added.

"Understood, I'll keep it in mind." He hung up.

I stared down at my phone, feeling like I'd regained some form of control over my life.

"Aren't you Tak Jensei?" someone asked from behind me.

I turned around and squinted when I saw a man standing a few feet away favoring his shoulder with one hand. "Yeah, what about it?"

It took a full second for me to realize he had lifted a gun with his other arm. "They said they don't care how, they just want you dead. So do me a favor and die this time."

Time seemed to slow down as he pulled the trigger.

"Tak." I looked right and saw Jazz running toward me. She hit my body just as the bullet exploded from the chamber. I felt her body jerk as we fell together and hit the ground hard.

"Shit," the stranger shouted as he turned to run.

The door behind me burst open and two shots were fired. "Get him," Pit shouted.

Roman and Ox took chase. I barely paid them any mind. My eyes were focused on the woman in my arms.

"Jazz," I shouted.

Sitting up, I watched her press her hand against her arm. Her face screwed up in pain. I felt my heart freeze at the sight of the blood escaping from between her fingers.

"I didn't think I would make it," she forced out.

Skittles walked over to our side. "We need to get her to the hospital.

"No shit," Jazz said with a pained laugh.

I moved to a kneeling position by her side and picked her up. "Can you drive?" I asked Skittles.

"Sure."

Jazz released a pained wince. "Don't worry, it just hit my arm."

"Shut up, don't talk right now or I may really fucking lose it."

I carried her over to my truck. Skittles ran ahead and opened the back door for me. "Thanks." I put Jazz inside and quickly got in behind her and pulled her into my arms.

Skittles walked to the driver's side and got in and tore out of the parking lot. My mind was a fucking mess as the image of Jazz getting shot repeated in my head over and over again. If the bullet had hit her somewhere else.

I gritted my teeth and told myself to focus on getting her to the hospital. I'd let myself think once she was safely in the hands of a doctor.

CHAPTER FORTY-THREE

His Story

Jazz

I held back from flinching as the doctor gave me a shot of anesthetic. I looked over to Tak who sat across from the bed I was on. Since he'd brought me here, he hadn't said a word.

The silence had grown almost cold. It would have been difficult to talk anyway. The minute we entered and the nurse saw my bleeding arm I'd been dragged off.

The doctor kept telling me I was lucky the bullet hadn't hit a major artery as he stitched me up. I closed my eyes. Even if the wound had been a bit worse, I wouldn't have changed my decision to save Tak. He suddenly stood up and with a dark expression he stepped out.

"Okay, you're good for now," the doctor said once he finished bandaging my arm. "We're going to have to ask you to stay and wait to speak with an officer. We have to report it when anyone comes into our building with a gun wound. Sorry for the inconvenience."

"No, I understand."

I avoided his gaze. Speaking with the police could put me in an iffy spot. As long as they didn't do any sort of background check on my identity, there shouldn't be any problem.

Just in case, I texted Dutch for help. The doctor left the room, leaving me alone with my gloomy thoughts.

Tak

As I stormed out of the room Jazzy was in, I ran into Skittles in the hallway. Seeing my expression, she grabbed my arms and stopped me.

"What's wrong?"

Where did I begin? There was so much going on in my head, I felt like I would explode at any minute. I'd watched as the doctor had exposed Jazz gunshot wound and the sight of her blood spilling down her arm had tapped into something I'd long ago learned how to pretend didn't exist.

Fear.

Skittles looked me over. She finally said, "Let's go outside. It took some work, but I got you this." She lifted her other hand and in it was a Twinkie. "Does this work?"

I looked from the Twinkie to her before I said, "It'll have to do, let's go."

Together we walked out of the exit that led to the break area. I made a beeline for the bench and slumped down and pressed the heels of both my hands to my forehead.

Skittles eventually took a seat next to me. "Want to talk about it?"

"Not really, but if I don't I feel like my head will fucking explode."

"Been there," Skittles said. "Let me guess, you're in love with the girl who saved you. Jazz, is that her name?"

I stilled and dropped my hands so that they rested on my thighs as I turned my head to look at Skittles. "Is it that fucking obvious?"

"Sure is, if you saw the way you looked at her, you'd make fun of yourself."

I groaned. "Fuck."

"Trust me, I completely understand."

I looked away from her and thought over my next words. "Skittles, I… I never gave a shit about my own life. I tried. I don't know how many fucking times to see just how much the universe was against me dying. I tried my best to test it over and over again, even the fucking night I met you and the others I was playing poker with the cards I'd been dealt."

"Tak," she said my name with a wealth of love I'd never received from those who shared the same blood as me.

"But I've never been this scared." I pressed a hand to my chest and squeezed. "I don't think they're any words to describe how my heart froze when she jumped in front of me or how much I wanted to murder that bastard who shot her."

The crinkling sound of the Twinkie package caught my attention before Skittles held it out to me and spoke. "That's definitely love. I think now you get it. How Pit and I feel about each other. What I was hoping you would begin to see. You're hopelessly in love, sweetie."

I took the Twinkie from her as she continued. "To be honest, it's scary as fuck to love someone to this degree. I was terrified when I admitted to myself that I was falling. I love Pit with my heart and soul. That man drives me crazy, but I couldn't go a day without him in my life."

"Wow, I feel like I'm listening to my parent talk about her love life." I took a bite of the Twinkie she handed me.

Skittles smacked my arm. "Shut up, I'm trying to be serious."

"I think I speak for everyone and myself when I say that you and Pit's love story makes me feel both nervous and fearful for my health."

She rolled her eyes at me. "Fuck it, just answer this. Do you love her?"

"Yes," I answered without having to think about it long.

"Then that's all you need, just don't fuck it up."

Eating the rest of the Twinkie in two bites, I shot her a cocky look. "I don't plan on it."

We went back inside to find Jazz in the hallway talking to a pair of cops. She looked so tired, she didn't even notice when we returned.

"Thanks for your cooperation, we'll contact you once we have more information." One of the cops said before he shot us a greeting as he and his partner left.

Walking over to Jazz, I gently grabbed her wrist and pulled her to my side. "How are you feeling?"

She wrinkled her nose at me. "We're talking again. I thought you were mad at me."

"I'm not mad at you," I said, flicking the tip of her nose. "I'm mad that you put your life in danger for me. I don't like seeing you get hurt."

With her wound-free arm, she smacked my hand away. "It's a part of my job and I don't like the alternative, which would be you getting hurt."

Both of us were so focused on each other, when Skittles cleared her throat, we looked at her in surprise. We'd completely forgotten she was there.

"Shit, I forgot you were here," I said.

Giving a chaffed look, she said, "Wow, and all the warm fuzzies from our heart-to-heart turns to smoke just like that." She turned her eyes to Jazz, her expression softened. "Sorry, I tried to raise Tak with manners, but he and the rest of the idiots in my crew just can't seem to use them."

"I am the best one out of the entirety of our crew. You're just bias," I complained.

Jazz laughed and said to Skittles, "Yeah, I've noticed his lack of manners."

"Jazz," I pouted down at her. "I've been very nice to you. Remember the move I did in the shower."

"So, your name is Skittles, right?" Jazz nearly yelled over me, giving me a warning look. I shot her a naughty look before I decided to leave her alone and I let her and Skittles talk.

"Yep, that's me," Skittles said.

"How long have you known Tak?" Jazz asked.

"Since he was a teenager and he thought it was cool to look like John Bender from *The Breakfast Club*," Skittles joked.

Skittles and Jazz both snickered together. An odd sense of contentment filled me from seeing the woman I saw as my older sister and the woman I'd figured out I loved getting along. The sound of a phone ringing cut in and Skittles reached into her pocket and pulled out her cell.

"Well, it looks like my ride's here. Jazz, it was nice meeting you and Tak make sure you call Pit when you get home."

"No can do, I'll be fucking my woman tonight."

Jazz smacked my arm. "Tak."

Skittles rolled her eyes. "Whatever, we reply to your texts while fucking all the time, make it happen, my man-child," she said before she left.

We followed her example, leaving the hospital to head home. It didn't take long for Jazz to fall asleep. I stayed up thinking about everything I needed to make sure her life was never in danger again.

CHAPTER FORTY-FOUR

The Reveal

Tak

I stood in the meeting room of the JS Records building, looking out the window. I'd debated for two nights after returning home with Jazz on whether I would tell Kole about what was going on or not. After thinking it over, I decided it would be smarter to tell him and the others.

Especially since I planned on using our concert as possible bait for my wannabe killers. The door opened behind me. I turned around and watched as Kole entered along with Chelsea and my band members. Jay gave me a searching look as he walked over to my side.

"Do you know how shocked I was when I got a text message from you this morning?"

"As shocked as I was when you insisted on buying the top you're currently wearing." I gave his shirt a disgusted look. It was covered in smiling kittens.

"Much better than wearing torn pants as a fashion statement," Jay snarked back.

I looked down at my jeans. "At least my balls can breathe, how are yours doing?" Clicking my tongue, I gave his crotch a pitying look. "Those poor suffocated balls."

"Did you call us all here to watch you and Jay argue?" Chelsea asked from where she'd taken a seat at the head of the table.

"No, I called you all here because I'm trying to catch the person who's trying to kill me."

Everyone looked at me with varying levels of flabbergasted expressions. Not that I cared, it was refreshing to finally be able to say it openly. I walked over to the conference table and took a seat.

Kole spoke first. "Are you saying you finally remember something?"

"Wait a minute, what the fuck are you talking about?" Jay says.

"I told you, my attempted suicide was someone else's doing." I took my phone out and placed it on the tabletop and slid it over to Jay. "The pictures on there are of them carrying my body to my room."

Pit's people had finally been able to get the untampered footage from the hotel. Jay picked up my phone and looked at it, his expression turned ashen. "How long have you known about this?"

"Well, I couldn't remember anything after entering the parking garage. So, at the time, I wasn't too sure, but when the studio light fell, I knew something was up. I called in a favor with a friend of mine to look into it."

Chelsea looked at me in worry. "Have you figured out yet who it is?"

"You're really a fucking asshole," Ark said.

I placed a hand on my chest in shock. "Now Ark, if your fans knew just how dirty your mouth was, they'd be disappointed."

He glared at me. "How the fuck could you hide this from us for this long? It's been nearly two and a half months since your suicide scandal. If you even suspected for a second that it was set up, you should have told us."

"You're right."

"Did you just say he's right?" Omar asked, clearly taken a back.

"Yeah, I've been in my own head and I just assumed you guys wouldn't believe shit I said. I've worked through it, which is why I decided today to tell you everything."

"We should contact the proper authorities and tell them what's going on," Kole said, looking to Jay who had handed him my phone.

I tapped my fingers on the table. "Well, last night when I went out to meet with some friends one of the guys from that night in Vegas showed up and tried to shoot me."

The silence was deafening.

I continued. "Luckily, Jazz managed to save me, but she put her life on the line to do it. There's already a police report in."

Jay turned to Ark, who's face had turned red. "I won't stop you if you punch him. In fact, I'll hold him down for you."

"Okay, I want to know why you decided to tell us now?" Omar said.

"Because when I initially started investigating, I thought it could be Kole, but I quickly abandoned that idea. Now that I still don't have answers, I've decided to play the role of bait to end this once and for all."

"If I wanted to kill you, I'd just cut your brake cables and treat you to my best whiskey," Kole cut in.

I gave him a long look. "Thought about it a lot, have you?"

He just gave me a mysterious smile in answer.

I squinted my eyes at him. "Okay, well in order to wrap this shit up and get our hands on the culprit, my friends and I have decided to use our concert as the bait. The goal is to give them easy access to me, so they can make a move and from there everything else should go smoothly."

"Are you sure about that?" Jay asked. "What if they don't come?"

"Then I'll turn everything over to the proper authorities," I answered easily.

"Why don't you do that now?" Chelsea asked. "If they are willing to shoot you out in the open, that means they're sure they'll get away with it."

"And that's why I don't want to hand it over to the authorities yet. Something tells me they'd get arrested then someone would get paid off and they'll be back on the street. Like what happened to the asshole who tried to cave my head in. This way, we cut the head off the snake."

"What makes you think your friends can do that?" Ark asked.

I gave him an amused look. "This is the kind of shit they're good at."

Jazz

Tak had left me sleeping and had gone to JS Records without me. I wanted to be angry, but there really wasn't any point. Especially when I considered the burning pain in my arm.

Getting out of bed, I walked into my bathroom. Tak had tried to bring me to his room last night, but I was determined to act like I at least wanted my job. Not to mention, with my wound, I knew I would probably spend the night tossing and turning.

I took a quick shower, while avoiding my arm. When I was done, I came out to my phone ringing. I picked it up and answered, "Hello?"

"We need to meet," Zeno answered. "I'll text you an address, be there in thirty." With that, he hung up.

I stared at my phone for a second before I tossed it back on the bed and went to my closet to get some clothes. Zeno had sounded more than a little upset.

Finished getting dressed, I called an Uber and headed to downtown Vander City.

***

Thirty minutes later, I sat across from my cousin Zeno in a small coffee shop.

"Let me get this straight. We told you to lay low, but instead, you go and get shot for some limp wristed rock star. You've done some ballsy stuff, but to think that you could take a risk like that without thinking twice about us is disappointing. You could have died."

I inwardly cringed at the anger in his voice. "How did you find out?"

"Julius told me."

"I thought he was busy investigating my dad," I said.

"He was down at the precinct dealing with another case when he overheard a cop mention your name," Zeno explained. "If it wasn't for that, he'd be here with me."

Honestly, between Zeno and Julius, I would have preferred it be Julius who'd come to chew me out. Julius wasn't as passionate as Zeno was. Zeno treated me like a little sister.

We were supposed to be going unnoticed, but my cousin with his Puerto Rican heritage and good looks had the eyes of every girl in the place on him. He was tall, a little over six-two, muscled, and kept his hair pulled up in a top knot. Zeno had been the one who'd reluctantly taught me how to steal cars and fight.

If Tak was the one who woke me up from my living coma. Zeno was the one who'd pulled me out of the ditch. He'd taken me under his wing and showed me the ropes of the world he lived in. So, I couldn't bring myself to look at him now. I hated to see the look of disappointment in his eyes.

"When Trisha told me what you were up to, I almost killed her and fucking Dutch, but I let it go. After we learned about some of the Ripaldi boys getting involved, I figured it was better to leave you with that guy. But now, this shit is getting too dangerous.

"Once people like that start using guns in public, it's a clear sign they don't care about who the fuck gets hurt. It's time you hand everything over to the police and bolt, Jazz."

"The same police who said my mother died by *accident?*" Indignation filled me at the fact he would even tell me to do such a thing. "I know the police well here in Vander City and Bridge Lake. They're the ones my father paid off to shut down the investigation into my mother's death as well as my accusations against him. I can't trust them."

"I'm sure they would actually do their jobs when it comes to your star," Zeno said, muttering something in Spanish.

I glared at him. "Is it so wrong wanting to protect someone I…" I trailed off.

Could I even say I loved him? Wouldn't Zeno say that my obsession had gone too far? He'd think I was crazy dragging a high school crush into adulthood.

"Look, I'm not going to leave until he's safe," I finished.

He weighed his words as he considered me with his dark gaze. "Okay, fine, I see you're going to be stubborn about this. I'm just going to ask you one thing. Does he still not recognize you?

"The guy you're doing all this for doesn't even remember you, Jazz. In my opinion, no matter what happens, he's not going to forgive you for lying to him."

I winced. His words hurt me far more then he knew. I looked away from him.

"Like I said before. I'm not doing this for him to remember me and as long as he's safe, I don't care if he doesn't forgive me for lying to him.

"I know I'm being selfish by insisting that I stay with Tak, but for the first time I can think of something outside of my father. I need this. I want to be near him."

"Do you love him?" Zeno asked.

I paused and looked away from him. "It doesn't matter how I feel."

"Dammit. If you're trying to live out some fantasy stop now. If you think he'll wake up one day and be madly in love with you, give that thought up. I've seen the gossip columns. Your singer isn't worth your loyalty."

"Good thing I'm not trying to make him my man then," I said, shooting him an annoyed look.

He didn't know anything about Tak. The one who was in the wrong here was me. I was the one who felt like I was playing with him.

"Zeno, it's not going to last more than another month. Once I get my hands on whoever it is trying to kill him, then I'll leave, don't worry."

He frowned before he suddenly stood up and pushed his chair back. "I'm going to give you a month to figure it out and after that, I'm going to drop a tip off to the police."

I followed his example and stood. "A month is fine. I'll figure it all out in a month."

He gave me a nod. Reaching out, he placed his hand on top of my head. Something he'd done since he'd taken me under his wing. "All right, don't get hurt and stay out of the cameras."

I smiled. "I'll try," I said, knowing things were good between us now.

Feeling my phone vibrate, I pulled it out of my pocket and saw it was Tak.

"Hi."

"Where are you?" he asked.

"I'm downtown at a café. I decided to meet with one of my friends." I walked with Zeno outside.

"Text me the name, I'll come and pick you up."

"Okay, I'll be waiting for you outside," I said before I hung up.

"Alicia, is that you?" I immediately lost my smile when I met the amused gaze of my half sister, Gloria.

I wanted to pretend I hadn't seen her, but that was nearly impossible with her standing right in front of me. Zeno had walked off, not bothering to acknowledge her. As the Liberius usually did when it came to my other family.

"I thought that was you. I almost didn't recognize you with these clothes." She looked over my cheap athletic wear. "And when did you cut your hair? Not to mention the contacts."

I looked around, trying to keep a low profile, and probably would have if she'd been dressed in nondescript clothes, but she was dressed from top to bottom in brands that drew the eye of everyone walking past. I glanced behind her and noticed a few men in suits who were just as eye catching. Feeling the growing attention coming in our direction made me nervous of being discovered.

"Do you know that dad's been driving himself crazy trying to get in touch with you?"

"No," I answered, replacing my phone in my back pocket.

She squinted her eyes at me. "You're making your life more difficult avoiding him like this."

I gave her a scornful look. "Shouldn't you be more worried about your life than mine?"

"What does that mean?" she demanded.

I shrugged, glancing at the road. Not seeing Tak's car yet, I looked back at her. "Nothing."

"Don't bullshit me, I know something's up. Let's be honest between sisters. Originally, Dad didn't seem to care about whether you were dead or alive.

"Now it's like all of a sudden he's become obsessed with getting back in your good graces. Personally, I think you should contact him and put him out of his misery. Then he'll stop stressing Mom and the rest of us out.

"It's been peaceful since you successfully ran away to your cousins, I want it to stay that way."

She'd wanted my attention and now she had it. "The reason your daddy is so interested in me is because he bit off more than he can chew and his company is about to go belly up," I snapped. "And he's looking for his daughter to fix that problem for him. Unfortunately, for both you and him, I have no interest in helping."

Her face turned pale. "You're lying."

I laughed. "Am I?" Spotting a familiar car, I added. "Do me a favor and act like you didn't see me here today." On that note, I walked toward Tak's car.

"You're lying," she said once more. I pretended to not hear her.

I opened the door and got in. Tak immediately took my hand in his and glanced at Gloria who I assumed was still standing there. "Someone you know?"

I shook my head. "No, she just wanted to know how to get to the mall."

Taking my answer as it was, he pulled off.

CHAPTER FORTY-FIVE

Lovers

Tak

After dealing with my band and Kole, the only thing I wanted to do was lay in bed with Jazz in my arms.

As I followed her into the house, I imagined all the things I would do to her once we were inside.

She took a right. I stopped her. "Where are you going?"

"My room," she answered, pulling at her button-down shirt. "I had to run out so fast. I want to take a shower and get some more sleep."

I pointed toward my wing. "My shower's bigger, go take one in mine."

She shot me a look, but instead of arguing with me, she walked toward my room. "The only reason I'm listening to you is because I've seen your shower and it is bigger."

"I'm going to check on something in the studio."

She waved me off as she walked away.

I watched her disappear around the corner before I took out my phone and texted Chelsea that I wouldn't be available tomorrow. Finished, I turned my phone off and tossed it on the couch. I didn't want anyone interrupting my time with Jazz.

Ever since I'd left her side this morning, I'd only thought about getting back beside her. After waiting a few minutes, I headed to my room.

The door was open and Jazz stood in the center of the room. I watched as she slowly took off her shirt. Her pants were already off and on the floor.

She paused as she tried to pull her sleeve down the arm she'd been shot in. I closed the space between us and wrapped my arms around her. "Let me help you with that." I leaned forward and pressed a kiss to the top of her head.

She looked at me over her shoulder but didn't say yes or no to my offer. I kept my eyes on hers as I reached up and gently pulled the shirt back off her shoulders and slid it down her arms, it fell to the floor without a sound.

"Tak?"

I walked around her and stopped in front of her. I reached up and buried my right hand in her hair and tilted her head back. Leaning down I took her lips with mine. She moaned into my mouth as she grabbed at my shirt. I plundered her mouth, tasting the sweetness that was Jazz, trying to consume her down to her soul.

I chased her tongue with mine. The soft sighs and sucking sounds filled my ears. With my other hand I rubbed and flicked her left nipple to a peak.

Breaking the kiss I straightened.

"Tak," she called my name, her voice thick with lust.

I smiled, more than pleased with myself for putting such a dazed look on her face. "Take off the rest of your clothes and lay on the bed."

Jazz didn't hesitate as she took off her bra and panties. I enjoyed the sight of her ass jiggling as she walked over to my bed and crawled onto it. It took everything in me not to jump her from behind. She was still injured, once she was healed up I'd fuck her from behind until she screamed my name.

"Turn around, love. Let me see your pussy."

She followed my orders once again. Turning around she sat down and spread her legs, presenting her pussy to me. I could already see she was glistening with need.

"Damn, baby. You're already wet for me."

She sucked her lip into her mouth.

I smirked. "Don't tell me I left you starving so much the mere sight of my dick makes you excited?"

She glared at me. "Shut up and fuck me already."

I laughed, but instead of doing what she wanted, I walked to the end of the bed. "You're so impatient, love. I've got to teach you how to take it slow." I licked my lips and narrowed my eyes. "I want you to touch yourself for me."

Jazz's expression turned shy and like always it made me want to make her dirty. "I... I..."

"Do it for me, love. Show me how you like to be touched."

She hesitated for a second, her lashes lowered as she scooted back a bit more so that her back touched the headboard of my bed. She bit her bottom lip as she brought her uninjured arm forward and slowly started to touch herself.

I swallowed, watching her as she pleasured herself. She circled and stroked her clit. Her short little pants of air filled the room. I balled my hands into fists at my sides to keep from touching her.

"That's my baby, show me what makes you come." At my words, she looked up and spread her legs wider. I wanted to be there between them. I just couldn't decide if I wanted to use my dick or my tongue first.

She grunted as she started to hump her hand, her fingers no longer rubbing her clit but dipping inside her. She panted, "Tak, I need more."

Shit, hearing my name on her lips nearly had me coming in my pants.

"What do you need, love? Tell me."

"You," she nearly cried as she continued fucking her hand. "It's not enough."

"Beg me," I ordered.

She didn't stop pleasuring herself when she nearly shouted, "Please, Tak. Fuck me."

I bared my teeth in a lecherous grin. "Good girl."

It took me no time at all to take my clothes off. My member bobbed. Shit, I was so hard I could break a block of cement with it. The best part was Jazz hadn't stopped pleasuring herself the entire time. Getting on the bed, I grabbed her hand and moved it aside. "That's enough, love. I'm here."

"Tak." Her eyes were bright with lust as she looked at me. "I need you."

"Fuck, same, love, same."

I nearly threw myself at her. I kneeled between her legs and placed my right hand on the headboard behind her shoulder then leaned forward. I sucked in a quick breath as she grabbed my length with her free hand and guided me into her hot pussy.

I bowed my head and watched as she slowly filled herself with my cock. Her head dropped back as she bit her lip, her lashes fluttered against her cheeks as a deep groan of pleasure escaped her. This was hands down the fucking sexiest thing I'd seen.

Watching Jazz take me inside was only second to eating her out. Sweat built on my brow as I held back from thrusting forward. I wanted to watch my woman pleasure herself on me.

This was about her, not me. She released me and moved her hand around my waist to my ass and as she lifted her hips she tugged. Her mouth dropped open.

"Fuck, yes."

Her deep-throated groan flipped a switch, breaking my restraint. I took control, snapping my hips forward. Placing my other hand on the other side of her head, I used it as leverage to fuck her into my mattress.

The bed squeaked with every deep penetrating dip into her delicious pussy. It sucked on me just like a mouth. Fire licked up my balls as I grinded inside of her. "Spread your legs wider for me, love," I managed to get out.

She shook her head from side to side. "I… I can't. Tak, I can't."

I let go of the headboard and stopped. Scooting back, I then wrapped my arms around her thighs and lifted them as I dragged her down. She let out a startled shriek as she slid forward.

I settled her legs on my shoulders and reached down to grab her hands to hold her still. I didn't wait for her to recover as I impaled her once more.

"Shit, that's it."

I gritted my teeth as I fucked her until she threw her head back and screamed my name. She slapped her hand at my thigh. Her pussy tightened around me and I paused, letting her orgasm run its course.

Grinning, I squeezed her hands as I waited for her. Those pretty eyes regained some clarity. "Jazz, baby, don't relax yet," I said.

"Huh… Tak," she cried my name out as I started the process all over again. I had every intention of making it so she couldn't walk tomorrow.

She'd been working for me about two months, and we had to make up for all that time missed. I was glad she hadn't insisted on my wearing a condom. Jazz was mine, and the idea of filling her with my cum and watching her body change with our child filled me with a dizzying lust and hunger. I offered a devil's smile as she pleaded for me.

"Don't worry love, I'm here. I'll always be here."

Jazz

"Fuck, Jazz, I missed this."

"Shit," I cried out as he once again thrust all the way to the hilt. I bit my lip as I tightened and tried not to scream through another orgasm. "Tak."

He gently pulled out, forcing me to feel every inch of him. "You feel so fucking good." He leaned forward and used his wicked voice to whisper in my ear. "You're perfect for me, you know that?"

My pussy clenched in response to his voice. He thrust in and started moving again. I could only hum as he brought my legs together and started grinding into me.

"Yes, fuck yes," I moaned.

I was completely under his control. Orgasming again, I closed my eyes, biting my bottom lip hard enough to break the skin. I tasted the blood in my mouth.

Tak didn't stop moving, his breathing came hard as he nearly sang my name in my ear. I rolled my eyes back as he pounded me right through one orgasm into another. It was like a live wire had been set on fire.

"Ah, fuck, I'm... shit, Jazz."

His shaft expanded inside me and I felt the warm splash of his semen filling me. I could only moan as he thrust forward twice more before he collapsed on me. I wrapped my arms around him as he lazily nuzzled into my neck.

"I love you," he breathed into my ear.

"I love you, too," I whispered, feeling a sudden wave of fear rush through me. I truly loved him, and I was lying to him.

CHAPTER FORTY-SIX

Plan C

Tak

Two weeks later...

The bar Ol' Bull was filled with the lighting and sound crew as they worked on the stage. A large banner that read, *In Honor of Mira* hung over the stage. The line outside wrapped around the building as fans had started arriving that morning.

Some were holding posters, other's had fan lights. I knew it would be arrogant of me to say that I'd expected it, but I did. I checked the time on the wall clock of our trailer that had been parked behind the bar. There was still an hour until the doors of the bar opened.

"Are you sure you want to do this?"

I looked away from the clock and met Ark's worried gaze. "It's still possible to report everything and let the police handle it."

"Ark, no. With the amount of security Kole has out there its more likely they won't even try anything."

Ark ran a frustrated hand through his hair. "Fine, I won't ask again."

"Thank you, because I sincerely don't want to answer you again," I said, coming to my feet. I walked over to the door and stepped outside. "Jazz."

She stood next to the exit along with a few other men, some belonging to our company, others belonging to Pit. I let the door to the trailer close behind me.

"Aren't you supposed to be inside the bar?" I asked.

"I was, but I'm giving the guy who was here a break," she explained.

I reached out and brushed her hair behind her ear. She flushed. Pride filled me from the sight. I was the only one who got the pleasure of making her look nearly bashful.

Chelsea asked me a few weeks ago about our relationship, and I'd been completely honest. I wouldn't lie about the singular most important thing to me.

"We're fucking and I have every intention of getting her pregnant and marrying her," I said as the makeup artist put final touches on my face.

Chelsea sighed. "I don't know why I even bother telling you to watch what you say."

I motioned to the makeup artist and my stylist, who continued to work as if I'd never said anything. "They're used to it and why should I hide it. The worst that will happen is you'll tell Kole and he'll fire her. Also, thank you in advance for that, because I'm more than a little invested in having her home so I can spoil her."

And that was the truth. I kissed Jazz in front of others and boldly told people we were dating every chance I got. For the first time, I'd hoped that fucker Kole would catch us and strictly follow the rules.

So far, I swear that bastard was acting like he hadn't seen anything on purpose. And my faith in Chelsea had completely evaporated since she'd obviously not reported anything. And so the weeks had passed like this and I'd grown more in love with her.

No matter how many times I'd told her she should quit and let me take care of her, she had ignored me, but that's what I loved about her. Jazz was stubborn and passionate about the things she cared about. Which is why I'd made sure no one told her about my plans tonight.

The last thing I needed was her throwing herself into harm's way. I couldn't deal with seeing her hurt again and I would protect her no matter what.

"Don't worry, I'm only giving him a restroom break," she said.

I wrapped my arms around her and hauled her to my side.

"Why don't we sneak off and do some personal training?" I gave her a heated look.

She returned my look with a stern one. "If your training is anything like the pep talk you gave me yesterday then you're going to miss your own concert."

I bit my lip, giving her a come-hither look. I leaned forward to whisper in her ear. "Don't act like you didn't enjoy it. Especially when I had your ankles up by your ears."

I staggered back from the force of her shove. Something I'd learned over the last few weeks was that Jazz had a real big kink for my voice. She would flush so hard, and her pussy would become a plush, wet welcoming home when I whispered sultry naughty things to her.

She glared at me before she looked at something behind me. "Look, he's back. It's time for me to go back inside."

She turned on her heels and walked into the bar through the back entrance. Once she was gone, I dropped my smile and pulled my phone out of my back pocket. Roman had texted me that everything was ready.

I replaced my phone and reentered my trailer. Everything would come to an end tonight and I would finally be able to enjoy peace with Jazz.

Jazz

I couldn't shake the feeling that something was going on I didn't know about. Everyone wore tense expressions. Even Ark didn't look like his usual cheerful self. I'd thought for the longest it might be nerves.

However, something in my gut told me that wasn't the case. I stood near the entrance of the bar and watched as the fans entered. Each one wearing a bright expression of anticipation.

A bittersweet smile came to my lips. Mitchell and Tony had slipped out of sight. Dutch hadn't found anything. The money that had been deposited into Tony's account had disappeared in what seemed like overnight.

I knew the time for me to leave Tak was coming closer and closer. I'd promised Zeno after a month I'd leave. Who knew that keeping such a promise would feel akin to tearing my heart out?

I tried on several occasions to pull back and build some walls between Tak and me, but it was impossible. I was already too in love with him to turn back now. The only option left for me was to accept the inevitable end.

"Hey, Jazz, the bar staff needs help moving some merch boxes to the front. Can you go help them?" One of the security guards asked.

"Sure, where are they?"

"The break room, it shouldn't take that long. The only reason I'm asking is because it has gotten too crazy for the rest of us to handle it. And there shorthanded in the back," he said.

I made my way to the back. The break room was across from the entrance to the stage where Tak would be performing along with his band. Pushing the door open, I spotted the stack of boxes in the corner. There weren't a lot. I walked over and picked up two and turned around to head back out.

Just as I reached the door, it opened. Taking a step back, I watched as an employee of the Ol' Bull entered with an envelope in his hand.

Spotting me, he asked, "Are you Alicia Roarke?"

I stiffened hearing my real name come out of his mouth. Seeing my expression, he hesitated. "Sorry, did I get the wrong person?"

Recovering, I turned and placed the boxes back down. Freeing my hands in case he wasn't as innocent as he seemed. "No, that's me. How can I help you?"

"Oh, thank God, for a minute there I thought I got the wrong person. The guy pointed you out, but he left before I could make sure he really meant you. Did you know you share the same name as a famous heiress in Vander City?" he said as he handed me the envelope.

I took the envelope, ignoring his question, and asked instead, "Do you know the name of the guy who asked you to give it to me?"

"No, he just said it was important," he said as he turned around and headed back through the door.

Once he left, I looked down at the envelope in my hand. I couldn't think of anyone aside from my cousins who would send me anything, but they wouldn't have risked my fake identity getting discovered by giving my real name. My father didn't know where I was, if he had he'd have already been knocking down Tak's door, not sending me mail.

Thinking it over, I flipped the envelope back and forth in my hand debating on whether or not I wanted to open it. I decided the only way I could end my curiosity was to open it. Breaking the seal, I then took a peek inside.

It looked to be a few photos and two pieces of paper. I took them out. My gaze landed on the first photo and my heart hammered. It was as if I'd lost all awareness of my surroundings as I stared at a picture of my mother at the bottom of the steps.

Her limbs twisted this way and that. My hands started to tremble. I quickly looked at the next picture of my father running away from our estate, his expression a mixture of anger and fear.

I moved the picture and looked at the two papers. The top of the first paper read, *Witness statement.*

As I slowly read through it, my head started to spin as a nauseous sensation filled my stomach. For years I'd known something wasn't right about my mother's death. And it turned out I'd been right all along.

A red haze covered my vision as I crushed the incriminating evidence in my hands. I ran out of the room, passing Jay who had been heading toward the back exit. Pushing the exit door open, I ran over to the street and looked both ways.

I frantically searched for a passing taxi. Spotting one up the street dropping off a few fans, I ran over to it. I nearly shoved the ones exiting out of the way.

My name was shouted behind me. I glanced over my shoulder, catching a glimpse of Tak who'd come from the same direction I'd just come from.

"Jazz, where are you going?"

I closed my eyes and turned away from the clear worry in his voice and got in, slamming the door. "Take me to Markers Street."

I'd explain everything to Tak later. All I could think about was the man who'd stolen the most important thing from me. I pulled my phone out and called Zeno.

"Jazz?"

"I'm going to kill him. I knew it was him who'd done it."

Finally, my shock abated, replaced by rage and sorrow. My throat tightened.

"What?" confusion colored his voice. "Slow down. What happened?"

"That bastard, Clark. He's the one who killed my mom, Zeno," I nearly yelled into the phone. "I knew it, I knew it."

"Didn't you agree to leave him to me and Dad. Look, wherever you are, stop and wait for me to come to you."

"No. I'm done with letting you and Uncle Carter handle everything." I looked down at the photos and papers crushed in my left hand. My tears slipped down my cheeks and fell on the back of my fist. "I'm going to end this. Once and for fucking all."

"Jazz? Jazz—" I hung up and put my phone on silent.

CHAPTER FORTY-SEVEN

Showtime

Tak

As planned, Jay and the others had already left my trailer. They were supposed to act as if they'd had another disagreement with me and had left me behind in a huff. Leaving me alone to get attacked, even the security that been hanging around had been told to drop back.

Pit had Roman place a tracker on me so they could follow my would-be killers if they tried to kidnap me. A few minutes had already passed and I was starting to grow antsy.

Where were they?

I couldn't shake the anxiety that crawled in my stomach. I kept feeling as though I'd missed something, something particularly important but for the life of me, I couldn't figure it out.

The door to my trailer was shoved open as Jay ran inside. He frantically looked around before his panicked gaze landed on me. "Oh, thank God, you're all right."

Releasing a breathless laugh, he pressed a hand to his chest. "When I saw Jazz run out this way, I thought something had happened."

"What?" I stood, walking over to him. Something telling me the feeling I'd had was right. "When did you see her running?"

He motioned behind him. "A few seconds ago, but she ran toward the street and not the trailer."

I pushed past him and ran out toward the street. I looked both ways and spotted Jazz holding the door of a taxi. I shouted, but she barely spared me a look before she got in and the taxi took off.

"Fuck."

Something wasn't right.

Spotting a familiar SUV across the street I ran over to it, ignoring the loud honks of drivers who'd been passing. Reaching the other side, I grabbed the door handle and snatched the door open. A gun met my gaze before Roman drew it back.

"Shit."

I didn't even spare him a thought as I got in. "Follow that taxi that just pulled off," I ordered.

He placed the gun down and immediately started the SUV, whipping into traffic. It didn't take long for a driver like Roman to get within a two-car distance of the taxi Jazz had gotten into.

"Does this have something to do with the two guys trying to kill you?"

I didn't answer him as I tried to call Jazz for the third time. Again, my call went to her voicemail. My heart was racing as my hands grew hot with sweat.

"Fuck, Jazz answer the phone dammit," I shouted.

Squeezing the phone in my hand, I almost broke it. My eyes zeroed in on the taxi ahead of us.

Where was she going?

My phone rang and I quickly answered. "Jazz?"

"Tak, where the fuck are you going?" Pit shouted. "Ox just sent me a message that you'd disappeared from your own fucking concert. What happened to the plan?"

"The woman I fucking love may be in danger." I swallowed, my mouth dry from the level of anxiety that ran through me. "I'm sorry but she's more important to me."

"Don't apologize," Pit cut me off. "I'll tell Ox to follow behind you to make sure nothing gets out of hand."

I shuddered and lowered my head. "Pit, I don't know what I'll do if something happens to her because of me."

"Nothing's going to happen to her. I'm telling you as your big brother, nothing will happen to her. And if those fuckers put their hands on her, I'll give every one of them a long good night personally."

That meant a lot coming from him. He didn't get his hands dirty for anyone that didn't own the name Skittles. Knowing Pit and the things he was capable of, I felt some of my anxiety melt away. "Thanks."

"You're welcome, now pull that pussy of yours together and go save your woman."

The phone line went dead. I wiped a hand down my face, regaining some of my composure. I'd find out what happened to Jazz and if it was someone who'd tried to use her against me. I'd kill them.

CHAPTER FORTY-EIGHT

Confrontation

Jazz

The taxi had barely pulled up to my father's house when I'd tossed the few twenties in my back pocket at the driver and got out. I didn't spare the gate guard a look as I walked up the long driveway to the front of my father's mansion.

"Ma'am, ma'am," he called after me. I didn't stop, my mind solely focused on getting to the person inside. A hand landed on my shoulder. "Ma'am, I'm sorry, but you can't... Argh."

I grabbed his wrist and with a two-step move, I twisted his arm behind his back and turned his hand so that he released a pained cry.

"I'm Alicia Roarke and I'm here to see my father."

I finished telling him who I was and shoved him away, I continued up the driveway to the front door and knocked.

After a few minutes, the door was opened by one of my father's staff. I pushed past them and entered the house.

"Where is he?"

The butler pointed to the right. "H… he's in the living room."

I had dreamed about the moment my father would pay for what he'd done to me and my mother. He was the reason behind the horrible nightmares I had into adulthood. He was the reason the place that should have been a home had become the site of my mother's death.

Every birthday I'd spent alone without her was because of him. He'd ruined my entire life overnight and acted as if nothing had happened.

"Tell Gloria if she can get her sister to visit, I'll give her another car," he said. "It shouldn't be this fucking hard to have my own daughter visit me."

"Don't forget about me, Dad. I'm the reason she actually came to the banquet," Aaron said.

I could see his peasant posture in my mind's eye. His mouth open and eyes greedy.

"Don't worry, the minute we get back to Vander City I'll give you the money you asked for."

Again, he was treating his mutt better than the daughter of the woman he'd betrayed. I stopped in the doorway and spotted a small iron statue with a sharp almost knife-like top on the table. Picking it up, I entered the room.

"You," Aaron exclaimed when he saw me. Obviously, he hadn't been expecting me to pop up so suddenly.

Clark looked at me with what seemed to be astonishment from where he sat on the living room couch.

"I warned you. I told you if I ever found out you had something to do with my mother's death, I would kill you," I said as I walked toward him.

I reached into my back pocket where I had shoved the papers and tossed them at his feet. "It looks like someone else had the balls to tell me the truth."

Clark's gaze fell on the pictures at his feet. I watched as recognition entered his eyes before fear followed swiftly after. He jumped up. "Wait, stop this, Alicia. Stop."

I tightened my hold on the statue and pointed it at him. "If it wasn't for you, if you didn't exist, my mother would be here."

"Don't do this, Alicia. You can't kill him," Aaron urged from the side.

I ignored him and continued walking toward Clark.

"You killed her. Don't you think it's only right that you die now? You've enjoyed a long life, while she... she didn't." My throat was choked by my tears.

I stopped right in front of him and pressed the pointed end of the statue against his throat.

"Alicia," he screeched. "Please, you don't want to do this."

An eerie calm came over me. "I do, I really do." My hand trembled so I grabbed the statue with both palms. "I want to do it for every birthday she missed. For every time I had to visit her grave. I have to because she never had a chance to see me become the woman I am today. Killing you won't bring her back, but at least you'll be dead too."

Shaking, he glanced behind me. I whipped around and pointed my weapon at Aaron who'd taken a step toward me. "Don't."

He recoiled immediately.

I glared. "Don't think I won't hurt you."

I turned around in time to catch Clark trying to run. Running after him, I cornered him against the wall. "Let's just end this now." I pulled my arm up.

"No." His eyes opened wide in horror.

"Jazz, stop," someone shouted. A set of strong arms wrapped around me and lifted me up in the air.

"No," I screamed. The statue slipped from my hands, hitting the carpeted floor with a muted thud. "No. Let me go." I managed to turn around in the person's arms and tried to attack them. "Let go."

"Jazz, baby, you've got to stop."

I could barely hear beyond the loud screams in my head to get my hands on my father. I pushed at the person who held me. I wailed as I lost strength.

"He killed my mother," I shouted. My body was gathered up, but I refused to stop screaming. "He killed my mother."

All I could see was my father smug face as he'd told me lie after lie. I wanted to tear his face off. As I was dragged back, I slowly lost my will to fight and stopped shouting. I could only turn my face into the chest of the person who held me. I closed my eyes and chose to sink into silence.

Tak

I held Jazz in my arms as her body trembled. Her screams still echoed in my ears. I looked over at the stone statue that sat on the floor.

If I'd been a few minutes later, the woman in my arms would have been lost to me forever. I tightened my hold on her as the man who she had attacked staggered, his features twisted.

"You… you." He pointed at me as he stared from Jazz back to me. "It's because of you she…"

His gaze went to the papers that were still on the ground. Running over to them he picked them up and started tearing them to pieces. "Lies, these are nothing but lies."

He turned his panicked expression to me. "This is payback because of you. If he didn't want you dead so badly this would never have happened."

I frowned. "You know who's trying to kill me?"

He sneered, his gray eyes showing nothing but disgust. "Don't you wish I did?"

"Well, whether you know or not, it doesn't change that you're going to prison for the murder of Lydia Roarke, does it, Clark?" someone spoke up from behind me with a faint Spanish accent.

I turned and found two men. One of them was an older gentleman with salt and pepper-colored hair. He wore a black suit and radiated a dangerous vibe.

I also noticed Ox had followed me inside. He had the young man who'd looked like he was about to sneak out the door in hand.

"Fuck, let me go," he shouted as he struggled in Ox's hold. "Do you know who I am, I am Aaron Bennington. If you don't let me go, I'll have your ass in court for assault."

Ox didn't even blink at the asshole's threat.

I frowned. "Shut him up, Ox."

Ox slammed a fist into the bastard's face, shutting him up instantly.

I turned my attention back to the older man and the other guy that stood next to him, who's eyes weren't on Clark, but Jazz who was in my arms. Not recognizing them, I turned so he couldn't look at Jazz.

Seeing my move, he met my gaze, a provoking smirk taking over his lips. I ignored the challenge in his eyes.

"Carter, what the fuck are you doing here?" Clark turned his accusatory glare toward me. "Did you bring him here?"

"This is my first time meeting you fuckers," I answered honestly.

To be even more honest, I was totally in the dark about what was going on around me. The only thing I knew for sure was Jazz was important to me and I'd didn't give a shit about anyone else in the room.

"Clark." The voice of the man I assumed to be Carter came out like a hiss. "You've been a thorn in my side for too long, so I'm going to tell you in detail what's going to happen.

"In the next ten minutes, the police are going to come through that door and you're going to tell them everything, from killing your ex-wife to drugging Jazz when she was a minor so that you could control her family's money, and how you manipulated her deteriorating grandfather. Don't leave a single thing out. If you don't do as I say, I'm going to handle you like I've dreamed of doing."

Clark sputtered. "You… you don't have any proof."

Carter smiled as he reached inside his suit jacket and pulled out a few pictures. "It looks like the same fairy godmother who delivered proof to Jazz also took the initiative to send me the same information." He tossed them to the floor in front of Clark, who stared down at them in astonishment.

"And don't worry, there are plenty of copies. Even a set sitting on my nephew's desk. You remember Julius, the prosecutor, of course."

Clark fell to his knees. "S… stop, please. I'll do whatever you say. Anything, anything you want. I didn't mean to do it. She just… just wouldn't listen to me."

All I needed was for her to give me a little bit of what she had… just a small amount, but she refused. She called me trash. Told me she wished she'd never met me. I… I snapped. I didn't mean to kill her," he begged.

I tightened my hold on Jazz when what this piece of shit had done started to click. I started to regret that I'd stopped her from killing this dickless fucker in front of me.

"You can tell the police all about it when they get here." He glanced at the man behind him. "Zeno, take Clark to see your cousin, he should be here by now."

"On it." Zeno walked forward and grabbed Clark's arm and dragged him toward the exit. He stopped only long enough to tell Ox to follow him out with Aaron.

Ox glanced at me, and I gave the go ahead. The two of them headed out. Clark seemed to have lost his mind as he continued to repeat over and over, "I didn't mean to."

I looked down at Jazz. I wondered if she was even aware of what was happening. She clung to me like a child, her eyes closed as she shivered.

"Are you taking her to the car?" Carter asked.

"Yes, I'm going to take her to the hospital."

He gave me a long look. "After this is handled, I'll come to the hospital. I think there are some things you need to know about my niece, Alicia."

Alicia?

I had questions all right, but I held them in. I needed to get Jazz some help. That was the only clear thought I had.

"Got it, I'll see you later," I said.

With that, I made my way back toward the entrance, running into Zeno who stood in the foyer talking with a police officer. He only gave me a passing look as I walked by him.

I spotted a picture hanging next to the door. It was of Clark and a little girl in a yellow dress.

I paused and looked at it for a second before I continued walking outside toward the gate. To my right I knew my family mansion stood only a few miles away, behind the tall trees and high walls. An old memory came to the forefront of my mind.

A little girl sat in front of me in a bright yellow dress, covered in grass stains. Her warm almond skin was flushed. She lifted her bundle of flowers up to me. "Look what mommy gave me."

I looked over her flowers and felt shy when I said, "Pretty."

She gave me a bright smile, her gray eyes shining with happiness. "Mommy said I'm like these flowers. Pretty."

I scratched at one of the scabs on my cheek. "What's your name?"

She screwed up her nose. "Alicia, but my mommy calls me Jazz."

I looked down at the peaceful expression of the woman in my arms. She'd snuggled into my hold. I lifted her up and pressed my lips to her forehead.

"I'm sorry I didn't recognize you."

Getting into the SUV, I said, "We need to get to the hospital."

Roman gave me a nod. I moved Jazz so she rested against my side. Taking hold of her hand, I promised myself I'd never let her go again.

CHAPTER FORTY-NINE

Liberiu

Tak

An hour later, I sat by Jazz's bedside staring at her sleeping face. The doctor had prescribed her some meds. He said to make sure she was fine they would keep her to monitor her overnight.
I'd already called Pit and everyone else to let them know what happened. Although, I'm sure Ox or Roman had filled Pit in.

From the video she sent, Chelsea had beautifully explained my absence to my fans and my band members had covered for me. For once, I didn't regret working with those three idiots.

My phone buzzed and a number I didn't recognize appeared. I answered, "Hello?"

"It's Alicia's uncle, come outside so we can talk." The phone clicked off.

I stared at it and then looked at Jazz. Standing up, I walked over to her side and pressed a kiss to her forehead. Turning away from her, I exited to see her uncle standing across from the entrance to Jazz's room.

"Follow me," he said, turning to go.

I glanced around before following him. "Where are we going?"

"Not far, I just wanted to walk a bit. It's been a while since I've gotten out from behind a desk. At my age, it's good to stroll every once in a while."

"Well, I'm not interested in your issues," I said as I stopped right before we reached the exit door. "You said you'd clear things up about Al… Jazz for me. If you're just going to waste my time, fuck it."

The old fucker didn't seem the bit ruffled by my words. He turned and faced me, a look of amusement on his face.

"Fine, then I'll cut to the chase. What are your intentions toward my niece?"

"I love her."

Carter's expression turned skeptical. "You love Jazz, the person she pretended to be. What makes you think Alicia "Jasmine" Roarke is the same as her? The Roarke name is synonymous with success and wealth. She's never worn anything that's not worth more than your entire paycheck. In her family's eyes the Nakamuras are nobodies."

I flinched when he said my real last name. This fucker knew a lot more than I'd first assumed. It was rare to meet someone who made me feel like they could see right through me.

The first person who came to mind was Pit. Still, this guy wasn't going to scare me away.

"I don't care about all of that. I choose to believe the woman who I made love to, watched gruesome zombies with, cooked with, and who kicked my ass running every morning is the same woman you're talking about. I love her and I have every intention of marrying her."

Carter stared at me steadily in silence for a long minute. It was like he was dissecting me with his eyes to see the love I had for Jazz.

"Very well. What do you want to know first?"

Thousands of questions popped up. It took me a moment to sort through them.

"What happened back there?"

I knew the Roarke name. They were one of the top business groups in Vander City. From restaurant chains to fashion stores, they owned a good chunk of Vander.

They were known to be so wealthy that if you entered business with the name Roarke backing you, there was no way you wouldn't succeed. They also were the ones behind the Roarke Foundation, where only the most elite businessmen could sit on the board of directors.

"Alicia is the only heir to the Roarke fortune," Carter continued. "She has been in a silent cold war with her father, Clark Bennington since she was eighteen. When Alicia was seventeen, she came home to find her mother dead and went into shock.

"Naturally, her father showed his concern. It took a year before we realized what he was really up to. Alicia was kept in a semi-vegetive state for a year by her own father's hands.

"She was held prisoner while her father used her to manipulate her grandfather to have the responsibilities of the company handed over to him."

Carter's expression turned dark. "At the time, my wife was out of the loop because she'd been disowned for marrying me. So, we never learned about this until Alicia suddenly came to her senses when she turned eighteen and managed to finally get away. Unfortunately, by that time her grandfather was half senile and couldn't do much for her."

I ground my teeth, trying to remain calm. I felt anger toward Jazz for hiding such a big thing from me and I was angry at myself for never asking more.

"Luckily, once she entered my household, I was able to help her get her inheritance back under her control and started the process of helping her recover from her stint with her father. If you'd seen how skinny she was then…"

He trailed off, his expression turning nearly black. "I'd have killed Clark then if he hadn't gotten a hold of some information that was dangerous for my family."

Carter shook his head. "Anyway, when she was nineteen, he went to court, trying to have them make him the conservator of her estate. He tried to claim she wasn't mentally well and couldn't handle such a huge estate and wealth on her own.

"He failed, of course, but he'd continued trying to get his hands on Roarke funds. Alicia decided to stop fighting over the foundation her mother had willed to him, in favor of looking into her mother's death instead.

"Still, that wasn't enough, he always hung around her, looking to get his hands on anything he could, like a damn rat."

"So, how did she end up as my bodyguard of all things?"

Carter laughed and gave me an amused look. "That's because she tried to steal your car, something she does for fun every once in a while to relieve stress from work. It's harmless, usually she goes for a joy ride and leaves the car somewhere for the owner to find it later, but this time she managed to steal your car by coincidence."

I immediately remembered the thief who'd stared at me in bemused shock as they stood by my car. She'd been the one who'd tried to steal my car?

Carter continued. "She saw the guys who took you and followed them and had my nephew Dutch call the authorities when she realized they were up to no good."

Carter reached over and placed a hand on my shoulder. "My niece can be reckless sometimes. Alicia thought she could take this chance to repay you by protecting you."

He gave my shoulder a solid pat before he removed his hand. "As to repayment for what, I think I should leave that to her to tell. I've been protecting her since she was a young girl and now it's your turn to do so. Don't give me a reason to have to visit you in the future," he warned.

"Don't worry about that, I'd protect her with my life."

"Ha ha, good. Tell my niece I'll be visiting her later."

"Will do."

He turned to go but stopped and turned back. "Ah, I almost forgot. It's a tradition in my family to handle a problem for the person marrying into it. I have a present for you if you're willing to come with me."

I debated for a moment before I decided to see what Carter had for me. "I'll come."

His expression was a pleased one. "I like a man who gets his hands dirty. Don't worry, I'll leave two of my own men to keep an eye on her." He smiled and turned. "Let's go, I'll have you back before she wakes up."

I followed Carter out of the hallway into the emergency exit. Immediately, I noticed the alarm hadn't gone off. I paused on the steps to glance back.

"Don't worry about the alarms," Carter said as he continued down. "Dutch took care of them. That boy has always been clever with computers. He's actually the reason we were able to get your present together in such a short time."

I didn't respond to this and followed him until we reached the first floor. It hadn't escaped my knowledge that someone would have had to assist Jazz in faking her identity to get the job with me. That person must have been this Dutch person.

Once we hit the first floor, we exited to find a sleek black car parked outside. The guy I'd seen earlier named Zeno leaned against it. His appearance casual and at ease, accept for the gun that was in his holster.

He didn't look at me, but at Carter. "Pop's, Cirah said we've got two hours before she has to take him back."

"Text her we're on our way," Carter said, walking around the car to the other side. "And show some manners, say hello to Tak."

"Yeah, whatever," Zeno said as he opened the door and got in. "I'll share pleasantries with the fucker after he deals with his shit."

Carter shook his head as he got in. I followed their example and soon we were driving through Vander City. I was too focused on where they were taking me and what I would find to give two shits about the barking coming from Jazz's cousin. I could make his life miserable later.

A while later we pulled in front of a steel warehouse. The large building had a few other cars parked outside. I spotted a woman standing in the center of a circle of men. Her pose was relaxed. The minute her eyes landed on our car, she moved forward.

Getting out, I finally asked. "What's here?"

Carter only offered me one of his mysterious smiles before he turned his attention to the young woman walking toward us. "Cirah, I knew I could count on you."

Cirah offered him a small smile. "Uncle, I wasn't sure how long it would take you, but me and the guys added some tools to make it a bit more interesting. I hope you don't mind."

He gave her an affectionate pat on the shoulder. "No, no, it's fine. This time it won't be me playing, but Jazz's fiancé. Lead him inside, Zeno, and I will wait here."

Cirah looked away from Carter to me. She gave me a once-over before she said, "Come with me."

I shot Carter a look, but the old man had already walked over to the group of men who were hanging around. Zeno had also left.

Seeing I had no choice, I walked over to Cirah. "Since those two didn't want to say, can you tell me what the fuck I'm about to walk into?"

She hummed before she said, "The best thing someone can give a victim."

Hearing the word victim, I frowned. I wasn't a victim. I tried to think over what she meant as we entered through the open door of the steel warehouse.

The first thing that hit me was the smell, it was thick and cloying. I'd say it was the stench of piss. Cirah's heels clicked along the cement floor as we walked past pile after pile of wooden pallets.

The second thing I noticed was the sound of masculine begging. Within minutes of hearing him, I saw him with his arms tied above his head by rattling chains. Two men were standing beneath him.

One man was holding the end of the chain that was wrapped around Sakai's wrists, keeping him suspended in the air. He held him low enough for the other guy to stuff his mouth with what looked to be a ball gag. Cirah's voice cut through the haze that was fast building in my head.

"We put some toys on that table over there." She pointed to where there was a table to the left, covered with different weapons and torture devises. "And if I can offer a recommendation, I enjoy the knives and nails personally."

I swallowed over the rage that threatened to choke me. "Are you sure you want to allow me to do this?"

I thought back to everything that son of a bitch had done to me. I could faintly feel the echo of pain that ran through my body just remembering how ruthlessly he had beaten me. If they let me loose, I couldn't be sure I wouldn't kill him.

I squeezed my eyes shut. "I might kill him," I bite out.

She laughed. "And if you do, we'll deal with it." She gave my shoulder a small pat. "After all, this is who you've really been looking for. He was behind it all. You've got forty minutes. Do everything you want and can think of. You're now one of us."

With that, she motioned to the two men. "Reeves, tie him down and let's leave Mr. Nakamura to it."

I stood alone with the monster from my childhood. He'd also tried to kill me and inadvertently continued to put Jazz's life in danger. I thought about it and finally, I walked up to him. I grabbed the ball gag and jerked it out.

"Fuck," he released a low gasp.

Terror-filled eyes looked at me in supplication. "Tak, Takuya, please help me," he begged, his face was bloated as spittle and snot slipped down it. Fuck, it was disgusting.

"I want to ask you something first."

For the first time, without drugs or Jazz, I felt calm.

He sputtered. "P… please, let me go." He frantically looked around the warehouse. "I… I'll answer anything you want if you let me go."

My lips curled up into a cruel smile. "Why?"

His gaze focused back on me; confusion clouded his eyes. "W… what?"

"I want to know why. Why you beat me up when we were kids. Why you decided I should die. What were you thinking when you decided killing me was a thing? I just want to know, *why* do any of it?"

Sakai's expression emptied of emotion, his skin lost color. He licked his lips as he seemed to search for an answer. After a few minutes of silence, I laughed.

"You can't answer, can you?"

I shook my head and turned around and walked over to the table. I perused the items there.

"Let me take a crack at guessing. When we were kids you knew my parent's didn't give a shit about me. You beat the fuck out of me because you could, and you knew no one would stop you. Not my parents, not the staff, and damn sure not your parents."

I spotted a set of brass knuckles and picked them up. "Shit, if I'd never fought back, you would have continued beating the crap out of me."

I slipped the brass knuckles on each hand and flexed my fingers. Then I turned back around and walked over to him.

"No, no, that's not it. I was stupid, just a dumb kid," he yelled, trying to explain himself.

I cocked an eyebrow. "Then are you saying your dumb now. Is that why you hired someone to kill me? Because you were too fucking stupid to just let me live my life." I shook my head, "No, I don't think so."

I reached up and grabbed the ball and shoved it into his mouth. "You know what, I've decided why you did it doesn't matter anymore." He shook and struggled against the chains, but there was nothing he could do. I moved back and pulled off my T-shirt and tossed it to the ground.

I took up a stance in front of him. "Cirah said this would be the best gift for me since I was a *victim*. At first, I was confused, but now I know what she meant."

Without another word, I slammed my brass knuckle-covered fist into his chest. I just wailed on him until my eyes ached from the tears and sweat that dripped down my face. For a moment, I just forgot where I was and who I was beating.

It was like with ever hit of my fist against his body another wound on my soul was expunged. This fucker had taken advantage of my broken home. He'd hurt me and the woman I loved.

If I didn't carve out at least a piece of his flesh, could I even fucking call this taking revenge? The only reason I stopped was because Zeno pulled me away.

"Enough, Tak, enough."

I struggled against him and that's when I realized I'd been screaming the entire time. I'd been yelling like a wild man. My cousin had long since lost consciousness and was swinging back and forth with blood dripping down his bruised body.

I stopped struggling against Zeno's hold. As soon as I did, he released me and backed away. My chest heaved as I inhaled and exhaled roughly, the ache in my hands drew my attention.

The brass knuckles were covered with blood and what looked to be a piece of flesh. I quickly pulled them off and tossed them away. Moving over to where I'd tossed my shirt, I picked it up and pulled it on.

Cirah and Zeno were both admiring Sakai's unconscious body.

"Well, shit, I guess you're not as limp wristed as I thought," Zeno said in amusement.

I didn't even acknowledge what he said. I left and headed straight for Carter who stood outside smoking. The crowd of men that had been hanging around had left.

Carter spotted me and casually tossed the cigarette down and stepped on it. "You're done?"

"I'm done," I answered.

Carter observed me steadily, his expression serious. "Good, now let's get you back to my niece and both of you can move forward from this."

"Yeah."

Together we left the warehouse and headed back to the hospital. I was more than eager to see Jazz, I needed to see her. She was my future and she was the singular thing that could center me.

CHAPTER FIFTY

Awaken to Truth

Jazz

Opening my eyes, I stared blankly at the white ceiling. Again, I woke up in a hospital bed. There was a heavy weight holding my arm down.

I looked over and found a headful of thick black hair filling my vision. I knew it was Tak. I wasn't sure if this was real or not, so I didn't move. The last thing I could remember with full clarity was the sight of my father cringing away from me in fear.

I licked my lips. My mouth was dry. I lifted my left hand and pressed it to my forehead. I wasn't running a fever. Lowering my arm, I tried to remember what happened. I'd wanted to kill my father and I couldn't do it. I gave up after a few more minutes of recalling nothing else.

I thought this frustrated tight feeling in my chest I had been carrying for so many years would disappear the minute he was gone. The memory of his scared expression should have filled me with joy. Instead, I felt empty. All my hate had been used up and now there was nothing left.

"You're awake." Tak's voice sounded raspy with sleep.

I watched as he pushed up and bit back a laugh at the sight of his messy bed hair. Even looking the way he did, with one eye open and a five o'clock shadow, he still looked handsome to me.

"What time is it?"

"I'm not sure," I said, giving a look around the room. "I don't even know how long I've been out."

He stood up and walked over to his phone and picked it up. "You were only out for a night. It just turned noon. Give me a second, I need to use the bathroom. I'll be right back."

"Okay."

He placed his phone back down and left. I watched him go, unsure of the situation. Shouldn't he be angry with me? How had he known where to find me to begin with?

I was pulled out of my thoughts when he came back after a few minutes. He walked over to me and cupped my cheek in his warm hand.

"How are you feeling?"

I offered him a tight smile. "Fine."

"Good."

He pulled his hand back, plopped back down, and bowed his head. He stared at the floor for so long, I started to get worried.

"Tak?"

"I met Carter last night," he said, not looking at me.

I paused in pushing my way up. "You did?"

He nodded, still not looking at me. This time I pushed myself up fully and scooted back to lean against the pillows. "Then I guess you know everything."

"I know who you are, but I'm still missing the most important thing," he said.

I decided to not cower away from this situation. "And what's that?"

"Why? Why'd you feel indebted to me and why did you so blindly protect me?"

I looked away from him. There were plenty of reasons, some practical, some not. "Do you remember me?"

"Yes."

I hadn't been expecting him to say yes. I turned back to him. "You do?"

"Once I heard your real name a lot of the shit I'd forgotten came to the surface. There wasn't a lot of positive shit I remembered from Bridge Lake. I think I got to the point that any memory in relation to that place, I shoved as far to the back of my mind as possible. Even the little girl who'd played with me in the meadow between our houses."

I looked down. "I remember everything about you, from when we were kids to when you barely said hi to me in high school. I remember the time you beat the shit out of the school's biggest bully. Those small and precious memories of you are what got me through a lot of the worse times in my life." My eyes burned as I tried not to cry.

"You want to know why I wanted to protect you? It's because your music saved my life. My father had a doctor keep me in a sort of woke coma.

"And at that time, I wasn't willing to fight against it. I was relieved that I didn't have to feel anything or think about anything. Then one day your voice filled my room.

"I just couldn't ignore it. It was like you could feel what I felt. At that moment, I wanted to know more about the person who could sing my pain so well. Since that day, I refused to let myself sink so low ever again."

He pulled me into his arms, and I continued. "I knew it was wrong to lie to you about who I was, but it was my only chance to be with you."

I pressed my hands into my covers. "I regretted lying to you, but I would do it all over again. I'd never thought for a second, you'd actually love me or even like me. I just wanted to be your number one fangirl for the rest of my life. Even if I couldn't stay by your side after you found out."

Tak gently grabbed my chin and forced me to look up at him. "And now that I've found out, what are you going to do?"

I reached up and grabbed his arm. "I want to be selfish and stay with you."

He pressed his lips against my forehead. "Then that's what you'll do." He retreated and gave me a dangerous smile. "I was worried that I would have to become one of those psychos who lock people in their basement."

Letting go of his arm, I wiped the tears from my face. "The scary thing is I'd probably be okay with that."

"And that's why we fit together," he said.

There was a bit of truth to what he'd said.

"I guess you're right."

"I'm always right."

After a few minutes of lying in his arms, I found myself wondering. "What happened to Clark?"

"Well, I was hoping your uncle would kill him," he said. "But unfortunately, he's not dead. I keep debating on paying someone off to kill him though."

I laughed. "You didn't have enough excitement last night?"

"It was okay. It was actually pretty tame in comparison to some of the things I usually get up to with my friends."

I thought over my own past. "Aside from occasionally needing to run from the cops in a car I'd stolen for a joy ride, my life has been pretty tame."

"Ah, the car stealing," he said.

I looked up at him with a sheepish smile. "They told you."

"Yep, your uncle exposed your entire thieving past to me."

"If I wasn't stealing cars, someone wouldn't be here now," I huffed.

"I know, and I love that side of you," he teased, pressing another kiss to my forehead. "And the crazy fangirl side." He pressed a kiss to my cheek. "And the bodyguard who won't take none of my shit," he said as he pressed the final kiss to my lips.

I lifted my hand, stopping him and his eager lips to ask. "Why do I feel like you're trying to distract me?"

He raised his brows and offered a look of innocence. "What?"

"Don't play with me. You followed me to my father's. What happened after I passed out? Shit, what happened with the benefits concert?"

He pouted. "And here I wanted to have a happily ever after with some kisses and fucking."

I rolled my eyes at him. "I'm not sleeping with you in a hospital, Tak."

"But my dressing room was okay?"

I held back from hitting him. Seeming to catch my dark look, he sighed.

"Fine, your uncle made him confess everything to the police. Bribing federal officials, tax evasion, embezzling, blackmailing and murder. Ah, and for being ugly as well and a horrible father."

"Tak," I drawled.

"Okay, so the being ugly thing is me, but let's be honest, I think both of us can say with complete authority our fathers are pieces of shit. Look at that, another reason we match so well."

I covered my mouth to keep from laughing.

His brow wrinkled. "You asked about my situation, well, check this out." He reached over to the small table beside me and picked up his phone and scrolled through it. Once he found what he was looking for, he set it on my lap.

I picked it up and squinted at the picture there and released a small gasp. "Isn't that your cousin Sakai?"

"Yep."

The picture was of Tak's cousin in handcuffs being escorted out of a house. His face looked like someone played shuttlecock with it.

"Dutch sent it to me. He's being charged with conspiracy to murder and soliciting murder. Apparently, he'd had a vested interest in killing me."

"Wait, when did you meet Dutch?" I asked, confused.

Tak shrugged. "I haven't. Your uncle told me about him and he was polite enough to send me this information so I could update you on everything. Since then, we've been texting each other."

I eyed Tak, suddenly worried about just how long he'd been with my uncle Carter last night and what did he mean by *texting* with Dutch.

"Anyway, fucker was scared I'd change my mind and return to the family and take over the company. Apparently, he didn't believe me when I said I didn't want anything to do with the family business. Oh, and why didn't you tell me the fucker your dad wanted you to marry was Gerald Harrison?

"Dutch told me and I nearly lost my shit. He was a pretentious shit in high school, good thing I didn't run into him now, I would have beat his ass."

I stared at him. "Tak, you did run into him."

He looked at me in confusion. "What? No, I didn't."

"Yes, you did. He's the guy you beat up at the broadcast station."

If I had my phone, I would have taken a picture of his stupefied expression.

He quickly recovered and shrugged. "Whatever, my Jazz has better taste than to fuck a dude in a suit."

"If I recall correctly, you were wearing a suit the first time we slept together," I said, more out of my desire to see him pout than anything else.

"Listen, you were untouched pussy," he retorted.

"Tak," I groaned, pulling my pillow from behind me and hitting him with it.

He caught it. "It's okay, love. My lips are sealed." He blew me a kiss.

I groaned. My face was hotter than a stove top. "You're such an asshole."

"I'm your asshole, love."

He smirked before lifting his phone once more. "Ah, you know about the guy, Tony, from Vegas. He was delivered to the cops with a ribbon on his head along with his best friend Mitchell, the fucker that tried to crush my cranium with a fucking light."

I frowned. "How do you know that?"

He gave me another innocent look. "Dutch, of course."

I mentally groaned, this was a budding friendship I knew I needed to end soon. I glared at him. "You're joking."

He smirked. "Nope, your cousins have been super busy."

"Tak?" I called his name.

He lowered the phone and shot me an inquisitive look. "Hmm."

"Can you kiss me already?"

Tak took my lips in a deep kiss. He lifted me into his lap. When we finally came up for air, he gave me a cocky wink.

"Are you really okay with me? I am a reckless heiress, after all."

"Doesn't matter to me, you'll always be Jazz to me no matter what anyone else calls you or what color your eyes are."

I wrapped my arms around his shoulder. "Kiss me again."

He leaned down. "Of course."

CHAPTER FIFTY-ONE

Manipulation

Sakai

Sitting in the cold interrogation room, I looked at the two-way mirror across from me on the wall. The surface reflected my battered face, one eye was swollen shut. With a wince I looked away.

I could deal with my aching body later. For that moment, I tried to think over everything I'd said and done over the past year, trying to get my alibi together.

There was no way they could pin this shit on me when I'd taken great care with covering my steps. Every time I thought of that little fuck I felt the urge to scream. I can't believe I'd been put in such a situation by an unwanted half-breed.

The door to the interrogation room opened. I looked up and stiffened.

"You." I was taken aback. "He sent you here to represent me."

The lawyer who'd entered walked over to the table and took a seat. He offered me a smile.

"No, I've just been sent to pass a message. My client isn't pleased with your last minute cancellation of the order for Tak's hit. We came to you to have Tak killed and offered you help. Instead of following through, you reneged. Which is why we took things into our own hands and contacted Tony ourselves and sent him the payment."

"What?"

What the fuck was he talking about?

"I… I was just trying to move with caution. Besides, with Tak not wanting the company, I thought we could try again later. I didn't renege, I just needed more time."

"And what makes you think you're the one to make that decision?" the lawyer across from me asked. "Mr. Sakai you overestimated yourself, which is why you'll be charged with attempted murder and soliciting murder. Tony Enson and Mitchell Rendon are at this very moment confessing to the police that you ordered everything, including Tony's last attempt to shoot Mr. Jensei."

He stood up. "It's been a pleasure working with you, but it seems that our cooperation ends here."

"Wait," I shouted, standing up. "You can't do this to me. You're the one who told me to do this. Wait."

Not sparing me another glance, he walked out just as two officers entered. Their eyes not glancing at him at all, I pointed at him.

"Hey, that's the guy who directed everything, he's the one who got me in touch with the hit men."

Still, they didn't even look his way as they walked over to me. One of them grabbed my arm. "Sakai Nakamura, you are being charged with conspiracy to murder and soliciting the murder of Takuya Nakamura."

I yanked my arm out of his hold, taking a step back. "No, no. Stop. It wasn't me, stop him. He's the one who planned everything. He's the one."

"Hey, shut him up," the other officer said. And the next thing I saw was a fist aimed for my face and I knew only darkness after.

CHAPTER FIFTY-TWO

Wedding Bliss

Tak
Three weeks later…

I stood in the church waiting for the wedding planner to give the signal for the wedding to start. If I were still the person I was in the past, I'd have broken out in hives and figured out a way to leave. Friends' wedding or not, there were some things that should be appreciated from a distance. However, I was no longer that man. I now had Jazz and a future ahead of me.

"What are you doing?" Jeff asked.

"Showing you what happiness looks like, behold." I flashed him a picture of Jazz and me kissing. "How does it feel to be a lonely, old man who exchanges pussy with the masses?"

His expression turned blank before he looked at Kelex who stood next to him. "Why did you introduce me to this post-term abortion? He shows up to my house without an invite and texts me weird shit all the time. I don't want him in my life anymore."

Kelex didn't reply. Instead, he answered his phone.

I replaced my phone in my back pocket. "Jeff, let's be serious for once. If I didn't come and visit you, you'd be that guy who died alone with his kittens. Your body would just sit there for years before anyone knew. I am doing you a favor when I visit you."

Jeff stared at Kelex then looked at me. "I have dogs. I hate cats, like you, they annoy me."

Kelex still didn't respond.

"But you are agreeing you'd die alone though?" I asked.

He glared at me in vexation. "How the fuck did you manage to bag the only heiress to the Roarke family. Is it witchcraft?"

I was going to tell him it was because of my handsome looks and perfectly proportionate dick, but a soft punch at my back disabused me of that thought. "Tak, are you driving Jeff crazy again?"

Jazz's soft voice came from behind me. I turned around and nearly swallowed my tongue. A common occurrence when I saw Jazz. I still couldn't believe this beautiful woman was mine.

Her short hair was elegantly done, while her off-the-shoulder pearl pink dress made me want to do naughty things to her. She still had the habit of wearing her contacts, but I'd started hiding them so I could stare into her gray eyes.

I refused to let her experience with her father mar any part of her. My Jazz was beautiful inside and out and no one could convince me otherwise. I took her hand and brushed my lips against the back of it. This was done so I could appreciate the engagement ring I'd given her.

"I'm trying to open his eyes to the beauty of love," I explained.

She gave me a side-eye, before she turned her full attention to Jeff with a questioning look.

"He wasn't," Jeff denied bluntly. "I only have one question, he doesn't have anything to do with the business ventures of the Roarke corporation, does he?"

"Fuck no," I said, giving Jeff a disgusted look. "I'm already dealing with JS, why would I want to add a whole conglomerate to my plate? No thank you."

Jazz chuckled. While I'd just recently learned Jazz was an heiress to big business, this was the first time I saw a calculating look come over her face. "Instead of answering you, how about I ask what business venture you want Roarke's partnership in?"

"Stop." I stepped between them. "This is a wedding. Jazz is not allowed to be a coldhearted businesswoman today." I grabbed Jazz's hand and dragged her away.

Her soft laughter came behind me. I stopped and turned around to face her. Seeing the mischievous look in her eyes, I grew suspicious.

"You did that on purpose."

She laughed some more. "Yep, Jeff was screaming for help. I had no choice."

"He's a big boy, he deserves to be harassed every once in a while. He sold me out to Chelsea. I'll be at his house tomorrow for breakfast."

"Tak." Jazz reached up and pulled on my collar. "Leave the man alone before he actually kills you. Besides, there are bigger things you should be worrying about."

"And what's that?"

Her expression turned soft as she leaned forward, her lips brushing my ear as she whispered into it. "Figuring out what to name our baby," she said as she leaned back and stared up at me nervously. "I was late, so I went to the doctor to check and that's when they gave me the news. We're having a baby... Tak?"

I looked down at her before what she said registered. A part of me prayed that Pit and Skittles' wedding didn't get canceled because of me. My head exploded with music and the last thing I saw was the woman I love's shocked expression as I fainted at her feet.

EPILOGUE

Here We Go

Tak

My woman wanted strawberry ice cream from the most random ass place in the city. If I had known operation, *Make-Jazz-Fluffy* would end up with me running out and buying her the most random of food, I would have said fuck it and checked myself into an asylum, but my Jazz is beautiful, funny, and gives the best head that no other motherfucker will ever experience, so for her I'll do any fucking thing.

Like, enter some cheap ass diner to get her their strawberry shake. I am convinced only my face and the quick flash of a fifty is what made the fuckers behind the counter make the shake to go. Turning to the side, my jaw dropped at the sight of the one person I would never expect to see around these parts.

Taking a quick look around, I beat a quick retreat to the hallway that led to the bathrooms. Pressing my back against the wall, I prayed to Jazz's cute as fuck angry face that Deacon came

367

and went with swiftness. I would be too embarrassed to explain I was running an errand for my girl, especially after all the shit I talked. Deacon would tell the others and I'd have to endure asshole text messages from the fuckers for weeks.

Nah, fuck that.

"How're you doing, Noni?"

I moved closer to the corner. Deacon was many things, but soft-spoken he wasn't. And I'd just heard him talk in a way I'd never heard before.

Leaning closer, I glanced a bit around the corner and frowned when I saw him take a seat in front of a woman whose back was to me. A part of me wanted to take a picture and send it to the others. Someone had to keep everyone in the loop and if it was Luke, he would share the bitch out of this juicy gossip.

I leaned back and after a minute pulled the small baggy of edibles out of my back pocket. I had assured my lovely fluffy wife-to-be I wouldn't touch any of this shit, but the idea of pouring grade A marijuana gummies in the trash was reprehensible, so I'm patiently eating them up until there's no more.

Leaning against the wall, I could hear their murmured voices. The high must be getting to me, because at some point I started to imagine I was invisible, and I could walk right past them without being noticed. I looked over to the counter and saw the drink they'd made for me sitting there on top.

Dammit, how much longer are they going to talk? Jazz milkshake will be soup if they take any longer—

"You're pregnant?" Deacon's shout cut over my thoughts.

I pressed a hand to my heart, unsure if I was surprised or having a heart attack. After a while, I was assured it wasn't a heart attack.

I tried to focus and heard Deacon roar, "Are you out of your fucking mind?"

I released a whistle and shook my head. "Ah shit, here we go again."

ACKNOWLEDGMENTS

Thank you for reading my story. I hope you enjoyed it as much as I did writing it. The two characters were quirky and fun to explore. So, I'm pleased that it came out so well.

I'd like to thank my mother for always supporting me. I also want to send a shout out to my sisters for always being there for my long calls. And as always I'm thankful to my pen sisters who have laughed and cried with me through it all.

This was my first experience writing in a group setting and I learned so much. I'm so grateful to have gained this opportunity thanks to Blue and I hope to continue to enjoy many more exciting things in the future with my pen sisters.

Once again, thank you for reading and loving Tak and Jazz.

ABOUT THE AUTHOR

Ivy Harper is an avid coffee drinker and storyteller. When not being a complete addict to either of these obsessions, she is bingeing Chinese historical dramas with the family or coming up with new ways to prank her sister.

Living as a virtual night owl, she has made it a hobby to live on the dark side of the moon. From highlighting the delicious gothic love her characters experience, to thoroughly immersing her readers in a book they will surely shiver from. Ivy hopes to bring her readers along with her on the twisted, winding path of romance and sensuality that you'll find yourself craving more than a hot black, cup of coffee.

Wait, there is more to come! You can stay updated with my latest releases, learn more about me, the author, and be a part of contests by subscribing to my newsletter at
http://www.authorivyharper.com/

If you enjoyed *Tak*, I'd love to hear
your thoughts and please feel free to leave a
review. And when you do, please let me
know by emailing me IvyharperAuthor@gmail.com

or leave a comment on Facebook
https://www.facebook.com/authorIvyHarper
or Twitter @IvAuthor
or Instagram @AuthorIvyHarper

More to come from Ivy Harper in 2021.
If you want to keep up with the Perceptive Illusions Publishing authors and releases, subscribe to the newsletter for updates
HERE.

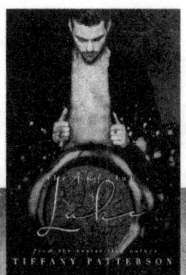

Continuing July 2022

A**hole Club

ARE YOU READY FOR THEM?